THE WIND SLAMMED INTO ITS CHOSEN, knocking Cam free from his physical body. With a joyous shout, Cam leaped into Its embrace. Together the two of them flung themselves over the battlements and away.

Cam had never felt so free. Of all the times he'd sent his mind out on the wings of the breeze, or reached out with his thoughts to the heart of the Wind, he'd never been taken up so fast or so far. When he broke clear of the Washe, his awareness spread out almost impossibly wide. He tore along the waves, but all too soon he sensed the confining presence of land before him, so, spinning in a great circle that sent the water churning into a whirlpool beneath him, his awareness folded back on itself until he was staring into the vast expanse of stars. With a whoop, he flung himself toward them.

It grew cold. Far away he felt a whisper of pain feather across his body, but he pressed on. Then something caught hold of him, arresting his ascent. He faltered. Far away he heard his name called and then he was falling. The sea rushed back toward him and, just before he plunged into its depths, he heard a triumphant voice.

"I've got him!"

He shot back into the air, anger granting him new strength.

"I can't hold him!"
"What do you mean you can't hold him! You gotta hold him!"
"We're losing him. . . ."

THE
GOLDEN
SWORD

Fiona Patton

DAW BOOKS, INC.
DONALD A. WOLLHEIM, FOUNDER
375 Hudson Street, New York, NY 10014

ELIZABETH R. WOLLHEIM
SHEILA E. GILBERT
PUBLISHERS
www.dawbooks.com

To Mum, for bragging

THE BRANION REALM
and Surrounding Countries 492 DR

THE COLUMBIAS

NORDANGER

Bryholm

DANELIND

BIERRE SEA

STORVICHOLM

HEATHLAND

SORLANDY

Lochaber

FENLAND

BACHIEM

Tarnbrook

KORMANDEAUX

St. Stephan's
Shrine

Forness Island

ANVRE

GWYNETH

Branbridge

GALLIA

Alderbrook

Guilcove

River Mist

ROLAND

Heronfort

BRANION

GASPELLIER

EIRION

PANISHA

TIBERIA

ESPALONIA

N

The Golden Sword
Principle Characters
In Order of Appearance

Chapter 1

Camden DeKathrine: Sword Knight.

Isabelle DeKathrine: Archpriest of the Wind and Camden's great aunt.

Collin DeKathrine: Captain of the Wind's Guard and Camden's uncle.

Alisha DeMarian: Royal Duke of Lochsbridge, fourth in line to the Throne, Camden's cousin through his aunt, the Consort Hadria.

Annie: Server at the Dog and Doublet Gaming and Public House.

Sarah Lambton: Owner of the Dog and Doublet.

Trevor: Bouncer at the Dog and Doublet and Sarah's nephew.

Kathlene: Owner of the Cock and Rabbit Tavern and Sarah's cousin.

Bonnie and Haden: Sarah's niece and nephew.

Alexander DeKathrine: Sword Knight, Duke of Guilcove from 495 DR, and Camden's oldest brother.

Joanne DeKathrine: Sword Knight, and Camden's oldest sister.

Amedeus DeKathrine: Sword Knight and Joanne's husband.

Alister DeKathrine: Sword Knight and Camden's cousin.

Elerion DeKathrine: Sword Knight and Camden's older brother.

Julian DeKathrine: Sword Knight, Elerion's Partner and cousin.

Stephan DeKathrine: Sword Knight and Camden's uncle.

Tatania DeKathrine: Sword Knight and Camden's younger sister.

Nicholas DeKathrine: Sword Knight and Camden's younger brother.

Margurette DeMarian: Sword Knight, Royal Duke of Kempston, third in line for the Throne and Camden's cousin through his aunt the Consort Hadria.

Nalani DeKathrine: Sword Knight and Camden's aunt.

Kassander DeKathrine: Sword Squire to Tatania and Nicholas and Camden's youngest brother.

Ellesanda DeKathrine: Sword Knight and Camden's great aunt.

Lorence DeKathrine: Sword Squire to Desmond DeKathrine (the younger) and Camden's cousin.

Desmond DeKathrine: Sword Knight and Camden's second cousin and later step-father.

Danielle DeKathrine: Camden's cousin.

Maia DeKathrine: Sword Knight, Duke of Werrickshire, First Admiral of the Aristok's Navy, and Camden's aunt.

Domitia DeKathrine: Sword Knight, Duke of Guilcove until 495 DR and Camden's mother.

Melesandra DeKathrine: Camden's youngest sister.

Celestus DeKathrine: Scholar, Viscount of Kairnbrook, Camden's great uncle and Danielle's father.

Atreus II: Twenty-fourth Aristok of Branion, Camden's cousin through his great uncle Desmond DeKathrine (the elder).

Clairinda DeKathrine: Captain of the Knights of the Sword, Hierarchpriest of Cannonshire, Duke of Cambury and Camden's cousin.

Marsellus DeMarian: Sword Knight, Royal Duke of Yorbourne, DeMarian Cadet, second in line for the throne and Camden's cousin through his aunt, the Consort Hadria.

Tatarina DeMarian: Sword Squire to Marsellus, Royal Duke of Clairfield, sixth in line for the throne and

Camden's cousin through his aunt, the Consort
Hadria.

Gabriel DeMarian: Sword Page to Marsellus, Royal Duke
of Roland, seventh in line for the throne and Camden's cousin through his aunt, the Consort Hadria.

Hadria DeMarian: Sword Knight, Consort to Atreus II,
Royal Duke of Lanborough, and Camden's aunt.

Kathrine DeMarian: Sword Knight, Royal Duke of
Kraburn, Heir to the throne and Camden's cousin
through his aunt, the Consort Hadria.

Mark: Groom at Kathrine's Hall.

Laura: Steward at Kathrine's Hall.

Jurin: Valet at Kathrine's Hall.

Ewan: Servant at Kathrine's Hall.

Historical Figures:

Kathrine I: Fifth Aristok of Branion. Reigned from 71-89
DR.

Braniana DeMarian: 1st Aristok of Branion and Avatar of
the Living Flame. Reigned from 1-63 DR.

Kathrine II: Sixth Aristok of Branion. Reigned from 89-
126 DR.

Chapter 2

Vakarus DeKathrine: Sword Knight and Camden's father.

Anastasia DeKathrine: Sword Knight and Alexander's
wife.

Quinton DeKathrine: Camden's second cousin.

Dianne DeKathrine: Celestus' wife, deceased.

Darnell DeKathrine: Flame Priest and Camden's cousin.

Chapter 3

Justin DeKathrine: Earl of Dorsleyshire and Camden's
cousin.

Brittany DeKathrine: Viscount of Dunmouth, Captain of
the ship *Kassandra's Pride,* and Camden's cousin.

Nathaniel DeKathrine: Captain of the ship *Sea Bear,* and
Camden's cousin.

Vincent of Storvicholm: Celestus' Companion.

Marna Jonstun: Steward at Tavencroft.
Jordan Jonstun: Cook at Tavencroft and Marna's brother.
Eban Croser: A servant at Tavencroft.
Ross Jonstun: A servant at Tavencroft.
Pri Gorwynne: Retired Priest of the Flame.
Kether Braithe: Heathland "Mirror."
Historical Figures:
Collin DeKathrine: (Collin Grey), uncle and Regent to Stephan 67-71 DR, Kathrine I 71-81 DR, and Kathrine II from 89-105 DR. The first DeKathrine, granted noble status by Kathrine II.
Edmund DeKathrine: 2nd century Kairnbrook Lord.

Chapter 4
Urielle DeSandra: Archpriest of the Flame.
Martin Wrey: Seer.
Osarion DeSandra: The Flame Temple's Deputy Seer.
Iwalani DeKathrine: Flame Temple Acolyte and Camden's cousin.
Allen DeKathrine: Flame Champion Squire and Camden and Iwalani's cousin.
Rysander DeKathrine: The Flame Temple Coadjuctor, Camden's cousin and Iwalani's father.
Lorien DeKathrine: The Flame Temple's Deputy Adjutant, and Iwalani's great uncle.
Kaliana DeKathrine: Captain of the Flame Champions and Iwalani's aunt.
Arthur: A Flame Champion.

Chapter 5
Tom Jonstun: Arms Master at Tavencroft.
Leilani DeKathrine: Earl of Essendale, Lord of Rowen's Keep and Camden's cousin.
Stephanie DeKathrine: Quinton's sister.

Chapter 6
Iain Jonstun: A "Cousin," an assassin and Marna's cousin.
Grand Prince Hilde: The Danelind monarch.

Chapter 7
Pri Garius: Dockside Flame Priest, deceased.
Brant: a poacher.

Chapter 8
Airik DeKathrine: A Flame Priest.
Pri Sandra: A Flame Priest.
Pri Gerald: A Flame Priest.
Pri Marcus: The Flame Temple's Deputy Provost.
Carla Armistone: A Heathland tinker.
Sister Maxine: Cleric at St. Stephan's Shrine.
Brother Duncan: Cleric at St. Stephan's Shrine.
Historical Figures:
Prince Atreus DeMarian: First born of Atreus II, now deceased.

Chapter 10
Bernard: A patron at the Dog and Doublet.
Traz: The cook at the Dog and Doublet.
Nani Jonstun: Chief Groom at Tavencroft.

Chapter 11
Pri Nadia: Head Priest at the Octavian Hospice.
Pri Breanne: The Aristok's Personal Priest.
Pri Zarion: The Flame Temple Liaison to the Palace.
Drusus DeYvonne: The Flame Temple's Chancellory Deputy.

Chapter 13
Eaglanter: Herald to the Duke of Werrick.
Pri Jacob: Priest of the Flame.
Pri Saldra: The Flame Temple's Night Seneschal.
Jarl Ansen: The Flame Temple's Senior Floor Polisher.
Randi Lea: Flame Temple servant.
Cory DeKathrine: The Deputy Marshal's Acolyte and Iwalani's cousin.
Janet DeKathrine: The Flame Temple Librarian and Cory's aunt.

Erna: Retired Flame Champion and chief Jailor of the
    Temple dungeons.
Pri Eylla: The Flame Temple's Deputy Interrogator.
Brairion: Pri Eylla's Acolyte.

Chapter 14
Devina: A Flame Temple Acolyte.
Gabrielle DeMarian: Duke of Gaspellier and the Aris-
    tok's cousin.
Tomi DeMarian: Duke of Anvre and the Aristok's great
    uncle.
Timothy DeMarian: Tomi's son and the Aristok's cousin.
Jeremy DeMarian: Tomi's son and the Aristok's cousin.
Rosalind DeMarian: Fifth in line for the Throne and Cam-
    den's cousin through the Consort Hadria.
Demnor DeMarian: Eighth in line for the Throne and
    Camden's cousin through the Consort Hadria.

I. Camden

The Sword Tower, Branbridge
Spring, Mean Boaldyn, 500 DR

THE late afternoon sun settled a veil of fiery light over the capital city. In the bell turret of the Sword Tower, a Junior Knight waited for its rays to flash through the copper circle atop the Royal Palace far to the west, then jerked the rope in her fist. The great hammer attached to Bran's Bell hit its metal side and the bell tolled.

The deep, rich note rolled across the city. Closing her eyes, the Knight waited for the echoes to fade, then cocked her ear for the answering toll of Dorian's Bell in its palace tower. The Aristok Kathrine the First had set up this system in the year one hundred and six to signal that all was well in the capital. In almost four hundred years it had fallen silent only once.

The Knight held her breath until the answering toll sounded from across the city and then jerked her own rope once more. Bran's Bell sounded again. Then Dorian's. Three times, four, and then, one by one, the subordinate bells of Branbridge added their voices to that of their leaders, calling the faithful of two major religions to their respective services: the Triarchs to High Sabbat Mass and the Essusiates to Devotions. As the multitude began to leave their homes and businesses for the many temples and churches across the city, the Knight leaned her arms against the tower's iron railing and peered down at the greatest metropolis on Braniana's Island.

Branbridge shone like a multifaceted jewel in the spring sunlight, pendants and standards fluttering over its copper-and-slate-covered roofs like so many gaudy butterflies. Brightly painted signs marched along each street declaring the industry of taverns, temples, artisans, and merchants, and the crowded docks along the sparkling River Mist were crammed with ships bearing the ensigns of a dozen countries. From the city walls the flags of the four Militant Orders—Sword, Shield, Lance, and Bow— flew beside the banners of the Aspects' Temples: Sea, Wind, Oaks, and the Active and most powerful and Senior Aspect, Flame; as well as the bannerets of the dozen Essusiate Churches. From the palace and the manor houses of the west to the warehouses and the great bulk of the Sword Tower to the east, the entire city shone with color and activity. A far cry from the fortified village that had once welcomed Braniana DeMarian, first Avatar of the Living Flame and soon to be Aristok of Branion, through its wooden gates so long ago.

Five hundred years had passed since Braniana had planted her flag here on the bank of the River Mist, formally naming the city as her capital and base from which to conquer the rest of the country. She'd reigned for sixty-three years and had passed a strong and united Branion on to her son and he to his daughter and so on down through the centuries in a sometimes frayed but never broken line of Avatar/Rulers. The twenty-fourth DeMarian to take the Throne and the Mantle of the Living Flame, Atreus the Second, had heralded in a golden age of unprecedented power and prosperity for the Island Realm. The celebrations that had begun last autumn would continue throughout the summer until Mean Lunasa and Atreus' fiftieth Coronation Anniversary. It was a number of great metaphysical importance, coming as it did during the five hundredth year of his family's reign, and the Most Illustrious Triarctic Order of the Knights of the Sword was to hold the position of highest honor among his Militant followers.

Leaning precariously over the edge of the railing, the

Knight watched the bulk of her Order mass in the chapel courtyard. The Knights of the Sword had over four hundred fighting members alone, and twice that of auxiliary and support staff, making it the largest Militant Order in the country. This five hundredth anniversary year had seen a flood of Petitionates, swelling the subordinate and nonmilitant ranks by another hundred and fifty. The Sword Chapel could barely hold half that number, so most—those who could not boast the Patronage of a Senior Knight—would be hearing Sabat Mass outside in the chapel courtyard.

The Knight snorted. She would much rather be outside in the cool spring breeze than suffocating in the small confines of the Sword Chapel proper but, as Bell Ringer for this month, she held a place of—to her mind—*overrated* honor below with the Senior Knights. That she could, at least, take the bell tower stairs directly to her stall rather than struggle through the press of Knights like a salmon fighting its way upstream was small comfort when the cool spring evening beckoned.

Squinting, she glanced toward the palace once again. The sun still shone through the copper circle, so, leaning her elbows on the railing, she played with the gold signet on her finger while she watched the Order negotiate its way toward the great ironbound doors of the chapel entrance. With so many Sword Knights in the capital for the anniversary celebrations, and most holding important positions across the country, rank and status were foremost in everyone's mind. The Junior Knights who moved grudgingly aside to allow the Seniors in ahead of them were often Earls or Viscounts themselves and there was considerable jostling amongst them as they sorted out who had the right to precede who. It wouldn't do to come in just before the Petitionates, or worse, to be told that there was no more room by the retired Keepers of the Doors. The Knight, herself too Junior to usually warrant any position at all, smiled happily, enjoying the chaotic spectacle below. With a few notable exceptions, most of the Knights bore the Sword crest on the distinctive bicolored surcoats of Branion's five Triarctic noble families: dark purple and red for the ancient DeLynne Lords, dark yellow and orange for the religiously split DeYvonnes, gray and light blue for the ever-scheming DeSandras, and light yellow and lavender for the newest family, the DePaulas; only one hundred and fifty years from their Continental heritage, but swiftly rising in favor. The dark blue and black of the Royal DeMarians was absent, but only because they were already inside, taking their ease with the Captain and the Archpriest of the Flame. But fully two thirds of those called to worship at the Sword Chapel wore the dark green and black of Branion's oldest and most powerful noble family, the DeKathrines.

Picking at the distinctive dark green braid of her own tunic, the Knight stared out at the many flags that bore the crest of her family's holdings across the capital. The story of Branion was as much the story of the DeKathrines as it was of the DeMarians. Granted noble status in 105 DR by Kathrine the Second, they'd been Royal supporters for far longer. A DeKathrine ancestor had accompanied Braniana from Danelind, another had married her son. Consorts, Regents, and Marshals, they were the foundation stones of the Crown's power. In this century alone their influence was unprecedented. They controlled nine of the forty Branion shires and three of the seven on the Tiberian Continent. Two of the four Militant Orders had DeKathrine Captains; three of the four Aspects' Temples had DeKathrine Archpriests. Their reputation was one of strength and loyalty to the Royal Family, the Triarchy, and the Living Flame; and the family guarded that reputation jealously.

Most of the family, the Knight amended.

A sudden breeze danced through her hair, drawing her attention west to the ancient Temple of the Wind, north to the newer Temple of the Oaks, then finally south to the Temple of the Sea on the banks of the Mist. For five hundred years the three Lesser Aspects had accepted their junior status below the Flame—with Its Royal Avatar and powerful ecclesiastical hierarchy—but in every century heretical Priests or ambitious Lords had labored to gain the secret of a Living Vessel for their own Aspect. In every century they'd been found out and crushed by the Flame Temple's Champions before their machinations could destabilize the Realm, but none had come so close to succeeding as the DeKathrine heretics of her own generation not four years past.

Sketching the sign of the Triarchy across her breast, the Knight sent a grateful prayer to the Living Flame that the danger to the Realm and to her family's honor had been averted, then glanced back to the west. The sun was just moving out from the copper circle. Giving one last jerk on the rope, she listened as Bran's Bell sounded its final call to worship, then turned, and made her way downstairs to join the rest of her Order for the first High Sabat Mass of Mean Boaldyn, 500 DR.

Across the river in the Dog and Doublet Gaming and Public House, one of the bell ringer's many cousins, Camden DeKathrine, squinted through the open window as the bells of the capital continued to sound. Their music filled the air with a symphony of chiming notes, so many that it was almost impossible to distinguish what hour they were tolling. Every Temple, Chapter House, and Guild Hall that could erect a tower had installed a bell this year, but Camden had ears for only one of their number. As the last call of Bran's Bell faded away, he raised his mug, toasting the Sword Tower on the opposite bank, then dropped it back onto the table with a hollow thump.

A tall and muscular man, his twenty years showing in the widening of his shoulders and the bulk just beginning across his chest and arms, Camden wore a plain, wine-stained shirt and the heavy brown breeches of a laborer. He might have been one of a hundred young masons or carpenters from the city, but his broad face and long, graceful limbs spoke of a lifetime of plentiful food and warmth and the heavy gold signet ring on his finger, with its engraved bear and passant alphyn, marked him as a member of Branion's most powerful noble family.

The cool spring breeze, wafting in through the open taproom door, whispered across three days' worth of stubble on his cheeks and ruffled his thick, golden hair in an intimately familiar gesture. Camden smiled in response, but his mind was still elsewhere. His blue eyes, red-rimmed from too much drink and too little sleep, were unfocused as he imagined the press of Knights entering the great vaulted Sword Chapel with the sun trickling down to mottle their multicolored surcoats with golden light. It was so real he could almost feel himself among them. He could smell the rich aroma of polished wooden stalls and sense the expectant hush that descended as the Aristok entered the nave to take his place behind the altar.

Atreus the Second would officiate at the High Sabat Mass of every major Temple in Branbridge until the first week of Mean Lunasa when he would sing his Anniversary Mass in the open, standing on the Branbridge Stone in the center of the city for all his people to see. Last month he had been at the Temple of the Wind. Barred from the Temple Proper, Camden had been to the ceremony regardless, although no one had seen him there, especially not the Aristok.

Built a hundred years before Braniana DeMarian had landed in Western Gwyneth, the Temple of the Wind had a dozen unused galleries and landings that looked down onto the central nave. Crouched behind the ornate wooden railing of the highest balcony in the Temple tower, Camden had watched the Avatar of the Living Flame speak the Triarchy's Blessing, then the Flame's and then the Wind's as was the custom in a Lesser Aspect's Temple. Sensitive to Its movements, he'd felt the Wind rise in response to the Aristok's power long before it began to ruffle the hair of the congregation. It had spiraled upward, Its metaphysical presence touching his mind as quickly as Its physical breezes feathered across his face. It filled him with Its ever familiar sense of rushing power, singing to him of the open sky, of tempests racing across fields to scatter across treetops and hillsides, of dust storms swirling over downs, and of waves tossed higher and higher by the force of the Wind's caress.

As he'd done so often in the past, Camden had sunk into Its embrace. His eyes sparkling with a pale gray light, his mind began to open, then he brought his control up just in time. He could not answer the Wind's call here with the Avatar of the Flame below. The Aristok would sense the shift in power and he would be discovered.

The Wind pressing against his resistance, Camden leaned his back against the cool stone of the tower wall, listening to the murmur of the ancient words below, and casting about his hiding place for something to distract him. His eyes lit on the marks of footprints on the dusty floor, and he smiled.

He was the only one who ever came up to this tiny balcony; was possibly the only one who even knew it existed anymore. Sitting in his family's private box, on a Wind's Festival Day, at age ten, an errant spring breeze had swirled about his face, drawing his gaze up along the tall spiraling temple pillars, past the main balconies and the thin graceful windows, past the vaulted ceiling with its richly carved stone buttresses, up the length of the wide Temple tower to the tiny balcony so far above his head that his young eyes could barely discern it. The Wind flowed freely up the tower's lengths and Camden felt the sudden, overwhelming desire to follow it to the highest place he would ever climb without wings.

He'd slipped away from his family after Mass that day and begun the search that would soon have him more familiar with the corridors and chambers of the Wind Temple than any of its Priests. Week after week he climbed stairs, exploring rooms and alcoves, seeking the one door that would lead him to his lofty goal. When he'd finally crept up that forgotten spiral staircase, his steps sending up little puffs of dust around his boots, and seen that small

wooden door, stuck partially open from damp and from
neglect, he'd felt the breath catch in his throat. Forcing it
cautiously open, he'd stepped inside. Then, gingerly
crossing the dusty, sun-faded floor, he'd knelt before a
stone-silled window carved in the shape of a rose and
peered down at the capital city laid out before him. The
breeze that had coaxed his vision up to this place now
sang to him more strongly than it had ever done below
amidst the overhanging buildings and crowds of people. It
was the most joyous moment of his life.

Had he been able, he'd have petitioned his mother that
day to allow him to enter the Wind Temple as an Acolyte.
It was not unusual—Great Aunt Isabelle was the Temple's
Archpriest and Uncle Collin was the Captain of its
Guard—but Camden had already sworn vows as a Page
four years ago to his eldest brother Alexander. And
Alexander was a Sword Knight, patronized by the Aristok
and therefore by the Flame, not by the Wind. All his
brothers and sisters were Sword Knights, so was his
mother, the Duke of Guilcove, and his father. They expected him to be the same, and until this day he had never
doubted the validity of that expectation. But as he left the
Temple, and his eyes were drawn inexorably back to that
tiny rose window, he felt an incredible sadness settle on
his spirit. He could visit the Wind Temple, he could worship in Its chapel, and find solace in Its gardens and tiny
upper landing, but he could not serve It. Not ever.

Ten years had passed since that day. Camden had returned often to his secret place, watching the imprint of
his boots from the day or the week or the year before
grow larger as he'd grown older. Slipping through the
door, he would first stand a moment by the balcony staring down at the altar far below and clearing his mind,
would reach out for the sense of sanctified peace that always came over him in this place. Then the Wind would
come to him. As his thoughts quieted, and the Aspect took
control of his mind, his senses would constrict, focusing

sharply on his immediate surroundings. He would feel the scratch of wood, long unpolished, against his palms, smell the moldy aroma of forgotten pennants and ragged curtains, piled away and left in a corner for the moths and the mice a century ago; watch the sunlight crawl along the floor and over the balcony railing like a living thing, and hear the warble of birds in the eaves. He would feel the cool touch of the Wind cleanse his mind and when It had filled him totally, he would move to the window and look down upon the capital. For one dizzying instant he would stand frozen, boy and Aspect in perfect balance, and then, the blue of his eyes obliterated by the swirling gray of Its power, he would fling his mind out on the tails of the Wind.

Together they would swoop over the tightly packed houses and shops, hover over the farmers bringing their produce and livestock through the North Gate, see the coaches of the nobility heading west toward the great manor houses, past the palace then beyond, across the fields and clumps of trees to touch the turret tips of the Wind Temple of Albangate barely visible in the distance. Each time Camden's mind strained to go farther, to reach the sea and dance along the waves, but that was as far as his untrained senses could take him. The Wind would move on without him and he would return to himself, crouched by the window on the tiny landing.

In the Dog and Doublet, Camden tasted the sea on this day's breeze and a flash of sadness came and went across his face. It puckered the faint scar above his left eye before it was swiftly banished. He *had* gone farther, all the way to the sea and beyond, and if he was earthbound now at least he had the memory. That was one thing they hadn't been able to take away. Raising his mug in a sarcastic gesture, he toasted the Sword Tower once again, then frowned. The mug was empty.

Glancing about he spotted the Server chatting amiably with the tavern's only other patron, a local cobbler well into his third tankard. Even here, most who could still stand attended High Sabat Mass in the single Triarctic Temple on the South Bank: *The Most Holy Shrine of the Living Flame and of the Lesser Aspects;* and so the tap-room was almost deserted.

Camden's blue eyes grew dark. *Lesser Aspects,* he snorted, as he drew the Server's gaze to him with a calculated stare. *According to whom?*

A whispered word, spoken in a voice long since silenced, fluttered past his consciousness.

"Heretic."
"Pawn," he answered gently.
"Read the signs."
"Go away."

He banished the voice with a shake of his head. The past was a closed door. It served no good to allow its ghosts into the present, even a ghost as beautiful and wise as Alisha DeMarian had been. Closing his eyes, he felt the afternoon sun caress his lids, then smiled as its warmth was swiftly brushed aside by the cool, spring breeze. Lesser or no, the Aspects were jealous of their own and, whatever his family might have wanted for him, he belonged to the Wind. Then and now. Alisha had known that, right from the beginning. So had his Uncle Celestus.

"Read the signs."
"You read them."
"Don't ignore them, Cam. Something's happening."
"So, let it happen."
"Read the signs."
"Bugger the signs."

"Cam?"
The words, spoken in the easy accent of the South Bank, drew him back to himself. He opened his eyes to see the Server leaning over him.

"What?"

She scooped up the empty mug. "I said, ya want I should get you another one, Cam?"

He shook his head, suddenly unwilling to cloud his senses any more than they already were. "Later, Annie. Is Sarah back yet?"

"She's jus' unloadin' now. Ya want I should I fetch her to ya?"

"Don't bother. I'll fetch myself to her."

Her face grew concerned. "She's in a right froth, Cam. Trevor didn't show up today. 'Sides, you know she don't like patrons goin' in the back."

"She'll make an exception for me."

Annie cast her eyes languidly up the length of his body and gave a snort. "I 'spect she will." Flicking a rag across the table, she watched as Camden rose unsteadily, gripping the back of his chair with one hand. He swayed for a moment but, as she threw one well-practiced arm up to catch him, he waved her aside. She frowned.

"You need help, Cam?"

He gave her a smile full of careless charm before shaking his head. "Not at all," he answered. "I do this every day. Walking, you know."

She nodded. "Yeah, walkin'." Watching him weave toward the storeroom, she snorted. "Staggerin's more like it." She watched him disappear into the back, then with a shrug, returned to her conversation with the cobbler. Camden DeKathrine was not her problem, he was Sarah's.

In the back storerooms, Sarah Lambton, the owner of "the Dog," as it was known to its regular patrons, hauled a sack of flour toward a stack by the wall then straightened with a groan as her left knee buckled. A lifetime in Branion's army had left her with a number of scars that acted up every spring. With a grimace, she leaned against a barrel of pickled herring. "I'm getting too old for this scorchin' crap," she muttered, running a flour-covered hand through her graying hair. "Where, by the Flame, is that useless nephew of mine?"

"Passed out at the Cock and Rabbit."

She turned with a growl, but the curse she was about to spit out at the intruder changed to a sour smile of greeting as Camden stepped into the room.

"Little bastard," she said without malice. "The least he could do is spend my brass in my own pub."

"I'll tell him that the next time we meet."

"You do that, but do it here at the Dog. I don't want to learn *you've* been frequenting some other tavern either or you'll find your credit drier than a dead fish."

He grinned at her. "It's the food, you see," he teased. "Your cousin Kathlene lays a good table. You'd know that if you ever went there."

"Like I have that kind of time with my people buggerin' off wherever the Wind takes them."

"One evening?"

"Don't you start on me today, boy," she warned. "I'm not in the mood. Kathlene has her own business to run and so have I." Catching up the sack, her knee buckled again and she swore vehemently.

"Scorch it!"

"Here, let me."

Moving past her, Camden hoisted the flour sack easily, flipped it into place, then reached for another. Never one to pass up an offer of free labor, Sarah fished through her tunic for her pouch and pipe, then stepped back to watch. Camden was a fine looking boy, she'd always thought. Strong-featured with brilliant blue eyes that lightened or darkened with his mood, and an easy smile. But his face was too often slackened by drink, his eyes clouded and his smile hidden by a bleak expression of melancholy. Tapping a finger full of fenweed into her pipe, she reached for a candle on the wall and considered what she knew of him.

He was wealthy and well educated; a Sword Knight and brother to the Duke of Guilcove. He looked to have every advantage a young man could want, but something told her that he found those advantages more of a burden than a blessing. It was said that he fought frequently with his Ducal brother who did not approve of the company he kept. With an inward snort, Sarah drew in a deep lungful of smoke. Who would, she noted to herself.

Camden frequented all the South Bank taverns, but came most often to the Dog. Sometimes he would talk, mostly about inconsequential things, but more often, like many of her Patrons he just came to drink in silence and stare at nothing. Sarah had yet to learn why he preferred the rough company and inferior wine of the South Bank to that of the more expensive and reputable establishments on Taverner's Row, but she would; the injured ones always confided in her eventually, and Cam's need to unburden himself of some painful secret was plain to be seen.

Finished with his task, Camden straightened, his thick, golden hair falling forward in a cascade of rippling sunlight and Sarah resisted the urge to reach out and run her fingers through it. He was young enough to be her grandson, she told herself sternly, and besides, she never got involved with Patrons, especially noble Patrons with drinking problems. She frowned. Annie had told her that Cam had been there all day. He must have had a serious fight with his brother to keep him here throughout High Sabat Mass.

Wiping the flour from his hands on his breeches, Camden gave her a questioning half smile, and she nodded to herself. That was it then, he wanted the key to the Dog's chapel.

Born and raised on the streets of Branbridge, Sarah was not a religious person by nature. Neither the Aspects nor Essus had lifted her from the squalor of her early life, that had taken a persuasive young recruitment sergeant in the pay of the Duke of Buckshire, but she recognized the need in others. When she'd bought the Dog, she'd turned one of the cellars into a chapel. Very few made use of it, but enough for her to keep it open. These days only Camden ventured into its tiny confines, but he never asked. He relied on Sarah to offer, knowing that she would.

With a sigh, the Dog's proprietor let out a long trail of smoke before passing a critical eye across his face.

"You look like something the cat dragged in," she noted bluntly.

He grinned at her. "Actually, he left me on the doorstep. I made my own way inside."

"Barely from the looks of you." She cast a sidelong glance out the dingy window. "Was that the bell for High Mass I heard?" she asked with studied indifference.

"The sun's just setting, so it must be," he answered in the same careful tone.

"You'll never make the Temple in time."

"Yes, it looks that way. I shouldn't have stopped to help you unload."

"Hm. Did you want to use the Dog's chapel then?"

"If no one else is there, I suppose I could."

"Help yerself." A jerk of her head indicated the line of brass keys on the wall and without meeting her eyes, Camden hooked the one he wanted off its peg and made for the door.

"Should I be expecting anyone to come looking for you?" she called after him.

His eyes flickered north toward the unseen Sword Tower for a quick moment and then he smiled faintly.

"Not for at least an hour and a half, I shouldn't imagine."

"And after that?"

"Probably. From Ler if not from Alec."

"I'll set some stew out for you, then. You'll be needing something to eat before you go back across the river."

"*Am* I going back across the river?"

"Yes, you are," she answered sternly. "For your own peace of mind, if no one else's."

He gave a short bark of laughter. "So, you know what's best for me now, do you?"

She ignored the sarcastic tone, catching his eye with a serious expression instead. "It's plain enough to see," she replied. "But go on now, you'll be late."

"It's a congregation of one. I doubt they'll start without me."

"Whatever, go anyway, I've work to do." She turned away and, after a moment, Camden left the storeroom, taking the worn cellar steps two at a time.

Sarah listened for the sound of the key in the lock, then she, too, left the storeroom. If they were going to host a DeKathrine messenger, they'd better be ready.

Annie was still talking to the cobbler, but stood when her employer limped into the room.

"You want I should finish the unloadin', Sarah," she asked, as the other woman began to rub her knee with an annoyed expression.

"No. I want you to head up to Watcher's Hill and keep an eye out for a boat coming from the Sword Tower."

"The Sword Tower?" Annie glanced toward the cellar. "Like that, is it?"

"Yes, and there may be more than one of them coming."

"You want I should get Cam out the back way when he's done?"

"No, just find Trevor first and drag him back here by the ear. I want all my people were I can lay a hand on them."

The Server chuckled. Trevor was over six feet tall already and as big around as a cart horse. He wouldn't be dragged back by any part of him if he didn't want to be, but Cam had got him out of more than one scrape with the South Bank Watch. He would come for Cam. Catching up her cloak, Annie tossed a quick look down the cellar steps.

"Is there gonna be trouble tonight, ya think?"

The proprietor jerked her head toward the door. "Of course not," she answered shortly. "I'm just being careful.

Now go and get Trevor. Have Bonnie and Haden carry
him if they have to. On second thought, have them come,
too, even if they don't have to carry him."

"Sure, Sarah."

As the taproom door swung open, Sarah cast a worried
look toward the Sword Tower. The last thing they needed
was to get caught in the middle of a noble squabble, she
thought pensively, but it didn't look like they had much
choice. The faint scent of incense wafted up from the cellar, and with a sigh, she reached for a tankard. It would all
work out, one way or another, she supposed, and if they
were lucky it wouldn't include broken furniture and random arrests, but with the Sword Knights one could never
be too sure; they were an arrogant bunch. But Trevor and
his two cousins should be enough to keep order; whatever
Kathlene's failings, she had birthed some intimidatingly
large children. Once Annie told her the story—which
Sarah was certain she would—she might even send a couple more. There was strength in family. Sarah hoped it
would be enough. Filling the tankard, she toasted the
North Bank with a sarcastic gesture much like Camden's
earlier motion, then drained the contents in one quick
swallow. It had better be enough.

The Sword Tower

Across the river, Camden's eldest brother, Alexander
DeKathrine, Alec as he was known to his immediate family, made his way through the gathered Sword Knights as
the echo of Bran's Bell faded away. The Senior Knights
had already begun their entrance to the Sword Chapel,
and he caught up with them quickly, casting a flat glare at
an unfamiliar cousin who was trying to maneuver in
ahead of him. Recognizing the Ducal crest on his kinsman's surcoat, the cousin quickly backed off with a swift
apology, and Alec headed up the steps two at a time.

Like many DeKathrines, Alec's face beneath its heavy

cap of dark auburn hair was broad, the expression in his stormy gray eyes serious. He was a tall, muscular man of twenty-nine, carrying the heavy ceremonial armor of his Order and his Ducal accoutrements with the ease of long familiarity. He'd held the shire of Guilcove for almost five years now, receiving the title and the position of Duke, after his mother, Domitia's, death. He took the advantages as seriously as he took the duties and responsibilities, and expected others to do the same.

Now, gently moving an older relative out from the doorway where she was chatting amiably with yet another older relative, he finally broke free of the press and entered the chapel's wide, sunlit nave. Tall even for a DeKathrine, he used his extra height to scan those gathered. Most of his immediate family should be here already. After a time, he spotted his sister Jo's graceful profile and made his way toward her.

Joanne DeKathrine was a tall, lithe woman three years Alec's junior. She shared his dark auburn hair and gray eyes, but where his expression was most often introspective, hers was more open. She was standing by one of the chapel's few stained-glass windows, conversing quietly with her husband Amedeus and their cousin Alister. Alec nodded to the two men, then turned to his sister.

"Everyone here, Jo?"

"Your wife's just arrived," she answered easily, knowing full well that he meant their four other siblings who held Knight's rank amongst the Swords.

He frowned at her and her lips quirked up in a smile. "I just saw Ler with Julian a moment ago," she conceded. "Over by the west transept. They should still be there."

Glancing across the nave, Alec caught sight of their brother Elerion, talking animatedly with his partner of five years and Uncle Stephan. Ler swept his own dark, auburn hair from his eyes with a smile just as Julian leaned over to make some jest. Ler looked much like Alec, green eyes and five years being the only discernible

difference between them. With a turn of his head, he
caught sight of his elder siblings and bowed slightly.

"Probably talking about hawking," Jo observed dryly.

"Probably."

After acknowledging Ler, Alec continued to sweep his
gaze across the chapel. "And the rest?"

Her lips quirked upward again. "Well, here come the
Flame Twins now."

Alec turned.

A murmur of appreciation preceding them, eighteen-
year-old Tatania and Nicholas DeKathrine entered the
chapel like a double shaft of sunlight. Known as Tania
and Nicky to friends and family, the twins were alike in
both height and coloring, long, blond hair, falling loosely
in thick waves of pure gold down their backs and pale
gray eyes warm and friendly. Their ceremonial armor
gleamed as did the metallic threads of both gold and silver
woven into their dark green surcoats, the DeKathrine bear
and Knightly sword embroidered in rich brown and red
tones. Although not identical, they enjoyed exaggerating
their similarities, presenting a beautiful picture of perfect
androgyny to the appreciative crowd.

Beside Jo, Amedeus brought his hands up to his face. "I
think I've gone blind," he joked.

Alister cocked his head to one side. "Should they be
wearing that much gold thread?"

Alec frowned. "No, they shouldn't."

"It's the style this year," Jo explained, absently turning
the signet ring on her finger. "You should see how much
gold Margurette, Duke of Kempston sports."

"That's different, she's a DeMarian."

Jo shrugged. "They're part of her circle."

"They waste too much money on clothing."

Alister chuckled. "I wouldn't call that a waste. I'd call
it a masterpiece."

Moving effortlessly through their peers, the twins
fetched up beside their older siblings, giving Jo identical
winks before greeting their brother with identical bows.

He inclined his head, acknowledging Alister's point with a grudging smile. No one could remain annoyed at the twins for too long.

"You were almost late," he chided gently as the Door Keepers began the delicate task of barring the chapel to further entry.

Tania smiled. "Aunt Nalani would never refuse *us*," she answered easily.

"Don't bet on it."

"But we did, Alec," Nicky answered easily. "Ler owes us five crowns apiece."

Their Ducal brother snorted. "He's a fool for risking it."

Tania smiled. "I did tell him that."

"Have you seen Cam?"

The sudden question caught them both off guard. The twins checked momentarily as the others grew still, then regained their composure. Both shook their heads, and before Alec could grill them further, slid off to greet their great aunt Ellesanda. Behind them, now that they had moved on, Jo spotted their brother Kassander, Tania's and Nicky's Page. His arms were laden with two heavy, dark green cloaks and Jo cast him a sympathetic glance.

"Still managing to keep up, Kasey?" she asked.

The ten-year-old returned her greeting with a wide, warm smile. Similar to Tania and Nicky in coloring, he was dressed much more simply but shone just as brightly. His nature was as effervescent as a mountain spring and it brought a smile to even the most somber of people, including his brother Alec.

"You look badly overloaded," he noted.

"I can manage," Kasey laughed in answer. "They're not that heavy, but they are awfully hot."

"Drop them in a corner, then, why don't you?" Alister suggested with a grin. "They've no real need for them today. It's beautiful out."

"Besides," Amedeus added, taking up the game,

"They've got so many, they'd never notice the lack of one each."

His smile as wide as ever, Kassander just shrugged. "I don't mind."

Jo looked down at him fondly. "Well, you can at least drop them off in the cloakroom. Get Lori over there to help you, but be quick, the Mass is about to start."

"Yes, Jo." Kasey caught the eye of his cousin Lorence, Page to their stepfather Desmond DeKathrine. The other boy caught up Tania's cloak and the two of them moved off together.

Alec returned his gaze to the gathered, seeking the last of his brothers, but the press of cousins, uncles, and aunts defeated him. He turned with a scowl.

"He's not here," he said flatly.

Careful to keep a neutral expression on her face, Jo shrugged. "I expect he's about, Alec," she answered lightly.

"You do?"

"He's probably on the other side of the chapel."

He's probably passed out in some public house on the South Bank.

The unspoken words hovered in the air between them. Neither would voice the suspicion out loud, but both believed it more than they believed that their troubled younger brother would be somewhere in the press of Knights. Alec had ordered him to be there; it was important that the family maintain a solid presence especially with the events of the past few years still fresh in everyone's minds. Alec had said just that, which was unfortunately the best way to ensure that Cam would not show up.

An inner bell sounded.

"That's the last call," Jo said. "We should get to our places."

"In a moment."

"He's here, Alec."

For a moment the identical expression of sadness that

had flashed in Camden's eyes flashed in Alec's. He shook his head.

Pursing her lips, Jo indicated that Amedeus and Alister should precede them, then turned to her older brother with a frown. "You can't expect him to come right up to you, Alec," she said impatiently, "not after the row you two had this morning."

"I'm not expecting him to come up to me," he growled back. "I'm simply expecting him to be here."

"He is here."

"Then where is he?"

Jo remained silent. They both knew that Cam, as tall as Alec and as golden-haired as the twins, was hard to miss. If he was there, they would have seen him by now, but she had no intention of indulging Alec in this mood. It wouldn't do any of them any good.

"Maybe he's outside, I don't know," she said finally. "But I do know that the Aristok's about to enter the nave and we have to get to our places. Come on." Taking her brother's arm, Jo drew him firmly toward their stalls as the gathered began to flow past them.

Grudgingly, Alec allowed his sister to lead him to the long row of box stalls on the left side of the chapel. He took his place, but once seated, continued to scan the gathered for his errant brother. There were plenty here who would notice if the family of the Duke of Guilcove were not in full attendance. Plenty who were just waiting for Cam to make another mistake to lower the boom of heresy on his head once again. So far they'd been fortunate. Cam was free to move about the country, unlike their cousin Danielle, under house arrest at her aunt Maia's keep in Werrickshire. Alec had tried to explain that to his brother, but Cam, as usual, hadn't listened. He never listened anymore.

Beside him, his late mother's husband, Desmond DeKathrine, took his place with a quick word of greeting. Alec nodded distractedly and, noting the thunderclouds in the other man's eyes, Desmond wisely left him alone.

Of an age, and friends long before Domitia—then forty years old—had taken the twenty-year-old Desmond as her husband, thus making him officially Alec's stepfather, Desmond had always deferred to his older second cousin. Things had not changed with her death. He still lived at Kathrine's Palace, their Branbridge home, along with his daughter, Alec's half sister, Melesandra. Levelheaded and objective, he was the negotiator of the family, able to defuse potentially explosive situations among his many stepchildren, but he'd met failure after failure mediating between the Duke and his brother Camden. Alec and Cam were too much alike if truth be told; neither would budge an inch. With a resigned shrug, Desmond turned his attention elsewhere.

Across the nave, in her own box stall, Jo watched the silent greeting between the two men, then studied her eldest brother, who with an impatient expression in his stormy gray eyes continued to sweep across the chapel. There would be another fight when Cam finally returned home, but glaring at everyone who wasn't their brother wouldn't help matters. Catching Alec's attention, she shot him a glare of her own, holding his gaze until he got the point and forcibly schooled his features into a less wrathful expression. Then he deliberately looked away.

Jo sighed. She remembered a time when Cam had worshiped his older brother. When the slightest word from Alec had been enough to bring a smile as wide as Kasey's to the boy's face, but that had all changed with the death of their father, eight years ago. Rubbing at a scar on her thumb, Jo frowned. Unable to deal with his own grief, Alec had turned away from Cam's. The boy had been hurt, confused, and then angry. When their great uncle Celestus had offered to host him at Tavencroft Keep in Kairnbrook, their mother had agreed. It had been the biggest mistake the family had ever made.

Across the nave, Alec raised an ironic eyebrow at her. Realizing she was now glaring about the chapel also, she schooled her own features as a young DeLynne, just come into his Knighthood, stood up in the front balcony and raised a horn to his lips. The gathered grew still. Savoring the moment, he blew one long, low call, then took a deep breath.

"His Most Regal and Sacred Majesty, Atreus the Second, Aristok of Branion, Southern Heathland, Kormandeux, Gaspellier, Roland, Anvre, Champsailles, San Valdoville, Count of Aquilliard and hereditary Earl of the Columbas Islands, Gracious Sovereign of the Triarchy, Most High Patron of the Knights of the Sword, Vessel of the Living Flame!"

The crash of ironshod boots hitting the floor was deafening as the most powerful Aristok since Braniana herself entered the nave, followed by an entourage of DeMarian and DeKathrine Knights.

Atreus the Second was a large, well-built man in his early fifties. Graying at the temples, his dark auburn hair—the legacy of his DeKathrine father—was worn long and loose, held in place by a thin silver circlet. It fell about his shoulders in a cascade of fire as if the Living Flame which pooled in his gray eyes had spilled out to create a nimbus of power about his head and shoulders. Despite the warm weather, he wore a heavy dark blue cloak trimmed in black fur, and silver-embossed armor over a silver-embroidered dark blue tunic and black breeches. His warrior's belt held two jewel-encrusted scabbards which housed the silvered and bejeweled Dagger of Divine Right and the more simply adorned Cor-Cairenn-Nemain, Bran Bendigeid's own broadsword. He wore two golden rings on his hands, the Seal of the Realm and the great Ruby of Flame. The crimson fire-wolf and three golden oak leaf clusters of the Royal Crest sparkled on his black surcoat and his polished black boots rang on the ancient temple's flagstone floor.

The Captain of the Sword Knights, Clairinda DeKathrine, Duke of Cambury, and Hierarchpriest of Cannonshire, followed at his right hand with the DeMarian Cadet, his son, one of Alec's closest friends, Marsellus, Duke of Yorbourne, at his left. Two of the Cadet's younger siblings, Tatarina, Duke of Clairfield, and Gabriel, Duke of Roland, who served as the Aristok's Squire and Page respectively, followed behind them. With four DeMarians present, the power of the Flame almost crackled against the walls.

The Consort Hadria, Duke of Lanborough, and three of the Cadet's remaining four brothers and sisters who held memberships in the Sword Knights would be officiating at other Masses across the city, with the Heir, Kathrine, Duke of Kraburn, standing in for her father at the Flame Temple to the east of the palace.

Pausing before the altar, the Captain banged one fist against her breastplate in salute. "Long live Atreus the Second!" she shouted.

"ALL HAIL THE ARISTOK!"

Atreus acknowledged the deafening greeting of his Knights with a salute of his own before making his way to the center stall before the altar. His children took their places to either side of him and, when all were ready, he raised his arms, calling down the blessing of his Aspect.

"May the Light of the Living Flame guide your arms. May it strengthen your resolve and free your spirit to better understand your duty."

Their faces raised to the skies as was the Triarctic custom, the gathered responded.

"And may we serve with honor and courage while there is still strength left in our bodies."

"I call on you now to declare yourselves in this company as True and Honorable Knights in the service of this ancient Order, the Crown, and the Living Flame."

The sound of three hundred swords being unsheathed was like a sudden rainstorm slicing down on the chapel. In his stall, Alec held his own weapon aloft, watching as it caught the late afternoon sun in a flash of silver. His father had given him this sword when he'd sworn his vows at age sixteen. Now, as he reaffirmed his commitment before their Royal Patron, he felt the power of the words fill him with a fresh sense of purpose. Putting all thoughts of the past and of Camden aside, he sheathed his sword as the Aristok began the Mass. If his brother were here, that was all to the good. If not, they would face the coming storm together as a family.

In the Dog's chapel, Camden set his own sword carefully to one side, staring sightlessly down at it for a long time. He could not have told Sarah the reasons for his avoiding the ceremony at the Sword Chapel any more than he could have told his brother Alec; that he could barely face the press of Knights who saw him as a heretic and a traitor to their Order, let alone reaffirm vows he'd been pressured into taking. It was too much.

> *"Read the signs."*
> "Go away, Lisha."
> *"Read the signs."*
> "I don't want to."
> *"Cam."*
> "Leave me alone."

The voice grew still. Closing the door, Camden began his own private Mass.

A small wooden altar stood in the center of the tiny chapel. It was bare, with no icon to identify its affiliation. Camden knelt before it, then turned his attention to a small shelf at hand's reach. It held a candle, a small bowl of water, a stick of driftwood, and a red grouse feather. Taking up the feather, he held it carefully in his hands a moment, then placed it on the center of the altar top. After a moment's contemplation, he took a deep breath and stared at its mottled markings.

The chapel's two wall sconces cast just enough light to see by. Camden concentrated until the blue of his eyes became two gray orbs, then he slowly closed them.

A breeze rose up from within his mind, sweeping all other sensations aside. He gave himself up to it, feeling the freedom of the rushing Wind flow through his

thoughts and into his body. His arms rose of their own volition, raised by the power of the freest of the Aspects.
Slowly the chapel faded from his awareness. A pale, gray
mist rolled in, and he opened his eyes.

A wide meadow appeared in the center of the mist, as
familiar as his own memories. He heard the ghost of
laughter as four youths, covered in daisy chains, chased
each other around a wide, old oak tree, bare feet trampling
the thick meadow grasses until they fell, panting, into a
sweet nest of wildflowers. They all had the look of siblings or cousins, hair of varying shades of blond or red
flowing out behind them, grass-stained shirts and
breeches holding no crest or symbol to interfere with the
morning's games. They could have been any four students
or Squires stealing an hour's play away from lessons except that the fire-pooled eyes of the youngest girl betrayed
their secret.

In the chapel, Camden smiled as he watched them rise
to run about again, but suddenly the surroundings grew
dark. The sky filled with clouds and, from their depths,
the wind grew cold. Two of the youths disappeared, while
the others mounted up and tried to make their way home
as it began to rain. The meadow faded, became a slick and
crumbling riverbank. The rain began to pour down in torrents and the remaining boy and girl fought to keep their
balance as their horses' hooves slipped on the suddenly
unfamiliar path.

In the chapel Camden felt the cold rain drive against his
face. His hair was plastered to his cheeks, obscuring his
sight. He tried to reach the place where the Wind lived
within him as Uncle Celestus had taught him, the place
from which he could reach out and take control of the
storm, bringing it into his own body where it could be absorbed, but he was too frightened to concentrate. Beside
him, he could feel the girl try to do the same, calling on
the Flame to surround them in protective warmth. For a
heartbeat they were safe and then the path vanished and

they were falling. Camden jerked backward as he felt the
sharp end of a tree branch score across his forehead.
Blood splattered into his eyes, and as the girl cried out,
her voice echoed across the Physical and Spiritual
Realms.

"Cam!"

He threw himself forward, scrabbling desperately to
find her again.

"Lisha!"
"Cam, where are you?"
"I'm here! I . . . I can't see you! Lisha, take my hand!"
"Cam! help me!"
The water closed over his head. His mind flung out on
the rushing Wind and screamed her name as his link with
her was suddenly cut off.
"ALISHA!"

"Camden!"

"Alec?"

The mist vanished. Around him the rain-drenched
downs of Guilcove stretched for miles. His face felt tight
and when he raised his hand to his forehead, it came away
bloody. He remembered then. Alec had gone hunting that
morning. He'd promised to take his six-year-old brother
along even though Camden's nurse had expressly forbidden it. So Cam had slipped from his bed and followed
him, running as fast as he could to catch the older boy. It
had begun to rain, but he'd pushed on, determined to join
him. Standing on the edge of a high chalk ridge he'd seen
Alec not a thousand yards away. He called to him, but
just as Alec turned, the ridge crumbled under Camden's
feet.

*   *   *

In the chapel Cam felt the catch of gorse bushes through his clothes and the pounding of the rain against his face. He struggled to free himself, to stand, but the earth beneath his scrabbling feet became slick and muddy. He began to slide farther down the ridge, but just as the gorse gave way to gravity, a hand shot out and caught him by the collar.

He shouted out with relief. Alec had come. Despite everything, his brother had come. Cam looked up to see Uncle Celestus standing before him.

"Cam?"

His eyes snapped open, the sound of an unfamiliar voice breaking through his Vision. For a second he was disoriented and then he remembered where he was. A faint stirring behind him made him jerk around to see Sarah standing in the doorway. In the background he could hear the faint sound of bells and knew that the city had been released to its evening. The Mass was over.

Sarah's expression showed worry, but she swiftly smoothed it over with professional ease.

"I didn't want to disturb you, Cam," she apologized, "but Annie's spotted a boat heading over from the Sword Tower with a DeKathrine Knight in the prow."

That was fast. His throat worked, but the Vision was still too fresh in his mind to allow for normal speech. He simply nodded.

"That'll be one of your family, I'm guessing, not a messenger?" she continued.

He coughed, then nodded again. "Ler . . . Elerion, likely," he answered hoarsely.

She nodded her understanding. "If you want to see him, Trevor's waiting in the taproom. He'll back you up."

Despite himself, Camden smiled at the thought of Ler's reaction to a South Bank Tavern Bouncer hovering at his younger brother's back like a giant bodyguard. "So you think I should rough up my own brother in a Public

House?" he asked, finding his voice in his amused incredulity.

She crossed her arms. "I *think* he might think twice before roughing you up with Trevor behind you," she answered curtly. "Bonnie and Haden are here as well."

"So I've my own private army, do I?"

She snorted impatiently. "You can look at it anyway you like, but the Dog takes care of its own, and I won't have my Patrons threatened in my own taproom if I can help it. Anyway, they're there if you need them."

Camden got stiffly to his feet.

"Thanks, Sarah, but if I'm going to face a brother, I suppose it ought to be the right brother, shouldn't it?"

"You're going home, then?"

"Might as well."

Reaching for his sword, he stared down at it for a long moment."

"He gave me this, you know," he said so quietly that she had to lean forward to hear him. "When I took vows as his Squire."

"The Duke?"

"Yes."

She glanced down at it, noting its plain, worn grip and short blade.

"It's a fine weapon," she replied after a moment.

He gave a short, bitter laugh. "No it's not. It doesn't hold an edge and it's too small. It was even then."

She frowned, unsure of what he wanted her to say. "So why keep it?" she ventured finally.

He shrugged. "He's never given me another. It was his place, you see. As my Knight. I've trained with other weapons; my uncle's Arms Master even offered me his own claymore, but . . ." With a sharp jerk, he thrust the sword back into its scabbard. "Stupid, isn't it? Or bloody-minded?"

"What is?"

"That I keep using it?"

"Just a bit childish, I'd say."

He glared at her, then his mouth drew up in a faint smile. "Trust you to always hit the nail on the head."

"Or the Knight, when he needs it."

"Him, too." He squared his shoulders. "And, on that note, if you'll distract Ler, I'll make use of your back door and go let Alec have his turn."

She nodded. "Trevor will see you to the river."

"That's not necessary."

She raised one eyebrow at him, and he held up both hands in mock surrender. "All right, my bodyguard can see me to the river." He moved past her, pausing to replace the key on its peg. Sarah's brows drew down.

"Why don't you just take it, Cam?" she offered. "I've got another."

He shook his head. "I'd only lose it somewhere. You keep it safe for me, will you, Sarah? Keep it as safe as you keep all my secrets?"

"What secrets? You've never told me any."

"Well, then, maybe I should."

She crossed her arms again. "Yeah, maybe you should. You need to tell somebody, that much is plain."

"Why? It's just a lot of childish nonsense like this." He gestured at his sword.

"Is it?"

He shrugged, unwilling to continue the debate. "Tell you what," he conceded. "If I survive my brother's displeasure, I'll be back tonight to drink your wine, regale you with tales of my misspent youth, and pass out on your floor, how's that?"

"Can you spare us the passing out part? You're not that light. Even Trevor has trouble lifting you."

He shook his head, golden hair falling into his eyes disarmingly. "Sorry. Passing out's part of the deal. No passing out, no life story."

"Fine. I'll just have him tip you into the horse trough for the night."

"Done."

The faint smile back on his face, but the look in his

eyes a mixture of relief and anxiety, Camden left through the back door without another word. After a quick glance at Sarah, Trevor trailed silently after him.

The sun was setting as Camden made his way back to the capital's North Bank. Above his head, the clouds flowed and merged in an intricate, wind-tossed dance which he ignored. The signs no longer interested him. They spoke of the past not the future, and he already knew the past. Alisha's words echoing in his ears, he turned away from the clouds, concentrating instead on the sound of his horse's hoofs against the cobblestones, but when the rhythm threatened to lull him into trance, he shook his head savagely. He would not See. The past was the past. He had no need of signs any longer.

By the time he made it to his family's ancient home, Kathrine's Hall was cloaked in darkness. Torches to either side of the main entrance illuminated the courtyard, casting shadows across the carved bear and rampant alphyn crest of Guilcove. They seemed to stare at him with eerie intelligence and Camden looked away as a groom came running forward. He tossed him the reins as he dismounted.

"Brush her down and feed her, Mark, but keep her ready. I'll probably be heading out again later."

The groom took the reins with a silent bow. Everyone in the household knew of the arguments between the Duke and his brother, and the groom watched with trepidation as Camden took the manor steps three at a time.

Nodding at the two guards standing sentinel before the door, Camden thrust it open, brushing past the Steward as she reached for the handle.

"Hello, Laura," he said in a tone of forced goodwill. "Any household news?"

The woman bowed, her expression as neutral as the groom's. "Your family's returned from the Sword Tower, Master Camden," she answered. "His Lordship, the Duke, was asking after you. I'm to announce you as soon as you arrive."

"Then I haven't arrived yet. I need to change first."

"And shave, Master Camden?"

"That, too. Send Jurin up, will you?"

"Yes, sir."

Camden headed for the main stairs. "So where are they all?"

"The Duke and Her Lordship Joanne are in the great hall with your stepfather. There was an upset regarding your sister Melesandra today."

Camden stopped in mid stride.

"What do you mean, an upset?"

"There was some disagreement regarding her placement as Page to your Uncle Stephan. His letter arrived today."

"Disagreement? Between who?"

"Between Master Sandy, I mean Her Grace Melesandra, and her elders."

"Well, that's hardly unusual. Where is she now?"

"She's run off to the orchards, sir."

"In the dark?"

"I sent Ewan behind her with a lantern."

Camden made for the back of the manor. "I'd better speak to her first, then."

"If you could convince her to come inside for her supper, Master Camden, her nurse would be most grateful."

"I'll do what I can."

"Thank you, sir."

Heading quickly down a side passage paneled in dark oak, Camden breathed in the faint smell of old rot with distaste. Kathrine's Hall was over four hundred years old and as far as Camden was concerned, a musty old firetrap, but it was the traditional home of the Duke of Guilcove and therefore his home also. Wishing sourly that he'd been born a shopkeeper's son, Camden pushed open a small side door, and headed for the orchards.

He found Sandy sitting with her back against the orchard's stone wall, throwing last year's apples at the dark trees beyond. The lantern was set on the wall above her head; that and the shadowy figure off to one side betrayed Ewan's silent vigilance.

Leaping easily over the wall, Camden hunkered down beside his six-year-old sister, the sight of her freckled face drawn into a scowl lightening his mood almost immediately.

"Are you defeating all your enemies?" he inquired with a smile.

Her auburn brows drew down as she hurled another apple at a branch without looking at him. It hit it square on.

"No," she replied emphatically. "I *haven't* any enemies, have I? I just have *family. They* only want what's best for me, and *they* think they know what that is better than I do just because they're *old.*"

With a half smile, Camden dug up a piece of fruit from the grass. "Well that's true enough," he agreed, hefting it in his hand before sending it flying at the same spot. "So what is it that they think is best for you?"

She narrowed her gray eyes, her broad, freckled face darkened by a furious grimace.

"*They* want me to be a Sword Knight and I *don't.*"

Much good that will do you, Camden thought, but he kept the words to himself. Pulling a rock out from beneath him, he made himself comfortable.

"So what is it that *you* want?" he asked.

"I want a white pony and dancing lessons and a dress that goes swish!" she declared immediately.

He blinked. It wasn't the answer he'd been expecting from his harum-scarum little sister.

"Can't a Knight have all that?" he asked finally.

She shot him an imperious glare. "A Knight *can* have all that, Cam," she said as if she were the adult and he the six-year-old, "But I don't *want* to be a *Knight.*"

"Why not?"

She crossed her arms. "Because they get all sweaty."

"All what?"

"All sweaty. They have to wear leather and I don't like leather, and they have to wear armor and I don't like armor, and I won't wear it!" She threw another apple at the branch, adding another spot of wet mush to the already growing stain.

Camden glanced over in admiration. "Pity. You have the aim for it."

"I don't care. I want to be a Scholar and study the physical sciences."

He blinked. "You want to study the what?"

"The physical sciences. Astronomy and geology. Master Grigori says I have a naturally analytical mind. He gave me a telescope all the way from Ekleptland that tracks the movement of the astral bodies. He could take me on as an apprentice, and I'd be a Scholar in only seven years, instead of ten for a Knight and he would, too, except that Alec would never allow it."

"I see."

Her eyes flashed dangerously. "Do you?"

"I think I do. Can you still have your pony that goes swish and your white dress if you're a Scholar?"

"Don't make fun of me."

"I'm sorry. Have you talked to your father about it?"

She kicked at the ground. "No. He'll just side with Alec, like always."

"You don't know that."

"Yes I do, Cam. And then Alec would send Master Grigori away and get me some stupid military tutor. You know he would. So you have to promise not to tell."

Sighing, he reached over and tucked her under one arm. "I promise."

They sat in silence for a moment, then he tugged at one of her long, auburn braids. "So what's your strategy?" he asked.

She shrugged. "Keep saying no, I guess. They can't *make* me be a Page if I don't want to be one. Even if they send me to Uncle Stephan's. *He* can't make me be a Page either. *Nobody* can."

He smiled. "You remind me of Mother."

Her face grew wistful. "What was she like? I can't remember her."

"Indomitable."

"What's that mean?"

"Nobody could make her be anything she didn't want to be, either."

"Good. I shall be indomitable, just like Mother." She drove her finger into the ground, digging out a small trench before looking up at him again. "But Mother was a Sword Knight, wasn't she, Cam?"

He nodded. "It was all she ever wanted."

"All the family are Sword Knights. I mean all of Mother's family, Alec and Jo and Papa and the rest."

"Yes."

"So I'm the only one who doesn't want to be one?"

He looked away for a moment. "No," he answered quietly. "There have been others."

"But they all became Knights, anyway?"

"Yes."

"That's not very indomitable."

"No, it isn't."

Tipping her head to one side, Sandy studied his face, then frowned. "Alec is awfully mad at you today, Cam," she said, changing the subject. "He was shouting and everything. How come you never went to Mass?"

"Who said I didn't?"

"Alec. He was arguing with Papa before Nurse went and told them about Uncle Stephan's letter."

"I never went to Mass at the Sword Tower, but I went to Mass."

"But you were *supposed* to go to the Sword Tower. Why didn't you?"

He shrugged. "I didn't want to," he said simply.

Chewing on one braid, she squinted up at him. "Did *you* want to be a Sword Knight, Cam?"

He gave a short laugh. "I am one, aren't I?"

Her answering look spoke volumes and he sighed.
"No," he said finally. "I didn't."

"Then why'd you become one?"

"I guess I'm not very indomitable."

"Cam."

"Alec thought it was best for me."

"Alec thinks its best for me, too, but he's *wrong*."

"Yes, I daresay he is. He was wrong about me, too."

"Then why didn't you *tell* him that?"

Camden sighed. "I did, Sandy."

"And?"

"And he didn't listen. You know Alec."

"Yeah." She tossed the braid behind her. "But he's
going to listen to me," she said fiercely. "I'm going be a
Scholar and I don't care *what* Alec says."

"Then you'd better shout louder than him and keep on
shouting until he listens."

Her eyes narrowed. "Oh, don't worry about that," she
growled. "I will."

"Good, but in the meantime, it's getting late. You
should go inside. Your nurse will be worrying."

"Let her, it's all her fault, anyway."

"Sandy."

"Oh, all right." She stood up. "Are you coming in?"

"In a minute."

"Cam?"

"Yes?"

"I think you're indomitable."

"You do?"

"Yes. You might not think so, but you are." Scrambling
over the wall, she headed back toward the manor without
another word.

Camden rested his head against the stone wall, his
mood darkening again with her absence. Before him, the
tree branches swayed in the wind, the wet circle of apple
pulp splattering droplets of prophecy onto the ground.
Once again, he ignored them. After a moment he heard
Ewan's footfalls approaching.

"Did you want me to leave the lantern, My Lord?

"No, I don't need it."

"Shall I have Jurin draw you a bath, then, sir?"

Glancing over at the tree, Camden picked up a piece of apple and threw it toward Sandy's target. It missed.

"Read the signs."

"I am reading them, Lisha."

"Sir?"

"Don't bother. I'm not staying."

"Yes, sir."

Taking up the lantern, Ewan moved off. As the orchard dropped into darkness, Camden rose, staring up at Sandy's astral bodies twinkling in the night sky. He wished her luck. If anyone could defy their older brother, it would be their fiery-tempered little sister. Even as a baby she'd never been afraid of anything.

"Indomitable," he whispered.

And the signs were there for her. He'd read them.

Walking alongside the wall, he felt the Wind feather against his cheeks and opened his mind to Its touch. His Aspect didn't fault him for his weakness—his cowardice—in letting Alec pressure him into an unwanted Knighthood. It didn't fault him for falling that day on the downs, breaking his leg and delaying his training in the process. It didn't fault him for losing his grip on Alisha's hand that night on the moors of Kairnbrook. It didn't blame him for the stain of heresy on his family's honor. But Alec did. And he couldn't face him. Not tonight. The signs had shown him that Alec wouldn't understand. He hadn't understood for eight years.

The Wind's chosen Avatar turned away from his home and toward another night of drinking and forgetting at the Dog and Doublet. Behind him, the trees swayed in the Wind, acting out the signs that Camden refused to read correctly.

2. Guilcove

The Dog and Doublet Gaming and Public House
South Bank, Branbridge

THE first thing Camden noticed when he opened his eyes was that the black-beamed ceiling above his head was swaying slightly as if he were aboard a ship. The second was the scratch of the rough blanket thrown over his shoulders. The third was the thin stream of sunlight sending a line of fire across his eyes. The physical sensations that crowded in next came too quickly to be individualized, but each rode on a wave of nausea. He groaned and closed his eyes.

After a while the roiling in his stomach eased; he opened his eyes again and took stock of his situation. He was lying on his back on a stone floor, his head and stomach pounding, his mouth tasting of vomit and wine. Around him the stacked flour and grain sacks told him where he was. The Dog's back storeroom, and it was sometime after dawn.

Reaching up to rub his face, he felt the pull of dried blood on his knuckles and the tender flesh around his eyes and mouth. That was a bad sign. Struggling to sit up, he almost vomited again, but managed to raise himself into a sitting position and drop his head into his hands. He felt terrible.

Trying to bring up the memories of the night before—he hoped it was only the night before—made his head spin in sickening circles. He remembered leaving his horse at the Paulin Wharf stables, the return journey across the river, the walk through the starlit streets of the South Bank, and of light pouring through the open doorway of the . . . His brows drew down. . . . of the . . . Cock and Rabbit.

That was definitely a bad sign.

There'd been a few taverns in between—he thought—until he'd finally returned to the Dog some time after three. The sounds of gaming and drinking had filtered out to him on a wave of fenweed smoke. He remembered a face looming toward him, a laughing, jeering face above a green tunic. That was all he remembered.

He swallowed against another bout of nausea. He hoped he'd done something intelligent then like pass out on the floor, but the bruising on his face and hands suggested that he hadn't. Sarah was going to be furious.

A sound behind him made him raise his head to peer blearily at a figure in the doorway. The tavern owner stood there, arms crossed, expression cold. They looked at each other for a long moment before Camden raised one hand in a wan apology.

Coming in to lean against the flour sacks, the Dog's proprietor studied him silently, then fished her pipe and pouch from her tunic. The smell of fresh fenweed soon filled the air, and Camden resisted the urge to swallow convulsively as his stomach twisted. The room began to spin faster. Sarah cocked her head to one side.

"So," she said, her voice sending little needles of pain across his eyes. "We've had the passing out part. Time for the life story part, I'd say."

He closed his eyes. "Sarah," he began wearily.

"Cam. You owe me for one broken table, three broken chairs, and four crowns as bribe to the South Bank Watch for not tipping you, Trevor, and the entire crew of foresters you got tangled up with into gaol last night," she stated bluntly, counting off the points on her fingers. "You owe me for not throwing you out of here for good and wiping my hands of you, and you owe me for getting

blood on my taproom floor, my storeroom floor, and my
horse blanket. You've never been that out of control before and, by the Flame, you won't be again, not in my
house. Time to pay up."

Her voice was hard, but the glint of worry in her eyes
made him feel ashamed. He looked away. "I wouldn't
even know where to begin," he answered lamely.

She shrugged. "Begin at the beginning."

He squinted up at her. "I was born in Branbridge," he
said, trying to lighten the mood.

"So was I. And?"

"And I grew up here and in Guilcove, in a damp, dark
manor house and a damp, dark castle. Any chance of an
ale? My mouth feels like a horse pissed in it."

She snorted, but turned her head to shout his order toward the taproom. After a moment, Trevor shuffled in,
looking as bedraggled as Camden. He passed over the
tankard, shot the other man a sympathetic glance, then
slipped out without meeting his aunt's disapproving glare.
Sarah waited for Camden to drain most of his drink, then
crossed her arms again.

He shrugged. "I had the same raising as most noble
children," he continued. "The same lessons, the same
challenges and the same advantages, only more of them
because I was a DeKathrine. The Aristok spoke at my
Adult Dedication and my fighting instructor was a Master
from the Bryholm school in Danelind." Staring into the
depths of the tankard, he smiled ruefully. "I was to be a
Sword Knight and a Lay Priest of the Flame, serve the
Crown, distinguish myself in battle, marry a DeKathrine
cousin with a title, sire as many offspring as she would
have, then die before I weakened, and lie in the family
barrows at Grayridge in Guilcove. Just like my father
did." Staring off into space, he rubbed gently at the scar
on his forehead.

"So, what happened to change all that?"

He shrugged. "Have you ever been to Guilcove?" he
asked instead.

"No."

"The harbors there aren't much, but the coastline is beautiful, all the same. You can lie on the edge of the cliffs, look up and see nothing but clear, blue sky." He closed his eyes, raising one hand slightly as if he wanted to reach out and touch the scene he was describing. "Below you the sea crashes against the rocks and you can hear the cries of gulls and kestrels fighting for nesting sites in the cliff face. And the wind . . . it blows all around you all day and all night. If you stand on the very edge and close your eyes, holding your arms out as wide as they can go, you can feel the Wind passing through you, filling you up with Its power, and you know that if you take one step forward, just one, you'll share in all Its secrets and all Its freedom in that single instant before you die."

He fell silent.

Sarah blew a ring of smoke into the air between them, waiting patiently for him to continue.

"My father died at Guilcove Castle when I was twelve," he said finally. "My mother couldn't bear to go back afterward. The family returned for her funeral three years later, but I couldn't visit the cliffs then. My uncle Celestus thought it was too dangerous. I haven't been back since."

Sarah frowned. "Too dangerous?"

He gave her a sly smile. "Have you ever heard of the Triarchy Heresy?"

"No."

"Simply put, it's the idea that all four Aspects should have equal representation by a Living Avatar."

Her eyes widened. "But the Priests say the Physical and Spiritual Realms can only hold up against the pressure of one Avatar: the Flame's. More would tear the Realms apart."

"The *Flame* Priests say that, you mean?"

"They all do, Cam."

"Yes, because the other three Temples don't dare go

against the Flame Temple and the Aristok, but the question's been debated for centuries, and in every century someone's put it to the test. And every time, before they could prove they were right . . ." He shrugged at her incredulous expression. "Or wrong," he added, "they've been arrested and executed by the Flame Champions, their followers scattered, and their words silenced. But the next century it's reborn again with new followers, and again and again, year after year. It won't be suppressed."

"But what does this have to do with you?"

"I was, I am, a follower of the Triarchy Heresy."

She pursed her lips. "I see."

"Do you?" he asked, echoing his sister Sandy's words from the night before. "I don't think you truly can see it unless you know it for the truth."

"But . . ." she paused, trying to decide what question to ask first. "Did you always believe it?" she asked finally.

"Deep inside, probably always, but I didn't understand that until after my father died."

Leaning his back against an apple barrel, he closed his eyes. The spinning room and the dull ache of the bruising on his face made it easy to call up that night eight years ago. Easier than he thought it would be, but he wasn't truly surprised. It was that night that had started it all. The night that the Flame had deserted his family.

It had been hot, stiflingly hot and close in his parents' bedchamber, he remembered as if it were only yesterday. He'd stood at the foot of his father's sickbed for hours, unseen beside his brother Alec, until his head had started spinning from the lack of air. He'd begun to hallucinate, his vision going from red to gray to black to red again, so that when his father finally gave up his battle with the Shadow Catcher, he'd missed it. But it hadn't really mattered. Vakarus DeKathrine was past noticing his family's grief, and his eldest son was too wrapped up in his own to notice his younger brother's. For the first time Camden DeKathrine knew what it was like to feel alone while surrounded by people. It was a feeling he would grow very familiar with.

Guilcove Castle, Guilcoveshire, Branion
Late Spring, Mean Ebril, 492 DR
Eight years earlier

The ancient castle was as quiet as a tomb. No one moved through its narrow halls as the family of Vakarus DeKathrine stood by his bedside, numb with shock. The husband of Domitia DeKathrine, Duke of Guilcove, was dead, couldn't be dead but was dead.

Vakarus lay as if asleep, his dark red hair spread out across the pillow, his strong, handsome face unmarked by any sign of injury or disease. His wife sat by his bedside, her own face pale, her hand gripping his as if her grasp alone could keep the Shadow Catcher at bay, but it was already too late. Beside her, her daughter-in-law, Anastasia, and six of Domitia's seven children stood unspeaking, the baby, Kassander, having been sent away in the care of his nurse. Elerion, sixteen and just come into his Knighthood, held his younger brother Nicholas and sister Tatania while they cried, eighteen-year-old Joanne—the most like their father of all of them—stood across from their mother, helplessly clenching and unclenching her fists, while at the foot of the bed, the eldest, Alexander, recently married and still grieving from the loss of his firstborn son not a week earlier, stood, his features white. He'd been there since his father had unexpectedly collapsed that evening and had not moved in five hours. Beside him, his brother and Squire, twelve-year-old Camden had stood for as long, trying to be a silent comfort to his elder brother while he struggled with his own disbelieving grief; fighting back the tears as, hour after hour, their father had writhed with the terrible pain that had sapped his strength so quickly.

Now it was over. The Physicians—mystified at his con-

dition and useless in his struggle—had gone, the family
Herald had been sent to Branbridge to inform the Aristok,
but still nobody moved. A cramp in Camden's left leg
made his eyes water, and he fought the urge to reach
down and massage it. He longed to open the window, to
breathe in the sweet spring breeze, to clear his lungs of
the smell of death and misery, but he didn't move. Alec
still stood like a statue, staring down at their dead father,
and as long as Alec did not move, Camden would not.

The boy risked one glance at his father's face before
turning his eyes quickly away, his head spinning. He
didn't understand why they all still stood there. It was
over, Da was gone. Couldn't they see that? The Shadow
Catcher had slipped in somehow, despite the tightly
locked window. It had oozed up through the floorboards,
or the crack beneath the door. In a heartbeat, It had stolen
their father's Spirit—a Spirit as strong as the mountains
themselves—as if it had been a child's, then slipped away
without a sound. Now all Camden wanted to do was slip
away himself, to leave this dark and gloomy fortress and
run across the moonlit meadows to the cliffs where the
wind could dry his tears, but he couldn't move. Not until
Alec moved.

Slowly, the room began to spin in front of his eyes,
then the floor came toward him very fast and made the
decision for them all.

The funeral was to be held a week later to give the
Aristok and his entourage time to make the journey from
Branbridge. Vakarus' carefully wrapped body was laid in
the larger castle crypt to wait, the family taking turns to
stand sentinel over their fallen kinsman. Camden did not
understand the reason for this ritual either. The Enemy
had already stolen the only prize worth having and no
mortal could possibly wish to creep inside that dark and
dismal tomb, but Alec took his place at his father's head
each evening and so Camden stood, unseen, beside him,

night after hollow night. And as the week passed, the damp, moldy air became even more unbearable.

During the day Alec went out alone to ride the narrow line of chalk downs, staring out at the marshes and mud-flats that made up so much of Guilcove, his gaze blank and unfocused. Camden would have gone with him, but Alec had refused his company that first morning, and every morning since. Confused and hurt, Cam had finally stopped asking. His bother Ler had taken the twins to Aunt Nalani's keep ten miles south of Guilcove Castle. Their mother was sequestered in her chambers with the family Flame Priest, and Jo spent all her time in the north practice circle hacking straw dummies to pieces. Camden found himself wandering the cliff edge with the softly blowing wind no comfort for the first time in his life.

Meanwhile, Guilcove itself began to fill up with family, as every DeKathrine who could make the journey in time swelled the castle's population. Aunts, uncles, and cousins by the score filled every corner of the keep and Camden quickly went from lonely to overwhelmed. As their only slightly subdued presence drew Domitia and Jo from their grief, brought Ler, the twins, Kasey, and even Alec home, it drove Camden farther into himself. There were too many people, too many voices, and no one to whom he could confess his growing sense of isolation. His older brother was still distant and cold with him. At first Camden had feared that Alec was angry because he'd fainted that night, or maybe that he'd made some unforgivable blunder in the crypt, or even that he was somehow responsible for their father's death, but finally, as resentful anger at his brother's silence slowly built, he'd thrust all these thoughts aside and returned to his cliffs. He didn't know why Alec wouldn't speak with him and he decided that he didn't care.

Then the Aristok's entourage descended from the capital. Shield Knights replaced the familiar House Guards of Guilcove, the local Priests were sent packing by a dozen Branbridge Flame Priests, and even Domitia gave up her chambers for the Aristok and his Consort. As each familiar face was replaced by a stranger, Camden's resentment grew. It felt like Guilcove had been invaded. When Alec curtly informed him that he was not to leave the castle grounds—with the Aristok in residence it was considered too dangerous—the invasion was complete.

That day, Camden disobeyed his eldest brother for the first time in his life: he immediately left for the cliffs. When he returned, Alec was too busy to see him until supper and then his shadowed gaze barely registered his Squire's presence at all. Fists clenched, Cam returned to his cliffs.

Now, as the gathered stood in a wide semicircle before the largest of the eight barrows on Grayridge Common, Camden glanced up at the cloudy sky. It was empty of birds. It would storm soon. He nodded grimly. He hoped it would. He hoped it would rain so hard that it would gut out the torches of the Flame Priests, wash the stinking funerary balms from his father's body, and flood the entire plain until there was nothing left but the tops of eight tiny hills. He hoped the litter would be hit by lightning and burn up and he hoped it would hail until the ashes were driven into the ground.

Expanding the carnage to include the Priests, Shield Knights, and Councillors of the Aristok's entourage, Camden failed to give the proper response to the first blessing or the second and, drawn by his anger, the Wind began to rise.

On the other side of the semicircle of mourners, thirteen-year-old Danielle DeKathrine watched the breeze swirl around her Guilcove cousin as he drove the toe of his boot into the ground. Her father, the Viscount Celestus of Kairnbrook, had had his eye on Camden for a long time and now Dani could see why. The Wind positively hurricaned around him. Strawberry-blonde brows drew down as she considered this. The Wind's power was definitely rising and, funeral or no funeral, the Priests were bound to notice the shift away from the Flame; and if they didn't, the Aristok surely would. Anyone with half an eye for the signs could read them. She risked one glance in their direction.

The service was winding down. The Priests' singsong chanting had risen in pitch and volume as they called on the Living Flame to bless Its servant, Vakarus DeKathrine, and Atreus was stepping forward to bestow it. They would be moving the body into the barrow in a moment, and Dani had a fairly good idea what Camden's reaction would be when that happened. Already the breezes about him were snapping at his hair and shaking the blades of meadow grass at his feet as the faintest of gray sparks began to shimmer in his eyes. He had to be distracted quickly.

She glanced up at her father. Celestus' lean face was composed into what she called his religious mask; outwardly respectful but with a distance which expressed, to the daughter who knew him so well, his total inward disdain. He was watching the Flame Priest carefully, but turned his black eyes to meet hers as the weight of her regard broke through his thoughts.

With the faintest movement of her head, Dani indicated Camden. Celestus' eyes tracked across the boy's face and the swirling grasses at his feet, then he nodded his consent. As the Archpriest of the Flame gave the signal for Vakarus' body to be placed in the barrow, Dani called up the power of the Sea and, turning her own black eyes full on her Guilcove cousin, willed him to look at her. The tiniest of blue sparks shot from her eyes to his. Startled, he met her gaze and when she had his full attention, she gave him a half smile and a shrug of sympathy.

That was all it took. The Wind receded, the threatened storm passed, and the Flame Priests concluded Vakarus DeKathrine's funeral, calling down the Flame's blessing without interruption from any of the other three Aspects.

Dani went looking for Cam the next day.

She found him at the cliffs, sitting with his back against a rock, his face lifted to the soothing wind and a huge white-and-gray herring-gull standing like a sentinel on the top of the rock above his head. It regarded her with one yellow eye and, always partial to seabirds, she returned its stare with a meaningful one of her own. It took flight with an uncharacteristically silent beating of wings and, with a smirk, she turned her attention to her cousin.

He'd not noticed her arrival. Barefoot and unarmed, his golden hair spilling across his shoulders, he remained motionless, eyes closed and hands clasped loosely over a simple dark green tunic that bore no crest or family device. His black breeches were faded and patched and Dani assumed they were old favorites, worn for comfort rather than for style, probably hand-me-downs from his older brothers. Never one for the frivolities of fashion herself, she nodded her approval and moved her scrutiny to his face. His expression was one of melancholy repose, and assuming he'd gone into some kind of light trance, Dani positioned herself between her cousin and the sun and waited for him to notice that he was no longer alone.

Unaware of her regard, Camden was far away, flying on the coattails of the Wind. It whispered through his hair, bringing the taste of heather and thyme to tickle against his nose and the sounds of birds and the distant hum of bees to still his thoughts. He could feel the beating of a hundred butterfly wings as the little blues fluttered about the turf and furze-covered hills and the minute resistance of thistles, trefoil, and clover as he brushed against their stalks. He hovered about the newborn lambs in the pasture fields, and breathed in the strong, familiar smell of wool and sunshine as they nuzzled against their mother's sides, then, in a single heartbeat, he was up and racing a mistle thrush across the downs. He soared into the air after it, higher and higher, feeling the last shred of grief begin to slip away. He reached out, felt his mind gather to leap the final gulf between human and Aspect just as a presence broke through his reverie like a dash of cold water. He swore. Eyes snapping indignantly open, he expected to see a castle servant come to fetch him home, but instead he saw a tall, freckle-faced youth about his own age, her tousled, strawberry-blonde hair sticking out in all directions and her black eyes staring disconcertingly down at him. He blinked in confusion, then, as he came back to himself, he recognized the girl from the funeral. She was dressed much as she had been yesterday; padded, dark green tunic with its bear and eagle crest of Kairnbrook on the front, black breeches and boots, and a dagger and short sword hanging from opposite sides of a worn belt. She looked capable and dangerous, but when she saw that she finally had his attention, she shot him her already familiar crooked half grin.

"I could've had you there," she said, her accent in the rich tones of the north country. "With you asleep and all."

"I heard you coming," he lied, as he tried to gather his scattered wits. "Besides, with all the Guards and Sword Knights around here, you couldn't be any kind of threat."

"No?" She dropped down to sit beside him. "I'm Dani," she offered.

"Cam."

"We're cousins."

"No kidding?"

"No, really. First cousin, once removed, twice over, to be exact. My da, Celestus DeKathrine, is your father's and mother's uncle both, so he's your great uncle times two, see?"

The physical world back in control of his mind and body, Cam nodded. His parents had been first cousins, as had one set of grandparents—a not uncommon arrangement among the DeKathrines—but one that complicated the family tree. He glanced over at her scabbard.

"You're a Squire."

"To my da."

"I heard he was a Scholar."

"He holds a Knighthood in the Lance from when he

was young." Plucking a small snail shell from the grass, she studied it carefully before tossing it behind her. "We live at Tavencroft Castle in Kairnbrook," she continued. "Da's the Viscount."

"You made good time from there," he noted, unable to mask a sour expression.

She ignored it. "We were in Branbridge visiting Cousin Maia when we heard the news," she explained easily. "We came down with her party."

"Oh."

"Are you a Squire, too?"

"To my brother, Alec."

"Why aren't you wearing your sword?"

He shrugged. "There didn't seem to be any point."

She frowned, but dropped the subject. Glancing around, she took in the cloudless sky, the unbroken line of green cliffs, and beyond them, the hypnotically inviting blue sea. "This is a beautiful spot," she noted. "All four Aspects together, Wind, Sea, Earth, and Flame." She poked him in the chest.

He squirmed uncomfortably. "The Flame resides in the Aristok and the Royal Family," he answered stiffly. "There's no Flame in me."

"No? You're angry, and anger is Flame in the emotional charting."

He squinted over at her. "In the what?" he asked, ignoring the reference to anger.

"The emotional charting," she intoned with mock seriousness. "All things can be placed in one of four categories, one for each of the four Aspects, even emotions, see."

"Says who?"

"My da. He knows everything, and he says anger is Flame."

"So what are the others?"

"Beats me." She picked up another snail shell. "How do these get up here?"

"Storms."

"Oh." She tossed it over the cliff edge. "Da and Quin—
that's your second cousin Quinton and my third cousin
once removed, you know, Cousin Clairinda's fourthborn—they know about all that stuff. Me, I mostly know
swords. And the Sea." She stood and peered over the
edge. "Is there a path down to the water."

"Back along that way." He gestured behind them.

"Good, I wanna go swimming."

"What?"

His melancholy forgotten in the face of this unorthodox
idea, he scrambled up and ran after her as she strode purposely to the small cleft in the chalk cliff which he'd indicated.

"You can't swim today," he protested. "It's Mean Ebril.
It's still way too cold."

"Just the way I like it." Her black eyes were challenging. "I'm not afraid of the Sea, Cam. Are you?"

"Not afraid, just respectful."

She smiled broadly at him. "I like that," she said. "Respectful." With another one of her crooked grins, she
began to make her way down the narrow path.

"Wait."

"What for?"

"Because . . ." He paused, unwilling to admit the loneliness that her presence had banished for the first time since
his father's death. "Because . . . they'll be looking for us
soon," he answered instead. "We don't have time and they
won't know where we've gone."

"Da will know."

She disappeared from view, her voice floating eerily up
to him through the outraged cries of the cliff-nesting
kestrels. "Are you coming or not?"

He hesitated for just a moment longer and then made
his way resignedly after her.

When he got to the bottom of the cliffs, she'd already
shed her clothes and was standing on the pebble beach,
her arms stretched wide as if to encompass the entire
seascape before her. She was a tall, muscular girl, with

small breasts and long, sturdy limbs. Her short, tousled
hair brushed against a wide scar on her shoulder and, as
his eyes tracked down, he saw two more on her arms and
one on her leg. As he watched, she dove headfirst into the
cold surf. He ran forward, only to see her head pop up a
second later.

"You're right," she shouted. "It is cold." With a whoop
of joy, she disappeared again and when she resurfaced,
her brows drew down in an impatient frown. "Aren't you
coming in?" she demanded.

"No."

"Suit yourself." Her head disappeared again.

Marveling at her ability to stay in the cold water, Cam
seated himself on an overhanging rock, waiting for her to
finish a series of somersaults. After a while, she swam
over to him. Leaning her arms on the rock, she paddled
her feet behind her as she studied him. "Don't you like to
swim?" she asked.

"Sure I do . . . in the summer."

She shrugged. "I've been in since last month in Kairnbrook and it's a lot colder there."

"Not everyone wants to freeze to death," he retorted.
"And then drown."

She grinned. "I can't think of a better way to die. To
give yourself up to the waves, to have the Sea enter your
body and fill it up with salt and sand, and take you out to
the very center of Its heart—"

"To be eaten by whales," Cam interjected.

"So what's the perfect death for you?" she demanded.

"No death at all."

A strange blue light swam in the black depths of her
eyes. "Don't be stupid, Cam, everyone dies, so if you
could choose how it would happen, what would it be—to
lie in some clammy bed at a hundred and one, I'll bet."

Her challenging look was back, but Cam ignored it. He
thought of his father's face, calm and peaceful for the first
time in hours, of his mother's grief, and of his brother's
cold silence. He shook his head.

"No."

"What, then?"

"I don't know."

"Sure you do. Everyone does. They just won't talk about it because they're afraid."

"Of course they're afraid," he snapped, her easy tone making him angry. "Death is frightening. It's sudden and it's final and it's horrible. The Shadow Catcher can take anyone at any time. Just like that." He snapped his fingers at her. "No one's safe from It, not ever. And no one gets to choose, not really. It's a stupid question."

Dani studied him calmly. "You're wrong, you know," she said after a moment. "Plenty get to choose: Physicians who treat contagious patients, soldiers who march to battle against overwhelming odds, or people just too injured by life to go on. It's not death they're afraid of, Cam, it's the *way* they might die. A *perfect* death is worth dying for, see, but hardly anyone gets a *perfect* death; that's what they're afraid of."

He shook his head. "So is that what *you're* afraid of? Not getting a *perfect* death?"

She flicked a handful of water at him. "Just answer my question, Cam. What's the perfect death for you? Come on, everyone has one."

He fell silent, thinking about his father again. Vakarus DeKathrine had been a warrior, a Sword Knight who'd ridden into battle beside the Aristok, year after year. He must have faced death a hundred times without flinching. Had he thought about it? Had he believed that a death in battle would be a perfect death, a death worth dying for? Cam snorted. Probably not. Nobody thought about these things. They just did what they had to do and hoped they'd get out of it alive somehow. Dani was crazy.

He glared down at his cousin, but she merely stared back at him patiently, waiting for his answer. He shook his head forcefully.

"To jump off the highest cliff in the land in the middle of a terrible storm," he snapped at her finally. "To be one with the Wind when It's at Its most violent and Its most powerful. There, happy?"

She laughed. "I knew it."

"Knew what?"

"Nothing." Pushing off the rock, she flipped backward under the water again.

"Knew what!"

But she was gone. Moments later she resurfaced some distance away and it was clear that if he was going to get an answer from her he'd have to go in after her. Suddenly he wanted to and, leaning down, he dipped his hand into the chill water. He supposed it wasn't *that* cold.

"Danielle!"

His cousin's name, shouted from the top of the cliff, jerked him to his feet. A tall, dark auburn-haired man in DeKathrine black and green was gesturing and when Cam turned, he saw Dani wave back.

"That's Da. I told you he'd know where we were." She pulled herself gracefully up onto the rock. Cam helped her dry off and dress and, by the time her father arrived on the beach, she was just doing up her belt buckle. She accepted a kiss on the cheek, then turned.

"Da, this is Camden DeKathrine. You know, Vakarus' fourth, your great nephew."

"Yes, of course." Celestus turned eyes as intense as his daughter's on Cam's face, but when he smiled, the boy felt the true warmth of his regard. "I was at your First Dedication, Camden," he said formally. "Though I doubt you'd remember me."

Suddenly inexplicably shy, Cam shook his head. "No, sir."

"Please, I'm your uncle and a familial title is much more pleasing to me than sir."

"Yes, Uncle."

"Much better." Celestus glanced up at the sky, smiling as the breeze brushed against his cheeks. "There were many signs that day as I recall," he noted. "The Wind was particularly active." His black eyes returned to Camden's face. "You're what, twelve years old now?"

"Yes, Uncle."

"Then you'll have had your Adult Dedication already."

Cam nodded.

"Did your Priest take notice of any particular signs?"

The memory of the Wind's whispering through his hair almost brought a smile to the boy's lips, but then he frowned. His mother's Flame Priest had officiated at his Adult Dedication and he'd not said more than three words to Camden himself. He shrugged. "No."

"How unusual." Celestus' expression was thoughtful. "Did you?"

"Did I what, Uncle?"

"Notice any particular signs that day?"

Cam shrugged, unwilling to share the memory of the Wind's embrace but somehow unable to lie about it to this strange new relative. "There were eight of us having the ceremony," he answered finally. "The signs could have been for any of us."

"Perhaps." Celestus allowed himself a faint smile. "Still, I was so sure the Wind had taken particular notice of you at your First Dedication," he mused. "It was quite a stormy afternoon, but then perhaps it was just a coincidence." He stared silently out to sea, watching a gull skim the surface of the waves. After a while, Cam shot Dani a questioning look, but she was also staring out across the water, her black eyes far away. Finally Celestus stirred. "I was so certain of it," he said, almost to himself, then his eyes found his nephew's face once again. "I keep abreast of most of the family's activities, you know. There was a time when I half expected to hear that you'd been sent to the Wind Temple to Squire under my nephew Collin. Imagine my surprise when I learned that you were to become a Sword Knight, sworn to the Flame. I thought Vakarus paid greater attention to the signs than that. He did as a boy."

Cam squirmed uncomfortably. "I'm Squire to my

brother Alec," he explained. "He's a Sword Knight, you see," he added lamely.

Celestus' thin face lit up. "Of course, that explains it. You were always very close to Alexander, as I remember. Domitia wrote that you were devoted to him as a boy and that your brother took you everywhere with him."

The relief turned in on itself and Cam looked away. Celestus exchanged a knowing glance with Dani before continuing in a kindlier tone. "You mustn't think your brother has forgotten his love for you, Camden," he chided gently. "He's just lost a son and a father this spring. It's a heavy burden to bear. He'll come around."

Cam's face worked between wanting to believe him and wanting to hold on to his anger. Finally he shrugged. "Maybe," he allowed.

"You just need to give him a little time." Glancing about again, Celestus smiled. "I haven't been to Guilcove in years," he said, changing the subject. "But I'm pleased to see that it's still as beautiful as I remembered. It's so very different from my own home. Kairnbrook hasn't the cliffs, you see. It's composed of rolling hills and the like."

"The water's warmer here, too," Dani interjected.

"I imagine it would be, it's not so deep. That must please you." He smiled down at her. "I sometimes think Danielle is a sea spirit's changeling," he joked, returning his attention to Cam. "She'll swim in even the coldest water." He glanced knowingly at the boy's dry hair. "I see, however, that you prefer the touch of the Wind to the touch of the Sea, yes?"

Cam nodded mutely.

"We all have an Aspect with which we feel the most comfortable. It's quite natural. In fact, to recognize and embrace such a bond strengthens the Realm."

Cam looked up. "Does it?" he asked almost eagerly.

"Of course."

"Um, do you? Have an Aspect you're most comfortable with, I mean?"

"I?" Celestus looked once more at the rolling seascape.

"I've loved them all in my time," he said quietly. "When I was a boy, I loved the Wind's freedom and the Sea's unpredictable changeability. Then, through my studies, I grew to love the ever faithful Oaks. I even went through a conventional period where I loved the Flame with Its raw, transforming power." He fell silent. "But my Dianne, Danielle's mother, she loved the Sea most particularly. She died in Its embrace, and for a long time I hated It for taking her away." With a sad smile, he looked down at his daughter. "Then Danielle taught me how to love It again, didn't you, my young porpoise? A good thing, too, since you're almost never to be found on dry land." He reached over to scoop her into a one-armed hug.

"It's a pity that Domitia is so locked into her worship of the Flame that she can't see her children have their own callings," he continued to Cam. "But then she always was a very conservative person, even as a child. Not that I mean to insult your mother, Camden," he added seriously. "I hold her in the highest esteem. But if we remain blind to the personalities that make up our family we weaken it, and that weakens the Realm. Don't you agree?"

"Uh, yes, Uncle, I suppose." Cam stammered. "I never really thought about it."

"No, you wouldn't. You haven't a Scholar's training. Fortunately for you." He smiled down at his nephew to assure him that he was not finding fault. "It can be very dull for those who haven't the love of it."

"Like Quin," Dani added.

"Yes, like Quinton. Has Danielle told you about him, Camden?"

"Just that he knows a lot of things . . . like you do."

Celestus smiled. "A daughter's praise is biased but treasured. Yes, Quinton does love his book learning. He lives with us at Kairnbrook, did you know that?"

"No, Uncle."

"I seem to collect young people. Sometimes even the most loving of families need time apart, and many have found some little peace at my home. Life moves more

slowly there, and I have few expectations and fewer rules.
Even your father stayed with me for a while when he and
your grandfather were having difficulties. He was about
your age, I believe. Now Quinton has been with us for,
what, six years . . . seven?" He turned to Dani.

"Eight. Remember, he came the summer after Mother
died."

"Oh, yes. Has it been that long?"

Celestus shook his head as Dani turned to Cam. "I was
lonely without her, see, so Cousin Clairinda sent Quin to
Kairnbrook to keep me company because we're the same
age. It was just us until Lisha came two years ago."

"Lisha?"

"Your cousin and my first cousin once removed, Alisha
DeMarian," she explained with her now familiar need to
set the introduced person firmly into the family tree. "You
know, the daughter of your Aunt Hadria, my cousin. She's
the Aristok's fifthborn. Lisha, I mean." She paused.
"Fourth in line for the throne now, since Prince Atreus
died in eighty-seven."

Cam nodded. His aunt was the Aristok's Consort and
between them they'd had nine children, one more than
Camden's own parents. But the Royal children were always counted among the DeMarians, not among the
DeKathrines.

"She's not anything like the rest of the Royal Family
though," Dani continued in a thoughtful voice. "She was
sick for a long time and it made her really quiet and
well . . . sweet, you know?"

"Sweet?"

"Well, nice anyway, not all arrogant and wild like the
rest of them. I think her illness harmed her relationship
with the Flame."

"And . . . her Highness lives with you, too?" he asked
hesitantly.

"She was feeling rather overwhelmed by siblings when
the youngest was born," Celestus explained. "I understand
he has a healthy pair of lungs."

Camden could understand that. "Are there . . ?" He paused, uncertain of how to phrase his question without sounding rude. "Are there . . . any others who live at Kairnbrook?"

"Any more nieces or nephews, you mean?" Celestus laughed. "No, just the two of them at the moment. And Danielle, of course. Plenty of room, though. Tavencroft is a huge, airy place and I do love to hear the sound of children's laughter in the galleries. Not that I'll hear it for much longer, they're all growing up so quickly." He tugged at Dani's hair and she grinned before pulling away.

"I did have a thought while watching the two of you from the cliff top," Celestus continued. "I wonder if you might like to visit Tavencroft for the summer. It would give your brother a chance to grieve without feeling guilty about ignoring your training, and it would balance the dynamic between my three bear cubs there." He leaned forward conspiratorially. "I'm afraid that Danielle and Alisha bully my poor Quinton most dreadfully."

"We do not!"

"And I think you might find it pleasant as well," Celestus added, ignoring his daughter's protest. "The Wind is very . . . powerful. Kairnbrook is famous for its winds, you know. It might be pleasant for you." He caught Cam up in his intense gaze once again. "We leave in a day or two and we'd love to have your company, if you'd like to have ours."

His face suddenly red, Camden looked away. The thought of running away from Guilcove Castle with its dark and gloomy halls that smelled of dust and death was almost too much to hope for. He'd liked Dani immediately and there was something about his Uncle Celestus, with his old-fashioned, almost formal speech, that was oddly compelling. He understood about the Wind and about peace, but . . . his place was by Alec's side. Just because he didn't want him now didn't mean he might not need him later.

* * *

"Why should later be any different than now," his mind retorted angrily. *"He won't even notice you've gone."*

"I'd notice."

"So notice at Tavencroft. You heard what Uncle Celestus said. It's huge and it's airy, and it has winds. I want to go. I can't breathe here."

"But my duty's here."

"Bollocks!"

Sensing his inner argument, Celestus placed his hand lightly on Camden's shoulder. "If you're worried that leaving so soon might be inappropriate, I could ask your mother and your brother myself. Sometimes these things are best broached by an adult, anyway. And, of course, if at any time they need you to come home they have only to send a messenger and I'll put you on the first ship back to Guilcove. As well, if you're unhappy or homesick yourself, you need only tell me. I'd understand. We believe in honesty over tact at Tavencroft, don't we, Danielle?"

"Yep."

Digging his toe into a cleft in the rock, Cam glanced up shyly. "My father visited you . . . like this?" he asked.

Celestus nodded. "Exactly like this. He stayed for the summer, and when he went home, things were much better between himself and your grandfather. Sometimes people just need some breathing space."

"You see?"

"Shut up."

"You'll talk to Alec?" Cam asked hesitantly. "You'll tell him that I don't want to run away from him or anything, it's just that . . ." He fell silent.

"It's just that you need time alone and so does he."

"Yes."

"Of course, I'll tell him." Celestus caught Cam in his dark-eyed stare. "He will understand, Camden," he said seriously. "He won't be angry with you."

"And you don't mind?"

"If I minded, I wouldn't have invited you. You're family, Camden, as precious to me as Quinton, or Alisha, or even Danielle."

Cam took a deep breath. "All right. I'd like to come with you, if Alec agrees."

"I'm sure he will." Celestus turned his dark gaze to the cliffs. "So, shall we return to the keep? I believe we're overdue in the banquet hall, and it wouldn't do to keep the Aristok waiting, now would it?"

His tone was oddly sarcastic, but Camden barely noticed as the three of them made their way back up the cliff face. His head was spinning and his stomach felt tight with anticipation and uncertainty. He felt a growing need to see Tavencroft and experience the winds his uncle had spoken of, but he hardly dared hope that Alec would agree.

Behind him, Celestus began to hum contentedly as he climbed, and Cam relaxed. His uncle would see to it; he had said he would, and suddenly Cam knew that anything Celestus DeKathrine put his mind to would be done. With the Wind tugging playfully at his clothes, Camden bent his attention to his ascent.

They took ship for Kairnbrook two days later. Cam stood on deck, looking back at the battlements of Guilcove Castle, unsure of whether he should feel relieved or injured that his brother had agreed to his leave-taking so quickly, but, as Uncle Celestus and Cousin Dani came to stand beside him at the railing, he smiled. The Wind danced through his hair and, as he turned to face the open sea, he put all his worries about Alec and home aside for the summer. He never noticed the figure standing stiffly on the gatehouse battlements, watching the ship depart with a worried frown.

Domitia's Personal Flame Priest and cousin, Darnell DeKathrine, stared darkly out to sea until Celestus' ship passed out of sight. He'd not approved of Camden's leave-taking, but could offer up no solid evidence for his disapproval beyond a vague sense of foreboding, and so had kept his arguments to himself. But now, as his gaze was directed by a shaft of sunlight to the small figure of Alexander DeKathrine riding alone on the downs, the sense of foreboding grew. He turned away, determined to discuss his fears with the Archpriest of the Flame. Something was not right, and it involved both the older and the younger brother.

Aboard ship, Celestus DeKathrine put his arm about his nephew's shoulders and smiled triumphantly toward the distant Flame Priest, then turned his attention seaward as they passed out of sight.

3. Tavencroft

The coast of Kairnbrook
492 DR

CAM spent the bulk of the two-day voyage to Kairnbrook leaning on the ship's railing, watching the
coastline slide past, and listening to Dani as she explained
the significance of every castle, manor house, and tower
between Guilcove and Kairnbrook. As dusk settled a hazy
orange glow across the distant hills on the first day, the
ship swung east to bypass Forness Island and Celestus
joined them at the rail.

"Shoreshill Port," he said, indicating the mass of
moored frigates and merchant ships to their left. "The
easternmost gauntlet for Branion's mighty sea-going fist."
He glanced down at his daughter. "The others being?"

"Breymouth, Barrowness, Kempsmouth, SeaWynne,
Grimscomb and Atreanusport," she answered promptly.

"Controlled by . . . ?"

She snorted. "The DeMarians. Except for Atreanusport;
that's Cousin Justin's, but he's followed the Aristok's lead
his entire life so it might as well be theirs. And Grimscomb, of course."

"Ah, yes, Grimscomb. Do you know its story, Camden?"

Celestus turned his intense gaze on his nephew's face,
and having been listening with only half an ear, Cam
started.

"Uh, Grimscomb?" His face red, he struggled to call up

the map of Branion his tutors had tried to instill in him with little success. "It's, uh, between Cambury and Linconford, isn't it?"

"Cambury, Linconford, and *Bricklinshire,* actually," Dani corrected.

"Right." Embarrassed, Cam looked away, and Celestus put his arm about his shoulders.

"Don't fret, Nephew," he said in a gentle tone. "We'll soon have you quoting political and geographical details with the best of my children. So, Grimscomb: nestled between three shires; each controlled by a separate family, DeKathrine, DePaula, and DeLynne. Harbor Treaty negotiated and therefore possible civil strife averted by . . . ?"

Camden brightened. "Collin DeKathrine," he answered promptly, recalling the old family story. "Acting as Regent for Kathrine the First, I mean Kathrine the *Second.*"

"Very good. So although Grimscomb is in theory controlled by three separate families, the family which extends the greatest influence would be . . . ?"

"The DeKathrines?"

"Exactly."

Celestus returned his gaze to the distant harbor, watching as the lamplighters began their rounds, illuminating each of Shoreshill's twenty wharfs, one by one.

"Every harbor in Branion—be it large or small—plays a vital role in the defense and prosperity of the land, and so it behooves us to take an interest in each and every one; to know its strengths and its weaknesses, its uses and who controls it. Each is important but most important of all are the seven Danielle has mentioned. Within their safe embrace the DeMarian Aristok has assembled the greatest Navy in the known world. Led by *Kassandra's Pride.*" He nodded toward the largest frigate. "His Majesty's flagship. Captained by . . . ?"

Wishing that he'd paid more attention to his studies, Cam peered into the gloom. "It's flying a DeKathrine standard," he observed hesitantly.

"A bear and two mastiffs. The Viscount of Dunmouth."

"Cousin Brittany," Dani supplied.

"She commands in the Aristok's absence. A steady, experienced Captain, a bit cautious, but a good balance to the Captain of *The Sea Bear* beside it."

"Cousin Nathaniel."

"Commanding in the absence of the First Admiral."

"Cousin Maia."

"The Duke of Werrick."

His head spinning with so much information, Cam concentrated on the distant ships.

"A lot of them are flying DeKathrine standards," he noticed.

"Most of them, actually," Dani offered smugly.

Celestus smiled. "DeMarian ships berthed in DeMarian harbors, but commanded by DeKathrine Captains. So, taking our discussion to its logical conclusion, what family would you say extends the greatest influence over these seven harbors, Camden?"

"Um, the DeKathrines, I guess."

"You guess?"

"Well . . ." Scratching nervously at his cheek, Cam tried to put into words the anxiety the thought provoked. "But they're DeKathrine Captains sworn to the DeMarian Aristok, aren't they?"

"Yes."

"So their influence is, uh . . . is . . ."

"Incapacitated?" Dani suggested.

"No."

"Impotent? Emasculated?" she offered with a grin.

"No . . . what?"

"Suborned to another's will," Celestus finished, with a faintly amused, yet reproving glance in his daughter's direction.

"Yes."

"The foundation stones of the Crown's power," Dani quoted in a sarcastic tone, ignoring her father's expression with calculated élan.

Cam gave her a questioning look, but she just crossed

her eyes at him, then turned to watch a large school of herring swim by as Celestus continued.

"So, we may then say that, for the sake of argument, the DeKathrines are, in actuality, the most powerful naval family in Branion. Combine that with our not inconsequential military and political might on land and we might say that the DeKathrines are the most powerful family on the Island, period. Yet we remain willingly subordinate to the DeMarians. Why do you suppose we've done that?" He looked at Cam expectantly.

"Um . . . for the good of the Realm?" he hazarded.

"Why is that for the good of the Realm, Nephew?"

"It, uh . . . unites us under one banner?"

"Whose?"

"Well, the Aristok's."

"So, once again, we come around to why. Why has the most powerful family in the country united under another's—that being the DeMarians'—banner?"

"Because the DeMarian Aristok is the Vessel of the Living Flame."

"Exactly. Because the DeMarian Aristok is the Vessel, or Avatar, of the Living Flame, and the Living Flame is the only Aspect which commands such an Avatar, yes?"

"Yes."

"So again, one might say, that the DeKathrines have signed a religious contract to serve the Avatar, or person, who wields an Aspect's power, in this particular case, the Flame. And that person, in this instance, is a DeMarian."

Cam felt his head begin to spin again. "Um, yes, I guess."

"The point, Nephew, is the word *willingly*. The DeKathrines have *willingly* suborned their power to that of the DeMarians." He returned his attention to Shoreshill Port. "But never forget that the power still remains, dormant, yes, emasculated," he shot Dani another glance, "never. Do you understand, Camden?"

"Uh, yes, Uncle."

"Good." He smiled down at him. "Enough of politics.

On to geography. How many Branion shires does the family control? Do you know?"

Still a little uncertain, but wanting to give the correct answer, Cam cast his mind back to his tutor's teachings.

Beside him, Dani's eyes swirled with a deep blue mist. "Willingly subordinate," she whispered, but only the Sea and the Wind heard her words.

The next morning, she pointed out a tall, gray stone tower built on the edge of a rocky promontory.

"That's Blacaster, the main watchtower in Hawn Candred," she said, her voice excited. When Cam gazed at her blankly, she sighed. "Hawn Candred is the easternmost coastal region of Kairnbrook," she explained. "We're almost home, Cam."

"Oh. Good."

"It was built in two-oh-three by Edmund DeKathrine, to guard against invasion from Gallia and it sent the very first warning south in two-fifty-four when Gallia did just that. See, there's the sentry on guard."

Squinting, Cam could just make out a tiny figure standing on the watchtower battlements.

"They'll pass the word to Wellsea Tower that Da's ship has come home," Dani continued. "Wellsea Tower will signal Brea Tower and so on until the news reaches Tavencroft. Then Vincent, that's Da's Companion, and the others can meet us, and Marna, that's our Steward, Marna Jonstun, can have everything ready." She rubbed her hands. "Boy, do I ever miss Jordan's stew. Jordan's our cook," she added unnecessarily. "He's Marna's brother."

Cam just nodded. "So we'll be there by tonight?" he asked, trying to mask the sudden anxiety in his voice.

"Oh, sure. We have to sail up the Whroxin River for a while, but then we'll really be there. You'll be able to see Tavencroft long before we arrive, though. It'll be all lit up, see, because Da's coming home."

"And the winds are really that strong?"

Dani grinned at him. "Some days they'll knock you right over. You'll love it."

"And the others . . . they won't . . . you know . . ."

"What?"

"Well, mind . . . that someone else is coming?"

"Of course not. Well, Lisha won't mind anyway; she likes people. Quin might—he's kinda funny sometimes—but if he gives you any trouble, just sit on him or something. You're bigger than he is. That's what I did when he first came. Besides," she added when Cam continued to look doubtful. "We're cousins, *family.* Da says that's the most important bond in the whole world, more important than vows or oaths or anything else. You'll be all right."

"But what do I call her?"

"Who?

"Her Royal Highness?"

"That'll do."

"Really?"

Dani sighed dramatically. "Not, not really, Cam. What do *I* call her?" she asked with exaggerated patience.

"Lisha?"

"Right. So what do *you* call her?"

He frowned at her. "All right, I get it, I call her Lisha, too, but she's fourth in line for the Throne."

"So when she gets there, you can call her Your Majesty, but in the meantime we're her cousins and we don't stand on formalities at Tavencroft. I told you we're family."

"But . . ."

"No buts, *fam–ma–ly.*" Turning her back on him, she leaned her arms against the railing, refusing to discuss it any further, and after a time, Cam grudgingly turned his own attention elsewhere.

They reached the mouth of the Whroxin River an hour before dark. As Dani had predicted, Cam could see the torches blazing at Tavencroft Castle miles before they reached it. It seemed huge, much bigger than Guilcove, with four, five-story turreted towers, and a massive gatehouse. It stood to the south of the main harbor town of Whroxmeir and, as their ship anchored mid-river, a small boat carrying a man and a woman came out to meet them.

"That's Vincent and Marna," Dani informed him.

A sailor threw down a rope ladder and Celestus descended immediately, with Dani clambering swiftly down behind him. Cam followed more cautiously.

When they were settled in the boat, Celestus gave the man a quick embrace, then turned. "Camden, may I introduce my Companion, Vincent of Storvicholm. Vincent, this is Camden DeKathrine, my great nephew, Domitia's boy."

The man, his rich clothes and languid stance marking him as one of Branion's elite contracted courtesans cum bodyguards, gave Cam a fluid bow with a sweep of long, dark brown hair. "A pleasure," he said, his accent in the rich tones of Danelind's south-lands. "I've heard a great deal about you." When Cam looked confused, he smiled easily. "From your mother's Companion, Jaqueline," he explained.

. Celestus gave a short laugh. "Always assume a Companion knows more than you think," he said. "And never speak loosely around them."

Vincent merely smiled in response. Turning, he held his arms open and Dani flung herself at him, rocking the boat precariously. Ignoring it, she gave him a fierce hug, then turned to Marna as the Steward began to row the boat toward shore.

"Where are Quin and Lisha?" she demanded indignantly.

Unperturbed, Marna jerked her head westward. "It's the half moon tonight, Danielle," she answered in a significant tone.

"Oh, scorch it! I forgot, they're at Brace Cottage." She turned to her father. "Do I have time to get there, Da? I don't want to miss *another* ritual."

"You have a new guest, Danielle," he reminded her.

"Cam can come, too. He could . . ." She waved one

hand, "I dunno, watch or something. He's ready. You said so yourself the other day."

"That was something we discussed in confidence and far from the point besides," he answered with a frown. "There are formalities to be observed, as you well know. Pri Gorwynne will want to meet with Camden herself to ascertain how much remedial tutoring he'll need." He turned to Cam. "The others take religious instruction from a retired Priest of the Wind four nights a month," he explained. "The classes are advanced and require a certain amount of background preparation before they can be fully understood." He returned his attention to his daughter. "By the new moon, Camden will be ready and you may take him then."

Camden opened his mouth, but shut it again as Dani gave her father an aggrieved look.

"But if I miss another ritual, Quin will get ahead of me, Da. He might even pass me."

Celestus snorted with disbelief. "You're so far ahead of Quinton, it would take months for him to catch up with you. Besides, with only Quinton and Alisha in attendance, you know Pri Gorwynne will be concentrating on Oaks and Flame. Which, I might add, you have little to no interest in.

"Yes, Camden, you wanted to say something?"

"I, uh, it's just that," Cam took a deep breath. "I'm not much of a student," he admitted. "I'm kind of slow to understand things like religious theory, sometimes."

"You mean orthodox religious theory."

"I guess."

Celestus smiled. "I believe you'll find this theory will come as naturally to you as breathing."

"It's just . . . well I probably won't be ready even by the new moon, so maybe I shouldn't take the classes at all, and I don't want to get in the way, so if Dani wanted to go tonight, I could stay behind. I don't mind."

Celestus sighed. "Close your eyes, Camden."

"My . . . ?"

"Eyes." He laid one hand on the boy's shoulder. "Close your eyes."

When Cam obeyed, Celestus gently turned his head so that he faced the prevailing wind. "Now, feel the breeze on your face, breathe it in, let it fill you up, let it freshen your mind. Can you feel it, Camden?"

Cam nodded.

"Feel nothing else. Feel only the breeze; feel only the Wind. Feel Its song and Its dance as it flies across the waves, across your mind, and through your body. Can you feel It?"

"Yes," Cam whispered.

"Can you feel it feather over the wings of birds and sweep past the chimney pots of houses and cottages? Can you follow It to the very tips of Tavencroft's turrets?"

"Oh, yes."

"And is everything well in my shire? Can you ask the Wind? Can you feel Its response?"

"Yes."

"What does It say?"

"Everything is well."

"Then open your eyes."

Camden blinked. He felt as if he'd been asleep for hours, dreaming of the Wind on the waves, but when he looked around he could see that the boat had moved only a few oar strokes closer to shore. Celestus smiled down at him.

"That's all there is to it."

"To . . . ?"

"To Pri Gorwynne's religious theory." He straightened. "With no formal religious training of any kind, you can already slip into trance and commune with one of the four Aspects. Imagine what Danielle is capable of with years of instruction behind her."

Cam turned to Dani, who gave him a sour half smile in return.

"You'll want to get Camden properly settled and familiar with the castle layout as a proper host ought to, won't you, Danielle?" Celestus continued, returning his intense stare to his daughter.

"I suppose." She brightened. "I could show him my tower."

"That's a thought."

Still feeling as if he were half asleep, Cam blinked again. "Your tower?"

"Well, *our* tower, actually. It's where we live. The top floor is where we . . . you know . . . go."

"We?"

"Quin, Lisha, and me. It's our presence chamber, in our tower." When Cam continued to look confused, she sighed in annoyance. "It's our special place where we go to be alone. Are you always this thick?"

"Danielle." Celestus frowned at her.

"Oh, all right, I know it's hard to pull out of trance at first. Didn't you have a special place back at Guilcove, Cam?" she asked with exaggerated patience.

"You know I did, you found me there, didn't you?" he retorted, stung by her now patronizing tone. "But it was just for me, where I could go to be alone, *by myself*."

"Well, our presence chamber is for just us, where we can go to be alone, only alone with three people instead of only one." She turned to her father. "We could have supper sent up and when Quin and Lisha get back, Cam could meet them there. Because you'll want to rest up from our trip and eat quietly alone with just Vincent," she added with a guileless smile.

Celestus and his Companion shared a laugh.

"That sounds like a fine plan."

"That way I can warn him," Danielle continued.

Cam turned. "Warn who?"

"You."

"About what?"

"Nothing, *really*. It's just that you should be . . . prepared."

"Prepared for what?"

"For meeting the others."

"I need to be prepared?"

She grinned at him.

"Don't let Dani unnerve you," Vincent interjected with a smile. "If you've survived her, I'm sure you'll survive the others just fine."

"Why would I have to survive them at all?" Cam asked suspiciously, as Dani made a face at her father's Companion. "What's wrong with them?"

She laughed. "*Nothing*. Will you please relax? I swear, you're so easy to tease, you'd think you didn't have any siblings at all."

"You'd think I had too many," he shot back.

"Maybe true, but stop worrying anyway. You'll fit in perfectly. The signs all say so."

"What signs?"

She waved her arm to encompass their surroundings. "The signs," she intoned dramatically, obviously mimicking someone else. "The signs are all around for those who have the eyes to See them. Will *you* See them, Cousin Camden?"

"I don't know what you're talking about."

She leaned back in the boat. "I know. But you will soon, right, Da?"

"That's right." Putting an arm around Cam's shoulders, he smiled down at him. "Don't worry, Nephew. It's nothing frightening. It will all be made clear to you soon enough, but in the meantime, just make yourself at home, and don't let Danielle get the better of you."

Camden smiled shyly back at him. "I'll try, Uncle."

"Good lad." Celestus turned. "And here we are at the dock already." He waited as Marna threw the rope to a waiting servant, then stepped easily from the boat. "Ah, it's good to be home." He turned. "Well, off you go. If you're going to show Camden your tower before the others return, Danielle, you'd better nip along."

"Right!" Dani jumped up and, without waiting for Cam, leaped from the boat and set off running down the dock. Camden allowed the servant to take his arm, then stretched his legs deliberately. When his uncle gave him a questioning look, he shrugged.

"She can't show me anything without waiting for me," he explained. "Eventually she'll figure out that I'm not behind her and she'll have to come back, so I don't have to rush."

Celestus smiled back at him. "You have a truly strategic mind, Nephew. And I think you've just passed your first survival test at Tavencroft," he added as Dani reappeared on the dock, an annoyed expression on her face. "You'll do fine."

It took all of ten minutes for the two youths to make it to the castle. They were expected, so both gates and the two portcullis on either side of the barrel vaulted gatehouse were open when they arrived. Dani hardly broke stride, merely waved at the duty guards as she sprinted across the huge main courtyard. Cam barely had time to register the overlarge windows in the three side ranges before his cousin had ducked under another portcullis in the far southeast corner wall. When he reached it, she was already heading up the tower's spiral staircase, shouting out the various rooms as they passed; storerooms on the ground floor, training and study rooms on the second, sleeping and living chambers on the third, empty on the fourth, and finally, their presence chamber on the fifth. Once there, Dani burst through the rough, wooden door and flung herself into a pile of sheepskin-and-fur rugs before the hearth.

"My tower," she announced breathlessly as Cam entered the room. "Danielle's Tower. It used to be called the Bricklin Tower because it overlooks the forest but now it's Danielle's Tower." Kicking off her boots, she tossed them into a corner. Her padded tunic followed quickly afterward. Then, dressed only in breeches and shirt, she dropped back into the furs. "And this is my presence chamber."

Cam looked about curiously. Dani's "presence cham-

ber" consisted of one large room, its floor covered with
heavy woolen rugs, its stone walls hung with faded tapestries depicting hunting and pastoral scenes in between tall,
open shuttered windows. A fire was lit in the large hearth
on the west wall and candles placed on a wide wooden
table in the northeast corner, obviously in anticipation of
their arrival. The occasional toy jutted out from untidy
piles of clothing. Books and weaponry were scattered
about on the floor, and a white-and-brown tabby cat
peered suspiciously down at him from the top of a large
wardrobe. Pushing between a wooden practice dummy
and one of several trunks set against the walls, Cam
glanced out a window.

"I thought you said this place belonged to all three of
you," he observed.

Dani shrugged with casual nonchalance. "Mine, ours,
what's the difference?"

With the fresh air spilling in through the window ca-
ressing his cheeks, Cam decided not to press the argument. Taking a deep, satisfying breath, he peered out into
the darkness. The half moon illuminated a short length of
field before sinking into the darkness of trees and bracken
beyond. Something moved at the very edge of his vision,
then melted away, leaving him with an odd sense of anticipation. He turned back into the room.

"So you all live here in the tower?"

"It's ours totally," she answered with a brief nod. "I
used to be in the west range with Da, but when Quin
came, he said we were too noisy. He said we could move
anywhere in the castle as long as it wasn't next to him, so
I picked the southeast tower. It was the last one built, see,
and it was built to house guests not guards because it
faced the landward side, so it's a lot more comfortable. It
has more rooms and more windows. The other towers are
all still watchtowers because they face the Whroxin and
the sea, and their windows are a lot narrower because they
were made to keep enemy arrows out. But back then there
wasn't any threat coming from the landward side and,

even if there would be, they'd have to swing west because of the Bricklin Forest, so we don't need this tower for defense. It was just built for symmetry, really. Quin likes it because it's surrounded by land, but you can see the Washe if you look out the north window, so I don't mind that. And it's got the biggest fireplace, so Lisha's happy, too."

"The air smells wonderful."

"That's because of the forest and because it's nowhere near a garderobe."

Cam frowned. "Where *is* the garderobe?"

"Why, you gotta go?"

"No, I just wondered."

"Two floors down on the southwest corner. You can either take the stairs all the way down or cross the fourth floor and take the *secret staircase*," she added in a voice of mock importance.

"We have a secret staircase?"

Dani grinned at his excited expression. "Sure. Tavencroft's riddled with secret places and boarded-up alcoves and doorways. You never know what might be behind any given tapestry. Edmund DeKathrine was a genius." She paused. "Well, kind of a paranoid genius; he thought there were sea spirits in the Washe who wanted to drown him, but he was still a genuine genius, all the same."

"Can we see it?"

"The Washe? There aren't any sea spirits there really, Cam, it's too shallow."

He shot her an impatient glance. "*The secret staircase.*" he said forcibly.

She grinned at him. "Later. When the others get back we'll show you everything. In the meantime we're waiting for supper. I'm famished; aren't you?"

"No."

"Tough."

"Come on, Dani . . ."

About to reply, his cousin snapped her mouth closed as footsteps sounded coming up the stairs. It was accompanied by heavy breathing and, moments later, an older, bearded servant, his face dangerously flushed, appeared in the open doorway. He was carrying a large tray of food and paused a moment to catch his breath before entering.

"Hullo, Eban." Dani said lightly.

Crossing the room, he set the tray down on the table. "Good evening . . . Your Grace."

"I thought Ross was supposed to be bringing our meals up from now on."

He grimaced. "I'm fine, Your Grace. Fit as a fox. Ross can go . . ." he paused. "Ross is needed elsewhere."

She grinned. Ambling over, she peered past his shoulder. "What's for supper?"

"Mutton stew and the last of this morning's bread."

"Smells wonderful." Turning, she waved at Cam. "This is my cousin Cam, Camden DeKathrine. Cam, this is Eban Croser, my oldest servant."

"*Your* oldest servant?" Cam asked after nodding in reply to Eban's bow.

She tossed her head carelessly. "Sure. He's always been mine, haven't you, Eban?"

"Since the day you threw up on me when you were two months old, Your Grace."

"See."

Dropping into a chair, Dani picked up a spoon, waving impatiently for Cam to join her.

"We'll need another chair for breakfast, Eban."

"Of course, Your Grace."

"And a bigger bed for tonight."

"Yes, Your Grace."

"And a bottle of Da's best brandy to go with the stew."

"Not if it was the last drink in the land, Your Grace." Smiling, Eban picked up the tray. "Enjoy your supper."

Dani shrugged amiably. "It was worth a try."

They were just mopping up the last of the stew with the bread when they heard the sound of more feet pounding

up the stairs. Dani leaped up and, tucking herself against
the wall by the door, laid her finger against her lips.

Moments later, a copper-haired girl exploded into the
room. Dani let her go, concentrating instead on her com-
rade who burst in a heartbeat behind her. Dani launched
herself at him. Cam caught a flash of dark auburn hair before the two of them went down in a struggling pile of
arms and legs.

With a grin, the girl skipped nimbly out of harm's way
and Cam got his first look at Her Royal Highness, Alisha
DeMarian, Duke of Lochsbridge.

A tall, willowy girl of twelve with thick copper hair and
a mass of freckles across her cheeks, Lisha's red-tinged,
blue eyes sparkled with the power of the Flame more
strongly than any DeMarian Cam had ever seen, save the
Aristok himself. It crackled about her, warping the air
around her head and shoulders and throwing up a fine
mist of crimson shadows that Cam had to almost squint to
see through. But his vision suddenly cleared as she smiled
at him.

"Hello," she said. "I'm Lisha."

Feeling as if a whole flock of fiery songbirds had just
spoken to him, Cam smiled back awkwardly. "Camden. I
mean Cam."

"Aunt Domitia's son."

"Yes."

"Then you'll be the one Pri Gorwynne spoke about
tonight."

"Oh?"

"Yes. She said the circle was now complete. I can see
what she means, the Wind just about dances around you,
doesn't It?"

"Does It?"

Dropping into Dani's chair, she cocked her head to one
side. "You can't Feel It?"

He blushed. "Well, sure I can Feel It, but, uh, I didn't
think anyone else could."

She nodded in understanding. "Don't worry. No one

else can, except those who've been trained to, like we have."

"We?"

"Those of us at Tavencroft. Great Uncle Celestus and his people, Dani and Quin." She indicated the combatants still struggling by the door. "Myself and Pri Gorwynne, of course. She's our teacher. Ordinarily we'd be at least an hour longer, but she had a Vision so she came back with us especially to speak with Great Uncle about it. When *they* stop wasting time, Dani will want to know that."

Cam watched the others strain against each other. For a moment he thought he saw a green and blue shimmer overlay them both, then it was gone as Dani got Quin in a headlock he couldn't break free from. His face turning a faint purple, he finally banged ruefully on the floor. She let him up and, throwing her arm over his shoulder, drew him toward the table.

"Quin, this is Camden, your second cousin. Cam, this is Quin," she said breathlessly. "If you're going to fight, do it now and get it over with."

The two boys sized each other up. Quin saw a large boy nearly six feet tall, his bright golden hair falling into shadowy blue eyes; deep with latent potential, the scent of the forest breezes all about him, and the bulk of the DeKathrines already showing in his arms and shoulders. Cam saw a boy of medium build with the family's gray eyes and thick auburn hair sticking up wildly in every direction. Dani had said Quin was thirteen, but he hadn't picked up any bulk or height yet and Cam towered over him. He smiled faintly.

Sensing his thoughts, Quin's eyes narrowed for just an instant, before he shrugged, a sardonic smile lighting the freckles he shared with Lisha. "Don't be a scorchin' moron, Dani," he answered. "He'd mash me, especially now that I'm so winded. Like to see him fight you, though. You'd finally get your comeuppance."

"I could take him."

Cam's gaze turned to Dani. Her expression was challenging. Quin and Lisha looked expectant and, for a moment, the air seemed to shimmer between them all. Cam heard the words of his uncle Celestus in his mind.

"Don't let her get the better of you."

He hadn't thought this was what he'd meant, but it might have been. He dropped his arms loosely at his sides. If it was, he was ready for it.

Dani's eyes grew bright with anticipation, then she laughed and the air cleared between them. "Not now," she said with a dismissive gesture. "I've already put the bookworm in his place, I'm too exhausted to fight the giant. You'll have to wait."

"Why don't you set up a proper wrestling match for tomorrow," Lisha suggested. "In the training yard. Great Uncle will want to see how well Cam fights, anyway."

Dani flung herself back into the furs. "Cam fights great. I mean just look at him, you can tell he does. Besides, he told me that he's better at weapons than he is at books, and I'm pretty sure he can read. You can read, can't you, Cam?"

He shot her an indignant look. "Of course I can read," he retorted. "Although I don't do it very often," he admitted.

Quin dropped down beside Dani, jabbing her in the ribs to make her move over. "You will here. How long will you be staying for?"

"All summer."

"Yeah?"

"He completes the circle, Quin," Lisha said pointedly.

The other boy's gray eyes stared into Cam's. "That explains it."

"Explains what?" Cam asked.

Quin turned to Dani. "How much have you told him."

"Not much. Yet. Da wants to wait for Pri Gorwynne's assessment. I say he's ready now."

"Pri Gorwynne had a Vision in the middle of our meditation," Lisha interrupted. "Quin thought she was having a seizure."

"She *was* having a seizure."

"She was having a Vision."

Dani narrowed her eyes. "About what?"

"About Cam, I'm sure of it. That's why we're home early. She came back with us."

Dani sat up straight. "What?" Smacking Quin in the back of the head, she scrambled to her feet. "Why didn't you tell me, kelp-for-brains?"

"I was too busy having them squeezed out my ears," he replied sarcastically.

With an impatient snort, she turned back to Lisha. "Did she say anything in particular?"

"She said she saw the one who would complete the circle and that all the signs have aligned. The tempest is near; all four Aspects rising up with the strength born of youth. You know who that means, don't you?"

"And she came right away?"

"She *rode,* Dani."

"She rode?"

"She rode very, very slowly," Quin clarified in a growled mutter. "She might as well have walked."

"Is she with Da now?"

Lisha nodded. "They're in his outer chamber. Kether Breithe is with them." She turned to Cam. "Kether's one of Great Uncle's . . . advisers," she explained.

"When Da tells her about Cam, she'll want to meet him," Dani said excitedly.

Quin pricked up his ears at this. "Do you think she'll want to perform the ritual right away?"

"Undoubtedly. She won't have come all this way just to say hello."

Cam looked from Quin to Dani. "What ritual?" he asked.

"The Seeking Ritual," Lisha explained. "It's, um, kind of intense."

"Kind of scorchin' painful, you mean," Quin corrected.

"What's she seeking?"

"Answers from the Prophetic Realm."

"And you get dragged right down into it with her. If you're not a Seer, which none of us are, it hurts like blazes," Quin continued.

Cam frowned at him. "What kind of answers is she looking for," he asked, directing his question toward Lisha.

"Answers about whether you're the Wind's Chosen . . ."

"He is," Dani interjected.

"Or just sensitive to Its touch."

"Chosen?"

"Like an Avatar, only we don't use that word."

"Unusually yet naturally drawn to a particular Aspect and able to more fully access Its power with your mind and body than most other people can," Quin explained.

"If you are . . ." Lisha continued.

"He is," Dani repeated.

". . . the Wind's Chosen, It will protect you in the Prophetic Realm. If you aren't . . ." The DeMarian girl fell silent.

"What?"

"Your head will explode," Quin answered gleefully.

"What!"

"Oh, don't be so stupid, Quin!" Dani snapped. "No one's head's going to explode. Cam's Chosen. We can all feel it. We all know it, just like we knew it about me and about Lisha and about you. The ritual's just a formality and not one Cam's going to walk into blind if I have anything to say about it."

"We don't have much time, then," Lisha pointed out. "If we're going to make him ready, we have to do it now."

Quin began shaking his head. "But you said Uncle Celestus wanted to wait for Pri Gorwynne's assessment."

"He didn't know she would be coming tonight," Dani replied. "Look, Quin, it's *our* Circle. Don't you think we should know more about who completes it than anyone else? Pri Gorwynne's going to try to break it because she's old and cautious, to break Cam, *our* cousin. Why should he have to face that unprepared? You didn't. None of us did. I say if we're a Circle, we should act like one. Agreed?"

"Agreed," Lisha answered promptly.

Looking from one to the other, Quin reluctantly nodded. "Agreed."

Cam coughed loudly and they all turned to him, suddenly conscious that they'd forgotten he was there. He crossed his arms.

"Don't you think that maybe someone should ask me," he demanded.

Dani frowned at him. "Ask you what?"

"If I *want* to be prepared."

"Believe me, Cam, the Prophetic Realm's not something you want to go into cold."

"Who says I'm going to go into anything at all. When Uncle Celestus invited me here, he didn't say anything about rituals or Circles or probings, just lessons."

"That's because he was waiting for Pri Gorwynne's assessment, like we said."

"Let's wait for it, then."

"You have no idea what that means."

"That's fine, too."

"Are you always this stubborn?"

"Only when I'm being dragged into things that weren't my idea."

"Oh, but it was your idea." Her eyes suddenly impossibly wide, Dani turned a gaze as intent as her father's on Cam's face. He felt a wave of blue energy wash over him, and then a power deep within his own mind rose up to sweep it away with a spray of bright gray light.

"Stop that," he snapped.

She gave him her familiar challenging smile. "You see, Cam. It's on the edge of your fingertips, sometimes even closer. When you answered my touch just now, you could feel it, and before this, at your father's funeral we both

knew right then that you were one of us. You can't deny
it."

The others grew still as she stood, the air about her
growing cloudy with a shimmering blue mist. "That's
why you came here, Cam," she continued. "You were
born to Feel the Wind on your face; to Feel Its power
touch your mind and answer It with your own abilities.
You need It, just like you need to eat and to breathe and to
sleep. No one else understands that and accepts it like we
do. The Flame Priests, even the Wind Priests, want you to
deny it—to starve yourself—just because they're afraid of
your potential, a potential they can only dream about. But
Da understands, and he can help you reach that potential
and be one with your own Aspect forever and for always.

"Now you've made your point, Cam. You're in charge
of your own destiny, and if you really want to throw it all
away, then go ahead, be stupid, don't be prepared, refuse
Pri Gorwynne's ritual, and go back home where they want
you to be just like them—if you can—but you'll be miserable forever and you know it."

She folded her arms.

Cam shot her a sour expression but, as long-winded as
her speech had been, she was right. He had come because
he'd felt the bond between himself and Dani by the barrow and on the cliffs, because he was lonely for others
who understood him, and because he longed to give himself up to the Wind and Its vast, sweeping power, and
Uncle Celestus had promised him that at Tavencroft it
would be possible. So why was he hesitating?

*"Because you think you're the only special person in
the whole world?"* his mind suggested.
"No."
"Because you like *feeling miserable and alone?"*
"No!"
"All that's left is that you're a stubborn idiot."
"That must be it."

*   *   *

He met Dani's eyes. "Would we be going into the Phrophetic Realm now?" he asked cautiously.

"No, just down through the Physical Realms. We can't get to the Prophetic Realm without Pri Gorwynne. Not yet.

"What would I have to do?"

"Trust us and come with us."

"To where?"

"The tower battlements. You should always do these sorts of things outside."

"Furniture tends to get flung around," Lisha added.

"We'll show you how to access your link with the Wind so that when Pri Gorwynne presses you, Its power will rise up in your defense. Otherwise it'll hurt. A lot."

"It'll still hurt a lot," Quin interjected. "Just not nearly so much."

"And you've already done this?" Cam asked, glancing about at the three of them. "Been prepared and gone through this Seeking Ritual into the Prophetic Realm and come out again? All of you?"

"Yes."

"Even Lisha?"

She nodded. "Just because I carry the Flame doesn't mean that I've ever been encouraged to embrace Its power, Cam," she said quietly. "His Majesty's Flame Priests don't dare compel us to deny our birthright, but they do say the Aristok is the only true Avatar. The rest of us are expected to turn our attention elsewhere. We're just secondary vessels, temporary and superfluous."

"Spares," Quin clarified at Cam's confused expression. "In case the Flame needs to pass; taught to ignore their potential. Just like the rest of us."

"The rest of us?"

"The whole country. Like we mentioned before, everyone can access it a little bit. Or did you honestly believe that Braniana DeMarian was the only person in the entire world capable of merging with an Aspect?"

"Um . . . yes."

"That hardly makes any sense, does it?"

"Enough." Dani chopped her hand down, cutting off further discussion. "We're wasting time. If we're going to prepare Cam before Da sends for him, we have to do it now." She glanced at him. "Have you decided?"

Feeling as if he was about to leap off a mist-shrouded cliff, Cam stood. "Yes. I'll do it."

"And you're coming with us of your own free will?"

"Yes."

"And you won't tell anyone what the four of us do, not Da, not Pri Gorwynne, not anyone else?"

Annoyance finally crowding out hesitation, Cam jerked his head sharply. "I said yes twice already, didn't I?"

"All right, then, come on." Turning, Dani headed from the room, the others in tow.

The moonlit sky was bright after the dark staircase below. The three Tavencroft youths emerged swiftly, crossing to the center of the tower battlements with the ease of long familiarity. Cam followed more slowly, pausing to peer over the northwest corner at the shrouded landscape below. Far beyond the dark outline of the castle gatehouse he could see the sparkling water of the Whroxin River, and beyond that the sea cupped by a vast expanse of star strewn sky. Everything seemed so quiet and peaceful that he could almost ignore the growing sense of anticipation that hovered in the air around him, but the rising wind that ruffled through his hair drove all other thoughts from his mind, and when Dani took him firmly by the shoulders he could feel the excitement through her fingertips. She drew him to the center of the tower and turned him to face the dark mass of the Bricklin Forest.

"Wind stands at the eastern point," she said, placing him in position. "Stay there. Oaks to the north, Quin take his hand."

The other boy obeyed her with a grin, taking up a position to Cam's left, and catching up his fingers. "Get ready," he whispered.

"Flame to the south. Lisha . . ." Dani gestured. The De-Marian girl moved quickly to Cam's right. They linked hands and she gave him a fast smile before returning her attention to Dani.

"And Sea to the west." Standing with her arms at her sides, she glanced at them all, her black eyes sparkling. "This is the first time we've all stood together," she said solemnly. "The very first night the Circle will be complete. Who knows what might happen, so be ready for anything. Cam?" She turned a wild, unfocused gaze on his face and he could already see the swirling blue mist beginning to grow deep within her pupils. "Don't be afraid, all right? You've done this before. Tonight's only different because you're with other people. When you feel the Wind's power, just give yourself over to It, understand. It won't hurt you, you know that. We'll be here to snatch you back if anything out of control happens. Remember, we've done this before, too." She glanced around the Circle again. "Everybody ready?"

As one they nodded; and so, with a deep breath, Dani caught up Quin's and Lisha's hands.

Contact came much faster than Cam had expected. The jolt of power that crackled through his body made him shout in surprise, and he would have fallen had the others not been holding his hands so tightly. For an instant, they were surrounded by a multihued red, blue, and green mist. Cam felt the others open their minds to it and, as he struggled to follow their example, a blinding gray light suddenly burst into being above them, knocking him backward. For a moment he was supported only by the iron grips of Quin's and Lisha's hands and then, as he felt the Wind rush toward him, he opened his mind to accept It.

Racing down the channel forged by the three veterans, the Wind slammed into Its Chosen like a sledgehammer, knocking his consciousness free from his physical body.

With a joyous shout, Cam leaped into Its embrace. Together the two of them flung themselves over the battlements and away.

Whistling past the castle walls, Cam laughed out loud. He'd never felt so free. Of all the times he'd sent his mind out on the wings of the breeze in Branbridge, or reached out with his thoughts to touch the heart of the Wind on the cliffs of Guilcove, he'd never been taken up so fast or so far. Unbounded by physical constraints, he sped along the Whroxin River, flattening the reeds and water plants along its banks as he went, then rushed headlong for the harbor and the open sea. When he broke clear of the Washe, his awareness spread out almost impossibly wide. For a time he tore along the waves, causing pure white crests to rise above the surface, but all too soon he sensed the confining presence of land looming up before him, so, spinning in a great circle that sent the water churning into a whirlpool beneath him, his awareness folded back on itself until he was staring into the vast expanse of stars he'd reached for on the battlements of Tavencroft. With a whoop, he flung himself toward them.

It grew cold. Far away he felt a whisper of pain feather across his body, but rather than turn back, he pressed on, racing toward the warmth of the distant stars. For just an instant they seemed to draw nearer, then something caught hold of him, arresting his ascent. He faltered. Far away he heard his name called and then he was falling. The sea rushed back toward him and, just before he plunged into its depths, he heard a triumphant voice.

"I've got him!"

He shot back into the air, anger granting him new strength. The sea rose up, long streams of water trying to ensnare him and, as he twisted away from their grasp, he heard the voice again, this time accompanied by another.

*   *   *

"I can't hold him!"

"What do you mean you can't hold him! You gotta hold him!"

"Shut up!"

He ignored the voices, bending all his will toward the open sky above him.

"We're losing him! Do something, Dani!"

"You do something!"

"I already tried, he won't come near me!"

"Cam! Cam, come back! Scorch it! Lisha, you try!"

The sea began to boil, transforming into a churning expanse of fire beneath him. It called to him, promising warmth and light and life. For a moment he was mesmerized by its power, and then the Wind rose up within him again and he was gone.

"I lost him."

"What do we do now, Dani?"

"Get Da. And Kether."

The voices faded away. Shaking off the last shred of physical sensation, he shot off into the night sky without a second glance.

The air was cold.

He'd given up trying to reach the stars and had been chasing clouds around a mountaintop, unfettered by thoughts or concerns of the physical world, since they'd relinquished control of the sky to the sun, but now the air was suddenly cold again, and he paused, uncertain what that meant.

About him, the Wind continued to play. It called to him, but as he turned to rejoin Its game, something—some dark, chaotic presence he could not identify—came between them, disrupting his intent, then winked out

again. Uncertain, he scanned the horizon. About him,
rocks and trees gave way to ocean and clear blue sky. The
breezes above the waves drew him and he moved toward
them, pausing to hover uncertainly over the ragged coastline. Reaching down, he absently stroked the white caps
on their crests and then a new presence rose up to gently
touch his mind.

He tasted salt, felt the spray of surf on his cheeks, and
heard a voice, soft and breathless as a summer breeze,
speak one word.

"Camden."

Puzzled, he moved toward the source of the sound. He
knew that word.

The presence grew stronger. It reached out for him and
he shied away, but before he could flee, it spoke again.

"Camden DeKathrine."

It was a name. It was . . . The Wind whistled past him,
whispering of the open sky, but this time he shook off Its
embrace, continuing to hover just out of reach of the presence, wondering what it might say next.

*"Camden, come back to us, will you? There's a good
lad."*

Come back? Come back where?

*"The others are waiting for you, they are. Come back
now."*

Others?

Something made him turn. Beyond the sea he saw the
hazy outline of a distant island. He knew that place. Its

name eluded him, but somehow he knew he was meant to be there. He began to drift slowly toward it.

"That's my good lad. You can go out again tomorrow, you can."

Tomorrow. His sense of time returned and with it a flood of physical sensations. It was cold. He was cold. He tried to move upward toward the sun, but the feeling had crept up to freeze his thoughts and he faltered. Now, conscious of his physical form, he began to fall, spiraling downward toward the rocks below, faster and faster as he remembered who he was.

"Alisha girl, catch him, will you?"

A plume of crimson shot into the air. He plunged into its midst and, as the warmth of it surrounded him, he slowed.

"Now, Danielle. Gently, look you! He's not a storm, mind, he's a breeze. Touch him now."

The fire took form, became a warm sea which buoyed him up and rocked him gently. He floated peacefully in its midst, the ghost of an ancient memory of warmth and safety enveloping him. He might have fallen asleep had the presence not spoken again.

"Quinton, your turn, boyo."

"'Bout time."

He felt himself rise up as land began to form beneath his . . . feet. He felt his feet, his legs, his arms, and when he tried to see, he felt his eyes open.

"He's back."

*   *   *

Blinking, Cam looked about.

He was lying in an unfamiliar bed in an unfamiliar
room. Sunlight streamed in the windows, blinding him.
His head spun and he felt bruised all over as if he'd been
repeatedly picked up and flung against the ground.
Which, possibly, he had. He groaned.

"He's coming out of it. Camden boy, can you hear
me?"

The gentle presence. He attempted to answer, but when
he tried to speak, all he could do was croak.

Something pressed against his lips. He opened his
mouth, allowing a small amount of liquid to flow down
his throat. He swallowed reflexively. The sharp odor of
wine burned his nostrils, but it gave him strength and he
drank. Finally, when it pulled away, he found he could see
a bit better.

A small, wizened old woman of well past seventy was
seated on the bed beside him. Her hair, fine and white as
the snow on his mountaintops, capped a face lined with
soft wrinkles. To Cam's youthful gaze she looked like a
tiny white bird, but the eyes that stared into his were two
gray, fathomless whirlwinds, the black of the pupils
barely visible within them. He felt himself sinking into
their midst, then she blinked deliberately and the spell
was broken. As the gray in her eyes became a soft, faded
hazel, she smiled at him, showing several gaps in worn,
yellow teeth. She smelled of lavender and fenweed and
the wind across the downs. An image of his great grandmother, Saralynne, whom he'd known for only four short
years, came into his mind, and he found himself smiling
shyly back at her as she withdrew one thin hand from her
shawl and pressed it against his forehead. Power flowed
from her fingers to spread across his temples. He shied
away from it at first, but as she bore down, the Wind,

which still moved through his mind, rose up to touch her fingertips and then whispered away like a fine stream of smoke. She withdrew her hand.

"That's better now. Welcome back to the world, little brother."

There was a stirring behind her. Carefully turning his head, Cam saw the others: Dani, Lisha, and Quin standing stiffly by the far wall. They looked haggard but relieved, and he gave them a wan smile.

"What happened?" he croaked, surprised by how weak his voice sounded.

Dani made to answer, but snapped her mouth closed as the old woman gestured.

"What do you think happened yourself, then?"

He frowned, trying to bring his sluggish thoughts in line with the odd cadence of her Gwynethian accent.

"I think . . . I went flying."

"You did that, and a long way you went, too, foolish child. We almost lost you, we did. Luckily, this old woman knows the Wind better than anyone alive, eh? And called you back, she did."

"Back."

The sudden sense of loss this revelation brought with it caused a painful lump to grow in his throat. He turned away so the others wouldn't see the tears in his eyes.

"Will he be all right, Pri?"

Cam recognized Uncle Celestus' voice but, afraid to see his expression, he kept his head averted.

"Oh, aye," the old woman answered easily. "He's strong, and the Wind only wanted to play, It did. Lucky for us. If it had been in a bad mood, he'd have been off sinking ships in the Bjerre Sea instead of playing about the Danelind mountaintops and home might not have seemed so attractive." She turned back to Cam. "Sleep now, little brother, and we'll talk more later, eh."

Her expression was gentle but commanding. Cam found his eyelids beginning to close of their own volition, but he fought the urge to sink immediately into sleep.

"Who are you?" he managed to ask around a yawn.

"Your new teacher."

"Pri Gorwynne?"

"Aye, that's right."

"The Wind Priest?"

"Retired."

"Then you know. What it's like."

"I do that. But I'm still that mad at you for not waiting for me, mind. Typical child of the Wind, you: impatient and imprudent. Though, I'll wager you were led astray by the Sea's Chosen, yes?"

"No. It was my choice."

With a snort, Pri Gorwynne glanced over at Dani. The others instinctively moved a step closer to their cousin, who shrugged. "We were all in it together," she answered defiantly.

"No doubt. Well, I'll deal with you lot later. Push off and get something to eat now. Then sleep. You'll need all your strength for the lessons I've got planned for you today."

Catching Cam's eye, Dani cocked her head to one side. He nodded once and, assured that he would not say anything he shouldn't, she led the others from the room.

Celestus stepped forward. "You'll be tired also, Pri," he said diffidently. "I've had the guest quarters prepared for you. You're welcome to stay for as long as you feel it necessary, of course."

Accepting his arm, she rose stiffly. "That's good. For I think I may be needed here and these old bones wouldn't take to riding up that hill every day." Picking up a worn, hawthorn cane from the bed, she turned back to Cam.

"Sleep now, boy. We'll talk later."

He nodded. "Pri Gorwynne?"

"What, lad?"

He glanced away. "Was I really in danger of being gone forever?" he asked hesitantly.

"You were that. You almost winked into the Prophetic

Realm, you did. We'd have been hard pressed to find you had you done that."

"I'm sorry." He finally glanced up at his uncle. "I didn't mean to. It just felt so . . . free."

Celestus nodded. "I know, Nephew. I've taken the Wind's path myself. Put it out of your mind for now. We'll teach you how to recapture that feeling without losing yourself in it, but in the meantime, I need you to sleep and regain your strength. Can you do that for me?"

"Yes, sir, but . . ."

"But what?"

"But what about the Seeking Ritual?"

"I'd say we have all the answers that we need. Yes, Pri?"

"We do at that. He's the Wind's Chosen as sure as he's lying here."

"You see. Now go to sleep. You'll stay a while, Kether?"

Cam could not see who his uncle was speaking to, but Celestus seemed satisfied with a nonverbal response because he nodded once and then left the room, holding the door open for Pri Gorwynne; when it closed, Cam found that he'd forgotten that his uncle had spoken to anyone at all. For a while he lay staring at the ceiling, feeling too ashamed to fall asleep, but as the summer breeze wafted in through the open window to brush gently against his face, his eyes closed and he slept.

Branbridge, 500 DR

In the Dog and Doublet, Cam fell silent as Sarah wordlessly handed him a bowl of broth. They'd left the back room about an hour before, trading the storage room floor for a small table in Sarah's counting room. Now it was nearing noon and the tavern was filling up rapidly. Sarah rose with a groan.

"Eat. I'll be back."

She returned an hour later. Cam was sitting playing draughts with Trevor, but one frown from his aunt had the Dog's bouncer up and gone. Setting two ales down on the table, the tavern owner resumed her seat.

"So what happened next?"

Cam lifted his mug. "I stayed at Tavencroft for the summer," he said simply.

"And?"

"And I spent my time doing what other boys my age do, more or less."

"More or less?"

Cam emptied the mug before answering. "My uncle had plans for us, of course. He'd sought us out, one by one, for our abilities and for our . . . vulnerabilities. He taught us that the primal power of the Aspects was the birthright of every Branion on the Island. That imbalance came in having only one Avatar instead of four. He said we should embrace the power for the good of the Realm, and we believed him."

Sarah frowned. "But you knew it was heresy, even then, didn't you?"

Cam shrugged. "Who cares? Uncle Celestus gave us a place to belong. He told us we were special, important. When you're twelve years old, that's everything in the world. It didn't seem like he was asking much in return for all that." Cam paused, staring up at a spiderweb hanging in the corner. The fine strands were torn and covered with dust, its spinner nowhere to be seen. He smiled sadly. "It still doesn't."

He straightened. "My uncle was, is, a very meticulous man. He knew we were changing the balance of power among the Aspects, and that the Flame Temple Seers, never mind the Aristok himself, would sense it immediately. We needed a protector, someone who could shield us from our enemies until his theories could be proven. So he brought in a Heathland Seer named Kether Breithe to keep us safe. I didn't really know him in those days. He was just one of my uncle's retainers. Most of the time we didn't even notice he was there.

"It wasn't until much later—in the Flame Temple Dungeons—" he added bitterly, "that I realized how important he was. And how close we all came to being found out that very first summer, even with his protection. But like I said, I didn't know that then. He was just one of my uncle's people and the Flame Temple was a lifetime away. We had no idea how close they really were, but Kether knew, even then."

He fell silent again, thinking of all the dramas that had played out without their knowledge and the quiet man who had shielded them from it all.

Kairnbrook, 492 DR

With Camden DeKathrine safely home from his first flight with the Wind, the Lord of Tavencroft and his children had retired to let him sleep. Unseen, in a chair by the door, a pale-eyed Heathland man watched the few remaining tendrils of the Wind's power rise and fall in time with the boy's breathing. Kether Breithe had been summoned to Camden's bedside as soon as Celestus had realized the severity of the situation. He'd placed himself in an out-of-the-way corner where he could slip into trance without being disturbed, and used to his ways, the Lord and his children had ignored him as if he wasn't even there. Which in some ways he was not.

Kether was a "Mirror," one of a very small number whose talents lay in reflecting and clouding the power of those with the Sight. The strongest could also shield others, and it was for this purpose that the Viscount had brought him to Kairnbrook ten years ago. Born on the rocky coast of Baltsgar Ness, the most northerly of Heathland's islands, Kether had no political nor religious leanings, no interest in the Viscount's philosophical stand, and none in his plans. He cared only for the large sums of

money Celestus paid him to hide his doings from the
Flame Priests of Branion each year, money which Kether
sent back to his family to shore up their defenses against
raiders from the north and the Mauley clan to the south. It
had been both an uneventful and uninteresting commis-
sion. Until today, he amended.

Taking an equal amount of a very potent infusion to
boost their respective powers, Pri Gorwynne had sent her
mind to the north seeking Camden DeKathrine while
Kether had turned his own attention southward, casting
his inverted vision out like a great net to ensnare any interest caused by the children's untimely Circle. Ordinarily
his presence alone was enough to shield the doings at
Kairnbrook, but the addition of the Wind's Chosen had
shifted the balance of power, rending a hole in his protection large enough to find them should any Branion Seer
be traveling in the Prophetic Realm at that moment.

Only one Branion Seer was; a solitary man just north of
the great shining sea of power that made up the Triarctic
signature of the capital city. Kether did not recognize him;
he was no Flame Priest nor Healer—Kether knew them
all—but he was strong enough to zero in on the con-
tention between the Wind and Pri Gorwynne. Kether deflected his questing easily enough the first time, but as the
retired Priest of the Wind struggled to bring Camden
home, the strange Seer returned again and again like a
dog on a scent. Each time Kether managed to maneuver
his own abilities between them, but as the time passed he
found himself using increasing amounts of power to keep
him at bay. Teeth clenched, he bent to his task, the other
man's persistence causing him to feel at first annoyed,
then angry, then worried. As Pri Gorwynne called the
three Aspects' Chosen into trance to help her bring Camden the last mile home, he felt the Seer leap toward them.
Gathering his own abilities, Kether reared up and, without
warning, smacked the other man's Vision away with one
great eruption of power. Taken completely by surprise, the
Seer's mind went spinning off into the void and, with pain

sending red-and-black streaks across his vision, Kether returned, gasping, to himself just as Camden DeKathrine opened his eyes.

It was some time before he was able to open his own. Mirroring was a passive, not an active talent, and the effort it had taken to knock the other man away had left him almost convulsing in agony. Clamping his hands to his head, he fought to bring his abilities back on track. Slowly the pain receded and, by the time he was able to raise his head, his innate abilities had settled over them all once more like a fine blanket of snow. Gingerly he reached out past the barriers of his protection. The unknown Seer was gone. Kether straightened and, when Celestus finally turned to him, he was sitting stiffly in his chair, his usual air of unfocused disinterest wrapped about him like a blanket.

None of them noticed the spark of wildness in his eyes nor the sweat which beaded across his forehead. None of them realized just how close they'd come to being found out, but he did and, when they left him alone with the boy, he forced himself to calm, then revisited the events of the night as objectively as he was able.

He'd always known that once the Viscount gathered all four of his Chosen together it would send flares of power into the Prophetic Realm, but until this moment he'd not realized just how strong those flares were going to be. It was clear that he'd have to be extremely vigilant in the future, especially if this unknown Seer returned.

His groin tightened with a mixture of concern and excitement. The other man was strong. He'd return. Maybe with others. He didn't know what he faced, only that it had proved more powerful than he was and that would be enough to spur him to return. Kether had run circles around dozens of Seers in the Prophetic Realm in the last ten years with none of them the wiser for it. This man would be no different.

The sweat broke out across his forehead once again. He'd proved more powerful than this unknown Seer, but by doing so he'd incapacitated himself and left the Viscount and his people open to discovery by any other Seer who might have been drawn to their struggle. That must never happen again. He was a Mirror; he deflected, he did not contend. Not ever.

Passing a hand across his face, he glanced over at the sleeping child. Unlike the others, Camden's Aspect hovered about him like dozens of tiny moths, growing thicker with each passing breath. He was going to be difficult to teach. The Wind had claimed him, and freest and most ethereal of all the Four Aspects, It resisted discipline and control. Camden DeKathrine would likely be the same.

His head still throbbing slightly, Kether rose with a frown. Teaching the boy was Pri Gorwynne's problem, he reminded himself. His was to shield him, most especially from the powerful Seers of the Triarchy's Flame Temple, trained to detect even the merest hint of heresy. And to do that, he needed discipline and control of his own, two characteristics that he'd believed he'd had in abundance until today. Two characteristics he planned to get back, but, for now, he needed sleep.

Glancing out the window toward Branion's Flame Temple far to the south, Kairnbrook's Mirror wondered how many would come seeking them that summer and from where.

4. The Flame Temple

THE Triarchy's grandest monument to Its Living Avatar, the Branbridge Temple of the Flame, was situated to the west of the capital, separated from Bran's Palace by three hundred acres of woods and field that served them both. Built on the ruins of a pre-Triarctic monastery, it had originally been used as a barracks for the companies of Danelind hill fighters brought over by Braniana to conquer the country. As the years had passed, and the First DeMarian's particular brand of Triarctic worship had grown, it had come to house the newly formed Knightly Order of the Living Flame's Most Holy Champions and their Priestly and Seer counterparts. Stables, granaries, dormitories, chapels, and libraries had been added until the complex was second only to Bran's Palace in size. By the year 492 it supported the most powerful and complex ecclesiastical and metaphysical hierarchy in Triarctic history, led by Urielle DeSandra, fifteenth Archpriest of the Flame. Initiating an aggressive policy of recruitment and renovation, under her leadership, the Temple population had tripled and with it, the Temple coffers. Couriers and visitors passing through its ornate public rooms were awed into silence by the grandeur of its architecture, the might of its military force, and the overwhelming sense of its metaphysical power.

The man who made his way through the crowded Main Audience Hall this day remained both unimpressed and uninterested in its might, its grandeur, or the radiant effects of its potency. He'd seen its dungeons, and knew the most affecting sight in the Temple did not come wrapped in either gold leaf or crimson-enameled armor. It hung on damp stone walls and smelled of dried blood. To his special Sight it was the plainest of objects in the Physical Realms that carried the strongest signature in the Prophetic, but he had to admit that there was no other place in Branion that caused him a greater psychic headache.

Ignoring the host of ghostly imagery that only he could see, he made his way through the crowded rooms toward the elaborately carved door at the far end of the Audience Hall.

People moved quickly from his path though he was neither a large nor an imposing man. Of medium height, age, and build, with wide dark eyes and light brown hair, he wore the plain, serviceable clothes of the capital's artisan class, but something in his demeanor and in the haunted quality of his gaze suggested that he was far more than a local smith or tailor come to beg an audience. Those Priests who chose to think of him knew him as Martin Wrey, a former Acolyte and Seer turned apostate and condemned to die. Martin referred to himself simply as the Archpriest's Man and tried to forget the days when he had gone by any other title.

Now, catching sight of the Clerical Deputy—the Priest in charge of granting the daily audiences—he gave him a brief jerk of his head and continued on, ignoring the host of ethereal images which fluttered nervously about the Deputy's head. The symbols of a man obsessed with detail and order, they needed no scrutiny. Their only relevance to the Archpriest's Man was that they represented the Deputy's fear that he would upset the daily routine— which he'd already done by arriving in the first place. Martin had no need to beg a meeting with the Archpriest;

he had a standing audience following Her Grace's morning meditation—he could arrive any day unannounced and be admitted, but it was a privilege he seldom exercised. His very presence sent the Temple into a frenzy of rumors and uncertainty and, whereas under different circumstances, he might have enjoyed the effect, he had no more wish to be at the Temple than the Temple wished to have him. After facing a lifetime of violently chaotic visions, then imprisonment and interrogation at the hands of his fellow Seers, the only thing in this world that Martin Wrey had left to fear was to see his condemnation rewritten in the pale, gray eyes of the Archpriest of the Flame. She'd granted him asylum in her service and he would serve her, but he feared to look into her eyes, so unless it was very important, he kept his distance. Today, however, he had news that Her Grace would want to hear immediately; news that only he could impart.

Pausing before her door, he waited for the Junior Knight on Guard to announce him, then followed her inside; his heart pounded shamefully loud in his chest.

The Archpriest's Private Meditation Room was dim despite the bright morning sunlight outside. Only one narrow window allowed enough light in to see by and it was partially blocked by the woman who stood, her back to the door, staring out at the gardens beyond.

Urielle DeSandra was a tall, austere woman in her late thirties, thick brown hair braided and wrapped in half a dozen fine, threadlike chains. She was dressed in a robe of crimson and gold, her badge of office picked out in a spread of tiny rubies. The gems sparkled with an almost living quality, made that much brighter by the reflection of the Archpriest's own abilities within their minute facets. To Martin's Sight she radiated a power so intense it made his head throb with a steady pulse of rainbow-colored pain.

The Archpriest continued her study of the gardens, giving no more indication that she'd noticed his entry than she ever did. Crossing to the center of the room, he went down on one knee and waited, his gaze locked on the fringe of carpet before her hearth. As always, he could not look at her, not before the audience was over and she'd indicated whether his service was still of value to her. Only then could he brave the brilliance of her presence to see if his life and sanity were still held securely in her eyes. In the meantime, he would wait as long as she demanded it.

After a moment he heard the faint rustle of cloth as she turned.

"Martin."

Her voice, rich and well-modulated, invoked a host of conflicting images and symbols that chased themselves around inside and outside his head. Forcing himself to concentrate on the red-and-golden pattern of her carpet, he took a deep breath to steady his mind before he answered.

"Your Grace."

"You had a Vision."

It was not a question. There could be no other reason for his presence, but he nodded anyway. "In a dream, Your Grace. Something's brewing to the north."

"In Heathland?"

Her words reached out to him on a fine thread of power, taking the form of an ethereal white dragon in the air between them: Merrone, Guardian of Essus and the people of the North.

He shook his head.

"No, Your Grace. In Branion."

The white dragon rose up on its hind legs and disappeared up the chimney to be replaced by a misty fire-wolf seated at the base of a huge oak tree.

"What sort of something?"

"Something powerful, Your Grace. The Aspects are stirring."

"To the north?"

"Yes, Your Grace."

He felt her turn back to the window. Her movement

caused the air to ripple about her, swamping the tiny tree and fire-wolf within its currents.

"Continue."

"Something touched my mind while I was sleeping, Your Grace, some presence, and for an instant I Saw what it Saw."

The images of his dream rose up to hover before his eyes.

"I Saw the Wind dancing on the waves of the Bjerre Sea, and as I watched, the waves became Flame and the Wind took the form of a child with hair as golden as the summer sun. Then the earth rose up, cupping the waves and the child in a cradle made of tree roots."

He paused. Between them, the imagery played themselves out like a ghostly pantomime.

"Then they were gone as if they'd never been there," he continued after a moment. "Something . . ." his eyes narrowed as he attempted to describe what he'd felt next. "A . . . not-thing came between us. It blocked my Sight. It didn't touch me, not at first, but we fought for what seemed like hours and, just when I thought I'd bested it . . . it hit me so hard that it knocked me from my Vision."

The Archpriest turned to regard him, her expression stern. "A not-thing, Martin?"

He raised his hands helplessly. "It had sentience but no substance, Your Grace, power but no identity. All I Felt for certain was that it was no image conjured up in a dream. It was real."

"An Aspect?"

Glancing at the Triarctic symbols which swirled before his eyes, he shook his head. "I don't . . . I can't."

The symbols merged into a solid mass which began to rotate slowly in midair. "No, Your Grace," he answered with more certainty. "I did See the Aspects, but that's not what the not-thing was. It was protecting them, blocking me from them, trying to hide their merging from my Sight."

The power about the Archpriest grew very still. "Their what?"

"Their merging, Your Grace, their coming together as one." He stared at the slowly revolving image before his eyes. It still bore elements of all four Aspects, but as he watched, their individual forms began to transform into a crude human shape. He shuddered. "I Saw the Aspects take on physical form and come together as one body."

"The body of a child?"

The image shattered like a glass ornament, spewing shards of power across the room. A number glanced off his vision, causing small explosions of pain to radiate across his Sight. He winced. "I don't know, Your Grace," he admitted reluctantly. "The child could be a person or the symbol of immature potential, a yet unrealized event, human sentience or humanity itself. I . . . just don't know."

She took one step forward. Even without meeting her eyes, Martin could feel the sudden intensity of her gaze. It caught hold of his mind, calling up his Sight and sending him into trance almost immediately. He felt her presence sink down into the Prophetic Realm with him, and as he had many times in the past, he waited for her questions to make sense of his Vision. She was not long in asking them.

"What do you See, Martin?"
"Chaos," he whispered.
"Is the child the key?"
Opening his eyes, he watched as her words became hands which reached in through his temples to effortlessly pluck the images from his mind. He opened his mouth, and the ghostly hands emerged with their answers.
"Yes."
"What does it represent?"
"An event in motion but as yet unrealized in the Physical Realms."

"An event involving the coming together of the Aspects in physical form?"

"Yes."

"And this is taking place to the north?"

"Yes."

"Where exactly?"

This time the answer was harder to retrieve. An image flickered just on the edge of his vision, but each time the hands reached for it, it melted away.

"I don't know."

"Is the event imminent?"

"Yes."

"How imminent?"

"I don't know."

"Who will bring the event into being."

The image flickered in the corner of his Sight once more. Once again he bent his attention toward it and once again it melted away, but this time he recognized the reason.

"I don't know. The . . . not-thing won't let me See it."

"What is the not-thing?"

"A . . ." He could almost See it, too, and then it also melted infuriatingly away. "I don't know," he sighed.

"What is its purpose?"

He took a deep breath as the Vision returned to normal.

"To protect and conceal the event."

"Why?"

Again it melted away.

"I don't know."

"How?"

"I don't know."

"Could you find it in trance?"

"I don't know."

"Would you recognize it if you encountered it again?"

There. For a split second he could See the not-thing's essence outlined in a tracery of light before it guttered out.

"Yes."

She released him.

The relief was like a rush of wind through his mind. He swayed and might have fallen if he hadn't already been on his knees. Throwing out one hand, he pressed it against the hearthstone, feeling the warmth flow through his fingertips and waiting for the spell to pass. After a moment he was able to look up. The Archpriest had returned to her place by the window and now she spoke without turning around.

"It's vital that we learn more about this not-thing as well as the event which is to bring the Aspects together in physical form. Whether this is within the body of a Living Avatar or not, it could have catastrophic effects across the Realms. You will prepare yourself to go into prolonged trance sometime this afternoon or this evening, possibly in concert with the Deputy Seer." She held up one hand as he opened his mouth to protest. "I expect your total obedience in this matter, Martin," she snapped. "I require both your Vision and Osarion's to make sense of this and you *will* obey me without compunction. Is that clear?"

He bowed his head. "Yes, Your Grace."

"Take rooms at the Dolphin Arms and wait for my summons. That is all for now."

He rose. Then, as he had at the conclusion of every audience she'd granted him for the past five years, he looked up, his need for her benediction held openly like an offering to a God. She turned.

Power radiating about her like a sunburst, she gave him a measured stare. Her pale gray eyes were bright with a searing luminescence, but deep within them he could See she still held his life within the bounds of her protection. Bowing deeply, he withdrew.

Making his way back through the still-crowded Main Audience Hall, Martin's entire body felt bruised but, as always, after an audience with the Archpriest, his mind felt clear. It would not last long, however, and quickly retrieving his horse from the Temple stables, he turned his

mount eastward toward the capital and the Dolphin Arms.
It might last long enough for a quiet meal and a few hours
of blessedly dreamless sleep. Then he would be strong
enough to face the Deputy Seer and the waves of hatred
and jealousy that came off the other man like oily smoke.

A faint smile flickered across Martin's face. The Archpriest had not said so, but it was obvious her Seers had
not Foretold the event nor Felt the not-thing. More impor-
tantly, the Deputy Seer, thought to be the most powerful
prophet in a hundred years, had not Felt it either. The
smile became a wide grin. Of all the Priests who'd turned
against him, Osarion DeSandra had been the most ven-
omous. Martin wished he could be there when the Archpriest met with her most illustrious Deputy Seer, and
maybe he could be.

Urging his horse into a trot, he passed under the Temple
gatehouse. A quiet meal and a few hours of sleep with
perhaps just one clairvoyant dream and he would be
strong enough to defeat both Osarion and the not-thing.
Then the former would crawl and the latter divulge how it
blocked the Sight of others so that maybe he might block
his own and finally be free of both the past and the future.

Straightening in the saddle, he turned onto the main
road to the capital. Just before he passed the first Branbridge milestone, however, the awareness of another's
Sight flickered across his mind. A flare of panic seized
him, but it vanished as soon as he scrutinized the source.
It was a small talent, the tendrils of its Vision barely able
to reach beyond the Temple grounds. Some young
Acolyte or minor Seer watching him from the Temple
windows, no doubt; unaware that Martin could sense another's Sight from a dozen miles off and react with a violent psychic slap before the other could disengage.

Resisting the urge to do just that, he simply shook off
the other's scrutiny. There would be time for retaliation
later once his duty to the Archpriest had been discharged,
but until that time, he needed all his strength.

Decided, the Archpriest's Man passed from the sight of

the Flame Temple, making for the Dolphin Arms and the scant few hours of Visionless sleep Urielle DeSandra had gifted him with.

Standing on the main balcony, Acolyte Iwalani DeKathrine watched the Archpriest's Man ride toward Branbridge, a frown marring her usually sunny countenance. His visits were rare and always spelled trouble for the smooth running of the Temple, and that would mean—as Assistant to the Flame Temple's Coadjutor—it would spell trouble for her. Or at the very least extra work.

Leaning against the stone balustrade, she absently plucked at the wall's ivy, just beginning to show green, before turning her attention to the young man at her feet.

"Well?"

His brown eyes—the legacy of his DePaula father—unfocused, her cousin, Allen DeKathrine, held up one hand and, with an impatient snort, she returned her attention to the road. Ever since they were children she'd counted on Allen's Sight to alert them to potential danger involving one escapade or another. He'd always come through in the past, but the closer he came to his Knighthood in the Flame Champions the less helpful he was becoming. This morning he seemed to be especially obtuse. With a short shove of her foot, she nudged him in the side.

"Well?" she demanded again.

His eyes slowly cleared.

"Nothing."

"There can't be nothing. *He* doesn't show up here for nothing."

"Maybe so, but there's still nothing that I can See."

"Try again."

"I've tried again."

"You weren't concentrating."

"Like you'd know anything about it."

"Allen."

He got to his feet before she could shove him again.

"What do you want from me," he groused. "I'm a Battle Seer not a Diviner. If you wanted me to cast for the best line of Sight to put an arrow between his shoulder blades, I could do that in a heartbeat, but I can't See why he came here. It's not . . ." He waved his hands in an attempt to explain the limitations of short-term precognitive Sight to the uninitiated and, in Iwa's case, the impatiently uninterested. "Maybe it's too far in the future, or maybe it's just too complex for my kind of vision."

"Can't you at least *Feel* if anything's going on?" she insisted. "You used to be good at that."

He shrugged. "I'm getting a vague sense of potential foreboding, like a thunderstorm in the distance. That's all. For all I know it *is* a thunderstorm in the distance."

Iwa peered past the balcony ceiling at the cloudless sky. "No."

"Whatever, the point is, I'm tapped out. If you want to know more ask the Deputy Seer, or go hover around the Coadjutor. He's bound to know why *he* came here by now."

Tossing the bit of ivy over the balcony, Iwa shook her head. "Father's been in a meeting with Uncle Lorien and Aunt Kali all morning. I'd have to have a *really* good reason to interrupt that."

"And the Archpriest's Man leaving so quickly isn't a good enough reason?"

"I suppose it is."

"Then go." Having successfully put her off, Allen leaned his head against the wall and closed his eyes.

"But you're coming with me."

His eyes snapped open. "Why me?"

"Because you saw him leave, too, didn't you? Father might want to question you."

"And I won't be able to tell him any more than I've already told you. Besides, if Aunt Kali sees me, she's bound to come up with something *useful* for me to do and I'm off duty for another hour."

Ignoring the protest, she began pushing him toward the

balcony doors. "You had that vague sense of foreboding, didn't you? Have you still got it?"

"Sure, but I think it has more to do with interrupting the Coadjutor, the Captain of the Flame Champions, and the Deputy Adjutant than anything else right now."

"Of course it doesn't. It obviously harbingers something big or bad or both. Besides, you might be the first to Feel this. You'll certainly be the first to bring it to Father's attention."

"How do you figure that?"

"No one else would have the guts to disturb the Coadjutor, the Captain of the Flame Champions, and the Deputy Adjutant with something this trivial," she answered with a grin.

"Thanks a lot."

"Will you quit griping. Have I ever steered you into trouble?"

"My entire life."

"And you've always survived it, haven't you? So come on."

"All right, all right, quit shoving." Indicating that she should lead the way, he followed her inside. "You know, you aren't going to be able to push me around like this when I'm a Flame Champion," he warned.

"Wanna bet?" She grinned at him. "As long as you're here, I can get you to do my evil bidding."

"Then I'll have myself transferred to Heathland. Or better yet, Danelind. A whole ocean between us would stop you."

"Don't count on it. Come on." Without waiting for him to close the balcony doors, she headed for her father's offices, knowing he would follow her as he always had and, with a sour grimace, he did.

Located in the oldest section of the Temple, the Coadjutor's official Audience Hall had been designed with both beauty and practicality in mind. A heavy Ekleptland carpet covered much of the stone floor while richly

woven tapestries adorned three of the dark-paneled walls
and a large, flagstoned hearth and two newly installed
stained-glass windows took up the fourth. The only furniture consisted of a long oaken table at the far end, illuminated by two standing golden candelabra, and several
ornately carved chairs drawn close to the hearth. The
three Temple Officials grouped about the fire glanced up
at the sound of Iwa's knock, but returned to their conversation when they saw who entered. The two youths stood
quietly by the door waiting for the Coadjutor to gesture
them forward.

Rysander DeKathrine had held the Branbridge Temple's Stewardship for a dozen years, serving under three
Archpriests of the Flame. Blond hair gone predominantly
silver, he'd managed the delicate task of running the
country's most powerful Temple with the bulk of the
Flame's Highest Officials in residence with a combination
of quiet diplomacy and quieter despotism. Known for his
even temper, most of the negotiations between the Palace
and the Flame Temple came through his office. Had it not
been for Urielle DeSandra, he might have been Archpriest
by now, but if he resented her meteoric rise to power, he
never showed it.

Now he gave his youngest daughter and her cousin a
distracted smile, waving them forward as he returned his
attention to the slow words of his uncle Lorien, the
Deputy Adjutant.

Lorien DeKathrine had served the Flame for over five
decades. A large man, still in his prime at age sixty-seven,
the only true sign of his years was in his thick once
auburn hair, now gone almost entirely white. He wore it
long and free-flowing as he had as a youth, and had the
habit of twirling it around his fingers when he was thinking deeply. He had a sharp mind and a devilish sense of
humor; most of the Temple Couriers under his command
believed he spoke slowly to annoy those who had to listen
to him without interruption, but in truth it had evolved
from a bad stammer as a child. He was Iwa's favorite rela-

tive, and she crossed the room to give him a kiss on the cheek before dropping a quick bow in her father's general direction. Behind her, Allen saluted their aunt Kali, Captain of the Flame Champions and—as her Squire—his direct superior. Leaning against the hearth, she drew slowly on a clay pipe before nodding once in response to his obeisance.

The youngest Captain in the history of the Flame Champions, Kaliana DeKathrine was a brilliant if temperamental tactician and a powerful Battle Seer. She'd earned her position on the fields of Brechburg in Bachiem, taking command of Temple forces when the former Captain had been cut down by enemy cavalry. She was quick-tempered and quick moving, but could be prudent if absolutely necessary. Now she turned her impatient gaze on her brother Rysander as he gestured his daughter forward.

"What have you got, Iwa?"

"The Archpriest's Man was here," she announced.

"We know."

"He just left."

The three adults exchanged a glance. "That was fast," Lorien observed. "Any inkling of what his visit might have been about, children?"

Both youths shook their heads.

"Ry?"

The Coadjutor gave a noncommittal shrug. "I imagine Her Grace will summon me if it involves the Temple."

"Of course it involves the Temple," Kaliana said tersely, blowing a puff of smoke toward the fire. "It always involves the Temple."

Lorien nodded. "It might be well for us to discover what we can before that takes place, Ry."

"Maybe so, but how do you plan to accomplish that?"

"Ask the Seers."

"I have Osarion's morning report. They experienced nothing unusual."

"Allen did," Iwa interjected eagerly. "He had a sense of danger."

"I had a *vague* sense of *foreboding*," the Flame Champion Squire corrected, shooting his cousin an annoyed glare.

Kaliana's brows drew down. "When?"

"Early this morning."

She turned to her brother. "So did I."

"This morning?"

"That's right. Nothing seemed out of the ordinary, yet I felt a faint sense of unease when I awakened."

"Martin Wrey's presence is certainly out of the ordinary," Lorien pointed out.

"True enough, and, given the way his Sight operates, I'd hazard a guess that he's experienced more than a faint sense of either foreboding or unease," Kaliana agreed.

"If that's why he came," Rysander corrected. "Remember, Martin Wrey is the Archpriest's Man in more than name. His visit might have been of a personal nature. It does happen," he added, glancing pointedly at his sister, who gave him a disbelieving snort in return. "Or he might have been summoned."

"Not using any of my messengers, Ry," Lorien countered.

"Regardless, the fact remains that his visit does not necessarily herald the end of the world."

"Were any of the Priestly Seers in the Prophetic Realm last night?" Kaliana asked.

Rysander shook his head. "It's not a ritual night, as you know, and there've been no signs or omens of any kind to warrant a special Seeking."

"And Osarion's morning report carried nothing unusual about last night." Kaliana reiterated.

"As I said, no ominous feelings, no strange dreams, nothing."

Twirling two fingers through his hair, their uncle grinned. "Looks like the Deputy Seer missed the prophetic boat last night," he said gleefully. "He must have been drunk."

Rysander shot him an irritated glance. "You know Osarion doesn't overindulge."

"He's wound too tight," Kaliana observed dryly.

"The fact remains, Ry," Lorien continued, "that the Archpriest's Man was closeted with Her Grace in her Meditation Room this morning, and you can bet they weren't rolling on the carpet. Her Grace scares him witless most of the time. He only comes here when something major rattles his Vision. We all know that."

"And Allen and Aunt Kali both felt something," Iwa persisted.

Lorien nodded. "Two Battle Seers, Ry."

"I know."

"I'll speak with my people," Kaliana offered. "See if anyone else has felt this sense of foreboding."

"And if they have?"

"Then it's a near future event involving either battle or the Flame Champions directly."

"In which case the Archpriest will likely send for you first, Kali," Lorien added.

"I imagine she'll send for Osarion first," Rysander interjected.

Lorien chuckled. "I'd give my left ball to eavesdrop on that conversation," he said gleefully.

"If you could give your left ball for anything, Uncle Lorien, you'd have given it years ago," Kaliana snapped. "It's one of your less endearing sayings."

The Deputy Adjutant just smiled at her as the Coadjutor turned to his daughter.

"Iwa, go to the Archpriest's Assistant and report on the Flame Captain's and her Squire's sense of foreboding. Tell him we're beginning an investigation, then go and make yourself useful around the Clerical Deputy. Find out if the Deputy Seer's been summoned to the Archpriest. If he has, come back here at once, if he hasn't, stay there until he is."

"Yes, Father."

Kaliana turned to her Squire. "Allen, begin asking the Battle Seers if any of them have felt a sense of foreboding or unease this morning or last night. Be quick. I want this information when I eventually meet with the Archpriest myself. Speak with Arthur first, he's the most likely to have felt something."

"Yes, Aunt Kali."

Allen saluted, and the two youths left together, Iwa shooting her cousin a smug glance. Allen aimed a kick at her ankle, and the last thing the three adults heard was the beginnings of their usual squabbling.

When the door closed, the Flame Champion Captain gave the two men a pointed look.

"So, what do we do now?"

Running a hand through his hair, Rysander sat back in his chair with an aggrieved sigh. "We finish the morning's business and then we wait for Her Grace to finish with the Deputy Seer."

"That might be some time, Ry," Lorien noted.

The Coadjutor shrugged. "Well, none of us is going anywhere."

"True enough."

"It's odd that none of the Priestly Seers had even an inkling of his visit, don't you think, Kali?" Lorien observed.

Pressing a fingerful of fenweed into her pipe, she nodded slowly. "The signs usually have more clarity than that."

"Perhaps they're looking in the wrong place."

"Perhaps."

As one, the three Officials turned to stare quietly into the fire, hoping one of the multitude of tiny signs in the flames might shed some illumination on the future as their physical forms illuminated the room.

In her Official Audience Room, Urielle DeSandra was also staring into the fire. Fingers steepled before her, she

watched the host of tiny symbols form and reform within
the flames. The signs spoke of chaos and confusion, but
that was hardly surprising. The Temple would be buzzing
with rumors about Martin's visit, and this news of the
Battle Seers' unease would just fan the flames higher. The
Temple Officials, Coadjutor, Deputy Marshal, and the
like, would be scrambling for information, all the while
waiting impatiently on her word. The Deputy Seer, however, would not be waiting. A man of powerful prophetic
ability, her third cousin Osarion would have gone Seeking
the answers to Martin's presence immediately. Ordinarily
she would have granted him enough time to complete his
vision, but she was not predisposed to be patient this
morning. He and his Priestly Seers had missed the first
warnings of a very dangerous possibility, and Osarion
would answer for their lack of vigilance.

A log rolled over in the grate, sending a shower of
sparks across the hearth. The Archpriest smiled coldly at
its rebuff. That she, too, had missed any sign of this threat
was immaterial. It was entirely likely that only Martin's
very sensitive Gift could have plucked it from the
Prophetic Realms at such an immature stage. However,
she answered only to the Aristok and Osarion DeSandra
answered to her, so he would do so.

A knock at the door interrupted her thoughts. At her
word her Assistant entered to announce the arrival of the
Deputy Seer and, setting her features into a mask of cold
disapproval, she gestured that he be sent in. A heartbeat
later he pushed past the duty guards and into her presence.

Like the Archpriest's Man, Osarion DeSandra was a
man for whom nature had combined average height and
build with unprecedented prophetic ability. Unlike the
Archpriest's Man, however, he'd been born into a noble
family and had never had cause to doubt the validity of
his life, his faith, or his Gifts. Arrogantly confident, he
had a violent temper and no patience for diplomacy. He
would have made an excellent Flame Champion, but his
Sight was so powerful that it precluded anything but a life

dedicated to Prophecy. If he had any weakness it was that his interpretation of that Prophecy was often dogmatically conventional, but his loyalty to the Flame Temple and its Archpriest was absolute.

Now he came forward at her gesture to stand before her, feet apart, hands clasped behind his back. His face was tightly neutral, but the Archpriest could see the unfocused cloudiness in his dark eyes that marked the Potion of Truth. She nodded to herself. It was as she'd expected. She came directly to the point.

"Martin Wrey has come to me with extremely disturbing news gleaned from the Prophetic Realm," she said. "News that has not been corroborated by my Temple Seers. You will explain to me why this is."

As expected, his face flushed angrily. "Because there's no corroboration to be made, Your Grace," he answered. "Martin Wrey is a madman whose Vision cannot be trusted."

"His Vision has proved accurate enough in the past," she countered. "Often more accurate, in fact, than more conventional Seeking."

His dark eyes burning, he nodded stiffly. "Perhaps so, Your Grace," he allowed, "but not this time. There's no disturbance of any kind to be found in the Prophetic Realm. None. All the signs continue to point toward a strong and prosperous season, just as I and the rest of Your Priestly Seers have been saying for months."

"Do they?" Briefly she outlined the elements of Martin's vision. "These images do not alarm you, Osarion?"

"No, Your Grace."

"And the foreboding felt by Temple Battle Seers this morning?"

"Is so vague that, had it not coincided with his visit, it would have gone completely unremarked."

"But it has coincided, and you will consider it."

"As you command, Your Grace, but forgive my bluntness, has any such imagery occurred in Your Grace's Vision to lend credence to Wrey's ravings?"

The Archpriest gave him a chilly smile. "I will forgive your bluntness for the simple reason that it is a legitimate question. No, I have not Seen these things, but Martin speaks of a presence he calls a not-thing which blocks the Sight of others. Have you ever encountered such a presence before in Vision or in study?"

"No, Your Grace. It's a twisted fantasy. There's no such thing."

"You're certain of this?"

"Very certain, Your Grace."

"And this isn't simply stung pride speaking?" She leaned forward. "Have a care how you answer, Osarion. This Vision of Martin's could herald the greatest threat to the Triarchy this Temple has ever faced, and I will not allow personal rivalry to undermine our ability to defeat it. If there exists even the most remote possibility that some outside force is interfering with the Flame Temple Seers, it is vital that we discover and neutralize it immediately."

The Deputy Seer's jaw tightened, but he jerked his head in recognition of her point. "What would Your Grace have me do?" he asked formally.

"Enter into a full Seeking in concert with Martin Wrey to discover the reasons behind his Vision, whatever they may be."

His expression registered resentment but no surprise. "Your Grace is aware that he and I do not work well together; that our individual Sight operates in opposition to one another's."

"I am aware of it, and I am also aware that this is caused by personal antagonism and not by prophetic leaning. You have worked together in the past—and you will do so again now for the good of the Temple. Is that clear?"

He bowed rigidly. "As Your Grace commands. I will require some time to prepare, however. His proximity creates a destabilizing effect within the Prophetic Realm.

One that I must prepare to overcome if I'm going to See clearly."

"As, no doubt, he will need time to overcome the effect of your proximity. Take what time you need."

"And Your Grace will instruct him to submit to my scrutiny of his Vision? Otherwise I cannot discharge my duty as you require it."

The Archpriest's luminescent gaze locked onto her kinsman's face.

"Martin knows what is required of him. He will cooperate with you as long as you remain within the bounds of duty. I know that I do not have to remind you of this."

His face twisted in disgust. "No, Your Grace, you do not. I would no more touch the hidden realms of his twisted thoughts than plunge my hand into a nest of poisonous snakes."

"Then go and make ready. I will have Martin summoned here for a Seeking at sunset. Will that give you sufficient preparation time?"

"Yes, Your Grace."

"Very well, then. You may go."

With another stiff bow, the Deputy Seer left her presence. The Archpriest returned her gaze to the fire, but she rose impatiently after a moment. If such a small prophetic vehicle could have revealed the future, it wouldn't have alerted Martin. Crossing to the window, she stared sightlessly at the gardens. Once she had reports from all quarters she would go into the Prophetic Realm herself, but for now, she must wait on the vision of others. She would begin with the simplest: the Battle Seers. Calling to her Assistant, she gave orders that the Captain of the Flame Champions be summoned to her at once.

That evening, as the setting sun sent long orange fingers of light to splay across the Temple courtyards, Osarion DeSandra and Martin Wrey prepared to enter the Prophetic Realm on orders from the Archpriest.

Seated at opposite ends of the Deputy Seer's Meditation Room—Osarion in a heavy oaken chair, Martin on the floor within the arms of a burly Acolyte—each accepted a bowl of the Potion of Truth from the Temple Herbalist. Osarion emptied his immediately, beginning the ritual breathing that would take him down into vision. Martin drank more slowly, fighting the urge to sneeze as the sharp, narcotic scent burned his nostrils.

Unlike the Deputy Seer, Martin rarely took the Potion of Truth. The ancient Gwynethian infusion sent his already chaotic Sight into spasms, causing the symbols and images which followed him everywhere to spin out of control. He preferred to cast his Sight out like a fisherman's net to ensnare what visions might come his way. However, to keep from being weakened by the Deputy Seer's hostile presence today, he needed all the strength he could muster.

Osarion's Sight was like a hard shaft of ice sent plunging down into the Prophetic Realm like a flung spear. To the Deputy Seer, visions were like prey to be hunted down and forced into submission, and Martin had no doubt that he would treat him the very same way if given half a chance. Shuddering as the potion took control of his mind, he reached out and began to weave his ability into a great, shining net capable of ensnaring both his vision and the Deputy Seer as well if necessary.

In the interim, having already descended into the Prophetic Realm, Osarion waited impatiently for Martin's presence. Capable of a much greater clarity of self in vision than any of his peers, he began to cast about, seeking the portents and omens that would lead him to the source of the other man's delusion. As he expected, the Prophetic Realm stretched out before him, as orderly and peaceful as it had been that morning. Tersely, he formed the symbols that would translate this vision into words, knowing his scribe would be faithfully recording everything he said. When he sensed Martin Wrey's chaotic presence, he didn't even bother to mask his disgust.

To the Deputy Seer, Martin's Sight was a mindless swarm of colors and imagery all spinning in random di-

rections. Its very proximity caused red shafts of light to
streak across his thoughts, and he reached out, determined
to force the other man's mind to some semblance of order.
Rather than fight him, however, Martin leaped forward to
catch him up in a maelstrom of chaotic energy. For a
heartbeat he was swamped by the force of the other man's
power, then his own abilities came to the fore and he
broke free. The two of them struggled until a tenuous balance was reached, then they merged; not compatibly, but
well enough to work together. Using Martin's Sight to remain linked and Osarion's to move forward, they began to
drop deeper into the Prophetic Realm.

Meanwhile, Kaliana DeKathrine had taken a dozen of
her Battle Seers to the Temple's topmost battlements. Just
over a third of their number—this third—had felt the
same sense of unease as their Captain. Now, however,
there was a general sense of excitement in the air. Temple
gossip had informed them that none of Osarion DeSandra's Priestly Seers had sensed anything amiss the night
before or this morning. Usually forced to acknowledge
the Priests' superior Prophetic abilities, the Battle Seers
were in a buoyant mood. Lined up facing the green hills
to the north, at Kaliana's order, each reached into a side
pouch for a fingerful of dried herbs.
    Short Distance Precognitives with little to no talent for
reading the vague and confusing symbols thrown up by
the Prophetic Realm, the Flame Champions did not seek
Visions in the quiet sanctity of a Meditation Room nor did
they take the Potion of Truth as an infusion. Taught to
reach into the near future to find an enemy's most vulner-
able spot or to discover a General's next battle order, they
caught their Visions on the fly amidst the distractions of
battle, and all worked best outdoors.
    Now, as the sun touched the tops of the distant trees,
each one took as much of the dried Potion of Truth as they
felt they needed and, as one, dropped into the Prophetic
Realm.

*   *   *

In his Meditation Room, Osarion jerked as his vision was interrupted by the burst of Sight from the gathered Flame Champions. Beside him, Martin remained unaffected. Such limited Sight was of little interest to him and he ignored it as one ignored a cloud of midges. Feeling the thought through their link, Osarion growled low in his throat and snapped his fingers. An Acolyte raised his bowl to his lips. He drank without coming up from vision, and with the added strength, shoved past the jumbled collection of Battle Seers.

With Osarion in the lead, the two Seers began a systematic sweep of the surrounding area, scanning first the Flame Temple, then the palace and the capital city itself. When Martin began to chafe against Osarion's restrictive methods, the Deputy Seer relented and the two of them moved northward, across Branshire, Werrickshire, and the central shires up to northern Yorbourne and Pennineshire.

They found nothing.

They pushed on to Essusiate Heathland and across the sea east to Branion's ancient rivals, Gallia and Panisha, then west to Triarctic but independent Gwyneth.

Again, nothing.

Now Martin took the lead, ranging randomly here and there, seeking the not-thing, the child, or anything that might bring his Vision into focus once more.

And again, nothing.

On the battlements the Battle Seers had fanned out, skimming across the near future like a wave of misty birds. Seeking the source of their own personal unease, they, too, scanned the Flame Temple, the Palace, and the capital, looking for traces of treason, intrigue, illness, or natural catastrophe. They reached out for the plans of Branion's enemies and the hidden thoughts of its friends. They, too, came up with nothing.

Returning to the Physical Realm, Kaliana dismissed

them with real disappointment, then went to report personally to the Archpriest.

Meanwhile, Osarion and Martin continued their search, each hour taking a fresh infusion of the Potion of Truth until the Temple Herbalist feared for their safety. Hours passed in total silence. The Scribes dozed beside the fire, while new Acolytes received Martin's limp form from the arms of the old. Finally, as the sun began to touch the horizon with the faintest of pale color, both men—pallid and shaking from prolonged exposure to the Potion of Truth—returned to the Physical Realm.

Standing erect but haggard before the Archpriest, Osarion came straight to the point.

"Nothing."

Her eyes tracked to Martin's face. Kept on his feet with the aid of an Acolyte, he shook his head wearily. "It's gone, Your Grace."

The Deputy Seer made a disgusted noise. "That's because it never existed in the first place," he snapped.

His eyes blazing, Martin rounded on the other man, his rage granting him new strength. "Why?" he demanded. "Because the great Deputy Seer can't find it?"

Osarion bared his teeth at him. "No. Because the *Archpriest's Man* is a liar."

His fists balled, Martin took one step forward, and the Archpriest slapped her hand down on her chair with such force that both men jumped. "Enough! Martin, you will wait in my Meditation Room while I speak with the Deputy Seer alone."

For half a heartbeat, rebellion fought against obedience, then Martin turned and allowed the Acolyte to help him from the room. The Archpriest turned to Osarion.

"Nothing at all?" she asked calmly.

Expecting a rebuke, he blinked tiredly. "None, Your Grace. We've searched for hours, together, apart, first with myself taking the lead and then . . ." he grimaced, "then with his leadership. We've scoured the Prophetic

Realm and found nothing." He shook his head, his face drawn with fatigue. "There is nothing, truly nothing, to See, Your Grace. Forgive me, but it has to be faced. Martin Wrey has finally lost his mind completely. He's delusional."

Nodding slowly, she rose to stand staring out her window at the dawn sky. "Thank you for your efforts, Deputy," she said formally. "We will consider this matter closed."

"Thank you, Your Grace." Too tired to show any triumph, Osarion DeSandra merely bowed and withdrew.

When the Archpriest entered her Meditation Room, she found Martin crouched beside the fire, his head pressed against the warm bricks beside the hearth. Indicating that he should remain where he was, she seated herself by the fire, staring into its depths for a long time without speaking.

After a while he stirred. "Your Grace?"

"Yes, Martin."

"It does exist, Your Grace," he said quietly. "I swear it."

She studied him silently. Between himself and the Deputy Seer, she had the two most powerful Seers in Branion at her command, but that in itself presented its own problems. As equally powerful Acolytes, both Martin Wrey and Osarion DeSandra had taken an instant and almost pathological dislike to each other. Their rivalry had reached dangerous heights, only easing with Martin's violent fall from grace. Now it only flared up on his rare visits to the Flame Temple.

Her eyes narrowed. Of the two of them, Martin was the easier to control. She'd offered him one slim thread of stability within the chaos of his unstable Vision, and he had grasped at it like a drowning man. He was unshakably loyal to her personally, and she had complete faith in his word. But not, she had to admit, in his sanity. If Osarion was correct and Martin had finally been driven mad by his

Visions, she had no more need of him. However, this had yet to be proved.

"I believe you, Martin," she answered finally.

His face drawn but relieved, he laid his head back against the hearth.

"I will find it again, Your Grace," he promised.

"Yes, you will."

He straightened. "But I can't find it here. Not with him. He's too hostile. He . . . clouds my Vision. Please, Your Grace."

The Archpriest sat staring into the fire for a long time. "Very well, Martin," she said at last. "Go home. Discover the answer to this riddle." She leaned forward, her eyes luminescent in the firelight. "Justify my faith in you."

To the collective relief of the entire Flame Temple, the Archpriest's Man left immediately. Once back in the peace of his Alderbrook tower, he gave himself over entirely to seeking the presence that had defeated him before. With the Potion of Truth and without it, he scoured the Prophetic Realm, growing steadily weaker as the days passed, but he persevered. He would find the not-thing, even if he had to enter into a bargain with the Shadow Catcher Itself to do so.

Meanwhile, in his own chambers at the Flame Temple, the Deputy Seer also searched, not because he believed in Martin's Vision, but because he knew the Archpriest believed.

As the spring of 492 gave way to summer, both the Priest and the Apostate continued to turn up nothing.

5. Brace Cottage

THE summer of 492 passed slowly at Tavencroft. As soon as Dani could coax the others into the water, the four youths spent most of their time down by the Whroxin River, swimming, fishing, eel-bobbing, or just lying about on the banks carving reed pipes and weaving chains of wildflowers. Sometimes Celestus would join them and, although his visits always included lessons of some kind, it seemed easier to learn outdoors. Generally he would rely on the youths themselves to do the teaching: Dani could reel off the strengths and weaknesses of every Branion Lord from Pennineshire to Wilshire, Quin knew reams of history from memory, and Lisha could win any debate on tactics or strategy he put forth.

At first Cam was too embarrassed by his lack of knowledge in any of these subjects to join in very often. He would answer if a question was posed to him directly, but for the most part, he would just listen, his head pillowed in Lisha's lap, one part of his mind following the flow of words while the other flitted about the water on the tail of the summer breeze. Celestus would draw him out occasionally, but for the most part he was content simply to watch the gray spark of the Wind's power rise and fall in the boy's eyes as he quietly absorbed the lessons buried in their conversations.

In the training circle, however, Cam lost his shyness.

Confident in his physical prowess and remarkably graceful for someone his age, he was naturally adept in a score
of weaponry from longbow to long sword and could out-
ride, outshoot, and outfight all three of the others combined. After the first month, Tom Jonstun, the Castle
Arms Master, having exhausted his knowledge of Branion
weapons, handed him his own Heathland claymore. The
only one of the four able to even lift the heavy weapon, it
quickly became Cam's blade of choice and he spent hours
alone in the outer courtyard learning to master its awk-
ward weight. Encouraged, Tom then introduced him to the
Heathland quarterstaff, dirk, and hunting bow and Cam
quickly grew proficient in each.

However, it was his time with Pri Gorwynne that he
valued the most. Sitting together on Tavencroft's upper
battlements, eyes closed, minds merging with the warm
summer wind, the boy and the old woman would cross the
length and breadth of the island, flinging chimney pots
from the roofs of Falmarnock, churning the waves before
Caristead Castle into froth and whispering prophecy into
the sleeping ears of the great gryphons of Gwyneth as
they dozed on the rocky tors of Bradyn Pass. They would
hover beside a butterfly as it perched on a rose in the Aristok's garden, whisper down Bran's ancient well in the cellars of the Sword Tower, then spin off to weave a
complicated dance though the ragged, old Kenneth Forest.
With the ex-Priest's steady presence at his side, Cam soon
learned how to give himself over to his Aspect without
losing himself in Its power as he had that first day at
Tavencroft. Pleased with his progress, Pri Gorwynne felt
certain that within the month he would be able to join the
others at Brace Cottage.

Sometimes, however, when he drew too near the capital, Cam thought he could almost feel the presence that
had touched him on the battlements that night. Kether
Breithe had told him the presence was the mind of a powerful Branion Seer who had linked with him and nearly
drawn him into the Prophetic Realm. At these times he

would feel the thread of fear interrupt his concentration, but Kether's mind was never too far away, as if he, too, could sense the man's proximity. He would come between them with the swiftness of a coastal fog, and Cam would fly away to swoop and dive off the cliffs of Morgwyr Penchen with the gulls and swallows.

If Cam'd had his way, he would have spent most of his time merged with the Wind, but Dani was jealous of his absence and adamant that he spend no more time with his Aspect than the rest of them did. When she felt his time with Pri Gorwynne was growing too long, she would position herself between him and the sun as she had the first day they'd met and stare at him, black eyes swirling blue with the power of the Sea, until he was so distracted by the constant plumes of water that rose up to smack against his mind that he'd finally return, scowling, to the world. Ignoring his mood with perfect élan, she would then drag him off for less ethereal pursuits: riding across the wide fields of Kairnbrook to the warrens or the fens, exploring the western edge of the Bricklin Forest, or most often, swimming in the Whroxin River. In the evening they would lounge about their presence chamber or drag a pile of furs up to the battlements and lie out under the stars, only coming down when Eban or Marna insisted. Then they would tumble into bed together and, after a certain amount of shoving, the three Tavencroft veterans would grow still.

Lying beside them with the night breeze whispering across his face, Cam would then close his eyes and send his mind out to rejoin the Wind once again.

Nearly a month after he'd arrived, Cam awoke to an unfamiliar sense of space. Beside him, Lisha slept soundly, her chin pillowed on his shoulder, Quin's arm thrown over her waist above the blanket. The dawn sun sent just enough light into the room to make out the sleeping forms beside him and he raised his head slightly, counting lumps. Only three, including himself. Sinking back down, he stretched his legs in relief. Four years younger than Ler, and gone from the nursery before the twins had left their cradle, Cam had been used to sleeping alone. He would have happily continued that way, but the others wouldn't hear of it. His first night Dani had insisted he stay in the large bed which dominated their sleeping chamber. It had been a tight fit then and it was getting tighter all the time. Sometimes he felt like he was part of a large litter of half-grown, ill-trained puppies. Dani thrashed, Lisha stole the covers and, sandwiched between the two of them, Quin was always complaining that he needed more room. Half the time Cam found himself sleeping with one leg or arm dangling over the edge, just to have some breathing space. He'd developed the habit of rising first, partly to have some time to himself, but mostly because he liked to sleep on his back and there was never quite enough room for his shoulders. He would slowly ease himself out from under Lisha, watching as she and the others slowly moved over to take up the vacancy, then collect his clothes and slip from the room.

The castle folk would already be going about their business as he'd make his way across the quiet inner courtyard toward the stables. Catching up a couple of last year's apples, he would saddle the young roan his uncle had lent him for the summer, then lead him from the keep, stopping a moment to greet the morning breeze, before mounting up and heading in whichever direction the Wind dictated.

An hour later the others would be gathered in the great hall—his uncle liked to take at least one meal a day with all of them together—squabbling sleepily because Quin and Lisha had dragged Dani out of bed much earlier than she'd wanted to be dragged, but after tucking into a hearty breakfast of oatmeal, bread, and honey, she would wake up enough to announce their plans for the day. This morning, however, the Captain of the Tavencroft youths was mysteriously missing. Rising, Cam threw on a tunic and went looking for her.

He found her talking earnestly with Marna Jonstun in the kitchen gardens. When she saw him, she waved a handful of greenery at him and he ambled over to meet them.

"What are you doing up so early?" he asked, glancing at the basket of herbs at their feet. "Are you sick?"

"Not a bit of it. I feel great." Dani grinned excitedly at him. "It's a very important day, Cam," she declared. "Maybe the most important day in Tavencroft history."

"Uh-huh." Used to her exaggerations by now, Cam seated himself on the low wall that separated the herb garden from the vegetable beds. "Why?"

"I just got my first flows."

Cam blinked. "Your first what?"

She rolled her eyes at him. "Flows, Cam, my first flows. You know, the first time a woman bleeds? You have an older sister, don't you? She must get them. And your mother?"

"Oh, yeah." He blushed. "Sure. It's just that's not what Jo calls it, er, them."

Dani looked interested. "So, what does she call it, er, them?"

He ignored the mockery. "Um, her scorchin' courses, usually."

"It's the same thing. Flows is just the Heathland word, right, Marna." Dani turned to the Steward, who nodded.

"And my mother calls them the blood mysteries," Cam continued.

"Why? Are they mysterious?"

"I dunno."

"Orthodox Triarchs attribute a woman's flows to the power of the Flame," Marna explained.

"Figures," Dani muttered.

"They hold special consecration rituals each month."

Plucking the head from a tansy flower, Dani shredded the petals thoughtfully. "What do they do in them?"

"I don't know, Danielle." The Steward leaned forward to pluck a weed hiding under a patch of motherwort.

"Only Triarchy women are allowed to participate. That's why they're called mysteries."

Dani gave an unimpressed snort. "Well, I'm not doing any drownin' consecration ritual for any Flame. *My* flows come from the Sea, or they don't come from anywhere at all."

"They come from your body."

"That works, too."

Dropping onto the wall next to Cam, Dani squinted up at the Steward. "So, what do Essusiate women do, then?"

"In Heathland, nothing in particular. The flows are just a part of life, no more or less mysterious than any other." She paused. "Of course, the first flows are special. They mark the passage from childhood to womanhood. Usually we have a ceremony and a celebration afterward, presided over by the girl's mother and her oldest female relative."

Dani cocked her head to one side. "Well, my mother's dead, and Aunt Ellesandra's in Branbridge, so maybe you could, you know, preside," she added with uncharacteristic hesitation. "If you wanted to. It being a Heathland celebration and everything."

"I'd be honored, but let me speak to your father first. He may have other plans. You are a Branion after all."

Dani tossed the shredded flower head away carelessly. "That won't matter. You know Da prefers Heathland customs to Branion. He says they haven't been corrupted by extraneous ritual." She turned to Cam. "Unnecessary observances added for pomp and circumstance interfere with the power called up by the original rite," she explained in imitation of her father's voice. "It corrupts the purity of the energy, see, so it's harder to use."

He shrugged. "Um, I guess. So what kind of energy will this rite call up?"

"Beats me. My guts feels all tight and crampy, like I've got to fart, but I can't, but here," she poked herself in the chest, "Here, I feel so powerful I can hardly hold it in. It's like the power of the Sea is so close it's going to just burst right out of me, like I could take on the whole world and drown it in one big geyser."

Her eyes were swirling with blue energy and Cam glanced at Marna nervously. "Is it always like that?" he asked.

She chuckled. "Sometimes, although usually it's only your husband you want to drown. But in this case I imagine it's because Danielle is the Sea's Chosen. She's a woman now, so she can access her power more completely. Alisha will come to this, too, but likely not for another year."

Dani was looking smug and Cam suddenly felt an irrational spark of jealousy. "Well, what about Quin and me?" he asked plaintively.

"What about you?" Dani retorted.

"Well, if you have . . . flows that make you women, what will we have that will make us men?"

Dani shrugged with studied indifference and Cam turned an aggrieved look on the Tavencroft Steward. She laughed.

"Your seed will become potent."

"My seed?"

She pursed her lips. "Have you ever seen young horses mounting each other in the pastures, lad?"

"Yes. They're trying to mate, but they're not old enough yet. Father used to say their seed hadn't . . . Oh."

"Exactly."

"Well, when will that happen?"

"How old are you now?"

"Twelve."

"Soon. Six months, a year maybe."

Cam looked disappointed but Dani just laughed. "Don't worry, Cam, " she said, her voice a mix of sympathy and amused condescension. "It'll happen for you soon enough, maybe even tonight," she hinted.

"Why tonight?"

"We have to do a Circle, don't we, to see how this changes the power dynamic. And maybe, just maybe, my having extra power will tip the rest of you over. If you're close enough, that is."

"You think it might?"

"No, it doesn't work that way," Marna admonished. "Each person comes to adulthood in their own time. The Aspects have nothing to do with it."

"But you said I could access more power now, so they must have a *little* something to do with it, right?" Dani countered.

The Steward scowled at her, but eventually shrugged. "Perhaps," she allowed.

"There you are."

"But Pri Gorwynne hasn't said I'm ready to join the Circle yet," Cam protested. "What if she won't let me?"

"I'll get Da to talk her into it. We need you in the Circle now to counter my added power, or the Sea will swallow everything else up. She'll *have* to see that." Leaping from the wall, Dani caught up the basket of herbs. "Anyway, right now, Marna's going to brew me up something to get rid of this farty feeling, and then I have to go tell Da about my flows, so why don't you go do whatever it is you always do this early in the morning and I'll see you at breakfast?"

Cam glanced at the Steward, who nodded and, still feeling strangely left out of something, he headed for the stables.

By the time he returned to the keep, the small dining hall where they took most of their meals with Uncle Celestus was in an uproar. Cam could hear Dani's voice all the way down the corridor and almost turned back but, after only a moment's hesitation, he made himself continue. If he didn't go in now, he would miss breakfast, and ever since his first morning in Kairnbrook he seemed perpetually hungry. It must be the winds off the Washe. On cue his stomach growled loudly. That settled it. He couldn't wait until noon, not even to avoid a squabble; he'd collapse. As he neared the room, he heard his uncle speaking in his familiar lecturing tone, deliberate and calm.

"I was not suggesting separate rooms, only separate beds. It's time the four of you slept apart."

One foot through the doorway, Cam froze. Peering in the room he saw Lisha standing by the sideboard, staring at her great uncle as if he'd just suggested they attack the local village, Quin was looking shocked, and Vincent amused, but it was Dani who gave voice to her reaction.

"But, Da, Quin and I have shared a bed for eight years!"

Celestus carefully spread honey onto a piece of bread before answering.

"That was when you were children, Danielle," he replied. "You're not children any longer, you're young adults now, and young adults sometimes feel the need to act upon the new and highly demanding physical sensations they're experiencing."

"So?"

"So," Vincent interjected, "acting upon these particular sensations can lead to childbirth, Danielle. With the advent of your flows, you're now physically capable of bearing children no matter how unwise that might be at your age."

"Oh, come on, Vincent!" Dani snapped back. "Even if I'm capable, Quin and Cam certainly aren't!"

Quin surged to his feet. "How do you know," he demanded.

She waved her hand dismissively at him. "Because if you could, you've have told me about it."

"I might not have. I don't tell you everything, you know."

"Yes, you do. And besides, your power hasn't changed one wit and Marna says it will."

"Oh." Quin subsided, muttering into his oatmeal, and Celestus sighed deeply.

"You're all getting far too big to share a bed anyway," he pointed out. Turning, he noticed Cam hovering by the door, and gestured him in with a reassuring smile. "One of these days, Camden is going to fall right out," he continued. "Or Quinton will get smothered. You may, of course, remain sleeping in the same room," he allowed, raising his hand to forestall another outburst. "Unless any of you feel the need for greater privacy. Camden?"

Suddenly the focus of the entire room's attention, Cam resisted the urge to back up a step. "Um, no, Uncle."

Celestus glanced at the others, who all shook their heads with various degrees of vehemence.

"Very well, then," he said. "It's settled. Ross will bring another bed up to your tower for Quinton and Camden, and I trust that you will all confine your physical explorations to those of the same gender. The last thing we need to contend with at this stage in our work with the Aspects is an infant, never mind a nine-month pregnancy. Isn't that true?" He glanced about the room and after each of the four youths had nodded, he picked up his cup.

"Excellent. Now I understand that Marna has a ceremony planned for your induction into adulthood, Danielle." He smiled sadly. "I'm so sorry your mother couldn't be here to share it with you. She'd have been so very proud of the woman you're becoming."

At mention of her mother, Dani's expression softened. "Don't be sad, Da," she said gently. "Marna will do. She's known me forever. Ma wouldn't mind."

"Of course she wouldn't. She trusted Marna from the day you were born. And so do I." He set his cup down, unemptied. "Well, well, the first of my children grown," he noted in a slightly melancholy voice. "It won't be long now before you're all men and women, and then what shall I do?"

"The same thing you do now, Uncle," Lisha answered, coming forward to wrap her arms about his neck. "We'll never leave you, will we?" She glanced expectantly at the others.

"Of course not," Dani answered. "We have theories to prove, right, Quin?"

"Right." He nodded and Lisha returned contentedly to her place at the table, but behind them, Cam frowned as the breeze from the dining room windows whispered another answer into his ear. Never was a long time, and he suddenly knew that they didn't have nearly that much time.

That afternoon the Tavencroft women took Dani off to the Whroxin River for her ceremony. Barred from attending, the other three hung about the castle sulking until the Arms Master sent them off to practice their sword work, but after Cam had beaten both Quin and Lisha twice, they withdrew to the tower to await their leader. On returning, her smug, *"I've got a secret and you don't,"* attitude did nothing to elevate their mood. Eventually, however, she talked them into riding out to the warrens to hunt rabbits.

Later, stretched out on a low hill, their mounts hobbled below and their catch hanging from the branches of a young ash tree, she allowed them to nag her into telling them what had transpired.

Afterward, her head pillowed on Cam's chest, Lisha squinted into the sun.

"I wonder how long it will be until I get my flows?"

Quin sprinkled a handful of daisy petals over her. "Years," he teased, and she smacked him.

"It probably will be years," she continued mournfully. "My sister Kathrine didn't get hers until she was fourteen, and Margurette was almost fifteen."

"You'll be thirteen in a month," Dani observed, "so it can't be *that* long."

"I think Stephie was about thirteen," Quin added. "Aunt Leilani wrote me about it. I could dig the letter out, if you like."

"How old was Jo?" Dani turned to Cam who was stretched out on the grass with his eyes closed. "Cam?"

He opened one eye. "What?"

"How old was *your sister Joanne* when she got her first flows?"

"I dunno."

"You were there, weren't you?"

"Sure, but she's six years older'n me. It's not like we talked about things like that. Besides, Marna said each person comes to adulthood in their own time. You can't predict it. It'll happen when it happens."

"Now, there's an intellectual philosophy," Quin observed.

Cam turned a baleful, one-eyed glare on the older boy. "Intellectuals spend too much time snooping about in other people's lives and not enough time living their own," he snapped.

"Don't fight." After banging the back of her head into Cam's ribs, Lisha shook a finger at Quin. "It's too hot. What did Pri Gorwynne say about tonight, Dani?"

The other girl grinned widely. "We're a full Circle tonight."

"What?" Cam sat up, spilling Lisha onto the grass. "All of us?"

"All of us. Like I said, we need you to keep the balance now that I'm so much more powerful than everyone else."

Both Quin and Lisha threw a handful of grass at her, but Cam just frowned. "Pri Gorwynne said I was ready?"

Plucking a long stick from the grass, Dani took aim at a large purple windflower. "Ready and able." She chopped the flower head off with one quick motion, then aimed at another.

Quin shot Cam a calculated glance. "Nervous?"

"No!"

The smaller boy laughed. "I was. I nearly pissed myself the first time I sank into the earth with Dani beside me. I thought she was going to pull me right down into an underground spring and drown me."

"So you just about caused a mud slide, ya little worm."

Quin ignored her with well practiced disdain. "When Lisha came, it was even worse. We weren't used to a De-

Marian. Not me nor Dani. She had more latent power than
both of us put together. You could hardly see it was so
bright. I though for sure she would burn us all up before
she learned how to control it."

Lisha nodded solemnly. "It's true. Our Aspects are all
so different it's hard to maintain a balance, especially at
the beginning. But you'll have Pri Gorwynne right there,
Cam. There's nothing to worry about."

"Besides, tonight won't be anything different than what
you've done already," Dani added.

"Sure but last time I . . ." He dug a pebble out from
under him before continuing. "You know."

"Can't happen again. You've been practicing for a
month now. Quit fretting. You were born for this." Brushing a bumblebee from her hair, Dani lopped off another
flower head before rising. "Anyway, it's time we went
back. I'm hungry and I think I have to change this moss
thing."

Used to Dani's abrupt change of subject, the other three
stood with various amounts of grumbling, and taking up
their catch, followed her down the hill toward the horses.

That evening as the sun hovered like a bright orange
ball just above the treetops, the four youths made their
way along the river path to Pri Gorwynne's.

They'd spent the early part of the afternoon training
with Kether Breithe in the great hall, learning to recognize
the presence of others through their link with the Aspects.
Kether had insisted they at least become familiar with the
subject, but the Heathland Mirror seemed even more
withdrawn than usual, and the warm summer day was a
distraction for them all. They tried—with limited success—to concentrate on his words and not on the breeze
which whispered in through the windows, bringing the
scents of meadows, trees, and water with it to tempt them
away, but one by one, their thoughts drifted to other pursuits.

* * *

"Anyone can temporarily deflect the attention of a Seer," Kether said for the second time, rubbing irritably at his temples. "It just takes practice. Take this man outside Branbridge, for example. How would you deal with him? Danielle?"

Dani jerked her gaze from the shaft of sunlight playing across the floor. "Stick a sword in him?" she offered.

"He's a little far away for that."

Quin and Lisha snickered.

"How would you deflect him with your mind?" the Mirror continued. "Camden?"

The smell of wildflowers was maddening. He could almost feel the bees buzzing over the blossoms, collecting the golden pollen on their backs and on their wings, then rising up on the wind to journey to the next and the next. Almost . . .

"Master Camden!"

Jerked from his reverie, Cam blinked. "Yes?"

"How would you distract this Branion Seer?"

"What Branion Seer?"

This time it was Dani's turn to snicker as Kether shut his eyes briefly. "The Branion Seer whose presence you felt on the tower battlements. The Branion Seer who's been trying to reestablish his link with you ever since."

"Oh. I dunno. I guess I'd just fly away from him until I lost him. Would that work?"

Kether nodded. "Likely it would." He turned to the others. "You see, you must make use of your individual talents. Quinton, you could send your mind sinking into the earth, Danielle into the sea . . ."

Kether's voice faded to become like the buzzing of the bees again. No matter how hard he tried to concentrate on what he was saying, Cam found it almost impossible to even keep his eyes on the man.

Finally, even Kether gave up on this method of teaching.

"Let's try some practical applications."

That met with even less success. Dani was wildly unfocused, her power as well as her control spiking erratically. She was constantly setting off Lisha—as the only Aspect with a Living Avatar in the Physical Realm, the Flame would not be overwhelmed by the Sea—and finally, with a headache sending his left eye into spasms, Kether stood.

"Go, leave. Do something restful for the afternoon. I'll meet you at Brace Cottage for the working."

The four youths didn't have to be told twice. They disappeared toward the Whroxin River, and the Heathland Mirror went to lie down in a dark room.

Now, having spent the day fishing and lolling about on the riverbank, the youths were restless and eager to get down to work. Walking quickly along the path to Brace Cottage, their bare feet sending up little puffs of dust with each step, the three Tavencroft veterans talked excitedly about the evening while Cam lingered a few paces behind. The path was cool, the overhanging trees creating a vast leafy archway above his head. It reminded him of the Wind Temple, and he craned his neck so that he could stare up into its midst as he walked. The summer breeze rustled the smaller branches, whispering of the adventures to come, and suddenly Cam knew that there would be no nasty surprises tonight. Lengthening his stride, he caught up to the others just as the trees opened up to a wide, sweet smelling meadow.

Brace Cottage lay at the far end, its accompanying herb-and-vegetable gardens barely visible above the tangled mass of blooming chicory and red clover. Conical, wicker beehives stood tucked against the line of trees while in the distance they could just make out the tops of several stone dovecotes. As they started down the path, a flock of geese fell into step behind them, following them like a suspicious House Guard all the way to the cottage.

Dani resisted the urge to shout at them only because Lisha
had her firmly by the arm—the last time they'd tangled
with Pri Gorwynne's geese, the geese had won. She released her only after they stood before Brace Cottage.

Pri Gorwynne was sitting on a bench beside a small
stone bakehouse, sharing a pipe with Kether Breithe.
Blowing a puff of smoke into the air, the ex-Priest jerked
her head toward the open doorway.

"Go in and make ready, will you. We'll be there after."

The two girls immediately headed inside, but Cam hesitated, drawing Quin to one side.

"Are we going to eat?" he asked in a whisper.

"Later. Why, are you hungry?"

"Well, sure, it's nearly suppertime. Aren't you?"

The other boy shrugged. "Yeah, but supper's not until
after the ritual."

"Why?"

"I dunno. That's how we've always done it. Maybe
having a full belly inhibits the complete merging of Chosen and Aspect."

Cam blinked at him.

"It makes you lethargic." Quin sighed. "You know,
sleepy, like it would if you tried to fight right after eating.
You'd lose your edge."

"Oh." Cam rubbed his stomach mournfully. "I'd think
I'd lose my edge more with an empty belly. It's distract-
ing, you know?"

"That's true. Hey, maybe we could sneak some honeycomb from Pri Gorwynne's cupboard. We helped her
gather it, after all."

"You think so?"

"Maybe, but we'd have to hurry before she gets there."

"Well, come on, then." Heartened, Cam pushed the
smaller boy through the door.

Brace Cottage was essentially one large room with a
stone hearth dominating the south wall and a large, open
shuttered window on the east. Bunches of dried lavender,
chamomile, borage, and cat-mint hung from the beamed

ceiling, while strings of garlic decorated the doorframe. The furniture consisted of a huge cherrywood hutch, its shelves laden with pots and jars of various sizes, a bed, table, chair, and several trunks pushed against the walls. A multicolored braided rug of red, blue, gray, and green lay in the center of the floor and in the center of that sat a slim, white cat with black ears. The table held a candle in a black iron lantern, two bowls, one ceramic and filled with water, the other wood, containing a mixture of sand and earth, and a large golden eagle feather. His eyes wide, Cam reached for the feather.

It was both soft and firm, the delicate bands of brown, black, and gold extending to the very tip. Cam brushed it lightly along his jaw, feeling tiny sparks of energy crackle against his skin. He turned a questioning look on Dani.

"Talismans," she said simply, picking up the bowl of water and carrying it carefully to the west side of the rug. "To help bond with the Aspects. We haven't needed them in a long time, but I guess Pri Gorwynne feels we do tonight because you're new."

"And because of your flows," Lisha added, picking up the lantern."

"Whatever."

As the DeMarian girl joined Dani on the rug, Quin slipped past her, crossing quickly to the armoire and pulling down a large earthenware pot.

The black of her eyes already growing pale with a fine blue mist, Dani frowned at him.

"What're you doing?" she demanded.

"Eating."

Lisha turned. "Before the ritual?"

"Cam's hungry." Reaching into the pot, Quin carefully removed two pieces of honeycomb. Handing one to Cam, he stuffed the other in his mouth with a grin.

"Pri Gorwynne's going to kill you," the DeMarian girl observed. "You don't eat before the ritual."

"S'e never thed that," Quin replied, honey dripping

from between his teeth. "'Ave thom." He held out two more pieces.

Dani glanced at Lisha. "I am kinda hungry," she admitted. "It must be because of my flows." Having come up with a convenient excuse, she caught the piece Quin tossed at her.

"Well, I'm not on my flows."

"But 'u 'ave to 'ave thom now," Cam added, already on his second piece. "We're a thircle, yeah?"

"That's right," Dani agreed. "We gotta stand together. Beside, you know how boring it is being the only one not in trouble. Might as well be hanged for a sheep, eh?" She bit into her piece with gusto.

Lisha glared at them all, but finally accepted the piece Cam held out to her. "I'm only eating this in the name of solidarity," she said primly.

"Whatever. Toss me some more, will you, Quin."

By the time Pri Gorwynne and Kether Breithe entered the cottage, all evidence of the unauthorized snack had been cleared away and the four youths were sitting cross-legged on the rug in the positions Dani had first arranged them in on the battlements. Dani and Quin already had their eyes closed, beginning the ritual breathing that would bring them in tune with their Aspects, but both Lisha and Cam seemed uncomfortable and slightly guilty. The ex-Priest frowned, studying their faces intently. They returned her scowl with equal expressions of wide-eyed innocence as carefully crafted as the cat's and, after a moment, she grunted and turned away, motioning to Kether who took up his usual position in the corner of the room. With a relieved sigh, Lisha closed her eyes, but unable to follow her lead just yet, Cam watched as the fur along the cat's back slowly rose in response to the increasingly focused power in the room. Finally, it stood abruptly and, with a low growl, stalked from the cottage. Cam smiled.

As he began to slowly relax, the sense of anticipation he'd felt on the battlements began to rise. Pri Gorwynne came to sit behind Dani, hands resting lightly on her shoulders. Dani opened her eyes briefly, but her gaze was already lost in a sea of swirling blue and after a second, her lids grew heavy and she closed them again.

The sense of anticipation grew.

"Now, my children," the ex-Priest began quietly in an almost singsong tone. "Tonight's an important night, it is. Danielle has made the crossing to adulthood, and things will never be the same again. The rest of you will follow soon enough, mind, but in the meantime, you'll find the Circle will be unbalanced in the Sea's favor, eh."

Dani grinned and, sensing her thoughts, Pri Gorwynne squeezed her shoulders.

"The other Aspects won't like that at all, them," she continued. "They're jealous, they are, and they'll be fighting your control, but don't let it fret you, you've all been well trained and I'll be there to help you stay focused, won't I? So just give yourselves over to your Aspects. You're their Chosen, and they'll accept your control after a time.

"Now, we'll not go far tonight, it being Camden's first true Circle, but we'll go deep, almost all the way to the Prophetic Realm, mind. But don't be afraid. We'll all go in together and we'll all come out together, us."

She glanced about at them all, her eyes bright and shining. "Are you ready, then, my children?"

Already floating in a faint trance induced by the rhythm of her words, the four youths nodded without speaking.

"That's good, then. Close your eyes now, all of you, and concentrate on your breathing as you've done before, then take hands. Danielle girl, you send your mind out to the Sea right off the biscuit, like. Tire it out, and yourself, too, eh. Go now."

With a whoop of joy, Dani took a huge breath and, as they all linked hands, she flung her mind out toward the Sea. Cam smelled fish, heard the sound of gulls, and then a great wave of salt water crashed over his mind. He couldn't breathe, couldn't see. He began to flail about in panic, then the Wind caught him up and shot him into the air. With a deep sense of relief, he gave himself over to It.

It was different this time than it had ever been before. Although free to soar above the clouds, Cam could still feel the connection to the world below him along the physical link of his cousins' clasped hands. He looked down through the gray mist that obscured his vision to see Quin, his face and chest already covered with brown bark, stretching out his arms to become the great green forests of Branion; Lisha spinning in a great fiery vortex as she merged with the Flame through the open channel of her birthright; and Dani already one with the vast ocean below him. They flowed around him and through him, lifting him up with the power of their merging. He could feel their combined presence radiate through each of the Physical Realms, mingling with their Aspects to create a vast rainbow of ever-moving colors. Together with the Wind, he played about in their midst for a long time, happily swooping and weaving aimlessly until a spark of light caught his eye. He turned.

Far below, the great shining net that was Kether Breithe's gift stretched out across the horizon. Cam slowly drifted toward it, mesmerized by the shimmering lights that traveled along its surface. He reached out to run his fingers along its length, and felt it thrum in response like a fine harp string. He smiled.

Something moved behind the net.

Cam squinted. Through the fine mesh of sparkling light he could just make out a faintly luminescent shape flitting back and forth like a ghostly sentinel. Drawn, he pressed against the net, feeling it slowly give way under the pressure of his mind and with a pop, he broke through into the Prophetic Realm.

Contact came so fast it nearly knocked him out of trance as a torrent of conflicting thoughts and emotions spewed out to hammer against his mind. Within them, the Branion Seer took form as a wildly gyrating moth the size of a man. Its great wings beat against his face and chest, threatening to smother him and, with his own panic rising, Cam's mind shot out along the link with his Tavencroft cousins. They responded. The force of their contact jerked them both to a standstill and in the split second of calm it afforded, Cam looked down to see the giant moth pressed against him, trembling with fear. He reached for it, and then Kether Breithe's ability rose up like a huge metaphysical hand and slapped them apart. Cam's last sight was the creature tumbling away, out of control once more, and then he was back in Brace Cottage, his head snapping back to crack against the wooden floor.

He began to seizure.

Alderbrook, Branshire

Martin Wrey came back to himself with a shriek of pain as a bolt of power crackled across his mind. His body snapped into a fetal position, scraping his head against the ground as he began to convulse. All he could do was ride out the attack curled in a tight ball, the tendons of his neck and arms standing out from the strain. Finally, with blood coursing down his forehead, he felt the seizure pass. He went limp.

He lay, panting heavily, for a long time, his face buried in a pillow of soft grasses, his whole body throbbing with the force of his expulsion from the Prophetic Realm. When he was finally able to move, he dragged himself up into a half-sitting position, his eyes glassy and staring.

He hurt everywhere, mind, body, and spirit. His head lolling sideways, he blinked uncomprehendingly at his surroundings.

He was sitting on a hill overlooking the town of Alderbrook. The oat and barley fields below were deep in shadow, the setting sun nothing but a bright orange glow on the horizon. Above him, storm clouds were beginning to gather. When he'd come up here this morning, the sun had been high in a cloudless sky, the warm summer breeze and gently undulating wildflowers promising hours of solitary prophecy.

He coughed.

He'd been seeking the not-thing and the Vision it was hiding for almost a month now. Night after night he'd roamed the Prophetic Realm finding nothing, but it was the daylight hours that were the most maddening. He would get flashes of color and sound, glimpses of places he'd never been; reeds along an unfamiliar riverbank or signal fires glowing on a cliff above the sea, and all from the strangest perspective: treetops from above, or the waves from below. One day fire erupted all around him yet nothing burned, and another day he seemed deep in the earth as if he had already died and been buried. And every time these flashes would come with a momentary sense of peace. The symbols that danced about his head would fade away and his mind would grow still and clear.

But then the not-thing would pass between him and his Vision and the chaos would return, stronger and more violent each time. It was infuriating. On those days he would return to his tower and brew up as large a dose of the Potion of Truth as he dared, but always it was the same, the Vision was gone, cloaked behind something he could not See.

He took to wandering the woods around Alderbrook, seeking help from the natural world around him: staring intently into the depths of the green trees or up into the sky. He would plunge his hands into the many small streams that crisscrossed each other through the bracken and down the hillsides, or drive his fingers into the mossy, leaf-covered earth beneath the trees. Still he came up with nothing.

The people of Alderbrook left bread and milk at his door—to help sustain their *mad Priest*—but he rarely touched it. He was seldom hungry anymore. He began to lose weight. His body felt light from lack of restful sleep, his mind faint from lack of food. But he still searched. Every day he came up to the hilltops and, with his back pressed into the crook of two worn rocks, sent his mind out toward the north, seeking the child, the not-thing, anything. When contact came, it had surprised him as much as it had them. But the not-thing had reacted first.

Wiping weakly at his face, his hand came away bloody and he grimaced. This was the second time the not-thing had hurt him, but this time—he bared his teeth at the north—this time he'd finally managed to See what it was. A man. A powerful man with the ability to block and deflect the Sight of another, but still, just a man. And he'd Seen the child, Seen him and touched him and knew him to be real as well.

His head throbbing painfully, Martin brought his knees up to his chest, staring blankly at nothing as the host of ethereal images and symbols that followed him everywhere surrounded him with new vehemence. But this time one image held his attention. A great moth, its wings beating frantically against the chest of a golden-haired boy with eyes as blue as a summer sky. The boy reached out, and as he touched it, the moth grew still. *He* grew still. Quiet. Peaceful.

It began to rain.

Blinking, Martin looked up into the evening sky. The world around him was in conflict; wind from the north, clouds from the east. He nodded mutely, understanding his vision at last. His duty lay in the east, amidst the gold-and-crimson-bedecked halls of the Flame Temple, but his future lay to the north, tied to a boy-child who could banish the chaos with a single touch, and a man who would kill him to prevent that from happening.

His head spinning in sickening circles, Martin stood. Rain pelted against his face and as it washed the sweat and blood from his eyes, he looked up.

The wind was from the north.

Looked down.

A wood lark singing in a nearby gorse bush suddenly took flight, flying . . . north.

He smiled, opening his mouth to accept the rivulets of

rain that tracked through a month's worth of beard on his cheeks. Then he turned his gaze toward Alderbrook, knowing what he would See.

Candles and hearth fires flickered from the windows of homes and shops. Before his special Sight the fires joined together to weave a swirling pattern which pointed . . . north.

He laughed out loud. The Aspects were in concert, and for the first time in his life he understood what they were saying. He would find peace, one way or another, in the north. He began to run down the hill toward his tower, eager to be on his way, but lightning flashing in the distance brought him up sharply. His Vision was to the north, but the lightning was from the east. There was danger to the east, danger from the Flame Temple and the woman who'd granted him life, pardon, and protection from execution. He froze.

The rain began to fall harder as he stood there, staring bleakly into the darkening sky. One by one, the symbols of each possible future played out their silent pantomime before his eyes, and finally he closed them, sudden weariness making him sway.

Thunder rumbled in the distance, in the east, and he bowed his head in obeisance to its command. He would go north as his Vision directed, but there would be no peace for him there. Only duty, and danger.

He opened his eyes.

"And maybe death at the end of it," he whispered. "That's a kind of peace, isn't it? Maybe death at the end?"

Shivering in the rain, he made his way slowly toward his tower to pack his few belongings for his journey north.

6. Celestus

THE sound of a furious argument filtered in through the windows of the keep's lesser hall. Busy with Kairn-brook's account books, Celestus smiled fondly as Danielle's voice rose above the din.

It had been just over a month since his daughter had burst into his inner chamber, gasping out the news that something terrible had happened. He'd followed her at a run all the way to Brace Cottage to find Camden seizing in Kether Breithe's arms. Beside them, her hands clamped to the boy's temples, Pri Gorwynne was deep in trace, try-ing to still his convulsions. Quinton and Alisha were in hysterics.

"See to the others, Danielle." Dropping to his knees, Celestus took the boy from the Heathland Mirror, wrap-ping his arms about him firmly.
"What happened here?"
Kether grimaced. "He slipped into the Prophetic Realm and linked with the Branion Seer."

Even weeks later the memory of his words caused the Tavencroft Lord's brows to draw down in a deeply wor-ried frown.

* * *

"How?"

"He got past me. The Seer was poking about as always, I was blocking him, and then the boy went straight through. Something drew him."

"What?"

"I don't know." Kether paused, working to maintain his usual stony expression. "I didn't anticipate that he would do that."

"No, you didn't."

The Mirror had not apologized. There would have been no point. He'd merely waited as Celestus had dropped down through the Physical Realms and, linking with Pri Gorwynne, had reached out for Camden's mind. After a long time, he'd spotted the smallest of tremors in the distance. He froze, projecting the image of a hot summer day out before him.

Nothing moved, not a leaf nor a blade of grass, the only sound, the heavy droning of bees. Beneath a tree, a fox panted in the heat, a drop of saliva dripping from its tongue to stain the dusty ground.

Everything about the image called out for a cooling breeze, and after a long time, the breeze responded. Camden stilled.

Celestus allowed himself the faintest sigh of relief.

"He'll be all right now. Let's get him up. May we use your bed, Pri?"

Her hazel eyes still swirling with gray, she nodded mutely.

"Danielle, Quinton?"

The two youths came forward at his word, helping him to lift Cam's limp form to the bed. Pulling a quilt over him, Alisha chewed anxiously on her bottom lip.

"Will he be all right, Uncle?"

"Yes. He's back now, he's just sleeping."

He returned his dark gaze to Kether's face.

"How much did the man See?"

"The boy's essence, a certain amount of his physical form, a bit of mine."

"Enough to identify either of you?"

"No."

"And our location?"

"Nothing."

"Will he be able to link with him again?"

"He'll try now that he knows what to look for. Complete, your Circle creates a much stronger signature within the Physical Realms than we ever suspected."

"And in the Prophetic Realm?"

"When Camden entered, it was like a cyclone in the night sky."

"Was this comet Seen by anyone else?"

"No."

"What of the Aristok?"

"His countenance was directed elsewhere."

"That's something at least."

The Tavencroft Lord stared intently at the other man.

"Can you protect my children from this ever happening again, Kether?" he asked bluntly.

The Heathland Mirror met his gaze.

"Yes, My Lord, I can."

"Then see that you do."

Celestus turned to Pri Gorwynne. "Aside from this little drama, how did it go, Pri?"

She made a sarcastic snort. "Aside from this, it went as I thought it would. They work well together. When the boy found himself in trouble, he called to the others and they came faster than gryphons to a kill."

She frowned at the cat who'd jumped up onto the bed and was now seated on Cam's chest, kneading the blanket and staring at his face with wide, yellow eyes. "But he needs more practice, mind—scat you! His discipline's as poor as you'd expect the Wind's Chosen to be, eh? He's *too easily distracted. Drawn to sparkly objects like a magpie, he is. Likely that's what happened tonight."*

"Then we'll just have to provide sparklier objects to keep him on track, won't we?"

"Aye, that we will."

The three youths exchanged a worried glance.

"We can do that, Da," Danielle offered quickly. *"He's part of our Circle; we'll look after him."*

He smiled at her protective tone, but when he spoke, his own voice was serious. *"I know you will, Danielle, and I have no desire to interfere with your autonomy, but this Branion Seer poses a very grave threat to us all."* He paused, his expression thoughtful. *"I will join you in your workings here at Brace Cottage."* He held up one hand as she started to protest. *"As an observer only, in exactly the same capacity as Pri Gorwynne."* His expression grew wrathful. *"If this Seer approaches Camden or any of you again, he'll find me waiting for him."*

"Maybe that's what it's going to take, anyway," the ex-Priest noted as she laid the back of her hand against Camden's cheek. *"If this fellow's going to keep after us, mind. Maybe we should bring the fight to him, eh?"*

"How would you suggest we do that, Pri?"

"Lie in wait within the Second Realm as you plan, then track him, find him, and kill him in this one."

Celestus nodded. *"It's worth considering. In the meantime, Kether, you will provide extra lessons for Camden in shielding his mind and, Pri, in maintaining his focus."*

The ex-Priest stood with a groan. *"Aye, we'll do that, but for now it's time we ate, eh? I'll wager the lad will likely rouse himself as soon as he smells food, mind. Will you be staying, Celestus?"*

Glancing down to see that the color was beginning to return to the boy's face, the Tavencroft Lord nodded.

"For a time, anyway."

Back in the keep, Celestus cocked his head to one side as Camden's voice now grew as loud as Danielle's.

*   *   *

As Pri Gorwynne had predicted, the boy had awakened, no worse for wear, as soon as he'd smelled food and after eating four bowls of stew, he'd gone back to sleep. He'd remembered very little of his experience in the Prophetic Realm, just a hazy sense of panic and loneliness. The others had been convinced to leave him there for the night under the watchful care of Kether and Pri Gorwynne. The Tavencroft Lord and his three veterans had taken the starlit path home together, speaking quietly of the evening's events.

The next month had passed quickly. True to her word, Dani and the others had kept Cam so busy he'd had hardly a minute to himself. At Brace Cottage they'd purposely stayed away from deep travel, concentrating instead on working together as a Circle. The boy never went into trance without at least one of the others right by his side. But it wouldn't last. Already Camden was chafing at the restrictions and, as a true child of the Wind, it wouldn't be long before he shook them off and returned to the open sky on his own. Celestus was actually a little surprised that he hadn't gone already.

As for the Branion Seer, Kether'd assured him he'd picked up no trace of him since that day. Perhaps his encounter with the Heathland Mirror had incapacitated him. Perhaps, but Celestus could not afford to take that chance.

Setting the white goose quill pen to one side, the Tavencroft Lord stared intently out the window at the cloudless sky.

They must proceed with the belief that their enemy was alive and planning a new form of assault. Although it was not in his nature to move quickly or dramatically, the threat this man posed called for drastic action, and so Celestus had wasted no time in sending for Marna Jonstun. The Tavencroft Steward had offered a simple solution.

"My cousin Iain'll kill him for twenty crowns."
"Send for him."

*   *   *

Ross Jonstun had been dispatched for Lochaber Castle in Dunduth immediately with orders to bring Iain to Kairnbrook with all possible speed. They were due any day now. In the meantime, Celestus, Pri Gorwynne, and Kether Breithe had come together to lay a trap for the Branion Seer. So far their enemy had not seen fit to approach, but they were patient. Eventually he would come, and then they'd have him.

Today, however, the Tavencroft Lord had a more pressing problem. His gaze dropped to the letter lying open on his desk. The letter from Alexander DeKathrine.

The Duke of Guilcove's oldest son had opened by thanking his uncle for hosting Camden over the summer. His absence, while painful to their mother, had allowed her to recover from their father's death more quietly than she might have done. He went on to mention the growing friction on the Continent between Triarctic Danelind and Essusiate Gallia over the religiously neutral Fenland Territories in between. Gallia's armies were on the move, and it was entirely likely there would be some form of armed conflict before harvest time. Prince Hilde had requested martial and financial aid from Branion and His Royal Highness Marsellus, Duke of Yorbourne, had been sent to the Danelind Court to begin negotiations. These were expected to last the winter and so His Highness had requested the company of his childhood friend, Alexander, and his wife. They were expected to leave within the week. Could Celestus send Camden to join them in Danelind as soon as he was able?

Rubbing the pen's feathers against his cheek, Celestus stared sightlessly out the window, his expression hard. He had no intention of allowing Alexander to spirit Camden off to the Continent at this stage in his training, but his response needed to be carefully worded either to convince him to change his mind or to suggest that Camden himself had refused to go. He frowned.

Originally he'd planned to write Domitia after the harvest and simply request that Camden stay the winter. He'd learned that her Cousin Leilani was hosting the twins, Tatania and Nicholas, at Rowan's Keep in Essendale and, knowing how she enjoyed celebrating the winter solstice with lots of children present, it was safe to assume they'd be remaining there until spring at the very least. With that in mind, Camden's continued presence at Tavencroft was almost a given. No subterfuge would have been necessary at all. He'd not counted on Alexander DeKathrine requiring his absent Squire in Danelind of all places.

He snorted. The Danelind capital was even farther north than Kether's family holding at the very tip of Heathland. It was cold seven months out of every twelve and the winter storms were legendary. Why the Grand Prince Hilde wasn't coming to Branbridge instead was a mystery.

With a grimace, Celestus threw his pen onto the desk. He had thought to take his four Chosen to the Continent as well this winter, but to Panisha or Espalonia, certainly not to Danelind.

His gaze softened. Southern Espalonia was beautiful in Mean Genver; sunny and warm, the rocky coast dotted with tiny inlets for Danielle and tall, cool trees to read under for him. They hadn't been back since before Dianne had died. He'd meant to return every winter since but somehow he'd never managed it. And now, with the advent of Alexander's letter, it looked as if they were going to spend another winter in Northern Branion. Danielle would be disappointed.

Thunder rumbled outside, and he looked up in surprise. The bright blue sky had darkened in the last hour although the sun still glinted off the keep's slate roofs. Just the sort of conditions for a sudden summer storm. He cocked one ear at the window. The yard had gone quiet. No doubt his four Chosen had gone off to find something to do indoors.

Eban entered softly to light the candles and Celestus' expression hardened again. He'd spent a lifetime finding the perfect four Vessels to prove his theories. He would not allow one of them to vanish again just because his brother believed he had a duty elsewhere. One way or another, the boy was staying here. Folding up Alexander's letter, he opened a small cherrywood box and tucked it inside under a pile of other correspondence, then picked up his pen again.

There was a knock at the door.

"Come."

Marna entered, a significant expression on her face.

"Iain's arrived."

"Where is he?"

"At my gran's cottage with Ross. Do you want me to bring him up?"

Celestus stood. "No. I'll go to him. The less who know about his presence the better."

She nodded brusquely. As they left the hall together, it began to rain.

Meanwhile, snug at the back of the stables, the four youths lounged about in the haymow, listening to the rain pelt against the thatch roof. Dani had wanted to view the storm from the top of their tower but had been overruled for once. Neither Quin nor Lisha had wanted to climb stairs, and Cam, with unusual surliness, had simply refused. Now he was lying a little apart from the others, staring moodily at nothing. Dani turned the full power of her dark gaze on his face.

"What is wrong with you?" she demanded. "You've been moping about like a fisher with no catch all week."

Stuffing the end of a piece of straw into his mouth, he just shrugged. "Nothing."

"Bugger nothing. Come on, Cam, we're a Circle, we're Chosen; we don't keep secrets from each other."

"Oh, no secrets, huh? So what have you and Lisha been doing lately?"

The two girls shared a grin.

"Nothing," Lisha echoed in wide-eyed innocence.

"Oh, sure, you can do nothing, but I can't?"

"It's a joke, Cam."

"And besides, it's not the same thing," Dani retorted.

"Why not?"

"Because our nothing is something good and your nothing is something bad."

"How do you figure?"

"Because otherwise you'd be happy instead of miserable."

She sat back against Lisha with a triumphant expression.

"So spill."

"I just have a lot to think about right now, that's all."

Quin rolled his eyes at him. "Bad idea, that," he said with mock concern. "Your brain might overheat."

"Shut up."

"Thinking about what?" Dani prompted.

"Nothing, all right, nothing. Just private thoughts. I am allowed one or two private thoughts, aren't I?"

"Is it about the Branion Seer?" Quin asked.

Cam started. "Why would it be?" he demanded angrily.

"You dreamed about him last night."

The girls glanced over curiously and Quin shrugged. "He was talking in his sleep."

"Why don't you all just mind your own business," Cam snapped, and Dani squinted at him with real concern.

"Is your seed getting potent like Marna said it would?"

"No!"

"Well, it better not be," Quin answered hotly. "I'm almost a full year older than him. I get to go first."

"Hardly, I'm twice your size," Cam scoffed.

"Yeah, and you're a hundred times a baby's size, too, but you're still acting like one."

"Sod off!"

"You sod off!"

Both boys stood, fists raised. Dani began to laugh, but Lisha immediately put herself between them.

"Enough fighting!" she insisted, her voice pained. "I don't like it when we fight."

The boys subsided, muttering. Dani looked disappointed.

"Cam doesn't have to say what he's thinking about if he doesn't want to," Lisha continued. "We'd like him to, but he doesn't have to."

They all glanced over at him and after a minute he looked back.

"What? Lisha said I didn't have to."

With an exasperated snort, Dani threw a handful of hay at the other girl. "Fine, whatever. Look, if we're not going to fight, let's change the subject. Da told me he was thinking about taking us to the Continent this winter."

Quin and Lisha both sat up straight.

"Really?"

"Where?"

"Panisha or maybe even Espalonia."

"But those are Essusiate countries," Quin pointed out. "Is it safe?"

"Espalonia's only marginally Essusiate."

"My father believes there may be war on the Continent," Lisha added. "Maybe even next year."

"So let it happen next year."

"But . . ."

"Look, Da says that if there's war it'll likely be between Danelind and Gallia. Espalonia's miles away. It won't affect us, especially not this winter."

Throwing herself back into the hay, she tucked her hands behind her head. "I hope we do go to Espalonia. Da says you can swim all along the southern coastline all year long."

Lisha nodded. "So that's it."

Dani scowled at her. "It's not just the swimming. It's *warm* there. You'd like to be warm this winter, wouldn't you, Cam?"

Dani turned to him for support, but he just shrugged.

"It doesn't matter. I'll be going home soon, anyway."

Lisha blinked. "What?"

"Why?" Quin asked.

"Because it's almost harvest."

"And?" Dani asked.

"And I was only here for the summer, remember?"

When the others just stared at his blankly, he shook his head. "So when the summer is over, I have to go home," he explained slowly as if he were speaking to three very young children. "That's what *for the summer* means."

Dani gave a dismissive snort. "Don't be stupid, Cam," she scoffed.

His face reddened. "Quit calling me stupid," he warned. "I'm getting sick of it."

"Then quit acting like it. You can't leave. You live here."

"I don't live here. Your father only invited me to stay for the summer. What part of that *not including the autumn* do you *not* understand?"

Her eyes narrowed. "The part where you figure that's what he meant."

"It's what he said."

Lisha looked up, an aggrieved expression on her face. "Do you want to leave us, Cam?" she asked.

"Of course I don't, but . . ."

"But what?"

"But . . ." he clamped his teeth shut, unable to express his feelings in the face of the hurt in her eyes.

"What about the Circle?" Dani demanded.

"What about it?" He jerked to his feet, causing clouds of hay dust to swirl about his legs. "Look, this wasn't my idea, all right? None of it was. We all knew it wasn't going to last. Just because you lot might have forgotten that, doesn't mean I have. *I don't live here!* It's over, all right." He chopped his hand down. "Over."

Leaping the low iron railing between the mow and the stalls, he stomped from the stables.

The others sat in shocked silence, then Lisha shook her

head. "So that's what's been bothering him," she noted sadly. "Poor Cam."

"Poor nothing, he's a moron," Dani scoffed. "Wait here."

She caught up to him halfway to the main gate.

"Cam, wait."

"What for?"

"So I don't have to throw a brick at the back of your head. That's what for."

He turned, his expression both defensive and downcast, and Dani sighed.

"Look, doorknob, you *do* live here. Don't argue with me," she snapped as he made to protest. "Da brought you here because you're one of us, all right. How many times do we have to tell you that? *One of us.* And you're the only one who thought it was just for the summer. We all knew it was for longer."

"But your father said . . ."

"Oh, do you honestly think Da would send you home with all the work we still have to do? You're the Wind's Chosen, for crap's sake! Who are we going to get to take your place?"

He shrugged with forced indifference. "Maybe I don't care. Besides, Quin says anyone can commune with the Aspects, remember," he answered with heavy sarcasm.

Dani glared at him. "If you don't quit with this *I'm not important* attitude, I swear I'll slug you," she warned. "We need you. I'm not going to say it again."

"But I have to leave sometime."

"Why?"

"Because *I don't live here!*" he shouted at her.

"Yes, you do, boyo."

The quiet voice behind them made them turn to see Pri Gorwynne leaning against the inner wall. "What's more important, mind," she continued when she saw she had his attention, "is that you belong here, like Danielle said, eh."

"You don't understand."

"What don't I understand?"

Quin and Lisha had come up behind her and now the four of them faced him. Cam just shook his head.

"Look, Cam, whatever's bothering you, we can fix it," Dani said earnestly. "We're family. We're a Circle. I don't know why you don't see that, but we are. Think of what we've accomplished together so far, and what we still have to do. We're on the brink of something really huge here. If the four of us can harness the full manifested power of the Aspects in concert, just think what that could mean. Really think of it."

She pointed at Lisha, "No more madness in the Royal Line." Then at Quin. "No more potential wasted because the Flame Priests don't want to share their power. You can't let this go, Cam. This is the greatest experiment in the history of Branion, and you're an integral part of it. If you don't believe me, ask Da."

"But . . ."

"But nothing. Ask him or shut up." Dani crossed her arms. "One or the other."

Cam glanced at each of them, then finally nodded. "All right, fine, I'll go ask him," he agreed through clenched teeth.

"And then cheer up, will you, you've been acting like a caged dragon all week."

"I said all right, already!" As Cam turned for the main keep, Lisha stepped forward.

"Wait, Cam."

He sighed. "What now?"

"Do you want us to come with you? I mean, if it's really hard for you to talk about how you feel and all . . ."

His expression softened reluctantly.

"No, I can do it." He tried for a reassuring smile. "Look, why don't you go up to the tower battlements and watch the storm before it stops raining. I'll meet you there afterward and tell you what Uncle Celestus says. All right?"

"Done," Dani answered immediately. When the others

hesitated, she caught both of them by the arm. "Come on. This is between Cam and Da."

As she dragged them off, Cam turned to Pri Gorwynne. She nodded.

"Go on, little brother. You've some conflict in your mind, more than just not belonging here, and you won't be easy till it's solved."

His eyes widened fearfully, and she shook her head. "No, I don't know what it is, but it's as clear as a gryphon's cry at night that it's tearing you up inside."

"It's nothing."

"Your tongue's a good liar, boy, but your face is too honest." When he would have answered, she just nodded toward the keep. "You go talk to your uncle, really talk to him, mind, not this make us go fishing for it nonsense. Whatever it is, he can help you."

Cam looked at her with an aggrieved expression. "I don't think he can, Pri. I don't think anyone can."

She chuckled sympathetically. "The young always believe that," she said kindly. "The problem's too big, too terrible, and always too unique, for anyone to possibly sort it out, eh, least of all an old man with years of experience?"

He gave her a sour look. "Maybe."

"Hog swallow."

"But what if . . . ?"

"What if what?"

"What if it is too big and too terrible, and whatever else you said. What if he gets mad and . . . ?" He struggled to find the words for a moment, then just shrugged.

"He's your uncle. He loves you, yes?"

"I guess."

"Then whatever it is, it's not so terrible that he won't help you, even if he does get mad, mind. So remember that and go."

With an unconvinced nod, Cam made for the keep.

* * *

As it turned out, he hadn't needed to screw up his courage at all. At the door to the great hall, Eban informed him that his uncle was not in the castle. Marna had come with a message and the two of them had left immediately.

Cam glanced out at the rainy sky and the servant shrugged.

"It seemed important. He didn't stop to say when he'd be back. If you like, I can come find you when he returns."

"No, thanks. I'll, uh, see him at supper."

"As you like."

Eban took his leave and Cam wandered out to the long inner gallery that ran along the south range. He didn't feel like heading back up to the tower just yet. The others wouldn't be able to spot him here from the battlements, and he badly needed some time to himself.

He grimaced as Dani's voice floated down to him from high above. They all thought he was being stupid. That whatever was wrong could be magically fixed by just talking about it.

"We're family."

"Yeah," he muttered. "That's part of the problem."

Leaning against the stone railing, he stared out at the strip of sky just visible above the gatehouse. Coming to Tavencroft had been like coming home. Dani and the others were more like siblings than his seven actual brothers and sisters had ever been, his uncle more like a father.

Scratching absently at a scab on his thumb he considered that. Vakarus DeKathrine'd had many serious responsibilities as a Sword Knight and a Peer of the Realm. He'd spent months away fighting on the Continent beside the Aristok, and when he was home, he was most often at Court with their mother. Cam hadn't seen much of him while he was growing up. But sometimes when he'd been little, he'd played under his father's chair and Vakarus had reached down and absently ruffled his hair or nudged him with his toe. Once they'd gone hunting rabbits together, just the two of them. Cam couldn't even remember why the others hadn't been there.

Two memories to last a lifetime. He frowned.

Sometimes he had caught himself remembering suddenly that it had only been one week, two weeks, three months, since his father's death. Realizing that he hardly missed him more now than he had then made him feel guilty and a little bit sad. Then a little bit angry. At these times he would go off by himself to try and sort out these conflicting feelings, but he never got very far. Dani invariably managed to ferret him out, demanding his participation in some adventure or another. More of a loner by nature than most of his gregarious family, it was starting to annoy him. So, as he had at Guilcove, he'd begun to draw into himself, keeping his thoughts from them as he had from his family back home.

Pushing himself up onto the railing, he leaned his back against a pillar with a snarl.

In the last month none of them had let him out of their sight, physically or metaphysically, and he knew why. They were afraid this Branion Seer would locate them and send the Flame Priests to arrest them all. Dani had been very blunt about it when he'd returned to the keep from Pri Gorwynne's. Leaning his head back he closed his eyes, remembering.

Two days after his return, the afternoon had turned rainy and dark. He and Dani were playing strategy while Quin read aloud from a book on Heathland battle tactics when Lisha burst into the presence chamber. Before she could catch her breath, Quin looked up with a frown.

"Weren't you s'posed to bring back sticky buns?" he demanded.

"Bugger that. Dani, the adults are having a meeting."

All three of the others turned to stare at her.

"Which adults?"

"Uncle Celestus, Kether, and Pri Gorwynne."

"What about?"

"Cam."

His eyes went wide with alarm. "Why me?"

"I don't know."

"Probably worried about this Branion Seer," Dani answered with a frown. "Where's the meeting being held?"

"In Uncle's outer chamber."

Setting the book down with an annoyed expression, Quin stood.

"We're going, then?"

Dani was already pulling off her boots, her own expression wrathful. "Of course, we're going. No one's holding secret meetings about *my* Circle without us being there."

"*Our* Circle," Lisha corrected severely.

"Whatever. Get barefoot, Cam."

"Wh . . . ?"

"Just do it."

The others had already shed their footwear and were now waiting impatiently for Cam to do the same. As he dumped his boots under the table, Quin shook his head in amazement.

"Cripes, your feet get bigger every day. No wonder there's never any room in the bed."

"You can always sleep on the floor," Cam snapped back.

"Shut up, both of you," Dani growled. "This is serious. Lisha, do you know if they've started yet?"

The DeMarian girl shook her head. "They're waiting for Eban to bring wine."

"Then we'd better get moving if we're going to hear it all." She made for the door.

"Get moving where?" Cam asked. "We can't just walk in." He looked around. "Can we?"

"Not exactly," Quin replied. "But we can *listen* in."

"What, like at the keyhole?"

"Secret chimney," Dani answered bluntly.

"Really?"

"Yeah. It was blocked up years ago, but it goes right down to Uncle's outer chamber," Quin explained as he followed Dani through the door. "We found it Lisha's first year here."

She snorted. "We found it because *he* nearly fell down it."

Already at the stairs, Dani turned to glare at them. "Hurry up."

The four of them headed quickly down the stairs to the fourth floor. Dani cracked open the door leading to the south range, then, keeping low, ran swiftly and silently along the empty gallery which overlooked the inner courtyard. The others followed. Fetching up before the door to the west range moments later, Dani put one finger to her lips.

"From here on no talking, understood?" She was looking at Cam, and he nodded mutely. They slipped inside.

The first room beyond the door turned out to be an empty outer chamber. The fireplace in the far wall had been bricked up, but much of the mortar was missing. Working swiftly, Dani pulled a dozen bricks from the opening, handing them to Quin and Lisha, until the hole was large enough to squeeze through. Then, without a second glance, she disappeared from view. Quin followed, then Lisha. Entering the hearth more cautiously, Cam peered through the hole into the darkness. He could just make out the faint sounds of climbing below.

Groping about on the cold stone wall, his fingers found several rough cuts in the stone. Hand and toeholds. Wondering—not for the first time—why he was blindly following a girl who thought drowning in the ocean was the best way to die, he squeezed through the opening and, reaching for the first toehold, began his descent.

In less time than he thought it would take, a hand caught him by the calf and guided him the rest of the way down. When his feet touched the dusty ground, he felt about, brushing against the other three almost immediately. The space was suffocatingly small, hot, musty, and pitch-black. Just before the rising claustrophobia sent him back up the wall, someone, probably Dani, took his head and turned it toward the faintest chink of light. Hands gripping the crumbling stone, he pressed himself against the wall, and closing one eye, put the other to the light.

He could just make out the furnishings of his uncle's outer chamber, the working hearth on the opposite wall, Kether's back and his uncle's arm.

"My garden won't stand the leaving of it right now. You'll have to come to me."

He jerked back in surprise. He hadn't realized Pri Gorwynne was standing right beside their hiding place until she spoke. Around him, he sensed rather than heard the others freeze. His heart pounding over loud in his chest, he pressed his eye to the tiny crack once again.

"Of course, Pri," he heard his uncle agree. "We can come to Brace Cottage each evening if you prefer. How is an hour before dusk, Kether?"

Cam saw the Mirror stir. "I've felt him in each daylight hour so it should do well enough. Eventually he'll come poking about. You lie in wait just beyond the veil to the Prophetic Realm, I open up a hole just large enough for you to catch his identity and . . ." he closed his fist.

"Will he sense our presence?"

"Not before it's too late.

"Will he sense the hole?"

"Oh, yes. He's been scratching about like a mouse behind the larder ever since Camden's first flight."

Pri Gorwynne chuckled. "So, like cats before a mousehole, we'll wait for him to peek his wee nose outside for a bite of cheese and then we'll have him, eh?"

"Essentially," Celestus answered.

"Can you kill him?" the Mirror asked.

"No, more's the pity," the ex-Priest replied. "Only the Aristok wields that kind of power, as a True Avatar, like. But we can wring him dry—and we can hurt him. Oh, aye, we're strong enough for that, we are. We can find out who he is and where he is and send this fellow, Sean?"

"Iain," Celestus supplied.

"This fellow Iain after him. And *he* can kill him the old-fashioned way."

"Will you be needing my protection over Iain as well, then?"

"Yes," Celestus answered. "Will that pose a problem?"

"No."

"Good. In the meantime, I'm concerned about Camden. This man has made contact with him twice now. Do you think he might have forged some link with the boy that's allowed him closer access to our workings?"

Cam tensed, then relaxed as Kether's back moved in a shrug.

"I haven't sensed one, but there could be. But that's for you active Seers to discover. I just deflect."

"If there is a link," Pri Gorwynne noted, "we may need Camden to draw him in. Did you want to bring the children in on this, Celestus?"

There was a mild scuffle in the hiding place behind him at the word "children," but it was swiftly stilled.

"Not in an active capacity just yet," Celestus answered. "If we don't turn up anything within the week, perhaps then. We do need to discuss this with them, however. I want the trap in place during their regular workings, so they need to be aware of it and the possible results of a capture. I want them well clear of any battle that might occur."

He took a seat. "In the meantime, since we're gathered now, I'd like to set the first trap immediately. Pri?"

She moved across the room to join him.

A hand gripped his shoulder so suddenly that Cam nearly jumped out of his skin. Dani. Listening, he could hear the faint sound of frantic climbing behind them so that when she moved her finger up the side of his cheek three times, he understood the message. And the urgency. If Uncle Celestus and Pri Gorwynne were going into trance, they'd sense them hiding nearby. They had to get back to the tower and quickly. With more relief than he cared to admit, he made his way up behind her.

* * *

Once back, Dani threw herself into the furs with a satisfied expression. "Well, that's it, then. Threat," she raised one fist, "canceled." She slammed it into the palm of the other hand. "We win, the Flame Temple loses. Ha!"

Seating herself at the table, Lisha frowned at the other girl, but said nothing. Quin laughed. Cam, having gone to the south window to stare pensively out at the Bricklin Forest, now turned.

"Who's Iain?"

"Marna's cousin. Ross' oldest brother."

"He's had *special* training," Quin added in a purposely dark tone. Dani shot him an angry look, and he raised both hands in a gesture of innocence. "What?"

"What kind of training?" Cam prodded.

"That's actually a secret," Dani answered evasively.

"So?"

"A *nationally* important secret."

"And building a Circle of Aspects' Chosen isn't?"

"Sure it is, but that's *our* secret. This is someone else's secret."

"Like Kether's abilities?"

"Sort of."

Cam's eyes narrowed. "Sort of." He nodded, suddenly understanding. "You don't want to tell me."

"It's not that."

"What is it, then?"

"It's not our secret to tell. Quin shouldn't have opened his big mouth."

"But he's part of the Circle," Quin protested. We don't keep secrets from the Circle. Do we?"

They were all looking at Dani.

"Do we," Lisha repeated.

With a grimace, Dani sat up. "No. We don't." She turned to Cam, her expression serious. "Iain is a professionally trained assassin," she explained. "He's part of an elite Guild called The Cousins, a *very secret* Guild. Da learned about them from Vincent and Marna. *We* learned about them from eavesdropping in the chimney. Da doesn't know we know. So now he doesn't know that you know, so you have to swear never to tell him, 'cause he'll want to know how we know. And we really don't want him knowing that."

Quin blinked. "It's a wonder your mouth doesn't seize up sometimes," he noted.

"Shut up. You've gotta swear, Cam. Telling *anyone* could get a lot of people in a lot of trouble. And not just us."

"Although mostly us," Quin added.

"Quin."

Lisha's softly spoken word quelled the boy's teasing smile and, schooling his expression to something more serious, he turned to Cam.

Under the weight of three pairs of eyes, Cam nodded.

"All right, sure, I swear I won't tell anyone. But if these professional . . . Cousins are so secret how does anyone know enough about them to hire them?"

Dani shrugged. "Who knows, who cares. All you need to know is that they don't like people talking about them." She pointed a finger at him. "For a price—for a very high price—they'll kill *anyone*. But those who talk about them to the wrong people, them they kill for free. And they *never* fail."

Refusing to react to her melodramatically delivered threat, Cam frowned thoughtfully.

"And Uncle Celestus is going to send him after the Branion Seer?"

"Looks like."

"But we're not even sure he's a real threat yet."

The others all stared at him.

"He's a *Branion Seer,* fool," Quin spat.

"Technically, so are we."

"No, technically we're *heretics,*" Lisha corrected somberly.

"And heresy is punishable by imprisonment, banishment, even death in some cases," Dani added.

"So why are we doing it?"

"Because we're right, they're wrong, and as soon as we're powerful enough to protect ourselves from them we can prove that we're right and they're wrong. Why else?"

Cam didn't push the point. The truth was he seldom thought about it, anyway. He loved the Wind. He was happiest in Its embrace. That was all. He didn't care about theories, madness, wasted potential, or being right. He left all that to the others: the thinking to Quin, the feeling to Lisha, and the reacting to Dani. It was easiest.

"And the Branion Seer is a *gigantic* danger," Quin continued. "Especially if he's managed to forge a link with *you.*"

His tone was vaguely accusing. Cam glared at him but said nothing as Dani snorted.

"Don't worry about that. We can break any link he might have made," she declared. "We're a Circle, and he's not part of it. You just tell me if you sense anything, Cam, and we'll come down on him like a thunderstorm."

"The point is," Quin carried on loudly, "that if this Seer finds out what we're doing and tells the Flame Temple they'll kill us all, except probably Lisha," he amended. "But definitely the rest of us. The DeKathrine name won't protect us. In fact our own relatives will probably tie the noose. You know that."

Thinking of his mother's unswerving devotion to the Flame Temple, Cam nodded reluctantly.

"So we have to kill him first," Dani finished. "It's the only way." She threw herself back into the furs. "Anyway, don't worry about it. He's as good as dead. I told you, The Cousins never fail."

Cam had dropped the subject. There was no point arguing with them, even if he had been able to put the vague sense of wrong Dani's words evoked into words. Besides, essentially they were right. If the Seer found out about them, they'd be in danger. The sense of wrong persisted, however, crowding out the more logical argument. It wasn't that simple. He just didn't know why.

He sighed. He probably wasn't smart enough to figure it out on his own, but there was no one else he could really ask. Both his uncle and Kether had questioned him about the Branion Seer the morning after he'd made contact. At first, he hadn't remembered much, and by the time he realized what he'd felt, he knew they wouldn't understand any more than Dani and the others would. Now, although lying to his uncle—lying to everyone, his mind amended—made his stomach twist, he'd remained silent for a different reason.

He'd had regular lessons with the Heathland Mirror since that day, learning to discipline his thoughts and his link with the Wind. Kether was convinced he would know if the Branion Seer made another attempt at contact before it was made, but Kether was wrong.

The night after their adventure in the chimney, with his mind drifting along on the midnight breezes as always, Cam had sensed the Branion Seer far below him. Wherever Cam went, the man followed, like the shadow of a bird on the ground below. Somehow their first touch had forged a bridge between their minds as his uncle had suspected. Cam didn't know how to destroy that bridge without Kether's help, and remembering the psychic blow he'd taken when the Mirror had knocked them apart the first time didn't make him too eager to give the man another shot. Instead, confident in his own abilities, Cam had allowed the Branion Seer to sense his presence. The response had been immediate. Again manifesting as a wildly gyrating moth, the Seer had rocketed toward him.

Cam had shot away, leading the other through the clouds for hours until, spent, the Seer had finally grown still. Then Cam had approached him as one would approach a wild animal, never getting too close, nor allowing the other to do so either. He'd hovered nearby, projecting a sense of peace and safety. As the nights passed, the moth's form had slowly faded to become a brown-haired man with dark, haunted eyes.

Cam knew then that he was no true threat to them. He was too . . . He struggled to find the right word amongst the host of chaotic thoughts and emotions that had swept over him in that first contact . . . damaged. The Seer's desperate need for stability, for peace, had drawn him to their Circle and once he'd Seen how close he was to madness, Cam could not turn him away. Instead, night after night, they'd flown silently together, never actually touching, until morning had separated them once again.

Cam hadn't tried to discover the man's name. He didn't want to know it, or anything else about him for that matter. Just being with him made Cam feel like a traitor. The others would never understand why he'd initiated contact with their enemy without telling them and, in truth, he wasn't entirely certain he understood either.

"They'd think you betrayed them," his mind supplied. *"They'd be right."*

It began to rain harder. Cam watched the droplets speckle the already full puddles in the main courtyard with an unhappy expression.

Throughout the past month, he'd remained close to the others during their regular workings, struggling to stay within a Circle of four instead of flying off alone. He could Feel the Branion Seer hovering far below them but, almost as if the man could sense the danger the others represented, he never approached Cam at these times. Cam was relieved. There was no way he could warn him about the trap his uncle and Pri Gorwynne had set without being discovered himself. All he could do was hope that their nightly flights were enough contact to keep the Seer away during the day, and especially during the evening.

At night, although he could sense Kether's net all around them, he'd resisted the urge to look for the trap himself. As long as he and the Seer maintained a certain distance apart from each other, the net was far away, but as soon as they drew too near, it rose up, ready to ensnare them. Cam did his best to keep them away from it altogether, but it was getting harder all the time.

A week after setting the first trap, his uncle and Pri Gorwynne had enlisted the Circle's help in drawing out the Branion Seer. Now when he flew, he not only had to avoid the Seer and the net, he had to pretend to *not* avoid them. That, combined with the strain of staying within the Circle and ignoring the growing need to just throw it all aside and fly away from the entire problem, was making him crazy. Something had to give.

Closing his eyes, he pressed his fingers against his temples. He didn't know how to sort out everything he was feeling and doing, all mixed up with everything he *should* be feeling and doing and wasn't. The Circle didn't keep secrets from each other, but by now he had so many secrets he didn't remember half of them. It was making his head ache all the time. It was keeping him awake, and when he did sleep, it was messing with his dreams. Fortunately, Quin slept as soundly as the earth he was so close to, because the bed had been a real mess this morning.

"You keep on like this you'll be no use to them anyway," his mind observed. *"Maybe you really should leave."*

"Shut up."

This morning it had all been too much. He'd had a terrible night. His dreams had been either frightening or flat out embarrassing, and his abilities uncertain. Suddenly he couldn't fly properly, and that had scared him more than anything else could. One moment he was soaring through the clouds under perfect control, the next he was shooting off in random directions, his power spiking chaotically, then dropping without warning.

The Seer had just made it worse. Relying on Cam for

stability, he was unable to adjust to the sudden change. He'd returned to the moth form, spinning and diving dangerously close every time Cam managed to get himself under control. The net kept flying in between them and finally Cam had forced himself to wake up.

Standing in the dark tower room, listening to the others' regular breathing, he'd decided the only way out was to go home. The strain of keeping secrets from them was too much. It had affected his flying and if he couldn't fly, he might as well be dead.

He'd gone to the battlements to stare morosely up at the night sky until the others had found him just after dawn and dragged him off to some useless pastime. He hadn't had time to tell them about his decision until they made for the stables and then it hadn't gone at all well. Now, with his resolve slipping away, he brought himself under control.

"You have *to leave,"* he told himself for the hundredth time since waking up. *"It's the only way. Beside, it* was *just for the summer. Uncle Celestus* did *say that. And even if he didn't, you can't keep lying to everyone. They'll find out and . . ."*

"And then they'll make you leave?" his mind supplied. *"Better to go on your own than be kicked out? Or worse?"*

"That's right."

A noise beside him made him open his eyes to see Pri Gorwynne's cat staring up at him with wide, unblinking eyes. Cam bared his teeth at it.

"What?"

The cat continued to stare.

"Oh, sure, it's easy for you, you were born here. The only responsibility you have is catching mice."

The cat turned and began washing its shoulder and Cam smiled despite himself. Somehow talking to something that couldn't make sarcastic remarks back made him feel a little better. Of course, if that wasn't a sarcastic remark, he wasn't sure what was. Picking up a straw, he scratched behind the cat's ears.

"What would you do, huh?" he asked absently. "Would you run home? After all, you'd have responsibilities at home, too, if you were me. Alec would need you, wouldn't he?"

"As if," his mind suddenly sneered.

"Shut up," he told himself harshly. *"He would so."*

"Then how come he hasn't written? Not once in three months. Why is that?"

"Because he knew I'd be back by the harvest and . . . and he didn't want to make me feel bad by . . . saying he missed me."

Even he wasn't convinced by that argument, and his mind pounced on it like a ferret on a kill.

"Just because you want him to need you doesn't mean he does, you know. He probably hasn't even noticed you're gone."

"Shut up! Shut up! Shut up!"

A sudden wind flung his hair into his face with enough force to knock his head backward. The cat hissed angrily and Cam forced himself to calm down.

"It doesn't matter about Alec anyway," he said out loud, stroking the cat's ruffled tail. "He isn't the problem."

The problem was his contact with the Branion Seer. Actually the problem was that he hadn't told the *others* about his contact with the Branion Seer. He frowned. He supposed he really had two problems.

His hand stopped moving, and the cat turned to stare at him again, but Cam's mind was elsewhere. When he thought about it, he supposed he really had a whole lot of problems; those two were just the biggest ones.

His eyes narrowed. Other than the whole heresy thing. But that wasn't actually his problem, it was his uncle's.

Unless they got caught. Which might easily happen if the Branion Seer told anyone about them. Unless *he* got caught by his uncle and then killed by Iain Jonstun. But Cam didn't want that to happen either. Although right at the moment he was so muddled he couldn't remember why.

"Because I like him, that's why. He's quiet and he doesn't call me stupid."

With a sigh, he began to stroke the cat's tail again. He really hated thinking about things. It usually only made him more confused.

"It all comes down," he said to the cat, "to the Flame Temple. If the others weren't so afraid of being found out, it wouldn't matter who I'd made contact with."

The cat said nothing as Cam considered it. He wasn't stupid, whatever Dani might think. He understood that what they were doing was heresy. It even had a name. The Triarchy Heresy. His uncle had at least two books on it in his library. Cam had read them. But he still didn't see what the big fuss was about. If everyone could do this, why shouldn't they? It wouldn't affect the Aristok's power. And wouldn't it make the whole Realm stronger like Quin had said it would?

His head began to pound.

"Don't think about it," he counseled himself as the cat came over to knead on his legs. "You can't do anything about what people think, so just forget about it. The Flame Temple isn't here, and if they find out about us, then that's Uncle's problem and not yours."

The cat stared up at him again.

"Right." His problem was the Seer. It was only a matter of time before he found the hole and, knowing him as he'd come to, Cam was pretty sure he wouldn't be able to keep him away from it once he did. He'd get caught. When that happened, Cam was going to have to decide whose side he was on and whether he was going to stand back and let the Seer be attacked or step in and try to protect him. Either way he'd be found out.

* * *

"Maybe you should just tell them now and get it over with."

"Yeah, bright idea. Did you forget about the having to leave part?"

"I thought you wanted to leave?"

"No."

The thought of leaving made his stomach hurt. Even with the strain of all these secrets, he was happy here, he was accepted. The thought of returning home to the dark, damp walls of Guilcove, of hiding everything he'd learned, of never knowing the freedom and the power he'd felt within Dani's Circle again made him feel sick. He couldn't go back to hiding his love of the Wind. He just couldn't.

"It's hide that or hide this."

"Then it's hide this."

"Glad we finally got that settled."

"Me, too."

The cat leaped off his legs. Seating itself on the railing, it wrapped its tail about its toes. Cam looked back up at the sky again. The rain had stopped during his argument with himself and he could just make out the end of a faint rainbow in the distance. The others would have a better view of it from atop Dani's tower and he almost decided to forget the whole thing and just join them, but as he made to rise, he saw his uncle and Marna Jonstun coming through the main gate.

His mouth went dry.

Catching sight of him, the two adults came forward.

"Alone this afternoon, Camden?" Celestus asked. "Where are the others?"

"Up on the tower roof, watching the rain. I, um, actually, wanted to talk to you about well . . . things, if you have time, Uncle."

Picking up the cat, Celestus took a seat on the railing. "I always have time for one of my children," he replied easily. He turned to the Steward. "We'll finish later, Marna."

She gave a short bow and headed for the main hall.

"Now, what did you want to speak with me about, Nephew?"

Cam stared out at the overcast sky. "It's, um, it's almost harvest time," he said without looking at his uncle.

"Yes, it is." Celestus studied the boy's face carefully. "Have you enjoyed your summer with us?"

Conscious of his heart pounding too loudly in his chest, Cam nodded mutely.

"So have I. You've been a fine addition to Tavencroft." Pausing a moment, Celestus suddenly chuckled. "You know, Danielle came to see me last night," he said in a conversational tone. "Did she tell you?"

Cam frowned. "No."

"She wanted me to write to your mother and tell her that you'd decided to extend your visit here throughout the autumn and possibly throughout the winter. When I pressed her as to whether this had been your decision or hers, she admitted that it was hers."

Cam gave a sour smile. He could see Dani doing exactly that.

"Has she discussed it with you at all, Camden?"

Cam's smile faded. "No, Uncle. Well, not exactly."

"I imagine it came to her suddenly. Danielle doesn't believe in letting sleeping dragons lie if she's walking past their caves with a pointy stick in her hand."

Despite himself, Cam chuckled. "No, she doesn't."

"I told her it wasn't as simple as my telling the Duke of Guilcove that her son wanted to remain in Kairnbrook, especially since I don't know if that is what he wants." He glanced down. "Is that what you want, Nephew?"

Cam stared out at the sky, feeling his stomach do a flip.

* * *

"It's now or never."
"Shut up."

He met his uncle's dark gaze as fearlessly as possible. "I don't want to leave," he said honestly. "But . . ."

"But . . ."

"But what would happen if I had to leave or if I got taken away? Would I be outside Kether's protection? Would the Flame Priests be able to get into my head and find out about us? About the Circle, I mean?"

Celestus gave him a curious look. "Is that what's been bothering you?"

The lie came more easily than he thought it would.

"Yes."

Almost.

"One of the things, anyway."

Celestus smiled. "Well, I wouldn't lose any sleep over this particular issue. Kether is a very powerful Mirror. He can protect you for as long as you need or desire protection, no matter where you may be: Kairnbrook, Branbridge, even Panisha or Danelind. And Pri Gorwynne will soon be teaching you how to conceal your thoughts and feelings from other Seers." He frowned. "This hasn't influenced your decision to stay, has it, the fear of discovery?"

"No. I was just thinking. I really don't want to go. This is the first place I've ever been able to just be who I am. In front of people, I mean. But . . ." he paused.

"But?"

Cam chewed at his lower lip, struggling to decide how much to disclose. "But everything's gotten so complicated," he explained. "I used to just fly and now I have to pay so much attention to everything else it's . . . I can't . . ." He shook his head, once again tangled up in a host of feelings he couldn't put into words. "Everyone's always so afraid of being found out," he began again. "They're afraid of the Seer, or they're afraid of the Flame

Temple. It's . . . it's not any fun anymore," he burst out finally.

"I see."

Cam looked up, his expression troubled. "I don't want anyone to think I don't want to stay with the Circle," he amended quickly. "I do. I just wish it wasn't so serious all the time."

Celestus cocked his head to one side. "Have you spoken with the others about this?"

Cam deflated. "No."

"Why not?"

"I dunno. They'd probably just say I was being stupid, or I haven't thought it through, or something like that."

"Have you thought it through?"

Cam's expression darkened. "I haven't done anything else *but* think it through. And all I can figure is what's the point of doing it if it isn't fun." He stared sullenly at his hands. "I know everyone else has these big important reasons, but I don't. Not really. I just want to fly. That's all. And now I can't even do that right."

"How do you mean?"

"I mean I can't do it." His voice rose. "I can't fly, not like I used to, it's all messed up. I can't concentrate, I can't make the power do what I want, I can't do anything. I had more control when I was little!" He stumbled to an angry halt, his breathing short and rapid.

Celestus turned his intense gaze on Cam's face. "How long have you been having this trouble, Camden?" he asked seriously.

"I dunno. A while."

"During the workings?"

"No, mostly just at night." He glanced away. "Mostly just last night," he admitted.

"You had difficulty controlling your abilities?"

Cam nodded.

"Power surges and sudden ebbs?"

"Yes."

Celestus did his best to hide a small smile that began to play across his lips.

"I think, Nephew, that your seed may have become potent."

Cam started. "That's what Dani . . . Really? I . . . Really?"

"It's possible. Have you been having dreams of a sexual nature lately?"

"Uh . . ."

His dreams had been either frightening or flat out embarrassing.

"Dreams that may have led to any nightly emissions?"

The bed was a real mess this morning.

Cam went red up to his ears, and his uncle smiled broadly. "I believe we may have another member of the Circle come to adulthood," he declared.

The blush faded as quickly as it had appeared. "Do you really think so?"

"Well, there's only one way to be sure. We'll have to do a working."

Cam began to grin. "Quin will throw a fit," he gloated.

Celestus smiled. "No doubt." He set the cat aside. "In the meantime, we must write to your mother and ask— and I do mean ask—that you be allowed to extend your visit here with us."

Cam looked up anxiously. "Do you think she'll say yes."

Celestus frowned. "Well, you have been gone for some months," he replied carefully. "I'm sure she was looking forward to your return, but, yes, I think she might if you and I wrote to her together."

"And Alec?"

"Ah, yes." Celestus pursed his lips. "I meant to tell you but I haven't had the chance. Your Cousin Leilani wrote to me last week telling me that Alexander and Anastasia had accompanied Prince Marsellus to the Danelind Court. They aren't due back until late spring."

Cam felt himself grow cold. "He went to Danelind," he repeated weakly.

"Yes."

Glancing away, the boy found his eyes growing wet. With an angry gesture, he swiped at the tears with his sleeve. Celestus gave him an understanding look.

"You're hurt that he didn't take you with him, that he didn't write?"

Cam shrugged, refusing to meet his uncle's eyes. "I didn't write to him either," he said with studied indifference.

"No, you didn't, but that was my fault, I'm afraid. I should have insisted that you write to your family at least once this summer, but . . . well, the time went by so very quickly. However, I can't believe that's why Alexander went without you. Perhaps there wasn't time to send for you."

"Maybe. Who cares."

"Do you want to write and ask him?"

"No."

"Did you want to join him there regardless? I could put you on a boat to Danelind within the week. If that's what you want."

Cam's eyes narrowed. "No, thank you, Uncle," he said with deliberate politeness. "If Alec had wanted me, he'd have sent for me. I think, if it's all the same to you, I'd rather stay here, where I *am* wanted."

Celestus nodded. "We should be happy to have you for as long as you want to stay, Nephew. We'll write your mother this very evening." He stood. "In the meantime, however, it's almost dinnertime. I believe Jordan's cooking up some fine eels that Drew and Eban caught last night. Why don't we find the others and go in to dinner. Unless there's anything else we need to discuss, that is?"

He looked at Cam who shrugged.

"There is just one more thing," he admitted reluctantly. "I, um, I need new boots. These don't really fit me so well anymore."

Celestus laughed. "Well, that problem's easily solved at least. Gressam is holding its market fair next week. Why don't we all go? You'll be needing some heavier clothes for the winter as well. No doubt, the others will also. There'll be juggling and games as well as horse racing and the like. Would you like that?"

"Yes, Uncle."

"Good. Then come, let's announce it to the others. That might take the sting out of your *other* news, I think."

Cam nodded and, feeling suddenly lighter, followed his uncle to the tower stairs. Nothing much had really been solved. The Seer was still out there waiting to be caught, Alec still didn't want him, and he was still hiding and lying to his uncle and cousins, but—somehow—none of that seemed important right now. He was an adult today. Once he got a handle on his new powers, his flying would settle down and then he could concentrate on sorting everything else out.

"It's gonna be fine," he assured himself. *"You'll see."*

For once, his mind had nothing sarcastic to offer in reply, and with a grin, he made for the stairs, eager to see Quin's face when he told them his news.

Beside him, Celestus DeKathrine allowed himself a faint smile. That had gone as easily as he'd expected. All he needed now to assure his Circle remained intact were two letters, one to Domitia DeKathrine from her son, the other to Alexander DeKathrine from his uncle. Everything was going perfectly.

From its place on the railing, the cat watched as the two of them entered Danielle's Tower, its expression unconvinced.

7. Martin Grayam

Halmouth Port, Kraburn
Mean Lunasa, 479 DR

*T*HE dockside Priest was drunk again. Seven-year-old Martin Grayam watched him dispassionately as he wove unsteadily back and forth along the wooden pier, each listing step to the right bringing him precariously close to the edge before an equally staggered step to the left returned him to safety.

Eyes narrowed, the boy looked past the Priest to the handful of tiny figures in the distance. The tide was out, exposing a stretch of dark, sandy beach for the cockle gatherers of Halmouth Port. Somewhere out there his mother labored with the rest. She'd have a good catch today. He had Seen it.

His gaze returned to the Priest. The man stood on the very edge of the pier, looking up at the cloudy sky, mouth agape, bloodshot eyes blank, expression slack. A week's worth of stubble across his cheeks made him look like some mad Essusiate Zealot come to harangue the sailors and dockworkers, but Pri Garius was neither an Essusiate nor a Zealot. He'd once been a respected Triarchy Seer until the drink had so addled his Sight that he was no longer of use to anyone. The boy frowned. He'd Seen the Priest in a dream last night. He'd Seen him fall off the pier. Now.

For a moment Pri Garius teetered on the edge of Martin's prophecy, then toppled over backward. The boy snig-

gered. Turning, he touched the old woman beside him on the shoulder to get her attention.

"He fell, Gram."

Eyes as vacant as the Priest's, the old woman bobbed her head without answering.

"Think he's dead, Gram?"

Under the worn shawl, frail shoulders rose and fell in a minimalist shrug.

"Think I should go look, Gram?"

Again the faint, noncommittal movement.

Tucking her shawl more securely into the crook of her arm, Martin crossed the worn, wooden planks to peer down at the Priest. It was a good six feet to the sand below. Martin had only Seen him fall, he hadn't actually Seen him get up.

Head pillowed on a clump of seaweed, Pri Garius lay as he'd fallen, eyes closed, limbs akimbo, mouth open. Snoring.

The boy seated himself on the pier. With his bare feet dangling over the edge, he stared down at the man.

A thin, wiry child, undersized for his age, with tangled light brown hair and great dark eyes, Martin had lived on the Halmouth Port Docks in Kraburn his entire life. His mother boiled cockles and whelks for the dockworkers when she was sober enough to work the brazier, his gram tended the tiny stall when she wasn't. They looked after Martin as best they could, but neither had spoken much since the spring of 472 when a predawn fire had raged through the waterside tenement where they lived, killing all but the three of them.

His mother, just sixteen, had been pacing the boardwalk with him in her arms, after a nightmare had awakened him screaming hysterically an hour before. She'd watched in horror as the blaze had engulfed their home in a matter of minutes. His gram had leaped from an upper story window, her youngest child tied in a shawl about her waist. She'd nearly drowned before being pulled to safety by local fishermen. The baby had not survived the fall.

Just four months old, Martin had stared out from his mother's arms, the conflagration playing out the tragedy he'd prophesied but had been too young to understand, while his mother's father and six brothers and sisters had perished in the flames. Martin had no memory of that night, but all his life his dreams had been haunted by fire.

Now he peered down at the sleeping Priest and wondered if he had any money left in his tattered purse. Pri Garius made a living blessing boats and babies and giving what comfort he could to the dying. He was usually to be found at the Green Whelk Tavern, but sometimes his faltering Sight brought him out into the light of day to mumble some few snatches of prophecy in the hopes of a copper or two.

His head cocked to one side, the boy pushed off the pier to land lightly beside the sleeping Priest. There was no response so, after a moment, he reached out gingerly for the man's purse.

The Priest rolled over.

Martin scuttled to one side, watching warily for signs of pursuit, but Pri Garius merely sat up groggily, rubbing his head with one hand and gazing blearily about.

"Something's going to happen."

He blinked.

"Or it already has."

His bloodshot eyes fixed suddenly on the boy. The two of them stared at each other for a long time, and then a bass rumble began from somewhere deep within the Priest's chest.

"Did it happen to you? Maybe, maybe it's yet to be. Yes, that's it. Begun but not birthed out in the world. Not yet."

He coughed and spat up a great wad of phlegm before gesturing at the boy.

Martin advanced a few careful paces. Pri Garius leaned forward.

"Have you ever Seen a ball of fire explode over a man's

head showering him with rose petals and golden coins?"
he asked in a hoarse whisper.

Martin's eyes widened.

*"Have you ever Seen a full complement of white ships
with dragons on their prows set out on a wind-tossed sea
only to be engulfed by a fiery vortex half a mile high?"*

Martin said nothing.

*"Well, I have. I've spoke prophecy for the Aristok him-
self, and I'll tell you something, boy, it wasn't worth half a
hogshead on a hot day."*

*His expression cleared. "You've got the Sight, don't
you, boy?" he rasped. "I can See it written all over your
destiny, poor little bastard. You've Seen the kind of things
I mentioned, haven't you? And more."*

"Maybe."

*"Maybe. Ha! You're a cautious one." He pulled a rock
out from under him and after a moment's scrutiny, flung it
to one side.*

*"Have you ever been to the Flame Temple of Bran-
bridge, boy?" he asked suddenly.*

*Martin shot him a condescending look. "Sure, every
day. I go in a golden coach."*

*"Ha! I'll bet you do. What did you think of it, eh? A
great drafty, rat-infested hole, wasn't it?"*

*Martin frowned at him. "I've never even been to Hal-
mouth's Temple," he answered scornfully.*

"Ah, but have you been there in your dreams now?"

Martin shrugged. "Maybe."

"I thought so."

*He fumbled in his purse and brought out one copper
helm. He held it out so that it gleamed dully in the sunlight.*

*"Do you know how many of these you'd need to travel
all the way to the capital city to actually see the Flame
Temple, boy?"*

*His expression avaricious, Martin shook his head. "A
lot?"*

"More than this, but maybe this." He shook the purse.

"I've a few coins left in here, you know. A few to bury me with or to drown me in drink. What would you do for them, boy, these coins of mine, eh?"

Martin's eyes narrowed. "I dunno. What would I have to do?"

"Help an old man up."

"That's all?"

The Priest began to laugh. "Oh, no, that's all for now." He scrubbed at his face. "I'll tell you plain, I'm dying. I've Seen it." He raised one finger in the air. "Seen my own death and pretty scorching close it is, too. But I've also Seen you." He poked the finger toward Martin. "I've Seen you speaking prophecy on the steps of the Flame Temple, much good it will do you in the end. And I've Seen how you get there." He shook the purse. "I'd rather it be a gift than a theft, so help me up and I'll tell your fortune."

He waved the boy forward and this time, Martin obeyed him, the jingle of Pri Garius' coins over loud in his ears. For an instant they became the rattling of chains and then the moment passed and he was taking the Priest's hand and helping him rise.

The Kenneth Forest, Leistonshire
Mean Lunasa 492 DR

The scrape of metal against metal woke Martin with a start. Rising to one elbow, he stared into the darkness, just able to make out the dull glow of a hooded lantern and the faint odor of fenweed smoke on the breeze. A figure off to one side stirred.

"Go to sleep, Seer. The storm's to the east. What you heard was just me lighting me pipe."

Martin eased back under his blanket. Around him the deep breathing of half a dozen others continued without pause as a rumble of thunder sounded in the distance.

The woman who'd spoken said nothing more. Martin closed his eyes again and tried to return to sleep.

He'd been traveling for a month, making his way slowly north along roads and riverbanks, following his vision. He'd made the southern edge of the Kenneth Forest two days before and had been hovering at its edge ever since, unsure whether to go around or through. His vision said north, but something intangible kept drawing him east. Finally, he'd followed his vision as he always had, hooking up with a family of Heathland tinkers willing to trade prophecy for the safety of numbers through the Kenneth Forest.

Rain began to sprinkle against his cheeks and he chuckled ruefully. It had been raining the day he'd set out from Alderbrook, hunting the boy with the golden hair and the not-thing which guarded him. In fact, it had poured for two full days after his decision to go north. Finally, he'd determined to leave the next morning at dawn regardless of the weather. It had been misty and cool, with a fine sprinkling of rain pattering against his face and hands when he'd set out.

Wrapping himself more tightly in his blanket, Martin fell asleep remembering.

Alderbrook, Branshire
Mean Mehefin
One month earlier

The fog lay on the ground in thick layers, turning the hilly land around the tower into a series of small islands peeking out from a white, rolling sea. Since coming to Alderbrook, Martin had set out on barely a handful of such journeys, walking east to Twick-On-Mist to hire a boat up the river to the Flame Temple. Today he turned north toward an unknown destination. Despite the uncertainty he found himself excited by the prospect. He hadn't made such a journey in a long time. Not since Pri Garius had sent him to the capital two decades before.

Ducking under the grasping branches of an old

hawthorn tree, he frowned. He hadn't thought about the Priest in years, and coming as it did at the advent of this journey, it had to mean something.

The fog parted to reveal the haggard countenance of Pri Garius before swirling back again. Martin grimaced. The day he'd become entangled with the drunken old man he'd helped him reach his small room behind the Green Whelk, but instead of handing over the promised coin, the Priest had begun rummaging through his things, muttering and coughing phlegm onto the floor. Martin had remained by the door, disgust evident on his face until the Priest had noticed him. Then his bloodshot eyes had cleared.

"C'mere, boy."

Martin remained where he was.

"I said, c'mere, I'm not going to bite you. I want to show you something."

Curiosity getting the better of him, Martin sidled forward as the Priest held up a worn, leather bag.

"Do you know what this is?" he asked dramatically. "The Potion of Truth. One pinch of this and you could See the future. A handful in a bowl of boiling water and you could speak Prophecy for the highest in the land and be believed. They make it in the Flame Temple Herbariums all across the country, and its ingredients are a carefully guarded secret." He held it out. "Go on, take it, have a whiff. It won't hurt you."

Martin accepted the purse warily. Inside he could just make out about a handful of coarsely ground leaves. The smell of it was sharp and acrid, and it made him want to sneeze. As he breathed it in, a tiny flame was born before his eyes and then disappeared.

The Priest chuckled. "Do you want it, boy?"

With a short shrug, Martin handed it back. "Why would I? I can See the future now."

"Ah, so you can, but . . ." He held a finger to the side of his nose. "There's so much more to this little bag than

*just Seeing the future. With it you can mold the future to
your own design. Do you know how?"*

Martin shook his head.

*"Change the ingredients just a little bit and although it
seems the same in scent and taste, you'll keep your wits
about you and you can tell your audience anything you
want them to hear. That's the secret of the Flame Temple's
power."* He leaned forward. *"Sometimes they take the Potion of Truth and sometimes they don't. Do you know
why?"* Before Martin could answer, he continued. *"Because sometimes the future doesn't suit their needs."*

He placed a finger to the side of his nose.

*"And the best of them, now they can mold the future
even with the Potion shrieking the truth in their ears.
They can open their mouths and have lies pour out like a
geyser of blood."*

*The boy cocked his head to one side. "You mean they
fake it, like ol' Ricky fakes fits to get money and food and
stuff."*

*"Exactly, only the Temple gains power and influence
rather than just stuff."*

*He straightened. "You remember I told you this, boy.
You'll need to remember it one day if you're to escape
your destiny. Now . . ." He straightened, suddenly all
business. "Sit down. I have a lot to teach you and no time
to do it in. You'll have to know the ingredients for both
potions at the very least." He turned. "Can you read?"*

"No."

*"Then you'll have to memorize it. Now pay attention.
Your life will depend on it. I've Seen it.*

Martin had never forgotten what Pri Garius had taught
him that day. The Priest had made him repeat the lists of
ingredients over and over, until he could speak them in his
sleep. He'd chanted them like a children's skipping rhyme
all the way to the capital that summer, and now, as he
made his way along the eastern bank of the Gable River,
he found himself repeating them again.

"Three hands rat-root, one hand worm-root, one hand holly berries, one hand . . ."

His walking disturbed a small wren, and it shot into the air past him, interrupting the litany. He smiled distractedly.

He hadn't known why he'd needed to memorize this strange little secret. His years at the Flame Temple had not given him so much as an inkling that the Priest's accusation had been correct. It had, however, tinged his acceptance of Temple doctrine with a strong dose of cynicism and suspicion, making it even harder to fit in than it might have been.

The sun began its climb over the alder bushes and birch trees by the river, and he stared out at the distant hills with a pensive expression. Pri Garius had been a powerful Seer in his day. Martin trusted his Vision, but there'd been times when he'd wished he'd never met the drunken old fool, that he'd become a dockworker or a sailor without the *benefits* of a Temple education. It might even have been possible until the day he'd come to that grubby little back room for the last time.

The Priest was lying very still on the unmade bed, a broken jug of cheap wine on the floor beside him. Martin peered down at him with a frown, then tried an experimental poke in the ribs. Pri Garius' eyes snapped open. He turned to hack a wad of bloody phlegm onto the floor, then waved his hand weakly. Martin helped him sit up.

"Drink," he muttered.

"There ain't none."

"Just as well."

He gazed up at the boy blearily. "Nearly time, now," he observed, "and about time, too, by all accounts."

He struggled to stand, then fell back heavily. "All right, fine. We'll stay on the bed."

His eyes cleared for a moment. "How's your mother," he asked suddenly.

"Same as always."

"She'll miss you when you go."

"I guess."

"And your grandmother, it was a grandmother you had, wasn't it?"

Martin just shrugged, and the Priest nodded shrewdly. "Seen her death, have you?" When Martin remained silent, he nodded to himself. "You're a powerful one, that's true enough. But you're not as powerful as you might be, boy, and not as powerful as you need to be to survive. Do you want to be that powerful?"

"Sure, who wouldn't?"

"Then you need one more thing. One little detail your mother should have seen to years ago, but I can See in your Vision that she never did. You need to be dedicated to the Triarchy, yet you never were. Why is that?"

Martin narrowed his eyes. "You're the great Seer," he sneered instead. "You tell me."

"Don't belabor my dwindling moments with nonsense, boy! Just answer my question. Why weren't you dedicated?"

Martin hesitated, then shrugged. "Our whole family got burned up in a fire when I was little," he answered in a careless tone. "Mam blamed the Triarchy, so she never went to Temple after that. That's all."

"Bugger it. So little time, so little time and so much to do. Well." Pri Garius clapped his hands. "There's nothing for it, it'll just have to be now. Fetch my satchel; it's over by the door."

Martin brought the musty leather bag over and watched as the Priest began rummaging inside, all the while muttering to himself.

"Sprig of rosemary, yes, cherrywood chips, yes, can't burn 'em, candle's gone out, but they'll do anyway. Dagger, yes. Bits of cloth, cream and red, um-hm. Water, water, oh, scorch it! Pass that bit of jug up here. Carefully now! Is there any wine left in it?"

Martin peered into the depths of the broken jug. "A little."

"It will have to do. Now rock for Oaks."

"Rock?"

"Don't interrupt." The Priest set a soft piece of limestone by the jug. *"Flame, hm. Really just needs ash. Bring some from the hearth."*

Martin obeyed, adding a handful of ash and charred wood to the pile of objects. *"You really need all this crap?"* he asked bluntly.

"Yes, now kneel down."

"Why?"

"Why? Because you're about to be blessed!"

"So? Why can't I be blessed standing up?"

The Priest glared at him, but after a moment, he shrugged. *"No reason at all. Here, hold this."* He stuffed the cream-colored cloth into the boy's hand. Martin scrutinized it curiously.

"What is it, a snot rag?"

"Well, yes, but it represents your dedication robe. The one you would have worn as an infant when this should have been done. Now be quiet." He raised his eyes to the ceiling, then blinked.

"Bugger. Your parents aren't here, are they? No. I suppose I'll have to stand in for them then; there's no time to fetch anyone else." He raised his eyes again.

"I bring . . ." he paused. *"What's your name, anyway?"*

"Martin."

"Martin what?"

The boy was silent for a long moment. *"Wrey,"* he said at last.

"I bring Martin Wrey before, er, me, to receive my blessing and be known to the Triarchy. What, er . . ." He paused again.

"I don't suppose your family has any heraldic animals?" he asked hopefully.

Martin gave him a sarcastic glance. *"Oh, sure, rats and cockles."*

"Hm. Better be the amphisbane, then."

"What's that?"

"The Two-Headed Serpent of Prophecy and Guardian of all Seers. So, um, who, I mean, I, um, I am Pri Garius of the Halmouth Port Temple, his, er, Patron . . ."

Martin snorted, and the Priest shot him a stern look from under his eyebrows.

"I speak for those who go before and those who will come after and, um, I'm known to the Triarchy."

He picked up the sprig of rosemary, dipped it in the jug, and after a moment's hesitation, sprayed it across his own face, dotting his cheeks with spots of red wine. His tongue darted out to lick them from his lips and he grimaced. "Crap. Be glad to go when the time finally comes. Look what I've been reduced to." He shook himself.

"All right, well, I suppose you'll have to answer these questions yourself. Will, um, will you be known to the Triarchy?"

"I guess."

"You have to answer 'I will.'"

"Why?"

The Priest gave an explosive sigh. "Because I said so!"

"All right, I will."

"Will you be guided and taught to heed your duty and your destiny?"

"Wha . . . ?"

"Just say I will."

"I will."

"Will you . . . wait, that won't work. Let's see, will you, um, let adults take care of you until you're old enough to take your place as an adult?"

"You're kidding."

"Just . . ."

"I'm old enough now. My mam works all day and my gram isn't right in the head. Who do you think looks after me now?"

"Good point. Well, will you take care of yourself until your Adult Dedication?"

"That's a really stupid question."

"Martin . . ."

"Fine, whatever, I will."

"Good. Here." He handed him the red cloth. *"This represents your acceptance robe."*

"So now I've got two snot rags?"

"Well, you're snotty enough to need them." He picked up the dagger and the limestone. *"Now, shut up, this part's important."* He chipped a piece from the rock and laid it against the boy's forehead. Martin winced slightly.

"Martin Wrey, I dedicate you to the Oaks whose roots dig deep into the earth and whose bones protect the people."

He tossed the rocks and dagger onto the bed and picked up the sprig of rosemary, dipping it in the jug again. The spot where the rock had touched began to itch but Martin resisted the urge to scratch at it.

"I dedicate you to the Sea which cradles the land and gives bounty to the people."

The Priest shook the rosemary sprig out over the boy's head and where the droplets touched, the skin began to burn. Clenching his teeth, Martin said nothing.

"Give me your hands." The Priest held them up. *"I dedicate you to the Wind that brings the rain which strengthens the people."*

Martin's hands began to cramp and, as soon as he was able, he snatched them away. His face was white and pinched by now, but he remained still as the Priest took up a fingerful of ash.

"I dedicate you to the Flame that birthed the world and brings warmth and comfort to the people."

Martin braced himself, but even he wasn't prepared for the explosion of power that burst into being between them as Pri Garius drew the sign of the Triarchy on his forehead. The Priest was flung aside like a rag doll and Martin was hurled into the air, his body outlined in traceries of fire. He opened his mouth to scream, and a great gout of light spewed from his throat to take the form of Merrone, the huge, white dragon guardian of Essus. It grew *until it seemed to encompass the entire world, then snapped its head down toward the boy. As Martin flinched aside, the amphisbane appeared with a shriek and streaked between them. The two ancient adversaries hovered, facing each other for less than a heartbeat, then slammed together with a deafening scream. The last thing the boy saw before the darkness took his mind was Pri Garius' crumpled body lying by the wall.*

Sunlight danced across his eyelids. He smelled reeds and water and heard the sweet call of warblers in the alder bushes about him. He opened his eyes.

He was lying facedown on the riverbank. Beyond the distant hills the sun was still partially hidden behind the line of trees, indicating that the seizure had been a short one. He sat up with a groan. It had been a long time since that memory had overpowered him. With a grimace, he leaned forward to splash water on his face. The river reflected back a man as haggard looking as the old Priest had been. Martin shivered.

Pri Garius had Seen his own death, but he hadn't Seen its particulars or he never would have dedicated an Essusiate boy to the Triarchy. At the best of times such a ceremony was tricky and dangerous. In that grimy little room, it had become deadly.

Wiping a streak of blood from his forehead, Martin sat up and pressed his back against a young birch tree. At seven years old, he'd never heard the word apostate, although he was to become all too familiar with it later. Pri Garius had said he needed more power to survive and Martin had wanted to survive. It hadn't occurred to him that the Priest wouldn't. And to be brutally honest, he hadn't really cared. He'd regained consciousness facedown on the floor and, after quickly rifling through the man's belongings, had fled the city before anyone could discover him, writhing tendrils of prophecy chasing him like a legion of ghostly snakes. He never did find out what had happened to Pri Garius' body, or to the rest of his own small family. He'd returned to Halmouth Port nine years later, but everyone and everything he'd known was gone.

Now, sitting by the water, Martin dismissed the host of past regrets as he'd done every day since the Priest's death, then rose and carried on along the river path before the snakes could find him again.

He passed through the village of Asford an hour later, then left the Gable River and turned east through lightly wooded country spotted with elm and beech trees until he reached the River Auld. Several beautiful willow trees grew bent over the water, trailing their long boughs in the slowly moving current, and he stood, leaning against the bridge's wooden railing, for a long while. As always, after a seizure, he felt light-headed and quiet, the wisps of Vision temporarily stilled. He watched a man collect willow wands on the bank, then shared a meal of bread and quail eggs with him before continuing on his way, through several small hamlets until he reached the village of Haminworth. It was a pleasant place with a single Coach House called the Hare's Kit where he had a bowl of mutton stew, then, not being used to so much travel, fell asleep under a large, shady oak tree at the back.

His dreams were disjointed and vague. Twice he felt the boy's presence, but the morning's seizure had left him weakened and he didn't dare alert the not-thing. Instead, his mind flitted about the north road, seeking any signs of difficulties to come, but again found nothing substantial. He awoke, cold and hungry, as the sun dropped below the hills and returned to the inn for a saddle of mutton and rather too much wine. As he fell into bed, his Vision rose up around him, but he was too tired to pay it much heed and slept heavily without dreaming.

He walked all the next day, pausing only long enough to eat a little bread and cheese before continuing on. As the sundown turned the waters of the Hind River a bright golden orange he bought a trout from a old woman outside the small hamlet of Little Hindon, accompanying her back to her cottage for supper. Her son, Brant, was a tall, lanky man of twenty-one, a year older than himself, and by the time the fish was eaten, they'd struck up an understanding. As the moon rose over the trees, Brant tipped his head toward the door. Leaving the old woman sitting contentedly by the fire with her pipe and a cat, they made for the shed at the back of the cottage.

Brant's eyes glittered in the moonlight.

"Know anythin' about coneys?" he asked.

"Some."

"Know anythin' about the Viscount Warrick DeSandra?"

Martin grinned. "I know he's on the Continent."

"For at least another two months. C'mon."

The wrought-iron fence about the Viscount's east park was easily scaled, his gamekeepers equally easily avoided. Three hours later they were back in the shed preparing a brace of rabbits by lantern light. Brant nailed the last of the pelts to a small frame and turned.

"It's not too late. Ma'll still be up. You wanna . . . ?" His eyes tracked to a small cot tucked in a corner by a neat pile of baskets and farming tools.

"You don't think it's too small?"

"Not if we don't move around too much. So what do you say?"

"Sure."

Brant wrapped his arms about him, breathing in the scent of Martin's hair before reaching over to close the lantern. In the sudden darkness, a dozen ghostly images appeared, illuminating the other man's face with a fine tracery of pale light that only Martin could See. The Seer reached up, smoothing the tiny figures of family and friends that danced across his cheeks together into one cohesive whole.

"You'll have a good life," he whispered.

Brant chuckled as he buried his face in the other's neck. "I already have a good life," he murmured. "C'mon."

He guided him toward the cot by memory and, with a
sigh, Martin sank back onto the old blanket.

They spent the night together having sex, drifting off to
sleep, then awakening to have sex again. As the dawn sun
poured in through the chinks in the wooden walls, Martin
watched three blurred figures dressed as Heathland Hill
Fighters appear above Brant's head. Each one touched
him lightly on the shoulder, then turned and disappeared
through the door, heading north. He gave a rueful snort
and bent to run his lips over the other man's eyelids.

"C'mon, wake up. I have to go."

Half an hour later, Brant walked him to the nearby ford
across the Hind River. They shared one last moment,
pressed against an oak tree, then Martin crossed the ford
without looking back.

He reached the town of Causlip by noon. It was market
day and he had pork pies, fresh plums, and hard cider on
the steps of the town's Flame Temple. Shepherds, farmers,
and fishers argued trade with the local merchants all
around him, and he lingered for a long time watching the
ebb and flow of their lives. Then, with the sky growing
cloudy, he set off across hilly country toward the town of
Mullen.

He was still in the hills when darkness fell. Making
camp beneath an elm tree, he snared a woodcock and ate
it roasted over a small fire, washing it down with the last
of the cider. Then, wrapping himself in his cloak, he fell
asleep.

His dreams were disturbing. Flashes of lightning illuminated the surface of a vast network of pulsing spiderwebs
stretching out across the Realms. He drifted cautiously toward it, then recognized it for the not-thing's net, grown
suddenly more menacing than it had ever been before. People hung entangled in its strands, staring out at him with
wide, milky-white eyes. They were clad in all manner of tattered clothing, from simple tunics to more elaborate courtly

garb. Some had been there for so long that graying bones peeked out from rents in their skin and clothing. As he drew closer, their lips began to move, working around the stiffening of death to whisper one word.

"Heretic."

He jerked back. The word took form, spilling out from each mouth on long lines of pale saliva. They reached for him blindly, each brushing touch against his skin leaving an icy scar behind. He felt his limbs grow cold. His eyes began to close, and then the boy's presence broke past the net like a shaft of golden sunlight. The webbing with its grisly prisoners disappeared, and he awoke.

It was a gray, misty morning, the overcast sky and chill wind off the hills threatening rain. Stiff and cold, he moved out at once, trying to shake the effects of his night's Vision from his mind but, as the day wore on, he found it harder and harder to concentrate on the path. Every indistinct shape in the mist writhed with unspoken prophecy and, as the threatened rain began to fall, whispering voices seemed to rise up all around him. He quickened his steps, keeping his eyes locked on the toes of his boots. He couldn't have an attack here, not in the open. He had to get indoors, but the nearest shelter was still miles away through the mist. Until then, he had to ignore the voices and the shapes that hovered closer and closer with every step.

By the time he left the hill country, he was almost running.

Suddenly a wrought-iron fence loomed up through the rain and he jerked to a stop, breathing hard. Gripping the bars, he pressed his forehead against the cold metal and forced himself to breathe deeply.

"Calm down, Martin."

His voice sounded strangely flat over the pounding of the rain. Behind him the hills continued to whisper their secrets and he squeezed his eyes shut as if that alone could silence them.

"You're almost there."

Opening his eyes, he squinted through the fence at the thick stands of hornbeam and oak trees beyond.

"You're on Evelynne DeKathrine's land," he continued. "This is her deer park, the one with the miniature hunting lodge in the center. You just have to walk east for half an hour and then you're at Mullen Town. There's a Flame Temple at Mullen, remember. You can collapse there, but you have to keep going until you get there."

Turning, he pressed his back against the bars, blinking up at the dark sky. He was soaked through. The rain had plastered his hair to his head hours before and run down his face and neck until he was as wet inside his clothes as he was outside. He felt like a drowned rat. A poor state for one of the country's most powerful Seers, but at least it was a good disguise. Neither the not-thing nor the boy would ever recognize him. His lips drew up in a sour smile.

"Still, I could use some of your golden sunlight right about now," he said, addressing the boy out loud for the first time.

The rain showed no sign of abatement.

"No?" He straightened. "All right. We'll just carry on, then."

Tucking his head down, he began to walk again, his left hand lightly pushing against the wrought iron fencing to keep himself on his feet. He began to chant the lists of ingredients once more, timing each word to each splashing footfall until he left the deer park and turned north toward the distant town of Mullen.

When he finally arrived, it took all of his remaining strength to stumble to the small Flame Temple in the center of town. As he collapsed in its tiny courtyard, he felt hands catch him up and draw him inside toward warmth and quiet. For half a heartbeat he thought he felt the boy's shining presence beckon him, but he was too exhausted to answer. With a tired sigh, he allowed the darkness to rush in and claim him.

8. Martin Wrey

The Branbridge Flame Temple
Early Autumn, Mean Fhomhair 479 DR

T HE Branbridge Temple of the Flame emitted the most powerful and awe-inspiring presence seven-year-old Martin had ever Felt. Even a mile away he could sense it throbbing in his head like a giant drum. It was all he could do to keep from running blindly forward, but instead, he made himself sit down on the opposite bank of the River Mist and study the grounds carefully.

Since fleeing from Halmouth Port he'd been traveling for over two weeks, heading in the general direction of the capital—ostensibly obeying Pri Garius' wishes because he couldn't think of a better way to make up for the man's death. Stealing food when he could, using the Priest's dwindling supply of copper helms when he could not, he'd walked until he'd grown tired, then slept until he was rested in dovecotes, sheering sheds, or under bridges; whatever offered enough shelter. He hadn't bothered to consider what might happen after he arrived, but now, staring at the Temple's bright copper turrets, he realized that he had no idea what he should do next. He couldn't just walk in and demand to be let in. Could he?

Staring into the depths of Pri Garius' purse, he frowned. He knew how the world worked. If you weren't born into a trade, you paid a master to take you on and teach you. If you couldn't afford a trade, then you hired out as a servant. The only other option was thievery. He'd never even

considered the Priesthood of either faith, but he'd assumed it was the same as tinsmith or barrelwright. If you
didn't have the money, you didn't get in.

"So what are you gonna to do?" he asked himself
bluntly. "Stay here and starve?"
"Maybe."
"You scared?"
"Yes."
"You're a Seer. You belong there. Pri Garius said so."
*"Pri Garius is dead. You killed him. If you go in there,
they'll find out and they'll . . ."*
"They'll want?"
*"I dunno, kill you back or something. Maybe even
worse."*
"There's nothing worse than being killed, stupid."
"Says you. Maybe they'll know something worse."

Propping his chin up against his palm, Martin abandoned the argument. He couldn't just walk in there for a
lot of reasons. But Pri Garius had said he belonged there,
so there had to be some way. His eyes narrowed. The old
soak had also said he was his Patron. Martin snorted. If
he'd been a real Patron he'd have lived long enough to
come with him or at least send him to someone else—not
left him to figure it out all by himself. Absently wiping his
nose with the red snot rag, he opened the Priest's leather
bag, hoping for some inspiration from the bits of Triarctic
junk inside.

His fingers tingled against the objects of his dedication,
and he quickly pulled his hand out again. Every night
since the Priest's death his dreams had been a battle-
ground between Essus and the—whatever Pri Garius had
called that two-headed snake-thing. The closer he got to
the Flame Temple the stronger the snake-thing got, but
that still didn't mean he could walk into the Temple
safely. And even if he could, his head would still probably
split apart from the pressure. The constant throbbing was

already making his left eye tic. It was stupid to have come here. He stood.

WAIT.

The compulsion was so strong he froze where he stood. "What?"

WAIT.

Squinting, he could just make out two people pushing a small boat into the water on the opposite bank. Two people in red clothing.

All his instincts told him to run. Whoever they were they had to be from the Flame Temple. Maybe they were guards, or worse, Seers. He took a step backward, panic overcoming the compulsion to remain. If they were Seers, they would know about Pri Garius' death. Maybe one of them was a Seer and the other was a guard: one to hold him and one to kill him. He took another step backward as the boat drew nearer.

"I thought you *wanted* to be a Seer?" he demanded, mostly to his feet.
"*No.* Pri Garius *wanted me to be a Seer.*"
"You went along with it."
"*So what? Now I want to run.*"
"To where?"
"*Who cares!*"

He stood rooted to the spot, arguing with himself until the boat drew close enough to identify the two people on board. The one rowing was an older man in a plain, red tunic, the other was an auburn-haired youth wearing the crest of a brown bear holding a ball of fire above its head. He stared at Martin intently. The boy's eyes narrowed.

QUIT IT.

* * *

The youth jerked his head to one side, then leaped from the boat as it ground up on the riverbank.

"I'm Airik DeKathrine," he said without preamble. "Assistant to Her Grace, the Deputy Seer. I've been sent to bring you to the Temple."

Martin's jaw dropped. "Sent?" His eyes strayed to the far bank. "How?"

Airik gave him a sardonic look. "By boat?"

"Very funny. I mean, how'd she know I was coming?"

"How do you think? Her Grace had a Vision. She informed me that a new Initiate was waiting on the south bank and sent me to collect you."

"Then how'd you know it was me?"

"You mean, besides the fact that you're the only one standing on the riverbank staring across at the Temple grounds?"

Martin glared at him. "Yeah. Besides that."

"You called to us."

"I did not."

"Your mind did. I could sense your presence all the way across the water—and your fear of us. That's why I asked you to wait. And now I'm to ask if you'll accompany me back."

"So I've got a choice?"

Airik looked genuinely puzzled. "Of course."

"What if I choose *not* to come?"

"Then I go back without you and you find your own way across later. But didn't you make the choice to come here in the first place?"

Martin shrugged. "Maybe. Maybe I've changed my mind."

"I see. Well, it's nothing to me whether you come or not, but it's going to rain. Do you have alternate lodgings?"

"What?"

"Another place to stay?"

"No."

"Then you might as well spend the night with us." Airik headed back to the boat. "What have you got to lose, anyway?" he asked over his shoulder.

"Oh, nuthin', just everything," Martin muttered, but after a moment, he followed him.

He was flying. The wind rushing past him billowed through his clothing, threatening to tear it from his body. He didn't care. He'd never flown before and the sense of freedom was intoxicating. Looking down, he studied the ever changing landscape, first land, then sea, then clouds, wondering if he would tell this dream to the Seer Provost in the morning. Probably not. Martin had decided a long time ago that the man in charge of the Flame Temple's Initiates was a useless git.

Sweeping past a strangely familiar castle, he made special note of the crumbling inner keep with its stick-figure defenders and crimson-armored attackers, and frowned. He knew enough about his Visions by now to recognize a portentous dream, but he'd be boiled for a cockle if he would tell the Seer Provost or his pretentious little Acolyte, Osarion DeSandra, about it. They would misinterpret it anyway, they always did. Turning his back on the castle, he headed for the open sky.

Martin had been at the Flame Temple for nearly four years now and had quickly learned two important facts; one: his fellow Initiates were a bunch of spoiled, arrogant, little brats who thought they knew everything, and two: the Temple Hierarchy wasn't much better. Except for Her.

Pale gray eyes illuminated by the most powerful inner Sight Martin had ever Seen, stared into his. He shivered.

When Airik DeKathrine had brought him before the Flame Temple Leaders to be accepted as an Initiate, he'd planned to lie, he'd planned to evade, possibly even to run, but when Urielle DeSandra, the then Deputy Seer, had turned her fathomless gray eyes on him, he'd given up everything without hesitation: Pri Garius' death, his Essusiate past, his dreams and abilities; everything. It had left him shaken and fearful, but accepted into their ranks with one proviso: the last of Essus' grip on his destiny must be broken. He'd agreed without truly understanding what that meant.

Each full moon for the next three years saw him kneeling before the Temple's main altar, rededicating his life and powers to the Triarchy, the Flame Temple, and the Living Flame. In between he endured endless lessons, lectures, and religious training made that much harder because the others his age were so far advanced beyond him.

"What do you mean you can't read and write?"

Pri Sandra stared down in horror at her newest student while the rest of the Initiates in the room tittered with laughter. Martin's jaw tightened.

"I never needed to learn," he answered stiffly, biting back the retort he might have made under other circumstances.

"What dockyard bastard does?"

Martin turned a look of cold fury on Osarion DeSandra. The noble boy just smiled.

"If I stared at you long enough," Martin grated, his eyes grown wild and dark, "I could See your death as plain as if it were just about to happen and . . ." he snapped his fingers and, despite himself, Osarion jumped, "it just might *happen."*

The older boy leaped to his feet, his fists clenched. Martin took one step toward him, then Pri Sandra had him by the back of his robe.

"I will not tolerate fighting," she snapped. "Osarion, you will sit down at once, and, Martin," she turned a jaundiced gaze on the younger boy, "you will report to Pri Gerald for reading and writing, and to learn the proper manner in which to address your fellow Initiates.

When you have mastered these basic skills, you may return to my classroom. You are dismissed."

Martin never did rejoin Pri Sandra's class. By the time he was ready for her teaching, his prophetic abilities had so outstripped the others that he'd been sent straight to Pri Marcus, the Temple's Senior Seer, who didn't care about basic skills or manners, only results.

He was adrift in a fiery sea of potential, fragments of prophecy floating all around him like pieces of a ship-wreck. He made to grab them, but they eluded him, riding along on the waves just out of reach. He ground his teeth in frustration.

"Martin, what do you See?"

Pri Marcus' voice tugged at him, drawing him back to the Temple room where he and a dozen other young Seers were skimming the surface of the Prophetic Realm. He shook the man's question off impatiently. If he could See anything coherent, he would have said so an hour ago. One image, bobbing up and down before his face, became a woman with coal-black hair, the tattoo of a dragon standing out on her left cheek. She beckoned to him.

"Martin, what do you See?"

The voice took the form of a ship, cutting through the waves and scattering the fragments in its wake. The woman disappeared to be replaced by a young man with long golden hair and a glittering sword.

"Martin? You're too deep. Come back up and talk to me. What do you See?"

Annoyance found his voice for him.
"I See an amphisbane having sex with a wyvern."

There was scattered laughter from the Junior Seers all around him.

"He Sees nothing. His Vision is tainted."

Osarion again. Martin almost growled out loud. Strong and talented, the older boy's Vision had remained tauntingly clear. Even when puberty had played havoc with the Sight of every one of his classmates, he'd slid through with barely a ripple in his abilities. It had grown as he had grown, perfectly and powerfully, without so much as a pimple to mark the occasion. By contrast, manhood had taken Martin completely by surprise, twisting his voice into an unrecognizable croak, lengthening his limbs out of all proportion to the rest of his body, and sending his already sensitive Sight careening out of control. More often than not these days his Visions were violent, frightening, and indescribable. Tainted, yes, but Osarion was wrong if he thought Martin Saw nothing. He Saw Osarion. And he remembered what Pri Garius had taught him.

With a word he made the DeSandra eagle rise up, beating its wings against the waves, then knocked it aside.

"I See an eagle," he reported dutifully.

"Yes?"

"I See it fall."

"How?"

"It overreaches before it's ready to fly."

"Is the eagle heraldic or personal?"

A thin rivet of prophecy played out before him, as far, far in the future a family pantomimed the events of its own self-destruction. Then it was gone.

"Personal."

"Who is it?"

Martin screwed up his face in a mock grimace of concentration.

"Osarion."

"He's lying," the other boy retorted immediately.

"Osarion . . ."

"He's lying, Your Grace, I haven't Seen anything like that."

"Pride blinds us to our own destiny."

"Shut up, you little wharf rat."

"Enough. Osarion, you will enter more deeply into Vision to search for this possibility. The rest of you are dismissed."

Coming slowly out of trance as he'd been taught, Martin allowed himself a tiny, private smile. His Vision might be swinging out of control these days, but its strength was the equal of Osarion's, and if he said he saw danger for the other boy, his teachers took him seriously. Osarion had at least an hour's searching ahead of him before Pri Marcus would agree that Martin was, at the very least, mistaken.

Stretching his legs, he followed the other Junior Seers from the room, leaving the older boy behind. Yes, it was petty, he admitted, maybe even stupid, but it would do for now, and one day, he promised himself, when he hit someone, he would hit a lot harder than this.

"I See the Shadow Catcher!"

He was fifteen and only eight weeks away from taking vows as a Flame Priest. In the last six months his studies had intensified; religion, politics, herb-craft, trance work, and dream and symbolic interpretation had been drilled into his head until he could speak prophecy in his sleep. Already acknowledged as one of the most powerful Seers to come out of the Temple in a hundred years, his abilities, although still wildly chaotic, could be brought under control with concentrated effort. All that remained was his first True Vision gained with the Potion of Truth. His teachers believed he was ready.

That morning, five High Temple Officials, including the Archpriest of the Flame, the Branbridge Coadjutor, and the Deputy Seer, gathered to witness Martin Wrey's first foray into the Prophetic Realm. Seated on the floor in the Temple's main chapel, two of his classmates to either

side in case his Vision became violent, Martin accepted a
bowl of the Potion of Truth from the Temple Herbalist. It
was hot and scorched his throat going down, but he finished the last of it, letting the bowl slip from fingers already gone numb. There was a loud thrumming in his
head and then something slammed into him with enough
force to knock the breath from his lungs. He fell for what
seemed like forever, then hit the shifting ground of the
Prophetic Realm with a crash. He lay, dazed, blinking up
at the world as it raced past him; trees, people, animals,
and creatures he could not identify flying by so fast he
could barely register their passing.

Far away, he heard Pri Marcus' voice.

"Martin. What do you See?"
He got to his knees.
"Concentrate, Martin. What do you See?"
He took a deep breath and reached out with his mind,
catching hold of his Vision and forcing it to steady.
Around him the images slowed, then melted away.
"I See a vast plain."
"What's on the plain?"
The voice echoed in his head, rippling out across the
world in tiny rivulets of sound.
"Nothing. Just . . . emptiness."
*"Look into the distance, Martin. What do you See in the
distance?"*
He squinted. Far away he thought he could See a tiny
speck of something. As he stared, it drew closer, rushing
toward him until the great snarling face of the white
dragon of Essus leaped up at him. He cried out, throwing
his arms up as he fell.

And the plain was empty again.

"Martin?"
He raised his head fearfully.
"Martin?"
Pri Garius' face hovered just before his eyes.

*   *   *

"Wait."

The Priest stared at him with rheumy, bloodshot eyes, his lips moving soundlessly. Forcing himself to calm, Martin turned all the power of his abilities on his dead Patron's words and after a moment, they became clear.

"Have you ever Seen a ball of fire explode over a man's head, showering him with rose petals and golden coins?"

"What?"

"Have you ever Seen a full complement of white ships with dragons on their prows set out on a wind-tossed sea only to be engulfed by a fiery vortex half a mile high?"

"I don't have time for this."

"Have you ever been to the Flame Temple of Branbridge?"

Unable to resist, Martin shot the figure a condescending look.

"Sure, every day. I go in a golden coach, remember."

"Ha! I'll bet you do. What did you think of it, eh? A great drafty, rat-infested hole, wasn't it?"

"Yeah. It is." He stood. "What do you want, old man?"

The Priest waved one arm to encompass the Prophetic Realm. *"What do you See?"* he intoned in a mocking voice.

Martin snorted. "That the God of my mother is still really pissed at me."

"Is that what you're going to tell them*?"*

"No."

"What, then?"

"I don't know. What *can* I tell them?"

"What do you want *to tell them?"*

"Something important. Something that only I could See." His face darkened. "Something that Osarion couldn't See."

The Priest's expression grew cunning. *"There is something,"* he answered. *"Something so terrible that the very*

*sight of It might drive a normal man, an average man,
mad from fear. You touched it once long ago as a very tiny
child and you might touch it again if you were quick. But
you'd have to be quick. It's nearly upon us."*

"What?"

"The Shadow Catcher."

Martin gave a sneering laugh. "Is that the best you can
offer, old man? Plenty of people have Seen the Shadow
Catcher."

*"Not like this. Not fully manifested, squeezing out from
the Aspect's Realm like some great evil being birthed from
the void, Its still hidden purpose laid bare to your eyes
alone. What do you say, boy? Do you want to have a Vision that not even the Archpriest himself will have?"*

The answer was easy enough.

"Yes."

"Even though it might drive you mad?"

"If I haven't gone mad yet, I'm not likely to now. Show
me."

"I See the Shadow Catcher!"

*The very nearness of the Death's Captain made his
limbs shake so hard he thought he was about to have a
seizure. The great metaphysical creature loomed threaten-
ingly over him for the space of a heartbeat, then descended toward the world on a gray thread of shadow like
a huge, swollen spider. Unable to pull away, Martin followed in Its wake. Together, they pushed through the veil
between the Realms, and suddenly Martin stood in a sunlit wood of oak and beech trees.*

*He blinked. In the distance he heard a hunting horn
and the crashing of some huge creature in the underbrush. He turned. A male dragon, blood and saliva covering its face, stumbled into a nearby clearing. Dozens of
darts and quarrels protruded from its legs and belly, but
there was also blood and matted hair in its claws, and
madness in its eyes.*

Far away he heard his own voice reporting what he Saw to the gathered Flame Priests as the sound of the hunting horn drew closer.

The dragon heard it, too. Rising up on its hind legs, it stood immobile like some great, three-dimensional heraldic crest. For an instant it glowed with an impossibly clear, white light, then the Royal Hunt came thundering into view.

At its head rode a tall, auburn-haired young man, clad in dark blue and black, his flame-pooled eyes bright with anticipation. He carried an iron-tipped spear like a lance and, as his eyes locked with his prey's, he raised one hand in salute, then urged his mount forward.

Martin spoke his name.

"Prince Atreus."

Atreus DeMarian, beloved firstborn son and namesake of the Aristok Atreus the Second of Branion, and Heir to the throne. As he bore down upon the dragon, it stood as still as a statue, its eyes glittering with a prophetic intelligence. The Prince raised his weapon to strike.

The Shadow Catcher dropped from the trees.

The spear took the dragon in the throat. It drove through and out and, as momentum carried horse and rider forward, the creature brought its clawed front limbs streaking down.

Blood sprayed across the clearing.

The hunt froze, horror-struck, as their Price was torn from the sadd!e. The dragon clutched him to its breast in a mockery of intimacy, then drove its teeth into his face.

Martin screamed.

The vision engulfed him. He felt an unbearable tearing pain as razor-sharp claws drove into his flesh. There was a wrenching in his head, and then the Living Flame rose up, boiled over, and spewed from his mouth and nose. The Shadow Catcher turned Its empty eye sockets on Martin's face. Then there was nothing but mind-numbing darkness.

*   *   *

When he came back to himself he was lying, tied to one of the infirmary beds. He hurt everywhere. His head throbbed, and his arms and legs felt as if they'd been wrenched from their sockets. Looking down, he saw that his blankets were soaked with sweat and spattered with dried blood. He tried to speak, but could only manage a weak, rasping cough. All around him, the ghostly fragments of his Vision rose up, then faded as he recognized the woman standing over him. He managed to croak out a few words past the burning in his throat.

"How long?"

The Deputy Seer gazed down at him, her expression emotionless.

"Four days."

"The Prince?"

"Dead. Killed by a dragon in the woods north of Branbridge while you were in Vision. The country is in mourning. They do not know that this tragedy was foreseen . . ." She paused, ". . . too late to prevent it. And they will not be told. All who were witness to this Vision have been sworn to secrecy, as you will be."

Martin's eyes widened questioningly.

"The Flame Temple Seers receive their Visions from the Living Flame Itself," she explained sharply. "The Flame is infallible, therefore Its True Visions are also infallible. If there is a fault, it lies within the Seer. Do you understand me?"

He nodded weakly. "The Flame . . . didn't send . . ."

"Pri Marcus believes that you reached into the Aspects' Realm and stole a Vision never meant for human eyes. I'm inclined to agree." She gazed down at him, her eyes glowing coldly. "The Aspects' Realm is an indescribably dangerous place as you well know. I will not have you endanger your service to this institution through reckless arrogance. You will not attempt this again. If you do, I will personally expel you from the Flame Temple. Is that clear?"

* * *

The room was on fire, smoke filling the air with a choking fog. A huge, frightening presence bent over his cradle and, as he screamed in terror, his latent abilities exploded outward, seeking help from someone, from anyone. A moment away from death, he caught a glimpse of a place so primordial it nearly destroyed his infant's mind, then he was awake and shrieking in his mother's arms.

"Is that clear, Martin?"
"Yes, Your Grace. Forgive me."

The years flowed over him like a rushing river. Each time he tried to surface, the current closed over his head again. He Saw Pri Garius lying like a broken doll in the back room of the Green Whelk, Saw his grandmother leap from a burning tenement house, and Saw the Shadow Catcher. crowned in flames, looming over him. The Aspects' Realm rose up, threatening to drive him insane with the intensity of Its light, then a hand reached down and pulled him to safety.
The boy . . .
They stared at each other for a long time, the other's blue eyes unaccountably sad, then Martin was alone.
He opened his eyes.

Sunlight streamed in through an unfamiliar window. For a moment he was completely disoriented, and then he remembered, it was the year 492. He was lying in bed in the small Flame Temple in Mullen Town. He'd been there for four days, falling in and out of Vision and raving like a madman. The local Priest and Physician had tended him night and day, but neither had been able to pierce the fog of prophetic nightmares that had engulfed him. Only the boy had been able to do that.

Martin frowned. He'd been flying with the boy for over a month now and in that time he'd learned the rules: remain calm, don't come too close, don't come too fast, and

avoid the bright and shining reflective presence that was
the not-thing. They'd made contact only once, and the
not-thing had reacted so fast it had nearly knocked him
into the next county. But when Martin had needed help,
the boy had responded. They had a link of some kind, a
link forged in the past, he could Feel it.

He closed his eyes, trying to call up the first time he'd
sensed the boy's presence. Not the night his Vision had
sent him to the Archpriest, but before.

*The wind rushing past him billowed through his cloth-
ing, threatening to tear it from his body.*

Maybe. Those dreams might have been the boy's
dreams. He was a flier. Maybe not a Seer in the true sense
of the word, but someone with an obvious affinity to the
Wind. This in itself was not unusual, many of the Wind
Temple Priests could claim such an affinity, but Martin
could Feel the Wind rise in power during the boy's flights
and that *was* unusual. If the boy were coming just close
enough to the Aspects' Realm to draw the Wind to him,
that would explain the link.

Scratching at three days' worth of stubble, he sat up
gingerly. As the Archpriest had said five years ago, the
Aspects' Realm was a powerfully dangerous place. In the
history of the Flame Temple it had only ever been successfully breached three times, and then only for the direst
of reasons involving the safety of the Realm. Each time
the Seers had not survived the experience. He grimaced.
There'd been rumors of other attempts; various heretical
groups who'd tried to harness the primordial power of the
Aspects for their own use, but he'd been taught that
they'd always failed and, like their Temple counterparts,
always died. No one touched that place and got away with
it unscathed. If the boy had become embroiled in something like that . . .

*   *   *

"I Saw the Wind dancing on the waves of the Bjerre Sea, and as I watched, the waves became Flame and the Wind took the form of a child with hair as golden as the summer sun. Then the earth rose up, cupping the waves and the child in a cradle made of tree roots."

It hadn't seemed that dangerous at the time. Perhaps it had begun innocently enough. Or still was.

The image shattered like a glass ornament, spewing shards of power across the room.

Innocent or not, it wasn't going to remain that way. He stood carefully, glancing about for his clothes. He had to go north. He had to find the boy before whatever was to happen happened. After thanking the Priest and the Physician, he made for the road again, ignoring the wisps of prophecy that followed along behind him.

He walked steadily northward for three days, careful not to overdo it, resting when he needed to rest, and spending each night in a proper bed in a proper inn. He made steady progress, reaching the small Essusiate Shrine of St. Stephan's just south of Albangate by dusk on the third day. He almost passed by, but, at the last moment, paused to listen to the thin streams of music coming from the open doorway.

It had been four years since he'd attended an Essusiate service here on this very spot. Four years and a lifetime ago. As the Cleric began the Greeting, he turned and walked to a nearby willow tree, kneeling down beside a small granite headstone and remembering.

"May Essus smile upon you."
"And also on you."
"Give your worship freely and freely will the God's blessings be showered upon you."

The Cleric lowered his arms. "Let us send our prayers to Essus."

As the gathered lowered their heads, Carla leaned over to poke Martin in the ribs.

"See, I told you your head wouldn't cave in if you crossed the threshold," she whispered.

His face white, Martin simply nodded.

It had been six months since his first True Vision. Four months since the Hierarchy, counseled by Pri Marcus, had decided to delay his vows. They needed time, they'd said, to assess whether his experience with the Aspects' Realm had damaged his Vision, but Martin knew what they really meant. They needed time to assess his usefulness to the Flame Temple. The Deputy Seer had told him as much. So Martin had waited, watching each of his classmates take vows and growing increasingly frustrated and resentful. By the time he'd met Carla Armistone, he'd been ripe for some sort of rebellion.

Wiping the sweat from his face with the back of his sleeve, he glanced cautiously about at the tall, bearded Essusiate men around him. This hadn't been what he'd expected when he'd first purchased the small packet of herbs from the tinker girl. He'd only wanted some respite from the headaches that had been growing increasingly debilitating since that day, the pain often so bad it made him sick to his stomach. He couldn't eat, then he couldn't sleep. Afraid of what the Hierarchy would do if they found out, he avoided the Herbalist, going instead to the tinker encampment just west of the Temple grounds. Carla Armistone prescribed a tonic of feverfew, vervain, and valerian to be taken once a day.

The herbs had helped. At first. But a month later the headaches were back in full force, driving him almost mad from the pain. Carla added worm-root to the mix, then ox-thistle. The combination of the two powerful narcotics finally did the trick. As long as he kept taking them.

He became a familiar sight at the encampment that

winter, sitting by the fire, listening to the local gossip, and talking to Carla. A slight woman two years older than Martin, she had long, coal-black hair, pale green eyes, and a tattoo of a dragon on her left cheek. She was sharp-witted and sharp-tongued and loved to dance and fight and argue about religion. Originally from Heathland, she and her family belonged to a small Essusiate sect which differed from the Continental Church in several key matters—including a more tolerant view on those with the Sight—which she was more than willing to explain at length.

Despite their many differences, Martin found himself slowly falling in love with her.

One evening, sharing a pipe of fenweed by the fire, he asked her about the tattoo. She just laughed.

"It's Merrone, the Dragon Guardian of Essus," she explained simply. *"Don't tell me you've never heard of Merrone?"*

Her tone was scornful, and Martin felt his cheeks flush.

"Of course I've heard of Merrone," he retorted. *"I've even Seen Merrone."*

Her eyes widened. "What, in a Vision?"

"Sure."

"What was It doing?"

He chewed on his cheek a moment. "Just things," he answered evasively. *"Metaphysical things. I can't talk about it."*

She nodded sarcastically. "I'll bet."

"No, really." He paused. "I Saw It there." He brushed his fingertips against her cheek.

"You did not."

"Sure I did. I Saw It, and you, in a Vision when I was fourteen."

"Yeah? What was I doing?"

"Gesturing to me."

"Like this?" She crooked one finger at him. "Or like this?" The other hand dropped to his thigh and moved up.

"Or this . . ." Taking his hand, she drew him to his feet, leading him toward the wagon at the far end of the encampment. Martin swallowed.
"Yes, like that."

That spring, his vows delayed yet another month, when Carla and her family left their winter camp for the open road, Martin went with them.

"You should come to the service."

Martin and Carla had been together for almost a year. They'd spent the summer months in Heathland on Armistone lands just north of the border, returning south when the nights began to turn cold. They'd wintered in Kraburn near Halmouth Port where he'd been born and now were heading north once again. At the Essusiate Shrine of St. Stephan's just outside of Albangate in Branshire, they stopped for a few days to worship and trade with the Clerics, Sister Maxine and Brother Duncan. Martin had remained with the wagons, speaking prophecy for the locals and watching the horses. Now he gave Carla an amused glance.

"Oh, sure."
"Why not?"
He laughed. "Because I'm a Triarch."
"So? You were born a Essusiate."
"Right, but I'm not one now."
"Once in, never out."
"That's my problem."
She nodded sagely. "I can see that."
"What do you mean?"
"I mean you can see the conflict tearing you up inside. Come to a service, you'll feel better. No one's asking you to convert, or rather return, but if you reconciled with the God, I'll bet your headaches would stop and your sleeplessness, too. Then you could ease off the ox-thistle."

"Yeah, I could ease off the ox-thistle because my head would probably cave in from the pressure of apostasy."

"Brother Duncan's awfully cute. My friend Tanner and I had him together two years ago."

"So?"

"So, we could have him together now. You know you'd like that."

"Again, so? I don't have to go to a service to have sex with some Cleric, you'd just have to bring him to our wagon."

"You scared?"

"To anger four Aspects, one God, an amphisbane, and a dragon? Oh, no, of course not."

"They're already angry. This way you might win over one of them at least, maybe even two."

"Yeah, the wrong two, no thanks."

She sat down beside him. "Why did you come with us, Martin?" she asked, her pale eyes serious.

"For the sex."

"You could've had plenty of sex at the Flame Temple. Why did you come with us?"

He took her hand. "For you. You know that."

"So you're planning on staying with me for a while, then?"

"Maybe."

"Maybe. Then what?"

"I don't know."

"Back to the Flame Temple?"

He looked away. "No. I doubt they'd take me back. Not now."

"Then you have to do something else with your life."

"What would you suggest?"

"Stay with us. Be a tinker and a Hedge Seer. Be my husband."

"I already am according to your mother."

"Be mine in my faith as well as in my bed. I'm an Essusiate. You used to be one. Come back to us. Stay with us. Stay with me."

She took his face in her hands and kissed him deeply on the mouth.

It took two days to convince him, but finally she won him over.

"They'll know I'm not an Essusiate," he protested weakly as Carla led him past the double line of poplar trees to St. Stephan's.
"How?"
"I, uh, I don't have a beard."
She began to laugh.
"What?"
"You're barely seventeen, Martin, you can't even grow a beard yet."
"I am shaving, you know."
She gave him an amused look.
"At least twice a week," he added.
"Here." Swiping at his hair, she dropped it over his forehead. "There, now you look thirteen if you look a day."
Angrily he shoved the hair back.
She laughed again. "Look, no one will notice," she reassured him. "No one your age wears a full beard yet. Even if they are shaving . . . at least twice a week. Come on."
They reached the Shrine as the first strains of music whispered through the door. Just beginning the Greeting, the Junior Cleric, Brother Duncan smiled out at them, and taking Martin's arm, Carla led him inside.

"Essus, we, your children, pray for your love and for your blessing always."
Sister Maxine raised her hands before the altar and the gathered stood, ready to speak the ancient reply.
"We pray for our poor."
"Grant them respite."
"We pray for our sick."
"Grant them healing."

"We pray for our dying."

"Grant them peace in your arms at the end of life."

"We pray for ourselves."

"We pray that you might see our needs and bestow fortune upon us."

She turned. "Let all who need ask, now ask."

Carla poked him in the ribs again.

He frowned at her. "What?"

"Ask?" she whispered.

"Ask what?"

"Ask Essus for healing."

"Are you out of your mind?"

"What harm could it do?"

"Plenty," he hissed. Three people turned to glare at him, and he lowered his voice. "It's not that simple. You can't flip-flop from one deity to another. It's too dangerous."

"You did it once."

"Yes, and it got a man killed, then took three years of ceremonies and prayer to fully dedicate me to the Triarchy."

"You were born to Essus," she insisted. "I'll bet it would take Brother Duncan a lot less time to bring you back."

"No." Clenching his fists, he pressed them against his temples. "I can't. I can't risk it."

"Essus, we stand before you in your consecrated Shrine to beg your indulgence and your blessing upon our brother, Martin Grayam. He has been long absent from your arms, yet we know that you have not turned your face from his spirit. We pray that you may receive him back into your keeping."

Carla's family had remained in Albangate for nearly a month so that she and Martin might be married at St. Stephan's Shrine. Brother Duncan had spent hours with the ex-Triarchy Seer, teaching him the ways of his

mother's God and praying on his behalf. Now Martin and
Carla knelt before the altar as the Cleric began the dedication ceremony.

*"Essus, we stand beside our brother, Martin Grayam,
who comes before you to pledge himself to your worship."*

*Around him the Shrine slowly faded before an ever-
growing white light. Having expected something metaphysical to occur, Martin brought all his concentration to
bear to keep from showing his reaction as he began his
own, silent bargain with the Gods.*

"Essus, I come to reconcile the worship of my birth
with the worship of my Vision."

*"We ask that you accept him into your keeping as your
child on this earth."*

*A sharp pain began to throb in his left temple as flames
began to dance before his eyes.*

"I ask that you accept me, flawed as I am."

*His head felt like it was about to split apart, the white
light so bright he had to squeeze his eyes shut to keep
from being blinded. Far above him he heard a high-
pitched whine, like a thousand midges hovering above his
head. The whine became a howling scream, drowning out
Brother Duncan's words. The veil between the worlds
cracked apart and Merrone, White Dragon Guardian of
Essus, took form to reclaim Its worshiper. Martin had to
make his thoughts shout to hear himself over the creature's triumphant shriek.*

"And divided in my loyalties, understanding that I cannot renounce the Triarchy which has gifted me with the
powers of a Seer."

* * *

*The crimson-scaled amphisbane appeared as quickly,
bursting outward from a nest of fire.*

*The two ancient enemies rose up on either side of him
as they had so many years ago, then came together with
an explosion of light and sound. Crouched beneath them,
Martin clapped his hands to his skull.*

*They fought for what seemed like hours, lashing out sav-
agely at each other, each strike resounding in Martin's head.
Something deep within his mind begin to tear and wounds
began to appear on his face and neck. He swayed. The world
around him darkened. Then he saw the Shadow Catcher
squeezing out from the Aspects' Realm. Turning Its empty
eye sockets full on his face, It began to slowly descend on Its
spider thread of shadow. Martin scuttled backward.*

"No."

*The Captain of the Dead drew nearer, called by the bat-
tle still raging between Merrone and the amphisbane.
Martin's mouth went dry.*

"Help."

It reached out for him.

"Help me!"

*His mind streaked out, seeking anyone who might come
between himself and the terrible manifestation. The Flame
Temple rose up before him. He Saw a Circle of Power,
Saw Urielle DeSandra standing in a swirling vortex of
fire, her gaze two pools of brilliant light.*

"Help me, please!"

* * *

They locked eyes for a single instant, then she smacked his Vision so hard the three metaphysical creatures were flung from the world.

"HE IS AT ST. STEPHAN'S SHRINE. FIND HIM AND BRING HIM BACK."

"Go together with Essus' blessing as husband and wife."

Martin blinked. Beside him, before St. Stephan's altar, Carla smiled as she took his hand.

He stared at her.

"They're coming," he whispered.

"Who?"

"The Flame Temple. They know I'm here. They're coming."

"You're not going alone!"

Martin continued to pull his traveling boots on, ignoring Carla's frantic words. Finally she grabbed him by the arm.

"Martin!"

He caught her by the shoulders.

"Six wagons can't outrun an entire company of mounted Flame Champions," he hissed. "We'd be caught, and your whole family would be arrested."

"Our whole family!"

"Fine, yes, right, our whole family. I won't put you all in that kind of danger."

"Then we run, just the two of us."

He opened his mouth to protest, and she almost slapped him.

"Don't you dare say it!" she shouted. "Don't you dare! You're my husband, my man! If you go, I go, or I'll kill you myself!"

He shook his head in frustration. "Tinkers! All right, fine, then. Hurry up and get packed."

*   *   *

If Osarion DeSandra hadn't been leading the company, they might have made it.

The Flame Champions ran them down on the banks of the Drey River. Kaliana DeKathrine knocked the knife from Martin's hand and, with one blow from the flat of her sword, sent him tumbling into the water. Airik DeKathrine caught Carla through the ribs. They dragged Martin's unconscious body from the river, then headed back for the Flame Temple, leaving Carla lying on the riverbank. A few minutes later, her family crept from the bushes. They took up her body and buried her beneath a willow tree beside St. Stephan's Shrine, Brother Duncan standing weeping silently beside them. Then they packed up their wagons and made for Heathland.

"Go in safety knowing you have Essus' blessing."

The service was over. When the small number of worshipers passed under the line of poplar trees, Martin kissed Carla's name on the front of the headstone, then rose and entered the Shrine. Resisting the urge to drop to his knees before the God's image, he made his way up the short central aisle.

The Cleric was tidying up the altar, blowing out the candles and folding up the altar cloth. He turned as Martin came up to the railing. His eyes widened.

"Martin?"

"Brother Duncan."

"A long time."

"Years."

"Did you, um . . ." The Cleric gestured at the railing hesitantly. "Did you want a blessing?"

"Best not. I'm on Flame Temple business."

"I see. They took you back, then?"

"After a while."

"Well, that's, um . . . You're looking good."

"You, too." Martin glanced up at the multicolored

stained-glass window behind the altar. "It's still so beautiful," he said wistfully. "I dream about this place sometimes, you know. Funny, isn't it? After all this time it still
brings me comfort."

"I'm glad." The Cleric looked away. "You never should
have left us," he said after a moment.

"I had to. You'd have been in danger if the Flame
Champions had found me here, you and St. Stephan's
both."

"I suppose. I'm just about to go in to supper. Did
you . . . want to join me?"

"I probably shouldn't."

"Sister Maxine's away. It would just be you and me.
We could catch up on old news." He came forward.
"You're always welcome, Martin," he said. "Not just for
Carla's sake, but for your own. Come for supper."

Smiling sadly, Martin nodded. "All right."

The next morning they shared an early breakfast of
bread and cold venison before Martin set out again.
They'd talked until well past midnight, Martin finally
breaking down in the Cleric's arms. Afterward they'd
made love quietly, then laid there talking about Carla until
Martin had finally fallen asleep. Now Brother Duncan
walked him to the road and handed him a full goatskin of
wine.

"Don't take so long to visit next time," he prodded gently. "Just because the Triarchy's reclaimed you doesn't
mean you have to forget your brothers and sisters in
Essus. You'll always be one of us."

"I'll remember."

"Good. Well, go in safety, brother." He raised one hand
in a brief wave.

"Remain in holiness," Martin answered with a smile.
"Brother."

He turned so he wouldn't see the blessing he knew
Brother Duncan would sketch behind him, then made his

way through the line of poplar trees and back to the north road.

He walked all day under a sky as overcast as his mood. Just before dusk he reached the Albangate Flame Temple, and with a sigh, climbed the short flight of stone steps and entered the central nave. The Triarchy must have Its worship in equal balance with Essus. That had been the bargain he'd struck in the dungeons of the Branbridge Flame Temple to keep what was left of his sanity, and he kept to it as best he was able in Carla Armistone's memory.

Ten days later saw him on Tilligham Common just south of the Kenneth Forest.

Since leaving St. Stephan's Shrine he'd dipped in and out of trance continuously, passing through small towns and smaller villages without a second glance. He'd crossed barley fields, pasturelands and apple orchards, watched a hawk hover almost stock-still over a field north of Eaverden, and listened to the faint sounds of a hunting horn far to the west in the Hopsfield Woods without really taking any of it in.

This day he'd walked for a long time along a poorly tracked road seeing no one except the occasional Coney Catcher in the distance. At noon he ate a light meal of bread and hard cheese, then continued walking until the sun set. It was a cool, clear night, perfect for traveling, and he carried on, staring up at the stars and thinking about his life and the choices he'd made. As the full moon rose over the hills, illuminating every blade of grass on the common, he could Feel the boy doing a working in concert with the others. Perching on a small hillock, he sent his mind out tentatively.

He hadn't thought much about the boy in the last few days; the past had had a much stronger grip on his mind than the future. The boy's abilities had grown since that night long ago when Martin had first Seen him in Vision. He was more proficient at handling the Wind's power, and at juggling Martin, the not-thing, and the others who worked with him to forge an increasingly strong bond with the Triarchy's Aspects. But each night he and Martin flew alone together, both content to keep their distance, neither willing to jeopardize their shared sense of freedom by getting too close, but soon . . .

With a grimace, he leaned his chin against his palm. Soon he would have to know just how far into danger or into heresy the boy had flown. On that night there would be no more flights in companionable silence. There would be only conflict, betrayal, and banishment from the peace and friendship they had known. As there always was.

Feeling overwhelmingly sad, he stopped for the night, building a small fire in the lea of a fallen beech tree and, wrapped tightly in his cloak, stared broodingly into the flames until he fell asleep.

The next morning dawned misty, cold, and drizzling with rain. He remained where he was, protected from the elements, until the fog began to burn off, then made for Crowsfield on the border of the Kenneth Forest. He spent two days hovering indecisively at the edge of the trees, until the sound of horse bells drew him to a nearby encampment. That night, surrounded by Heathland Tinkers once again, he dreamed of the boy.

He was spinning chaotically out of control, one moment soaring through the clouds, the next falling suddenly without warning, the next shooting off in random directions. His instability sent Martin into a similar tailspin, forcing him into the moth form for the first time in weeks. Gyrating like a dervish, he kept dropping dangerously close to the not-thing's net which sprang up, eager to trap him like a fly in a spider's web, and finally the boy broke contact.

Martin awoke with a jerk, listening to his heart echo the rumble of thunder in the distance, and realizing that whatever was to come it was now out of his hands. The boy had crossed over into manhood and the Wind had claimed him, just as both the amphisbane and the white dragon of

Essus had claimed Martin four years before. The Gods would play out their game with what pawns they chose, but if they were very lucky, the pawns might come out unburned for once. But he doubted it.

Lying back down, Martin pulled his blanket more tightly about his shoulders and willed himself to sleep. He had a long road still to walk before the game was over. He'd need his rest.

9. The Trap

Tavencroft Keep, Kairnbrook
Mean Fhomhair 492 DR, early autumn

BY the end of the summer the trees of Kairnbrook were beginning to turn. The orchards were laden with nearly ripened apples and pears, the barley heads had begun to droop, and the rye fields had transformed the landscape into a sea of undulating yellows and browns. As Cam led his horse from the keep, he turned his face to the warmth of the rising sun and breathed in the faintest taste of frost. It would be an early winter; he could feel it on the breeze.

He glanced up at the sky, checking the movement of the clouds. Kairnbrook would be far different than Guilcove or even Branbridge in the winter; colder, more prone to storms—windier. He could look forward to that now that his mother's letter had confirmed his stay until spring.

A stray cloud passed over the sun.

Now that *Alec's* letter from the Continent had confirmed his stay until spring.

He could look forward to it, he told himself firmly, and he would, for as long they wanted him to stay away. He glared out at the unoffending hills. He could stay here forever if he wanted to. His uncle had said so. This was his home. He was with family. He *was* family. Mounting up, he forcibly pushed all thoughts of his brother aside, then turned his horse west toward the Washe.

The disappointment over Alec aside, it had been a mo-

mentous summer, the changes he'd gone through so
dizzying it made his head spin just to think of them. It
seemed like forever since he'd knelt alone before the
Wind Temple's tiny rose window and sent his mind flying
out over the streets of the capital. Forever since he'd felt
the feather light touch of the Wind on his thoughts and
nothing else. Now, when he reached out for the breeze, he
was buoyed up by the combined might of all four Aspects
working in concert within the Circle of Their Chosen
Champions. He could Feel Dani churning the ocean
waves into froth, Quin sinking deep into the earth, and
Lisha burning with a heat so intense it was almost white.
If he needed to, he could call on any one of them to add
the power of their abilities to his, and they would respond.
It had enabled him to soar higher and fly farther than he
ever had in his life, but some days he found himself long-
ing for the solitary peace he'd known when it was just the
Wind and the clouds and the birds.

But there was no going back now. Two weeks after his
entry into manhood, Quin's abilities had also begun to
peak. This had left Lisha lagging behind, but Vincent had
assured her that the DeMarians often matured late. She
would cross over soon enough and then the Circle would
be balanced by four adult Champions able to access the
full breadth of their Aspects' power. When that happened,
nothing could stand in their way. Nothing except one
man. Camden frowned.

The Circle had continued to meet every evening at Pri
Gorwynne's cottage, the youths acting together to
strengthen their working bond, while the adults waited to
spring their trap on the Branion Seer. So far they'd met
with frustrating defeat. Although the Circle could sense
his presence, since Kether had smacked him away from
Cam, the Seer had kept his distance, never coming too
close, but always there, like a shadow in the corner of the
eye that disappeared when looked at directly. The others
had grown so used to his constant presence that they'd
begun to slowly relax their vigilance as Cam had hoped

they would, but his uncle was not so easily mollified. Each evening he and the other adults set their trap, and each evening they came out of trance disappointed. It was only a matter of time before the Seer found the rent in the Mirror's net, but with Iain Jonstun waiting to be sent out, Celestus had decided it was time to go on the offensive.

"The dark of the moon is tomorrow night. This will strengthen your bond with the Aspects and strengthen our bond with each other."

Seated at Pri Gorwynne's table, Celestus regarded the four youths seriously. "Camden, you will initiate limited contact with the Branion Seer and draw him toward the trap. From what we know about him, he should follow you readily enough. The rest of you will remain close by to shield Camden should the man attempt greater access and to help him disengage once the trap is sprung. The Seer may attempt to pull Camden into the trap along with him. If that happens, I rely upon you all to keep him safe."

Lisha looked up, her flame-sparked eyes concerned.

"What would happen if Cam did get caught in the trap, Uncle?"

Quinton chuckled. "Maybe his head would explode," *he offered gleefully.*

Cam glared at him. "What is it with you and heads exploding?"

"Nothing. It just stands to reason, doesn't it?"

"What does?"

"That it's bound to happen sometime."

"Well, maybe when it does, you won't like it so much."

Refusing to be drawn into a fight, the other boy just laughed. "Maybe."

"This is a serious matter, boy," *Pri Gorwynne snapped.* "If your cousin were to get caught in the trap, his head certainly would not explode, but his mind might very well be injured, eh?"

"And that injury would reverberate throughout the Circle and impair its efficiency," *Kether added.*

Lisha nodded. "What affects one of us, affects us all."

"Especially in the link," Dani concluded.

Quin shot them both a sour look. "I was only joking, all right? I don't want to see Cam get hurt any more than the rest of you do."

"Then stay vigilant," Celestus replied, "and protect each other. Once the trap is sprung, I want you all out of trance and waiting for the adults to conclude the Seer's capture, preferably out of the cottage altogether. This man has powerful abilities. He'll fight us, and I don't want any of you close enough to be harmed. The safety of the entire Circle is of the utmost importance here. Do you understand?"

They nodded.

"And, Camden, I need you close enough to draw him toward the trap, but not so close that he gains so much as an inkling of your identity. This is very important. If you feel you haven't gained enough finesse to accomplish this, you need to tell us now."

Camden met his intent gaze.

"I can do it, Uncle," he answered.

"Very good. So we will meet back here tomorrow evening and see if we can't put an end to this man's continued interference. In the meantime, I think Jordan will have supper waiting for us by now."

"Aye, and I've a hot toddy that's waiting for me," Pri Gorwynne added.

"We'll say good night, then."

Standing, Celestus led the way from the cottage.

Splashing over the Washe, Cam stared down at the tiny bubbles in the sand with a pensive expression. His uncle had given him the perfect excuse to—if not stop, than at least delay—the attack against the Branion Seer. No one would have blamed him for not having the necessary control yet. He'd only just got used to the power fluctuations his entry into manhood had caused. Except that he was used to them and he did have the necessary control. Even if the rest of the Circle didn't realize this, Pri Gorwynne must. To deny it would mean that he didn't trust his own abilities, he believed he wasn't as powerful as the rest of them, he had something to hide, or he was afraid. Quin would believe the latter. Dani might, too.

Dismounting, Cam looped his horse's reins around a dead tree branch and, walking to the water's edge, he drew his sword. The blade gleamed in the dawn sunlight, and he squinted sullenly at his reflection. He wasn't afraid, he told himself, not of his powers, the Seer's powers, or anyone else's powers. And he hadn't gone along with his uncle's plan because he was afraid not to either. It was simple logic. They were going to catch the Seer anyway. If he didn't help them, they would think he wasn't committed to the Circle and they'd make him leave. And since Alec didn't want him, where would he go?

He pointed the sword's tip out level with the waterline and began a series of slow figure eights. He didn't know the Seer, his thoughts continued. Why should he risk everything to protect him?

He looked down to see the giant moth pressed against him, trembling with fear.

Cam took a swipe at the air. So what, he argued. The Seer was an adult. And a really powerful and dangerous one, too, according to Uncle Celestus. He should be able to break free of any trap even if it was three against one.

His last sight was the creature tumbling away, out of control.

That wasn't his problem, he countered. If the Seer was so fragile, how come he was messing about where he shouldn't be?

The Seer's desperate need for stability, for peace, had drawn him to their Circle, and once he'd Seen how close he was to madness, Cam could not turn him away.

*   *   *

"Well, you should have turned him away," he said aloud. "If you had, you never would have got tangled up in all this in the first place."

Night after night, they'd flown silently together, never actually touching, until morning had separated them once again.

"I don't care," he retorted, driving his weapon into an imaginary assailant. "I don't need anyone to fly with. I'm happiest flying by myself. I always have been."

He let the sword point drop until it drove into the sand at his feet. "Besides," he added, addressing himself sternly, "You're a heretic. *Heretics* don't make friends with *Seers* because eventually the Seers get the heretics arrested and executed. That's the way the world works. So if you don't want to be arrested and executed, and you don't want your cousins to be, you'll get yourself to Brace Cottage tonight, and you'll help Uncle Celestus catch the Branion Seer and take him out because he's a gigantic threat to you and your family just like Dani said he was, no matter what he *Feels* like. And you won't feel guilty about it, and you won't ever think about it again. So just shut up."

Thrusting the sword back into its scabbard with unnecessary force, he returned to his mount, still unconvinced.

That evening the six of them made for Pri Gorwynne's cottage after the sun had fully set. With no moon to guide them, Celestus carried a lantern in front and Kether behind, but the light was still scant and they moved in silence, concentrating on the shadowy path beneath their feet.

Walking just behind Lisha, Cam touched the breezes wafting around them, absorbing the messages they brought to him about each of them. His uncle, grimly determined to succeed tonight, Dani and Quin openly excited whatever the outcome, Lisha, calm and confident, her DeMarian nature buried deep beneath an unusually stable exterior, Kether unreadable as always, and Cam himself, nervous and fretful, trying to ignore an increasing sense of guilt as the path brought him closer and closer to his part in the Branion Seer's imminent capture.

An owl flew silently overhead, intent on the hunt and Cam touched its mind briefly, enjoying its sense of simple purpose before leaving it sitting in an oak tree. He couldn't be distracted tonight as much as he wanted to be. There was too much at stake. The owl stared after him as he left the trees, his own mind bent toward a decision he still hadn't made.

He'd worried about the evening's working most of the day. Breakfast was nearly over when he returned to the keep with storm clouds chasing him from the Washe. By the time he'd finished the plate Jordan had saved for him, it was pouring rain. After a desultory morning of academic lessons which pleased no one but Quin, the four youths took their noon meal in the tower room, then lounged about, staring morosely out the one unshuttered window at the rain pelting against the gray slate roofs, and sniping at each other. Finally Dani had surged to her feet, intent on a fight.

"I'm bored!"

Quin glanced up from the book he was reading. "So what do you want to do?"

"I want to go swimming!"

Crossing to the south window, she leaned her arms on the sill and glared at the dripping forest beyond as if it were responsible for ruining her day.

Quin shrugged. "It's too cold. Besides, it's raining."

"No kidding?" She turned, her tone sarcastic. "I hadn't noticed."

Quin raised his hands. "Don't take it out on me, it's not

*my fault. You're the Sea's Chosen, why don't you make it
stop?"*

"You think I can't?"

"Did I say that?"

*Seated at the table, Lisha and Cam exchanged a
glance.*

"I could," Dani continued.

"Sure, you could."

*Quin's tone was deliberately condescending, and Dani
took a step forward.*

*Lisha rose. "No one can change the weather, Quin. You
know that," she said in a conciliatory manner. "Why don't
we just explore the keep."*

*"I've been over every square inch of the keep," Dani
retorted. "I'm bored with exploring the keep."*

"We could play hide and seek," Quin suggested.

She gave him a withering sneer. "That's a baby game."

*He rose, his face flushing angrily, and a sudden wind
surged through the window between them with enough
force to knock their hair into their eyes.*

"Cut it out."

*They both turned on Cam, who returned their allied in-
dignation with a dark expression. Setting down the knife
he was sharpening, he stood. Dani balled up her fists, but
Quin just shook his head.*

*"What I meant to say before Captain Tactful here
started on me was we should play hide and seek but with
a twist. One of us hides and sends out a call through the
Circle. The rest of us spread out and try and pick up the
call to find them. That way it's not a baby game."*

*Intrigued, Dani nodded. "Good idea," she said,
smoothly reversing her position. "That way if we get
nabbed by an adult we can say we're practicing, 'cause
we are."*

*"But Lisha hasn't crossed over yet," Cam pointed out.
"It wouldn't be fair."*

*"Oh, right." Quin glanced over at the DeMarian girl in
apology.*

"Lisha has more power than all three of us put together even without crossing over yet," Dani countered before her cousin could answer. *"Right?"*

Lisha shrugged. *"That's what Pri Gorwynne says."*

"Then it's settled. Come on. We'll start in the kitchens."

Quin grinned. *"About time, I'm starved."*

"You just ate, you greedy pig."

"Shut up."

"You shut up."

"You make me."

"Don't think I won't . . ."

Dani and Quin's argument continued down the tower stairs as Cam pulled Lisha aside.

"Are you sure?" he asked seriously.

She nodded. *"I've always had more power because I'm a DeMarian. This might actually be the last time we're really balanced. Besides, like Dani said, it's good practice and something we should be doing anyway. We might not always be together, so we should work on a distance link."*

Dani's and Quin's continued argument floated up to them, and Lisha took Cam's hand.

"Come on before they push each other down the stairs."

Catching up his knife, he replaced it in his belt sheath with a snort. "We couldn't get so lucky."

They started in the east range kitchens, and after prying Quin away from the dripping pan, they set the rules. As usual Dani would begin. She would find an out-of-the-way place in the keep somewhere, and in exactly five minutes the others were to head out in opposite directions. Five minutes after that, she'd send out the call. If the others hadn't found her by the time the north tower bell rang, they would meet back at the kitchens.

She took off at a dead run.

Lisha counted off the minutes, then sent first Quin and then Cam out after her.

* * *

Leaning against the east range balcony, Cam studied the inner courtyard. Quin had probably gone north—the Oaks' metaphysical direction, so he decided to go south. Passing their tower entrance, he pushed open the heavy oaken door to the south range storage rooms then, without bothering to take a candle, made his way down the wide, stone steps.

The storage rooms were cool and damp. In the heat of the summer the youths had often gone exploring under the keep. Dani knew every unlocked door in the place and could open almost any locked one. They'd spent most of the rainy days teaching Cam the keep's secrets, leaving him to find his own way back on more than one occasion.

One day when they'd all disappeared, Cam had found himself walking down a long, rough-hewn corridor under the south range, his candle flickering sporadically. It had begun to climb and soon he'd come to a small, wooden door. It was barred from the inside and, curiosity getting the better of him, he'd removed the bar, then taken hold of the rusty iron handle and pulled. The door had opened into the rocky, gorse-entangled underbrush below the keep. Off to the right, a small creek meandered its way underneath a tiny barred gate, heading for one of several wells inside. Cam had enjoyed a few moments' fresh air. Then, having got his bearings, he rebarred the door and returned to their tower without telling the others what he'd found. It became his special place where he came when he didn't want anyone else to find him; where he could be alone to think things through without being interrupted by cousins so much faster at it than he was.

Now he walked quickly down the corridor, running the fingers of his left hand along the wall to keep his balance in the darkness. When he came to the end, he removed the bar, forced the door partially open, then turned and tucked his knife into a corner next to a tin box holding a few candle stubs and a flint and tinder. He liked to think of this place as his own private bolt-hole—even though he sup-

posed his uncle Celestus knew it was here—and was
slowly collecting the things he thought he might need
should he ever have to make a run for it. Once he'd
brought a bit of bread wrapped in a handkerchief, but
when he'd returned, it was gone. Rats, probably. He supposed he'd just have to remember to bring food with him,
but he needed a knife. If he was running from the Flame
Champions, he might not have time to grab a weapon.

He straightened, staring out at the gray sky with a pensive expression. And the fastest way to end up running
from the Flame Champions, he told himself, was to forget, even for a moment, the very real threat the Branion
Seer posed. To trust him, feel sorry for him, warn him.

Squatting down, he leaned his back against the door,
feeling the rain patter against his cheeks.

He should turn around right now, go back to the more
populated areas of the keep and wait for Dani's call and
leave the Seer to his own devices.

He closed his eyes. His mind slid easily into a light
trance, floating just above his head on the tiniest of
breezes. He would reach for Dani as he was supposed to
do. That was all.

His thoughts rose over the keep. He felt the presence of
the others below him, muted by Tavencroft's stone walls.
Bending his thoughts toward Dani's signature, he reached
down, then slowly turned toward the Bricklin Forest. He
would send one visual warning then disengage. He owed
him that much at least. Opening his mind, he threw himself onto the tails of a strong head wind going south and
was gone.

At first all he could sense were trees and brush, deer,
birds, and the clumps of unknown people gathered around
rivers and streams that represented hamlets and villages.
Then, very faintly, he sensed a familiar presence. He
reached out, touched the Seer's thoughts and . . .

COME TO ME!

* * *

Dani's call sent a bolt of pain ricocheting through his head, snapping him back into his body. Grabbing for his temples, he sent an angry query back, but the reply was no less vehement.

"NOW!"

Forcing himself to stand, he reached out to the south again, but all sense of the Branion Seer was gone. Shaking his head, he made his way back along the corridor, heading for the gatehouse where he'd Seen Dani waiting. Obviously, this wasn't going to work. He'd have to try again later.

He never got the chance. The others were already there when he arrived, Dani so excited that she dragged them off immediately to report their triumph to her father. They spent the rest of the afternoon working on distance contact with Celestus keeping careful track of their individual progress. Too soon, it was time to leave for Brace Cottage.

Walking between Lisha and Kether, Cam tried to put his feelings of guilt and doubt aside. The Seer would just have to take care of himself. Cam had run out of time to warn him.

Pri Gorwynne was waiting for them at the door. The cottage was dark, the only light coming from the low fire in the hearth, and smelled of elder wood and basil. As they entered, the ex-Priest handed both Celestus and Kether cups of steaming brandy.

"For strengthening, eh."

Dani gestured the others toward their places, then turned.

"None for us, Pri?"

"You're too young."

Celestus smiled at her indignant expression. "The

young are always strong enough," he said. "It's only the old who need assistance."

Mollified, Dani took her own place. The others had already begun the ritual breathing and now she joined in, counting off each breath until they were all moving in unison, then, without waiting, she dropped into trance. Quin followed, then Lisha.

Still unsettled, Cam continued to breathe, watching the subtle changes that came over his cousins as they merged with their individual Aspects. If he concentrated hard enough he could See Dani's consciousness leave her body and seep through the cottage walls toward the Washe and the open Sea, Quin's, with hands pressed flat against Pri Gorwynne's braided rug, sink down through wool and wood to the dark earth below, then spread up through the branches of the Bricklin's many oak trees, and Lisha's dancing hypnotically in time with the flickering fire, the hearth glowing with a deep, metaphysical, crimson glow. Only Cam still remained within the confines of his own body. He could Feel the Wind waiting for him, calling to him, urging him to throw all his troubles away and come and play. That was all he was waiting for. With a deep breath, he made himself relax, then flung his own consciousness out through the window. The freest of the Four Aspects caught him up in a fierce, swirling embrace, then the two of them raced off to tear a jagged line through a nearby rye field.

For a long time Cam was content to simply fly, stretched out across the sky on the wings of the strongest wind, but eventually he turned, spinning about a hilltop bier until he caught a delicate breeze and whispered down into a meadow of tall grasses. He scattered the raindrops across a badger's pelt, whistled through a shepherd's alder pipe, then drifted along a mousehole, ruffling the fur of the tiny creatures inside. Having merged completely with the Wind, he'd forgotten all about the Circle and its intent that evening, but soon enough, he Felt the others reach for him.

He ignored them. Mesmerized by the ripples his passage made against the surface of a mountain pool, he drew closer and closer until the water reared up to swamp him, then he soared away to rustle through the fallen leaves in the Kenneth Forest. The brush tried to entangle him and he evaded it easily, his laughter dancing over the clouds. He swirled around the lamplighters of the capital, hovering just close enough to send the flames flickering madly, then shot away before they could catch him, knocking over chimney pots and loosening roof tiles all along the road to Westborough. Then, spinning around the Flame Temple spires, he tasted the awesome psychic power housed within. He paused, and the Wind swelled with another presence.

"CAMDEN!"

Pri Gorwynne's angry voice nearly knocked him back into his body.

"RETURN AT ONCE!"

For an instant he rebelled, then, as her summons came again, he flew back sullenly, sending a gust of wind whooshing down the cottage chimney before dropping down through the Physical Realms.

His surroundings blurred and changed as he drew close to the Prophetic Realm. Kether's protective net stretched out above him like a giantic web, the three adults crouched in the center like spiders. Around him, he could Feel his cousins waiting for him, and although there were no physical directions in this place, somehow he knew that they had arranged themselves to the west, north, and south as they always did.

He reached out for them, and they responded at once.

His sense of self disappeared as the four of them came

together, bands of red, green, blue, and gray energy flowing around them and through them and binding them together into one bright circle of power. As Cam gave
himself over to their embrace, he lost all sense of doubt
and fear.

Far away, in Pri Gorwynne's cottage, the four youths
breathed in perfect unison as, in their own Realm, the ancient Primordial Aspects of Wind, Oaks, Sea, and Flame
rose up together to merge with their Chosen Champions.
Filled with an overwhelming sense of unity, Cam gave
himself over to the sensation.

As usual, it was Dani who took command, sending a
power pulse of memory rippling through the Circle to remind them of their duty. The others made ready as Cam
obediently formed an image of the Branion Seer in his
mind and reached out for him.

Contact came immediately. For a single heartbeat the
two stared into each other's eyes, sharing each other's
thoughts and feelings, then under the pressure of the Circle's compulsion, they turned and Saw the trap.

The hole stood out like a jagged, black eye in the midst of
the net's reflective surface, and Cam Felt the other's sudden
eagerness to be complete. Unable to resist, the Seer shot toward it. Before Cam could react, the adults attacked.

The Tavencroft Lord in the lead, they slammed into the
Seer with a force so violent it sent shock waves crashing
through the Physical Realms. Pri Gorwynne cast a dozen
bands of power, as strong as steel, out to ensnare him as
Kether covered them all in layer upon layer of thick fog to
confuse his Sight, all the while Celestus hammered at his
identity like a battering ram.

The Seer fought back, throwing all of his own formidable abilities against them, but his control disintegrated as
his desperation grew. As Celestus closed in, he flung his
mind out, seeking help from any source, and found Cam.
His need scored across the youth's mind and, instinctively, Cam jerked forward, but forewarned, the others
snatched him away, cocooning him in a tight ball of pro-

tective power. They began to drag him off, struggling to leave trance as Cam fought their constraint, fought to reach the Seer whose need now battered against his mind in a desperate tattoo. Pressure built inside his head, pressing against a gateway he'd never known was there and, with a sudden snap, he broke free, shooting down an ancient link between them, a link made of prophecy and fate forged before he'd been born. For an instant they were face-to-face, the dark-haired, haunted-eyed man and the golden-haired youth, and for Cam everything suddenly froze. He Saw the adults ready to strike a final blow, Saw the Seer reach for his aid to fend them off, and Saw his cousins ready to pull him to safety. For a single heartbeat, he stood poised on the brink of indecision, then his mind shot back down the link and into the arms of the Circle. The last thing he Saw before they burst from trance was the trap slamming closed with the Branion Seer on the other side. There was an explosion of light behind his eyes and then nothing.

He hovered in oblivion for a long time before his senses began to reassert themselves. A spark of light zipped across his inner vision like a comet, his heartbeat grew loud in his ears, and he smelled the sharp odor of autumn leaves, before he tasted both copper and salt on his lips. He stirred.

"He's coming 'round."

A voice. Groggily, he opened his eyes. Indistinct shapes hovered just beyond his vision, blanketed by a thick, gray veil.

"No, he's not. Look at his eyes."

Another voice. He blinked and some of the veil faded away.
A blue-haloed blob peered down at him.

*   *   *

"Will you please stop doing this, it's becoming a really annoying habit."

Dani. Her voice floated up to him from somewhere far away.

He blinked again, hard.

Somewhere far . . . above.

Physical sensations returned to him more swiftly now. He realized that she was sitting on his legs, pinning them to the ground. His rear was cold and damp. A rock pressed into his left thigh. But his back was warm. He stirred and felt the pressure of someone holding his arms tight to his chest and cradling him against their body.

Cam opened his mouth to speak, but the only sound that emerged was a rushing of air. It streamed out as a fine gray line, and where it touched, the veil disappeared a little bit more. He looked up. A freckled face surrounded by a bright green halo grinned down at him.

"Welcome back to the land of the living."

Quin.

Afraid that the stream of air would blow his cousin's face away with the fog, Cam just stared up at him. Quin shifted his grip on him.

"Well, your head didn't actually explode, but I appreciate the effort."

Cam managed to find his voice. "Maybe . . . next time," he croaked out. The working of his mouth and throat caused his ears to pop suddenly.

"Maybe," Quin answered in a hopeful tone.

"What . . . happened?"

"You tell us?"

Dani.

"Can we please see if he's all right first before you start interrogating him?"

Lisha. Uncharacteristically angry. He turned his head and her face, covered by a red mist, swam into view. Concerned.

"I'm . . . all right," he managed.

She shook her head. "Sure you are."

Dani chuckled as she moved off his legs. "C'mon, Cuz, let's get you up."

The ground fell away. For a second he hovered above it, then somehow he managed to get his feet properly set up and he stood, swaying dizzily. Hands gripped him.

"C'mon, Quin, let's get him back inside."

His left leg gave out under him.

"Scorch it! He weighs a ton. Help me on this side, will you, Lisha."

More hands took hold. He felt himself being moved and somehow he managed to get his feet working under him enough to help. The darkness of the yard became the darkness of the cottage and more hands caught hold of him there.

"Here, sit him down quick, children, before he falls down, mind."

Pri Gorwynne. She peered worriedly down at him, her eyes a bright, shining gray and he flinched away from their light.

"Here now, easy, boy."

The hands helped him into a chair.

"Lisha girl, have a look in that jug, will you? Is there anything left in it?"

"Yes, Pri."

"Get it in him, then."

He felt his head being tilted upward and then strong wine poured into his mouth. He almost spewed it back, but at the last moment he remembered how to swallow. The room cleared slightly.

"Is he all right?"

His uncle. He turned, his head lolling slightly to one

side. Celestus was surrounded by a riot of colors, no one hue more brilliant than another. He grinned sloppily.

"Pretty."

Celestus frowned. "What did he say?"

"Gurble," Quin translated.

"He said, *pretty,*" Dani corrected, shoving Quin with her elbow.

"Sounded like gurble to me," he answered.

"No, it didn't."

Cam turned his eyes on her, watching her own halo flow back and forth across her features like the tide. He laughed. "Pretty," he repeated. Then he frowned. "I'm all right." He tried to stand, but his feet slid out from under him and he sat down hard. "Mostly."

Celestus peered into his eyes. "He hasn't fully left trance yet, Pri."

The ex-Priest joined him and Cam raised one finger to touch her gently between the eyes.

"Like me," he said. "Gray. Like the Wind."

"Aye, lad, like you and the Wind." She pursed her lips. "Can you close your eyes, Camden, eh? Can you do that for me?"

Cam obeyed, allowing the darkness to flow over him again. Pri Gorwynne's voice came to him as if from far away.

"What do you See, lad?"

He blinked. "Fog."

"Gray fog?"

He nodded.

"Is there anything in the gray fog?"

He frowned as a single image took form. "A tunnel, I mean a . . . corridor I think, like the one in the south range."

"Can you follow it?"

"Yes."

"Where does it lead?"

"To a door."

"Where does the door lead? Don't open it, mind, just tell me where it leads."

The fog was very thick. He was quiet for a long time, then he nodded. "To the Branion Seer."

"That link we felt, eh, Celestus? Does the door have a lock, Camden, or a bar maybe?"

"Yes. A bar."

"Is the bar in place?"

"No."

"Put the bar in place."

"Why?"

"So you'll be safe."

"Aren't I safe now?"

"No, lad. Now, put the bar in place like a good boy. Is it in place?"

"Yes."

"Good, now take my hand and come back out of trance. All the way out this time, mind, or I'll be right cross with you. Have you come out?"

"Yes."

"Then open your eyes."

He obeyed her again, moving his head back as five people, the lights around them dimmed to faint lines, leaned forward to stare at him.

"What?"

Pri Gorwynne straightened. "He's all right now. You're a sensitive one, you are," she added with a chuckle. "I can See all sorts of defensive work in your future."

He frowned. "What happened?"

Dani dropped into a chair beside him.

"You mean just now?"

"No, I mean with . . . the Seer." He turned to his uncle. "What happened with the Seer?"

"We caught him."

"Is he . . . ?"

Celestus tipped his head to one side. "Dead?"

Cam could only nod.

"No. The three of us haven't enough power to effect

that manner of assault, but we did hurt him, and we did discover his identity." His gaze encompassed them all. "His name is Martin Wrey and he's no more than a Priest of the Flame. Physically, he's no more than four days' distant, to the west in the Kenneth Forest."

Kether now came forward, the line of light around him silvery like the fine mirror he was named for. "You'll be sending Iain Jonstun out, then?"

"Yes, at once."

"I think we might want to take a short journey ourselves," he suggested. "With that link still in place, however tightly locked up, he might try and call on the boy again, especially if his life were in danger. Distance should negate the threat of it somewhat."

"Where do you suggest we journey to?"

"Heathland."

"Lochaber Castle." Dani's tone was aggrieved. "But it's Mean Fhomhair. We'll freeze our asses off!"

"Danielle."

"But, Da, you said we would go to Panisha this winter!"

"And we may yet, but for now I concur with Kether. We need to put immediate distance between ourselves and the Branion Seer. So pack warm clothes. We're going to Heathland, and we're leaving first thing tomorrow morning."

With a sour glare at her father, Dani stood. "All right, fine, but if I get frostbite swimming in the North Bjerre Sea, it'll be all your fault."

"I'm prepared to shoulder that responsibility."

"I'll bet." She turned to Cam. "Can you walk yet?"

"Yes."

"Good. Well, c'mon, then. If we're gonna pack, we'd better get home."

With one last frown at her father, she led the way through the door.

*   *   *

Walking between them in the darkness, one hand clasped firmly in Lisha's, Cam sent his mind tentatively south. Nothing. He envisioned the corridor, the door, the bar removed and leaning against the wall. Again nothing. Reluctantly, he brought his attention back to the task of walking down the dark path without treading on Dani's heels. He would try again later.

That night, and every night afterward, his dreaming mind searched the skies for signs of the Branion Seer. Both on the road and later in the heavily fortified Jonstun castle of Lochaber in Heathland, he would fly out on the tails of the Wind, calling him by name, but the Realms gave back nothing save an eerily echoing silence. Cam wouldn't Feel Martin's presence again for almost four years.

10. The South Bank

The Dog and Doublet Inn
Branbridge South Bank
Spring, Mean Boaldyn, 500 DR

CAM fell silent, staring pensively into his drink. Sarah leaned her elbows on the bar.

"And?" she demanded.

"And what?"

"And what happened next?"

Cam finished the contents of his tankard before making a dismissive gesture.

"We went to Heathland, like I said, and spent the next three years with the Jonstun family learning to be hill fighters."

"What about the Branion Seer?"

"What about him?"

"What happened to him?"

He waggled a finger at her. "That would be telling the story out of sequence."

She regarded him sternly for a moment then conceded the point. "Fine. What did you do in Heathland?"

He shrugged. "What most youths do, we studied, we trained, we expanded our abilities, both together and individually, especially after Lisha came into her own." He smiled. "It was during a skirmish with the Maccus Family. She nearly set an entire rye field on fire. Scared the wits out of everyone." He laughed. "We fought, we played, we had sex. We had *a lot* of sex," he added with a grin. "We grew up."

"And you never went home in all that time?"

"No."

"Why not?"

"There was no reason to. Alec was in Danelind trying to help Prince Marsellus avert a war that broke out anyway, my mother was at Court. Ler wrote me when she married Alec's best friend Desmond. The family wasn't too happy about it apparently, but I didn't care."

Sarah cocked her head to one side. "Why not?"

"Our father was dead, why shouldn't she marry again?"

"Wasn't there almost a twenty-year age gap between them?"

"So what? My mother always did have . . ." he shrugged again, "appetites. Besides, she was the Duke of Guilcove, the only permission she needed was the Aristok's, and he gave it easily enough. They had two and a half good years together. I wouldn't have denied it to them. They had Sandy—my sister Melesandra—in four-ninety-five, and then she died, thrown from her horse on a Royal Hunt south of the capital. Broke her neck. Aunt Maia sent us a message with Eaglanter, the First DeKathrine Herald, but we still had to scramble to get a ship south to Branbridge in time for her funeral."

"So you did go home for that?" Sarah's tone was faintly sarcastic, but Cam just nodded as if he hadn't noticed.

"Oh, yes, we were all there. Like I said, she was the Duke of Guilcove. Her status alone demanded full attendance. There must have been seven hundred people at her Funerary Mass. Two hundred DeKathrine relatives and a dozen DeMarians made up her Honor Guard back to Guilcove, including the Aristok himself." His expression softened as a faint gray light began to wash over his eyes. "As the sun came up and hit all those red sails, it looked like we were a fleet of spirit ships sailing out from the Shadow Realm. You could Feel the power of the Flame pulsing all around you, it was that strong. Lisha got so drunk on it we had to hide her belowdecks. It was the same at the interment."

"Did Alec attend?"

The gray light blinked out as if it had never been there.

"What?"

"Your brother Alexander, did he make it back from Danelind in time for the funeral and the interment?"

"He was the new Duke of Guilcove. Of course he made it back. He came with the Prince Marsellus on *Kassandra's Pride*." He paused. "They'd have waited for him anyway," he continued after a moment. "Our family always was very important to the Realm." With a shake of his head, he drained his tankard. "After all, we're the Foundation Stone of the Crown's power, aren't we?"

Sarah ignored the bitterness in his voice.

"Did the two of you speak?"

"What?"

"You and Alexander, did you speak?"

"No."

"Why not?"

"He was too busy."

"Cam . . ."

"He was *too busy,* Sarah. He had a great many responsibilities, not the least of which was hosting twelve members of Branion's Royal Family. He barely had time to piss, never mind chat with each one of his seven brothers and sisters."

"Chat?"

"You know what I mean. Besides, I had the Circle. I didn't need anyone else."

"Uh-huh."

"Sarah?"

"What?"

The tavern owner turned as Annie set a tray of clay mugs onto the bar. The Server jerked her head toward the taproom. "Jake and Marnik are about to set to again."

"Scorch it! Trevor!" Sarah snapped her fingers at her nephew, then headed around the bar with a snarl. "It's not even burning sunset. You," she turned a fixed gaze on

Cam's face. "Don't go anywhere. We're not finished talking yet."

"I've been talking all day. What am I, a traveling player?"

"You are today. Annie, don't let him leave."

She headed for the taproom with murder in her eyes as the Server took Cam's empty tankard with an even expression. "You want another one, Cam?" she asked.

He nodded. "I might as well. And some dinner, too, while you're at it. Confession's hard work."

The sounds of a struggle filtered in from the taproom.

"Good for the spirit, though," Annie noted.

They turned to watch as first one, then another body went sailing out the door.

"And better than the alternative," Cam agreed dryly.

"It is that." She leaned around to glance through the kitchen at the hearth. "Traz, is the joint ready yet?"

The cook shook his head and she turned back to Cam. "We got some cold lamprey pie in the larder. Will that do?"

"Admirably."

"Huh?"

"It'll do fine."

"Right."

She filled his tankard, then headed for the kitchen as Cam sipped his ale, wondering if Jake and Marnik had survived their flight. The sudden pounding on the door suggested they had.

He leaned back in his chair. Sarah was going to have her hands full for some time, but it looked as if it would be an entertaining evening. He supposed he could stay for a little while longer.

As it turned out, it was several hours before Sarah made it back to her place at the bar, and then she only stayed a few moments. With the five hundredth year anniversary celebrations well under way, the South Bank never slept and the Dog and Doublet was no exception.

The taproom was filled with sailors, traders, workers, even the occasional Knight or Priest, looking for revelry, and the Dog was happy to oblige, its prices rising with the noise level as the evening wore on.

Cam spent the early part of the night drinking with Trevor and helping him keep order but, as the moon rose over the River Mist, he grew bored and slipped away. He'd be back before Sarah noticed his absence, and even if he wasn't, she'd forgive him as long as she didn't have to fish him out of some flea-infested rat hole.

With that in mind, he headed for the docks.

Half a dozen open doorways beckoned to him along the way, but with some reluctance, he left them behind. He would do as Sarah wished even though he wasn't entirely certain why. He would sit and think and clear his head, then return to the Dog after the midnight crowd had passed out. She could pick his brains to her heart's content then if she had a mind to—much good it might do either of them. Turning his back on the rows of alehouses and brothels, he made for the abandoned Essusiate wharf of San Teres where it would be quiet and dark.

Stacks of lumber and empty packing crates impeded his progress as he picked his way carefully along the rotting pier, but eventually he reached the end. Sitting with his back against a mooring, he listened absently to the muffled cheering coming from the nearby dog-fighting pit. The Wind off the river caressed his cheek with the intimacy of a longtime lover, bringing him the taste of blood and wine and the heady sense of violence. It was a potent mix, one he hadn't tasted in a long time. Leaning his head back he closed his eyes, allowing the memories to resurface.

It was summer in Heathland. The Cheviot Hills were ablaze with blues, purples, and yellows, all mixed together in a riot of unfamiliar colors. The first time Celestus had allowed the four youths away from Lochaber Castle they'd stared, entranced, at the vast expanse of heather, gorse, and pine trees stretching out before them. Everything in Heathland seemed bigger, grander, or wilder: the trees, the lakes, even the wildlife. They pulled huge trout from the rivers, hunted roebuck twice the size of anything they'd ever seen at home through the dark, entangled forests, and stared up into the painfully blue sky to watch eagles and gryphons soaring high above their heads. Even the domesticated animals were exotic. For three years they'd gone on raids against the Maccus and Armistone family holdings, returning with dozens of the region's strange, red-haired cattle; DeKathrine cows, as Quin had called them. In spring and fall they'd followed their Jonstun hosts to battle, fighting on foot with the heavy dirk and claymore Tom Jonstun had taught them how to use. In winter they'd sat before the fire, wrapped in sheepskins and bearskins while storms that could last as long as a week tore at the slate roofs and pounded on the shutters. Marna knew a hundred stories of ancient Heathland, and night after night, she'd kept them entertained with outlandish tales of the great Jonstun Chieftains, powerful Battle Mages who could call the Hill Dragons down from their craggy peaks to do their bidding in the days before Essusiatism had enchained the Heathlanders as surely as the Triarctic Priests had enchained the Branions. And in summer when they'd gathered together in the meadow above the castle to join with their Aspects it was as if the physical world simply melted away. Cam had never felt so happy in his entire life.

The days before they were called home were some of the most beautiful they'd ever experienced. Free to roam through the hills, the four youths had trained and wrestled and run through the meadow grasses, until exhausted they'd flung themselves to the ground. The long summer days outdoors had tanned their skins and lightened their hair, Cam's and Dani's becoming almost white, Lisha's and Quin's a brilliant fiery copper. They'd quickly adopted the Heathland tunics and long braids and, although only Lisha had actually earned the battle right to

weave in the small pieces of her enemies' clothing—cour-
tesy of her fire in the rye field—they all had stories of bat-
tle to tell and retell to each other. Day after day they
would lie in the meadow, Dani and Quin absently throw-
ing clots of dirt and grass at each other while Lisha wove
tiny wild daisies and violas into Cam's hair.

This day Quin leaped over a collection of rocks before
spinning about on his heel, sliding sideways on the slick
grass just as Dani caught up to him. She barreled straight
into him and the two went down in a jumbled pile of arms
and legs. Moments later Cam and Lisha flung themselves
onto the pile.

Once he got his breath back, Quin laughed out loud.
"Heathland's a marvelous country," he declared, tossing
a pebble into the air. "The hills are so wild and unspoiled,
you could lose yourself in them forever and never miss the
sight of another human being."

"And starve to death," Dani added.

"Never. There's a hundred rivers to feed you, and in the
meantime, there's hills to climb, meadows to make love
in . . ." He winked at Lisha. "Fires to make in the
evening." He turned back to Dani. "Tell me you don't
miss Espalonia."

"I will not."

She aimed a swing at him just as Ross came running
through the bracken.

"Word's just come in," he said breathlessly. "Armis-
tones have raided a Jonstun farm south of here. Took
everything and burned the barn up. The Chief's called a
battle council. You're wanted at once."

"Excellent!" Quin leaped up immediately, the others
more slowly. Although Quin loved the battle councils with
their discussions of strategy and tactics, his cousins pre-
ferred action. Cam himself had no interest in talking
whatsoever, but as they'd make their silent way through
the hills toward some unsuspecting keep or farm, he
would feel his heart begin to pound with excitement. Then
he would send his mind outward to sense any stray Armis-

tone or Maccus sentry on the Wind, relaying his findings through the link before rushing down with the others. Then, after the fighting, as they made their way home along the dark, winding paths, the stars above them seemed to burn infinitely brighter, packed so densely in the clear sky that there was barely a speck of black left to be seen.

On the South Bank pier Cam opened his eyes, staring blankly up at the cloudy sky. He missed the Heathland stars terribly. On those warm summer nights they were so close it felt as if you could reach up and snatch a handful right out of the sky. The stars of Branion's capital were much paler, colder, and far more distant. They stared down at him accusingly, reminding him of every betrayal, every misjudgment, and every lie he'd told since leaving those free and innocent days behind.

He frowned angrily. He'd needed the lies to stay alive, he told himself harshly. There was no shame in that.

"And the lies you told Sarah tonight?"

"What lies?"

"The lies about Alec."

"They weren't lies."

"Weren't they?"

"No. Alec was busy at the funeral."

"And afterward?"

"Then, too."

"But not too busy to seek out his younger brother to comfort him. He came to you. You wouldn't speak with him."

"I couldn't."

"You mean you wouldn't."

"No. The others were there. I couldn't . . ." He shook his head in futility, unable to explain his rationale even to himself. *"I just couldn't . . . not with the others there."*

"And now?"

"Now it's too late."

                              *   *   *

The moon passed behind a bank of clouds. In the sudden darkness he almost heard his mind's reply spoken in Alisha DeMarian's voice.

"It's never too late while you're still alive, Cam."

He stood.

"Yes, it is, Lisha," he whispered sadly. "Because you're not alive."

Turning his back on the river, he headed for the Cock and Rabbit.

Bran's Bell had long since tolled the curfew before he made his way back to the Dog. The crowds had slackened off somewhat, the revelers giving way to the more serious drinkers, but there was still plenty of light and noise coming from the alehouses. The taverns might close down at eleven on the capital's North Bank where the close proximity of manors houses and upper class merchant businesses demanded a greater vigilance by the Town Watch, but here on the South Bank where the inns' only neighbors were cockfighting rings and gambling houses the Watch was more likely to be found inside than outside.

Cam was just drunk enough not to care where the Watch spent their time, but not so drunk that he was prepared to seek them out to start a fight. Weaving his way along the street, he took in a deep breath of the late night air, feeling it whisper through his lungs.

Something's happening.

Leaning against an unlit lamp pole, he allowed the Wind to tell him in Its own way.

Someone's crossed the river.

                              *   *   *

The misty image of a man wavered before his eyes, his identity just out of reach. With a recklessness caused by drink, Cam opened his mind fully, the Wind rushed into him, and the image snapped into focus. Elerion. His eyes gone completely gray, he turned to stare at the Dog's stout wooden door. Elerion was inside.

For a moment he considered returning to the Cock and Rabbit, but as the Wind played out its message completely, he reluctantly crossed the street. Something was happening, something important. His eyes returning to their more usual bloodshot blue, he entered the tavern.

The two DeKathrine brothers spotted each other at once. Elerion stood, his broad face concerned, but Cam gestured him back into his chair, then dropped down across from him.

"What are you doing here, Ler?" he asked bluntly.

"Looking for you. You have to come home, Cam."

"Tomorrow."

"No, now. Alec wants you."

Cam gave a faint snort. "It's the middle of the night, Ler. Only drunkards and heretics do business at this hour. All the righteous people are asleep in their beds."

"Not all of them."

"Then they should be. Whatever it is, it can wait until the morning."

"No, it can't." Elerion leaned forward. "Eaglanter's at Kathrine's Hall with an urgent message from Aunt Maia. Danielle's escaped from Broughgard Castle."

Cam grew very still.

"When?"

"Two days ago. Eaglanter's orders were to give us an hour's advance notice, then report to the Flame Temple, and you know what that means."

"Flame Champions."

Elerion nodded, his green eyes dark with worry. "She hasn't contacted you, has she, Cam?"

The younger man shook his head. "I haven't heard

from Dani in four years," he answered bitterly. "Alec saw to that."

Elerion flushed angrily. "Alec saw to it that you wouldn't end up in a heretic's prison or worse," he snapped back. "He probably even saved your life. Or had you forgotten that the daughter of the Aristok died four years ago?"

A flash of pain came and went across Cam's face. "No, Ler, I hadn't forgotten."

His brother took a deep breath. "Look, Cam," he said quietly, "I don't understand what happened between the two of you back then, and right now I honestly don't care. But you *have to come home.* Alec thought he might be able to keep Eaglanter at the Hall for an extra hour, but no longer. She'll be at the Flame Temple any minute if she's not there already, and with news this important they'll awaken the Archpriest at once. *She* won't waste time talking. She'll send her Champions out to scoop you up so fast you won't have time to blink. The family can protect you at home, but we can't protect you here."

Cam bared his teeth at the other man. "I'm not asking the family to protect me anywhere," he growled.

"Are you expecting *them* to?" Elerion's gesture took in the entire tavern. "Could they resist an armed company of Flame Champions?"

Cam snorted. "No one here would be stupid enough to try."

"They wouldn't have to be. If even so much as one drunken patron raised a voice in protest, the Flame Champions would arrest every last one of them for conspiracy. How many people could you watch dragged out of here, knowing what's in store for them, before you surrendered yourself? You, at least, have the protection of a noble name. What do they have?"

Cam remained silent.

"This is a family matter," Elerion continued urgently. "If you want to keep your freedom and protect the people you care about, you have to come home and let us stand together as a family."

Cam gazed at him blankly. "Like you did the last time?"

Elerion shook his head wearily. "I *tried* to see you, Cam," he replied. "*Jo* tried to see you. They wouldn't let any of us near you. Alec had to personally petition the Aristok to even get a message to you. Do you want that to happen again?"

Cam just shrugged, and Elerion rubbed at his face in frustration. "Look," he tried. "It isn't just Alec and me. Sandy's worried about you, too. She woke up when Eaglanter arrived, and she refuses to go to bed until she sees you. It was all I could do to keep her from coming with me, and I don't want to have to go back and tell our baby sister that her favorite brother was arrested in a South Bank tavern and she may never see him again."

"And it would be better for her to see him dragged away by her Aunt Kaliana?"

"We wouldn't let that happen."

Cam shot his brother an incredulous look before bursting out laughing. "What are you going to do, Ler? Fight off a company of Flame Champions? Oh, yes, I'll bet Alec is on board for *that* plan."

"We don't have to fight them off," Elerion replied hotly. "Aunt Kali can question you at Kathrine's Hall. If she has any doubts about your loyalty, we can hold you under house arrest by Alec's word as the Duke of Guilcove until she's satisfied. That much we *can* do." He stood, his fists clenched. "Now, I'm through with talking to you, Camden. You're either coming home with me of your own volition, or I'm carrying your bleeding body home—*but you're coming home now.*"

Cam glanced past him toward the bar. Sarah, Trevor, and Annie had been silently watching the exchange, and now the tavern owner's hand dropped to the cudgel by her nephew's side. He shook his head. He was wrong, he thought with a faint smile. They *were* stupid enough to fight off a company of Flame Champions. He'd better get out of here before they got into trouble. He stood. "All right. Let's get it over with."

With a relieved expression, Ler dropped his fists. "Do you owe anything here?" he asked in a mollifying tone.

Cam gave a bark of laughter. "More than you could possibly know."

"Then you'd better settle up; you may not be coming back."

"Oh, I'll be coming back." A tiny gray light began to flash in Cam's eyes. "Flame Champions or no Flame Champions, I'll be coming back." Gesturing his brother out ahead of him, he gave the Dog's owner a brief nod, then followed him from the taproom.

At the bar Sarah watched them go, then jerked her head at Trevor. The bouncer left immediately, and she turned to the Server.

"Can you get to Kathrine's Hall ahead of them?"

Annie snorted. "I should hope so. Cam's so drunk he can hardly walk straight."

"Then go. Find out from your cousin Ewan what's going on, then get back here straight away."

The younger woman snatched up her cloak. "What'cher gonna do, Sarah?" she asked, her eyes wide.

"Whatever I can do, but I need information first. Go."

The Server headed out at once, and with a dark light flashing in her own eyes, the Dog's proprietor took a seat behind the bar and poured herself a gin.

"Whatever I can do, but I need information first."

Her eyes narrowed. Camden DeKathrine wasn't the only one with family in Branbridge. There wasn't a Guild, Order, Temple, or Military Company in the entire city that didn't have at least one servant or hireling with links to the South Bank; there were no secrets in the capital; you just needed to know who to ask, and Sarah Lambton always knew who to ask—or who to bribe. Fishing out a silver helm, she caught the eye of a young man lounging by the fire. He approached with a smile.

"His Grace, DeKathrine the Beautiful in some trouble?" he asked smoothly.

"He could be. Are you still seeing that floor polisher at the Flame Temple?"

"Now and again."

"How about tonight?"

"It's late, but I could probably manage it. He'll be hard at work in the main hall—it's always a mess after the Di Sul audiences." He grinned. "I could help him buff it up."

"I'll bet." She handed him the coin. "Another like it for as much as you can learn about Camden DeKathrine's predicament."

"Done." He turned to go.

"And Bernard?"

"Hm?"

"By dawn."

"I live to service you, I mean serve you."

"Just go."

He sashayed out the door, and Sarah finished her drink with a thoughtful expression.

"Whatever I can . . ."

She sighed. It wasn't going to be much, not against the Flame Priests and their Champions, but still, she'd managed twelve releases and four breakouts from various Branion and Gallian prisons in her time; anything was possible, and although she doubted she could get Cam out of a Flame Temple Dungeon without getting caught herself, she could at least bribe the guards and the kitchen staff to treat him with some kindness.

The door opened, and a waft of cold night air sailed in behind a couple of sailors. She snorted.

"So, what are you doing mucking about in here," she admonished sharply. "He's *your* Chosen. Go help him."

She couldn't be sure, but she thought she might have seen the Wind sail out again.

And on that note a little metaphysical help for herself wouldn't be amiss right about now either. Rubbing her leg, she stood with a groan.

"Traz, watch the place," she called toward the kitchen. "I'll be in the chapel for a few minutes."

"Sure, Boss."

Catching up the key, she made her way slowly down the stone steps, wondering which one of the Aspects was likely to bother responding.

"Probably Flame," she muttered as she turned the key in the lock. "As if that's going to be any help at all."

In the taproom hearth, the fire gave its answer, dancing across the coals in a complicated series of ever changing signs, but there was no one left in the tavern to read them. Camden DeKathrine was on his way home to Kathrine's Hall, and he'd turned his back on the signs ever since the spring of 496 when one of his closest friends had been sent into the arms of the Shadow Catcher, breaking their Circle forever.

With a sullen glow, the flames hunkered down over the coals once again. Death was never truly the end and the Circle was not yet truly broken, but no one, not even Cam, had any way of knowing that yet.

Standing by the river as Ler gestured a boatman over, Cam thought about death and Circles, casting his mind back to the last funeral he had willingly attended. It had been wet and cold the morning they'd consigned Domitia DeKathrine, Duke of Guilcove, to the main barrow on Grayridge Common, the swollen clouds threatening rain. Standing like a stone, Cam had cast his gaze across the barrows, his expression hard.

The mist off the downs clung to the grass, parting with reluctance as the double line of Flame Priests took their places to either side of the body on its funeral carriage.

Before them, the wide semicircle of mourners waited for the Aristok to give the first blessing, while behind them, the barrow's dark entrance with its stone doors stood, the lintels hung with whitethorn boughs to summon the Shadow Catcher's entourage, the interior strewn with special grasses and herbs. Later, when the Priests had laid the body inside the main crypt, the grasses would be taken up and burned, but for now they perfumed the entire area with the strong scent of the Shadow Realm.

Standing within the protective circle of his cousins, Cam resisted the effect of the funerary herbs. He didn't want to be drawn into the ceremony's false promise of comfort, and as he passed a stony gaze over each of his family, it was clear to him that, despite their outward show of piety, they didn't either. He wasn't surprised. The children of Domitia DeKathrine did not show weakness in public.

To the right of the Aristok, Alec stood as hard and unapproachable as he'd been at their father's interment three years ago. Jo was just as angry. Despite his new relationship with his fourth cousin Julian, Elerion's demeanor was pale and distant, and flanking their Aunt Leilani, Tania and Nicky stared blankly at the body, their jaws set. Even five-and-a-half-year-old Kassander stood straight and still beside his uncle Amedeus.

Only their mother's husband Desmond showed any emotion. Standing between his new family and his mother, the Duke of Cambury's, he held his twenty-month-old daughter tightly, his broad face drawn with grief. The others did not approach him. They would comfort him later, but not here in front of Dukes and Princes and Sword Knights. Later, in private, where it was safe to show weakness.

The Aristok raised his arms. As he began the blessing, the sun broke through the clouds, wreathing his dark, auburn hair in a halo of fire. An appreciative murmur rippled through the gathered, and Cam bared his teeth.

About him, he could sense the Circle's reaction through

the link and their impiety comforted him far more than the Flame Priests' empty words: Lisha's attention was riveted on her father as she struggled to tamp down her hunger for the growing manifestation of Flame, Quin was very still, his mind wandering through the barrows, touching each of the DeKathrine dead, one by one, and Dani, standing with her eyes half closed, was far away, one with the cold waves of the Bjerre Sea. Uncle Celestus stood behind them all, maintaining an air of perfect solemnity, but Cam could feel his disdain resonate all around them.

He himself felt nothing.

A sudden breeze rose up, ruffling his hair and catching at his clothes. With a sigh, he gave himself over to It, confident that the Flame Priests would not notice the subtle change in his attention and that his uncle would draw him back if he were needed.

The Wind carried him over and through the thoughts of the gathered, much as the Oaks were carrying Quin through the barrow. He caught snatches of words and images, moments of profound grief and scraps of barely concealed boredom: Aunt Maia was remembering his mother as a child, Cousin Valius was thinking about sex, Alec . . .

He jerked away, hovering instead over his uncle Celestus. For a heartbeat he felt all his uncle felt, saw all his uncle saw, and then he was flying over the cliffs, trying to lose himself in the simple thoughts of the seagulls and terns, his mind already denying what he'd touched on.

"Cam."

The funerary banquet had been a subdued affair, the reception afterward equally quiet. Alec'd had his hands full accepting the condolences of his guests, but now, as many of them withdrew, some to Domitia's private chapel, others to an impromptu hunt led by the Crown Prince Kathrine, the new Duke of Guilcove moved through the crowd seeking his siblings.

Cam eased back behind Dani and found himself sandwiched between his great uncle Darnell and his cousin

*Clairinda. When he turned, Alec was standing in front of
him.*
   "Cam."
   He said nothing.
   "Cam."

Tavencroft Keep, Kairnbrook
Winter, Mean Gearran, 496 DR

"Cam!
   "Cam, c'mon, move over, you great lummox!"
   He blinked.
   "Wha . . . ?"
   "Move over, you're hogging the entire bed!"
   Quin.
   He shuffled over a few inches, then lay, trying to get his
bearings, while his cousin dropped almost immediately
back into slumber. It was dark and stuffy, the shutters
closed against the weather. For a moment, he thought he
was back at Guilcove and then he remembered. The funeral had been over four months ago. They were back in
their tower at Tavencroft. They were home. They were
safe.
   Staring up at nothing, he took a deep breath and, as
he'd done almost every night for the past three years, he
reached out tentatively for the Branion Seer.
   Nothing.
   He closed his eyes, imagining the passageway under
the south range, feeling the cool stone wall beneath his
fingertips, breathing in the damp, motionless air. When he
came to the door, he reached out and removed the bar,
then took hold of the handle and pulled. It slid open
soundlessly, and he sent his mind out on the tails of the
midnight breeze.
   Again nothing.
   He squinted. The door was still closed, the bar still in
place. Even after they'd returned home and he'd traversed

the passageway in person, removed the bar, and physically pulled open the door, it had remained closed in his mind. Pri Gorwynne had blocked the entrance as surely as if she'd used brick and mortar. Perhaps forever.

He frowned into the darkness. Uncle Celestus would not discuss what had happened with Iain Jonstun and his mission to track down and murder the Branion Seer. Cam could only assume that meant the assassin had failed, but as Dani had pointed out, it more likely meant that he'd simply carried out his orders and gone home. Cousins did not fail.

"Besides, if Da'd wanted us to know, he'd have told us. Obviously he has a reason for keeping it secret."

Quin gave her an incredulous look. "This from the girl who discovered how to spy on her father at the age of eight?"

She shrugged. "So how's this answer, then? Who cares? Has he ever tried to make contact with you again, Cam?"

"No."

"Then he might as well be dead. See? Let's go swimming."

Dani's answer to everything. "Who cares, let's go swimming," translated into "I don't care. I want you to come do what I want to do." Which was always swimming.

Cam couldn't explain why he needed to know what had happened to the Seer, so he'd dropped the subject, but every night, he'd sent his solitary thoughts out looking for any sign that the man might still be alive, and every night he'd found nothing.

He closed his eyes, trying to will himself back to sleep, but it eluded him and, after a few moments, he opened them again.

Since they'd returned to Tavencroft, their training had been intensive. Uncle Celestus had hinted that they were almost ready to ascend to a higher level of power, but had refused to go into detail. He'd said only that, by the time of the full moon, they would know everything they needed to know.

The full moon would be tonight.

The others were wild with excitement, but Cam was more reticent. A higher level of power meant a higher level of synergy, of conformity, within the Circle, and as far as Cam was concerned, he'd conformed more than enough already. Ever since his mother's funeral, he'd felt less conflicted, but also less inclined to accept things at face value. However, the others, especially Dani, would brook no discordance so once again he'd dropped the subject.

Now, as he lay staring into the darkness, he wondered why it was that he never seemed completely happy about anything, and why this so often came to him in the middle of the night. He closed his eyes.

When he opened them again, it was just before dawn. The few birds that wintered in Kairnbrook were piping outside the one, unshuttered window and he lay for a few minutes listening to their singing before slipping quietly out of bed. As usual, Quin moved over to take up the extra space without waking up. Cam pulled on a pair of leather breeches, a shirt, and a wool tunic and jacket, then caught up his boots and crept from the room.

The tower stairs were icy cold. He took them swiftly, pausing only long enough to pull his boots on at the bottom, before heading across the inner courtyard at a quick jog. The sky was a steely gray despite the dawn sun. As he reached the stables, he thought he felt a sprinkling of snow on his face.

Nani Jonstun, the chief groom, looked up from the colt she was examining as Cam ducked in the side door.

"Mornin', Master Camden."

"Morning, Nani. How's little Clovis doing today?"

"Better. The early children are always a bit dodgy, but he's out of danger now, I'm thinking. He took his milk straight from his mam this morning without my help. That's a good sign." She glanced over at him. "Take Tara, will you, she's in need of a good ride. You know how testy she gets when Vincent's away."

"Sure, but Vincent came back late last night. Don't you think he might want to ride her himself."

The groom raised a questioning eyebrow at him. "The man's been away for over a fortnight, boy, I think His Grace may have other plans for him today, don't you?"

Cam grinned. "Probably." Running his hands over Tarra's broad chest, he reached for a saddle blanket. "Looks like we may get some snow," he noted.

"Aye, the fields saw a touch of it in the night. There'll be a dusting more today, I'm thinking, though not likely as much; nothing like a good old-fashioned Heathland storm, that's for sure. Still, you might not want to go too far. The spring's chancy, even in Kairnbrook."

"I won't."

Cam walked the horse from the stables, mounted up in the courtyard, then turned her head toward the gatehouse. He wouldn't go far, but if Nani were right, he wouldn't have to hurry back. Breakfast was likely to be late. Heading for the road, he made his way slowly riverward.

The light snowfall had ceased by the time he cleared the gate. Keeping Tara to a sedate walk, he nodded to the few villagers making their way sleepily up the path, and they nodded back.

Cam often wondered about the castle folk. Most of Uncle Celestus' people were from Essusiate Heathland, but the few Branion villagers who came to help in the stables or bakehouse were Triarchs. They paid their yearly tithe to the one, small temple in Gressam, but Cam had always gotten the impression that they did this more out of habit than out of piety. In fact, no one at Tavencroft seemed even remotely pious. There hadn't been a single Sabat Mass or Essusiate Service celebrated in the keep since he'd been there—Uncle Celestus preferred open debates about religion, philosophy, or politics rather than blind obedience—and yet, when the Kairnbrook Lord had taken all four youths across the shire that first year Cam was with them, he'd witnessed no evidence that the people were suffering from a lack of divine assistance. He'd seen lush fields of grain, neat rows of fishing boats, and wide stretches of domesticated rabbit warrens. He'd met charcoal burners, shepherds, farmers, weavers, smiths, and shopkeepers, all industrious and content. If the Kairnbrook folk even knew about their Lord's unorthodox leanings, they kept it to themselves. They were prosperous and safe; what more did they need?

Cam wondered if they'd fare as well if the Flame Priests ever got hold of their shire, but supposed they would manage to survive somehow. Like the land itself, the people would carry on regardless of which Lord they paid their taxes to. In the end it wouldn't matter one whit.

Turning Tara off the main path, he headed for the river. As the waters of the Whroxin came into view, he allowed his thoughts to wander off again.

The Jonstuns at Tavencroft itself also knew how to take care of themselves. If the Flame Champions ever did attack the keep, they, along with Celestus and his family, would simply flee north, disappearing into the Cheviot Hills where the thick, thorny underbrush and violently territorial residents would keep any heavily mounted company from following. Celestus had spent hours with the four youths going over the various escape routes north. If they ever got separated, they were to make for Lochaber Castle where they would be hidden until he could get word to them. This special relationship with the notorious Jonstun reiver clan was one of the foundation stones of Celestus' plans and one which he'd spent a lifetime cultivating.

Reining up on the small rise before the riverbank, Cam relaxed the reins, allowing Tara to bend her head toward the short grass. Dropping his hands into his lap, he stared out at the water, thinking about foundation stones. The

DeKathrines were the Foundation Stones of the Crown's power; the Jonstuns of his uncle's. The DeKathrines received political favors, the Jonstuns received money—and probably the chance to stick it to Triarctic Branion, his mind added cynically. Give and take, power to gain more power, money to make more money.

Even his uncle's four Chosen fell squarely into that philosophy. Dani received her father's praise, Quin, the chance to prove himself smarter than everyone around him, Lisha, overwhelmed by a family where exceptional ability was commonplace, was made to feel special, and he had been given free rein to ignore his responsibilities and duties and give himself over to his first love, the Wind. In return they'd offered up their abilities to Celestus to mold and make use of as he saw fit. Give and take, power to gain more power, money to make more money. When something happened to interrupt that cycle or a participant decided they wanted a better deal was when wars broke out.

The snow began to fall again. Feeling unusually perceptive, Cam let his mind follow the path of each individual snowflake as it floated toward the ground. The Jonstuns, Pri Gorwynne, Kether Breithe, Dani, Quin, and Lisha; he understood everyone's motives for following his uncle into heresy, even his own. In truth, the only person at Tavencroft whose motivation completely escaped him was Vincent of Storvicholm's.

He watched as a single snowflake fluttered down to rest, brilliant and beautiful, on his horse's mane.

Highly skilled and very highly paid contracted Courtesans, Companions served the most powerful nobles in the land as lovers, advisers, and bodyguards. Although many had been with their individual Lords for years, they owed their loyalty to the Companion's Guild. That Vincent could be involved in the Triarchy Heresy without his superiors being aware of it was almost unthinkable. That they could be aware of it and not inform the Flame Tem-

ple was impossible. And yet Celestus trusted him completely.

Cam frowned. Dani had told him that Vincent had been
with her father since before he'd met her mother. He was
loyal to their interests. She left it at that. Although he believed her, it rankled him that he couldn't figure out why.

*Ever since his mother's funeral, he'd felt less conflicted,
but also less inclined to accept things at face value.*
*"Ever since you touched your uncle's thoughts on
Grayridge Common, you mean."*

That was true enough. Whatever Uncle Celestus' academic or altruistic reasons, the cold truth was that he'd decided he wanted a better deal. He'd reached out for the
power of the Aspects, believing that was to be his path toward power, and had gathered as many like-minded people as he'd needed to achieve it, including four children,
each with an affinity for a different Aspect, the first being
his own daughter.

Chewing at the end of one braid, Cam wondered which
had come first, his uncle's theories or Dani's abilities.

*". . . taught to ignore their potential. Just like the rest
of us . . . the whole country . . . everyone can access it a
little bit. Or did you honestly believe that Braniana De-
Marian was the only person in the entire world capable of
merging with an Aspect . . . that hardly makes any sense,
does it?"*

No, it didn't. His uncle could have steered Dani toward
an affinity with the Sea without her ever being even remotely aware of it. The same with Quin and the Oaks. As
for the Flame, Atreus DeMarian had nine children. All
Celestus needed was for one of them to feel overwhelmed
by the family and he had his Flame. For all Cam knew,
he'd chosen Lisha first and then encouraged the feelings
of isolation and restlessness in her.

A hawk cried out above him. Craning his neck, he watched it methodically searching the fields below. With a pensive expression, he wondered how long his uncle had searched before he'd found his Wind.

"I was so sure the Wind had taken particular notice of you at your First Dedication. It was quite a stormy afternoon."

"No time at all."

Frowning, he shook his head. "You're being awfully paranoid this morning," he told himself gruffly.

"Am I?"

"I keep abreast of most of the family's activities, you know. There was a time when I half expected to hear that you'd been sent to the Wind Temple to Squire under my nephew Collin. Imagine my surprise when I learned that you were to become a Sword Knight, sworn to the Flame. I thought Vakarus paid greater attention to the signs than that. He did as a boy."

"Am I?"

"Shut up."

Taking up the reins, he urged Tara down to the water's edge. As she bent her head to drink, he glared down at his misty reflection.

"Even if that is true, who cares?" he growled. "Uncle Celestus gets to harness the power of the Aspects, and I get to fly with the Wind whenever I want to. He gets what he wants, I get what I want."

"Give and take? Power to gain more power?"
"That's right. Why not?"
"And tonight when you reach a higher level of power.

*What then? What does Uncle Celestus actually want done
with that power? Do you know? Did you See?"*

"No."

"Are you sure?"

"Yes."

"Do you care?"

Cam was silent for a long time.

"No."

Ignoring his reflection's unconvinced expression, he
took Tara back toward the keep.

As they made their way back to the rise, he wondered
why he was dwelling on such a melancholy subject. His
uncle had given him a place to belong; a place where his
need to be with the Wind was understood and encouraged.
Why should his personal motives matter at all?

"It's just safer to know, that's all."

"Not necessarily. If the Flame Champions ever catch up
with us, not knowing would be a lot safer."

*"No, it wouldn't. It would probably be equally danger-
ous."*

"Then it doesn't really matter, so just shut up, will
you?"

Before the internal debate could degenerate into a series of "you shut up, no, you," a fleck of moisture touched
his cheek. He glanced up at the cloudy sky with a grimace. It was probably the weather, he determined. It
should be spring. He needed it to be spring. He wanted
green hills and warm breezes, not brown, bare trees and a
cold Wind that didn't so much touch his mind with a special intimacy as It wormed Its icy cold fingers through his
clothing like It did to everyone else.

Crouched in the lea of some barren Heathland rock
pile, he'd often wondered why Pri Gorwynne hadn't
taught him how to do something useful with his Aspect
like calling up a warmer breeze or heating up the spaces
inside his jacket instead of striving to catch the sounds of

an enemy encampment or sensing if a river or stream were behind the next hill. If he wanted to know these things, he had only to send his mind out on the tails of the Wind, but the ex-Priest who'd accompanied them to Heathland—despite complaining all the way that she was too old to "go farting about the countryside like a tinker"—insisted they know how to work within a limited scope. Cam hadn't seen the point, but also hadn't been willing to defy her. Now he wished he had. He could have used a warm breeze right about now.

A sound above him made him jerk his head up, and he was startled to see Lisha on her own mount coming down the rise. She reined up beside him with a faint smile.

"I couldn't sleep," she explained in answer to his curious expression. "My dreams were too vivid, so I thought I might join you. You don't mind, do you?"

He shook his head. "No, of course not, but, um, it is dawn, you know?"

She nodded.

"Dawn," he repeated with a smile, "not dusk?"

"I know."

"I was just making sure because I wouldn't want you to get confused when you saw the sun on the horizon twice in one day."

"Oh, do shut up." She aimed a mock kick in his direction, then, dropping the reins, allowed her horse to snap at the cold grass. After a moment, Cam followed her lead.

"Is this where you usually come on your rides?" she asked.

"Sometimes."

"It's very pretty. I like how the sun turns the hills over there all pink."

"Like fire in the distance?"

"I suppose." She turned to stare at him, her flame sparked eyes intense. "Why do you go riding alone, Cam?" she asked suddenly. "What do you get out here all by yourself that you can't get with us?"

Her question took him by surprise and he turned away

with a guilty start. "I don't know," he answered after a moment. "Just some quiet time, I guess. It takes me longer to think about things than it takes the rest of you."

"Alec rides off by himself a lot, doesn't he?"

He glanced back at her sharply. "So?"

"So is that why you do it? To be more like him?"

He frowned. "No. Why?"

She shrugged. "It's just that I used to do things to try be more like Kathrine and Marsellus. To be more like His Majesty. More DeMarian, you know?"

He shook his head mutely.

"Well, I'm not very DeMarian, am I? Everyone else in the family seems to, I don't know, resonate . . . with the Flame I mean. It seems to burn inside them like a forest fire. I'm not like that at all. I'm so much more like Mother's side of the family, the DeKathrine side: solid, stable . . ."

"Dull?"

She smiled. "No."

"Predictable?"

"Maybe." She stared out at the rising sun. "And yet, I'm probably more in tune with the Flame than any of them, save His Majesty himself," she mused. "And yet . . ."

"And yet?"

"And yet it still doesn't matter. I'm still not like them. I guess I never will be."

She turned suddenly.

"Are you nervous, Cam?"

He started. "How do you mean?"

"About today, about the new level of power that Uncle's told us about. Are you nervous, scared that we won't be ready for whatever he has planned?"

Cam considered the question in light of his earlier thoughts. Paranoid? Yes. Nervous? No.

"Not really," he replied. Then he laughed. "I've been knocked out, kicked around, and over absorbed by my Aspect so much that I can hardly think of anything else It could do to me. Why? Are you nervous?"

"A little." She watched a snipe hunting snails on the riverbank with a frown. "I don't know. Sometimes I think I should be more like Dani."

"You mean bossy and demanding?"

"No, just confident. She's never afraid she's going to get lost in it all. Quin isn't either."

"In what all?"

"In the Circle."

"That's because they've spent their whole life working together."

"I suppose. It's just that, well, up to this point it's always been just me and the Flame in trance. Oh, I know we all have the link, and I can operate within it just fine, but when I join with the Flame, I lose all sense of the physical—mine, your's, everyone's. For a while I'm only spirit, only Aspect. And during that time I know what it means to be truly DeMarian, to be one with the Living Flame. It's all encompassing. I feel like I could set the entire world on fire, I'm so powerful. I love that feeling. And I love Uncle Celestus for giving me the opportunity to feel it. I can't imagine a higher level of communion other than the one His Majesty shares with the Flame as Its personal Avatar, and that's what I'm worried about. Uncle's talked about a gestalt before. I'm afraid he has some kind of total merging with all four Aspects in mind. I'm afraid I'll lose that feeling, that my link with the Flame will get lost in this new gestalt. That I won't be . . . DeMarian anymore, just when I've discovered what it's like to truly be DeMarian." She fell silent.

Cam chewed on his lip, uncertain of what to say. Finally he glanced over at her shyly.

"Have you told Uncle Celestus about this?" he asked.

She looked away. "No."

"Why not?"

"I don't know. I guess I didn't want him to think that I didn't want to be part of the Circle, that by wanting to be

DeMarian I didn't want to be DeKathrine. I didn't want him to . . ." She trailed off.

"Cut you off from the Circle?"

"I suppose."

"And if you were cut off from the Circle, you might get cut off from your Aspect?"

"Maybe."

"I get scared of that, too, sometimes."

"You do?"

"Sure. I guess that's why I come out here every morning. To remind myself that even though I have doubts and even though I may not be much like my brothers and sisters or even much like my cousins, I have a connection with the Wind. In a way that makes me a little like the Wind and nobody can take that away from me; not Uncle, not anyone." He smiled at her, his eyes swirling with gray light. "And if the worst does ever happen, if Uncle breaks us up because you and I aren't as confident or as totally committed as Dani and Quin are, or if the Flame Champions come and arrest us all and raze Tavencroft to the ground, we'll both still have those connections. We were born with them. Right?"

She smiled a little. "Right."

"Right. You still nervous?"

"A little."

"Me, too. I'm nervous that I'm going to die of hunger if I don't get back to the keep soon and get some breakfast, I'm that starved. So— race you back?"

"Sure."

They turned their mounts but, just as Cam raised his hand to give the signal to start, Lisha caught hold of his arm.

"You'll remember that, won't you, Cam?" she asked seriously. "If the worst ever does happen, you'll remember what you said about the connection and not let anyone ever try and sever it? Not ever?"

"Well, sure," he answered, unnerved by the sudden intensity of her gaze. "Why wouldn't I?"

She shook her head. "No reason. I just had a dream that's all. A stupid dream. Still, if you remember what you said and I remember it, too, then everything will work out fine, right?"

"Right."

"Right."

Clucking her tongue, she urged her horse into a trot.

Cam watched her go with a slight frown, then, after a second, he shook himself. Right. He'd remember it and she'd remember it and everything would work out fine. Whatever everything was. He had enough of his own thoughts to confuse him without adding Lisha's on top of them.

Urging Tara forward, he followed his cousin back up the rise, the sudden growling of his stomach forcing out all other less earthy concerns.

Behind them the Wind whispered over the riverbank, translating Lisha's dream into the language of the Aspects before dissipating in a flurry of snowflakes.

Nani was wrong. Both Celestus and Vincent were down to breakfast when Cam and Lisha returned, although the Companion was looking unusually pleased with himself. Pri Gorwynne and Kether Breithe were also at the table. They'd waited for Cam and Lisha before beginning, and Dani gave both her cousins a dark look as they took their seats. Lisha smiled back, the picture of smooth innocence. Faced with a platter of kippers, Cam ignored her.

Little was spoken until breakfast was over, then Celestus leaned back, a cup of tea cradled in his hands.

"Many years ago," he began, "I, Vincent, and my late wife Dianne, your mother, Danielle, formed the theory that, within the proper environment and with the proper tools, anyone could access the power of the Aspects and harness them in the Physical Realm. After extensive travels throughout the mountains of both Danelind and Gwyneth where the veil between the Realms is the weakest, and after much experimentation, we found this to be the case, albeit on a very limited scale—as you yourselves have discovered individually. We then extrapolated that four participants, each with a strong affinity to each of the four Aspects, and working in concert, could manage an even greater degree of intimacy with the Aspects, one almost to the point experienced by an Avatar."

Setting the cup down, he swept his gaze across the table.

"I'm very proud of you all," he continued. "You've worked extremely hard these past three years and progressed very well, both individually and in concert, and now it's time to put that progress to the test; to stretch your abilities to the limit and reach for a new level of potential. To finally prove these theories correct. But don't misunderstand me," he amended as Dani began to bounce up and down in her chair. "This level is both challenging and dangerous. It will take all your skill, all your strength, and all your commitment to each other to achieve it, and it must be done under absolute secrecy. Up to this point we've never actually broken any laws . . ." He smiled tightly. "Although the Flame Temple would certainly debate that. However, this is about to change. You're adults now, and it's time to make adult choices. If you agree to this new challenge, there will be no going back, but I can promise you, you'll never wish to. I believe you're committed to our experiment and up to the challenge. So does Pri Gorwynne. I'm hoping that you feel as confident as we do. But if you don't, now is the time to tell us."

He passed his intense gaze over the four youths.

Grinning excitedly, Dani tossed her braids behind her back. "I was born confident, Da," she declared.

He smiled back at her. "I have no doubts on that account. Quinton?"

"You know I'm always ready for a new challenge, Uncle."

"Alisha?"

The DeMarian girl smiled hesitantly, but after a quick look at Cam, she nodded her head. "I'm ready."

"Are you sure? I don't want anyone here to feel pressured."

"I was just . . ." She straightened. "I was just a little worried that the intensity of my link with the Flame might fade if we entered a stronger gestalt, but I spoke with Cam this morning and now I know it won't. I'm ready."

"Good. Camden?"

Cam returned his uncle's stare with a serious expression of his own.

"I think it's far too late to travel backward now," he answered in a neutral tone.

The others about the table turned to look at him as Celestus pursed his lips thoughtfully. "Would you really want to?" he asked with a frown.

"No. But I still wish the flying was as simple and as private as it was when I was a child. I miss it."

"That's understandable. But children grow up and their lives become complicated and interwoven within the lives of other adults. That being said, are you still committed to our experiment?"

"Yes. I was committed that day we spoke in the gallery. I haven't changed my mind."

Celestus held his gaze for a moment longer, then nodded slowly. "Very well." He turned to take in the entire table again. "As you know, all the Triarctic Orders, as well as the Street Seers and others of their ilk, indulge in various forms of Prophetic Vision, but only the Priests of the Flame and their Champions do so with the added enhancement of certain powerful visionary herbs. These herbs heighten their bond with the Flame and allow them to pierce the veil between the present and the future. Those herbs are called the Potion of Truth and its composition is a very carefully guarded secret. Until now. Vincent?"

With a smile, the Companion reached down and lifted a heavy, leather satchel to the table.

Quin almost shot from his chair.

"That's not . . . ?"

"It is."

"And you know the composition?"

"I do."

Dani caught her breath. "But how?"

"How do you think?"

"Sexual favors?"

Vincent laughed. "As talented as I am, I'm afraid that isn't quite enough to tempt your average Flame Temple Herbalist to commit heresy."

His hands held tightly at his sides to keep from making a grab for the bag, Quin looked up. "What is?"

"A great deal of money."

"How much money?"

"More than you can possibly imagine," Celestus answered, "but well worth it in the long run."

Both Cam and Lisha had remained silent during this revelation, and now the Tavencroft Lord turned to scrutinize their reactions. Lisha looked stunned, Cam thoughtful.

"This is not the composition used by the Aristok," he assured his DeMarian niece, "only that used by the Flame Priests."

Slowly Lisha turned her fire-washed eyes to meet his. "I can Feel its potency from here," she whispered. "It calls to me."

Dani nodded, her own eyes wide.

"Can we use it now, Da?"

"Tonight."

"How could we possibly wait that long?"

"By spending the day in preparation. I've had some experience with the Potion of Truth in Storvicholm as a young man and I can tell you that this will be unlike any trance you've ever experienced. You'll be traveling in the Prophetic Realm extensively and exclusively. Images will have greater clarity, colors will be more vivid. You may have Prophetic Visions of the future or revealing Visions of the past. You'll be able to access a far greater storehouse of power. This may cause you to momentarily lose conscious contact with each other, and even with yourself, but don't be alarmed; your link is still strong. It's a bond of blood as well as of ability. If you reach out, you'll find that the others have not gone as far away as you imagine. As for your experiences, they will be highly individual. Try and speak them aloud if you can, Vincent and Pri Gorwynne will record as much of your outer reactions as possible. And don't be afraid. You've done this before, only without the benefit of visionary herbs. Also I'll be traveling with you to monitor your progress. If anything unusual happens, reach out for me and I'll guide you home. Do you have any questions?"

Without taking their eyes from the bag, the others shook their heads, but Cam turned to regard his uncle with an even expression.

"Yes, Camden?"

"You said, almost to the point of an Avatar, Uncle, why not all the way?"

A look of intense greed suddenly flashed across both Quin's and Dani's faces, and Celestus shot a frown at their younger cousin.

"To fully meld with an Aspect as a True Avatar would require entering the Aspects' Realm," he explained tersely. "Many have tried over the centuries, but only the Aristok Braniana has ever succeeded, never mind survived." He caught Cam in an intense stare. "You will not attempt it. You are not strong enough. Even the DeMarian Vessels themselves are not always strong enough." His gaze swept across the table. "None of you will so much as approach the Aspects' Realm. If I discover that any of you are even considering it, I shall be very angry and the experiment will terminate. Is that clear?"

He caught each of them in a dark-eyed stare and each of them nodded quickly, their excitement subdued by his unusual vehemence. He held Cam's gaze the longest.

"Is that clear, Camden?"

"Yes, Uncle."
"Very clear."

It was full dark before they made their way south of Tavencroft to the edge of the Bricklin Forest. The four youths had spent the day trying to remain calm and patient, but none of them had managed it very well. Dani and Cam'd had a huge fight immediately after breakfast, and it had taken all of Lisha's mediating skills to keep them from coming to blows. True to her mercurial nature, Dani had quickly forgotten about it, leaving Cam to sulk for a couple of hours before Quin dragged him off to have sex. Afterward they managed to work on their link until supper. Now, dressed warmly in leather and sheepskin, they followed Celestus into the forest.

It was dark under the trees despite the full moon filtering in through the leafless branches. As they made their way along the narrow path, Cam could feel the energy beginning to build all around them. It made his breath catch in his throat and, opening his mind to the link, he sensed the others reacting to it as well. Lisha's hair danced and twitched across her shoulders, and Quin began to walk with a queer hopping step as if the power coming up from the ground was too much for him to take in through the soles of his boots. Only Dani moved as if she wasn't affected, but Cam could feel that her mind was elsewhere, following the path of an underground spring deep in the earth beneath them.

Three hundred yards into the trees, they broke through into a small clearing where Vincent, Kether, and Pri Gorwynne were waiting for them. Furs had been arranged in the center around an unlit bonfire built before the weathered stones of a ruined tower and a nearby pool of water, with moss-covered fallen branches poking out from the ice. The Wind, whistling through the trees, commingled the scents of earth, leaves, and algae with the sharp odor of the Potion of Truth bubbling in a hanging pot inside the ruins. Even after three years of trance work in the open air of Heathland, Cam was nearly overwhelmed by the naked power of the place.

He turned a wide-eyed stare on Dani.

"Did you know this was here?" he whispered, watching, mesmerized, as his breath puffed out in a stream of tiny images.

She shook her head mutely, moving past him to stare through the ice into the depths of the pool.

"No one does," Celestus answered for her. "Except for Dianne and myself. It's a very old Pre-Triarctic site, probably a place of worship, certainly a place of power. We used to come here to perform our own rituals when we were first married, but it's stood empty for many years since. Now it will be revitalized again." He turned. "Come and take your place, Danielle; there'll be time enough to explore the pool's secrets later."

Reluctantly, she tore herself away, dropping down onto the furs to the west without a word. Equally awed into silence, Quin and Cam followed her lead, taking their usual places to the north and east, but as Lisha made for the southern place, Celestus held up an unlit torch.

"Oaks, Sea, and Wind are in equal balance already," he said. "That leaves only Flame. Alisha, my dear, will you do the honors?"

"Now?"

"Now."

She accepted the torch hesitantly.

"Do I need to say anything?"

"No, just light it from our small fire over there, then thrust it into the heart of the bonfire. Your presence alone will be enough to sanctify it."

She obeyed him quickly. For a moment nothing happened, and then smoke started to pour from the opening between two logs as, first one, then another tongue of flame appeared. As she took her place to the south, the smell of burning cherrywood filled the clearing.

Pri Gorwynne now began to throw handfuls of basil, mugwort, fireteeth and calling-thistle onto the fire. Their powerful aroma made Cam's head spin, but rather than re-strict his breathing, he sucked in a huge lungful of air, be-ginning the ritual breathing that would eventually steady his vision. Meanwhile, Vincent filled four bowls with the Potion of Truth. As he set them before the youths, they steamed invitingly and as one, they reached out.

"Not yet," Celestus admonished. "Kether, if you will take your place behind Alisha, please—of all of us, she will need the greatest shielding—Vincent, you will aid Quinton, Pri Gorwynne, you will be behind Camden, of course, and I will aid Danielle."

As the adults took their places, Cam stared into the bowl before him, watching the bits of dried herbs floating on the top merge into the image of a tiny flock of birds. He fidgeted impatiently. His mouth was dry in anticipa-tion, and his whole body tingled. It felt like all his pores were opening—as if by absorption alone the Potion would send him into trance. Finally, when all the adults were set-tled, Celestus raised one hand.

"Drink."

Cam caught up his bowl, ignoring the heat which played against his fingertips. The cold air had cooled the liquid and he sucked it in greedily, then allowed the bowl to fall to the ground. He never felt Pri Gorwynne wrap her arms about his chest to keep him upright.

His drop into the Prophetic Realm was almost instanta-neous. The world disappeared to be replaced by a spin-ning cacophony of colors and images. He gasped. Every sense was alive and ringing. Sounds, smells, physical sen-sations, even the flavor of the Potion of Truth in his mouth, seemed to explode all around him. He plummeted downward, then, taking the form of a huge golden eagle, he shot back into the air.

The world around him steadied. Below he Saw the bare and brown landscape of Branion laid out like a quilt, above the clouds rushed past him, vividly painted in the hues of a thousand dawns and dusks. He Saw the rose window of the Wind Chapel as he'd never seen it before, alive and breathing in and out with the rhythm of Its congregation. He Saw people and places, some he knew and some he didn't. He Saw a tiny figure standing on the cliffs of Guilcove and, with a start, he realized it was himself as a child. He Saw his father and his mother, his grandparents and great grandparents, stretching back in an almost infinite line of green-and-black clad warriors. He Saw a man, his hair the color of burnished bronze, helping a woman with flames pouring from her eyes and mouth leave a cave in the hills of Gwyneth, and then he Saw his uncle Celestus.

"You are too close to the Aspects' Realm, Camden. Move away."

He shot back into the air, leaving the past behind him. The clouds rushed in. For an instant, he faltered in their midst, then the Wind came up and blew them away and he stared into the future. He saw a dockside tavern and a woman with worried hazel eyes; he saw his brother Alec and his sister Jo dressed for battle, Saw the fields of Kairnbrook stained with blood, and then everything went dark and still.

He hovered in the blackness, uncertain but unafraid. Everything was quiet and peaceful, as if he was asleep or possibly dead. Reaching inside his own mind, he Felt the Wind lying dormant within him and, raising his arms, began to spin, allowing the Aspect to flow from his mind like the long, thin ribbons on a maypole.

He began to pick up speed, whirling faster and faster and faster. Far below he felt the others merge with their own Aspects, and as they did, the world came back into being. Spinning almost unbearably quickly, he and the Wind took the form of a giant cyclone.

He shot across the sky, sucking up the clouds like wisps of candy. Below him, the landscape shook and cracked apart as Quin and the Oaks reached out for him. He touched down, scooping them up into his spinning embrace along with acres of dirt and rocks and trees, then he and Quin together made for the open ocean. Dani joined them in a huge water spout half a mile high. It took less than a single heartbeat for them to merge completely, and then they went looking for Lisha. Towering over the hills of Gwyneth, they Felt the Flame far beneath the earth call to them in their cousin's voice and together they slammed down through soil and rock.

The world began to shake apart, the Physical and Prophetic Realms winking in and out of their conscious minds, and suddenly Cam was shooting down the south range corridor at a dizzying speed. When he reached the end, he slapped the bar away and crashed through the door just as the cyclone touched the Living Flame.

There was an explosion of fire. Cam went spinning away, like a comet burning out of control. He tried to scream, tried to jerk out of trance, but as the firestorm engulfed him once more, he lost all control. His mind began to crack apart, and in desperation, he shot down the nearest link and into the tormented mind of Martin Wrey.

For an instant, they stared at each other and then the Branion Seer yanked him from the maelstrom. The Circle collapsed and Cam came back to himself screaming and writhing in Pri Gorwynne's arms. As real darkness rushed over him he heard each of his cousins cry out as they, too, were jerked out of trance. Martin's shadowy features hovered above his head, but just as Cam reached out for him, he became the stern and fanatical form of Urielle DeSandra, her hands stained red with blood.

Branbridge's North Bank
Spring, Mean Boaldyn, 500 DR

The terrible image bled through the memory and into the present, staining the clouds above the capital a dark crimson. Forcibly jerking his gaze away, Cam covered his eyes with one hand as he collapsed against an upturned boat.

He began to vomit.

*   *   *

The Vision had overtaken him as he'd stepped onto the capital's North Bank. Assuming that he was just drunk, Elerion had let him fall. Now, as he slowly came back to himself, he passed a shaking hand over his face. That had been the first time he'd Seen the women who would be in charge of his interrogation in the dungeons of the Flame Temple and who, no doubt, now waited for her Champions to bring him to her there again. Ler had promised that the family would protect him, but Cam had no false hopes in that regard. The only person who'd been able to help him in those terrible days after the Vision in the forest had gone so wrong had been Martin Wrey, and only Martin could help him now. But that wasn't possible.

With a deep breath, Cam pushed himself to his feet.

Elerion looked over, trying to mask his concern.

"Are you all right?"

Cam just nodded.

"Do you need help? Can you walk?"

"As far as I have to."

"Then we'd better hurry."

Together, the two DeKathrine brothers headed for the dockside stables and from there to Kathrine's Hall and the waiting Flame Champions.

11. The Temple Seers

The Flame Temple, Branbridge
Spring, Mean Boaldyn, 500 DR

MARTIN stood on the Temple's main balcony staring sightlessly into the darkness. Far away to the east, Bran's Bell tolled four. It would be soon.

Closing his eyes, he took a full breath of the clean spring air. He'd been standing here for over an hour, watching the road to the capital and waiting for the Duke of Werrick's Herald to arrive. He had Seen her in a vision that very night, Seen her mission, and the side trip she'd made to Alexander DeKathrine, Duke of Guilcove, to warn him that the Champions of the Flame would soon be seeking his younger brother just as they had four years earlier. Fate wasn't finished with any of them yet. The Triarchy Heresy was raising its banner once again and none of them would emerge unscathed from this latest battle. He'd Seen that, too.

Behind him, the Flame Temple slept peacefully, unaware of the explosive events about to take place. No one, not even the Archpriest herself, had been able to See this single strand of prophecy. Only Martin, with his tenuous link to the Wind's Chosen had been sensitive enough to catch it and follow it down to its most likely conclusion, but this time it was imperative that he keep it to himself.

It was time.

He opened his eyes, ignoring the wisps of Vision that

danced before his face. The Herald should be coming into view . . . now.

A figure appeared in the distance.

Satisfied, he returned inside. As he crossed the main gallery, he glanced down to see the Temple floor cleaner chatting with a young man. As Martin watched, the two of them disappeared through a side door into one of the smaller meditation chambers. Martin smiled faintly. Even in a place as hallowed and lofty as the Flame Temple there were always tiny, little irreverences going on. Heresy was only a matter of degree, and Apostasy a matter of timing. Or the lack of it. Passing under a small arch, he made his way back to his room in the south wing tower.

Once seated by his own fire, he leaned his head back and closed his eyes. Flashes of light scuttled about behind his eyelids, each one sending a thin shaft of pain shooting down his neck and arms. With effort, he made himself relax. The pain eased.

Ever since the attack in the Kenneth, his Visions had been incredibly clear, people and events parading before his eyes like marionettes acting out a pantomime, but each had been accompanied by a blinding headache. He'd spent the first month after the attack tied to a bed in the Octavian Hospice on the northern edge of the forest, raving and witless. Afterward it was as if his mind had been cracked open like an egg. He'd Seen the man sent to kill him weeks before he tracked him down. By that time Martin was well prepared to meet him.

"It will be tonight."

Martin stood before the head of the Hospice, his dark eyes clouded with prophecy. Setting the book she was reading to one side, Pri Nadia regarded him seriously.

"What should we do?"

"Retire early. Lock your doors. And wait. It will be over by morning."

*She frowned at him. "And there's no way you can sim-
ply incapacitate this man?"*

*"None. My Vision has only two paths, both leading to
death, his or mine. I'll have one shot. But whether I succeed or fail, no one else in the hospice will be harmed."
He attempted a smile. "You'll just have someone's burial
to contend with in the morning."*

*"That is of dubious comfort." She stood. "Nonetheless,
we will trust in your Vision. We will retire and allow you
to handle this man as you see fit. May the Flame Protect
you, Martin Wrey."*

That night, as he'd lain in bed listening for the almost
soundless footfall that would signal the man's approach,
he'd thought about the past month.

The not-thing and its compatriots had taken him completely by surprise. He'd made contact with the boy as
usual, and as usual they'd flown together, careful to avoid
the others hovering nearby. They'd come a bit too close to
the not-thing's net and that was when he'd seen the small
rent in its defenses, standing out against the reflective surface like a tiny, fathomless eye. The need to discover what
lay behind it was too great. He'd shot forward. The rent
opened like an iris and he was through. For an instant he
thought he saw an old woman with eyes as gray as spring
storm clouds beckon to him, then another presence
slammed against him so violently that he was nearly
knocked back into his body.

Before he could react, a dozen gray bands snaked out
of nowhere to pin him to the net, while the presence battered against his mind. For an instant, he hung there
dazed, and then his own formidable abilities came to his
defense. With one blow, he hammered the presence away,
but as he turned his attention to the bands, a dense fog
rose up to obscure his Sight. The presence attacked again,
hitting him from a dozen directions at once.

Martin could feel his control slipping in the face of the

barrage. In desperation he flung his mind out, seeking help from any quarter. It shot down an ancient link and, for an instant, he Saw the boy surrounded by spinning gusts of power. He reached out for him, and time froze. He Saw the indecision on the boy's face, and then the decision; Saw him turn toward the others, and Saw them surround him in a multihued cocoon of power just before the presence attacked again. It drove into him as a gryphon might drive into a corpse on the battlefield and tore his identity free. In the split second that it was distracted, Martin jerked himself out of trance.

He'd awakened in the Octavian Hospice six days later and it took a month to recover the use of his mind and body. His memory of the attack was hazy, the only clear image was of the boy leaving him in the trap he must have known about. His betrayal had made Martin angry at first, but eventually, he shrugged it off. Had he been more successful in discovering *the boy's* identity, he would have given *him* up to the Flame Temple—with great reluctance, maybe, but he would have done it. Would do it. Nothing had really changed.

A month after the attack, Martin felt confident enough to return to the Prophetic Realm. But to his private relief, the boy was gone. The links, old and new, had been severed.

Each night since, he'd taken to the skies searching for any sign of the boy's presence and each night he'd found nothing. Instead he dreamed; dreams of the past, of the future, of Pri Garius and Pri Marcus, of Carla and her family, and of an Essusiate man, with blood-spattered hands and death in his eyes, creeping toward his door.

He felt rather than heard the man enter the Hospice. Half in trance, he watched him make his silent way down the corridor, pause, then reach for the door. Eyes slitted, Martin carefully brought a loaded crossbow up from beside the bed. Someone was going to die tonight, and it

was not going to be him. He had one shot. He would not
miss. Silently he released the safety as the door opened.

When he was five years old Martin had seen a man
killed.

He'd gone into the Green Whelk Tavern, searching for
his mother. She'd been sitting with a group of sailors and
had actually lifted him onto her knee while she talked.
He'd sat there, taking small sips of her drink, not understanding what was going on around him, but happy to be
in her company. The room was smoky and loud even
though it was the middle of the day, and so only Martin,
with his sensitive mental gifts, had turned to look when
the burly man had entered the tavern.

The woman seated by the door had barely glanced
around. She'd simply stood and driven a knife into the
man's chest with one blurred motion, then shoved him out
the door. It had all taken less than a single breath.

Martin had seen the surprise on the man's face and the
jolt of realization and pain before the door had closed on
his falling body. This would be no different.

The door opened. Martin saw the figure from his
dreams and pulled the trigger.

They buried the man the next morning, placing him as
far from the Triarctic dead as possible. Martin spoke the
Essusiate blessing and, for a moment, he thought he saw
Carla standing beside the grave, the dragon tattoo on her
cheek staring at him with tiny, yellow eyes.

Staring into his fire, Martin watched the dragon wraith
across the flames, then laid his head back. The Archpriest
would be sending for him soon, and though this meeting
would proceed differently from the last one, the consequences could be much the same. He needed to dream
what she was going to say and what he was going to
reply.

In the fire, a log collapsed into coals, spewing out a

surge of images both past and present. As they rose up to spin about his face, Martin fell asleep in his chair.

Breymouth Port, Staffolk
Spring, Mean Boaldyn 493 DR

He had spent months searching for the boy in both the Prophetic and the Physical Realms. As autumn gave over to an unusually harsh winter, he'd remained in the Octavian Hospice, speaking prophecy for the Physicians and patients and helping out where he could. Pri Nadia had told him that she'd sent a message to the Flame Temple when he'd been brought in and had received one terse note in reply. They were to give Martin what assistance he required, and when he was strong enough, he was to continue on with his mission. Martin wasn't certain whether he was relieved or worried that he hadn't been called back to give an account of his failure, but when winter gave over to the spring of 493 he left the Hospice and headed northeast.

   He walked all the way to the coast of Wiltham, then headed south and, although much of the terrain seemed familiar, especially in Kairnbrook, he found no physical evidence to suggest the boy or his compatriots had been anywhere nearby. After a week of fruitless searching in the Prophetic Realm, he carried on through Clairfield, skirting the edge of the Bricklin Forest.

   He walked for over a month, half in trance and half in the Physical Realm, following where his Vision led him. At dusk he took shelter where he could, then rose at dawn to continue on. He bathed when a convenient stream or brook widened out enough to immerse himself and ate when he could find food. He hadn't bothered to shave since he'd left the Hospice and most of the people he met on the road assumed he was some kind of Essusiate Pilgrim. Those who were of that faith took him in, fed him, prayed over him, then let him go on his way. At these times it seemed as if Carla was walking beside him, leading him by the hand. At other times it was Pri Garius who urged him on, promising success over just one more hill.

His strength finally gave out at Breymouth Port in northern Staffolk. He collapsed against a pylon on Collin's Wharf, his mind reaching out on its own for the most unlikely rescuer: Osarion DeSandra.

The Flame Temple, Branbridge

The Deputy Seer stood on the edge of the Prophetic Realm, staring out at a clear, crystal plain. There was no sound, no color, no physical sensations except the softest feeling of sheets against his body which told him that he dreamed. Patiently, he waited for the dream to become prophecy.

The landscape's indistinct features solidified. He was standing on his private balcony looking out at the Temple's inner courtyard. Far away he could feel his lips move, reporting the imagery even though there was no scribe to record it.

"Something which will affect the heart of the Flame Priests."

The sky above was dark with rain clouds, the flagstone paths between the neatly trimmed flower beds below already spotted with moisture.

"It will be dramatic and has already begun."

In the center of the courtyard, a hooded figure stood staring up at the Deputy Seer, power swirling about his head and shoulders. As he lowered the hood, the torches lining the surrounding cloisters illuminated his face. Martin Wrey. His dark eyes were filled with blood. Osarion's own eyes narrowed.

"Melodramatic, don't you think," he asked coldly.

The words formed little ice pellets which sprinkled against the other man's upturned face. Martin never blinked.

"What do you want?"

The courtyard opened up to become a vast expanse of wooded coastline. In the distance a great, gray cyclone drove a ragged path of destruction through the trees, unearthing a stand of ancient oaks like they were seedlings, then turned to score across the rough waves of the Bjerre Sea. Great gouts of water, intertwined with fire, were sucked up into its core until it was a ponderous mass of swollen potential hovering over the world.

"Is that meant to suggest that something involving the Aspects is occurring some distance from here?"

The figure never moved.

"Well? Will this . . . whatever it is dissipate or will it explode in an earth-shattering catastrophe?"

Not surprisingly, the cyclone tore itself to pieces, covering the landscape in darkness. A single, faint light illuminated Martin's face. Osarion looked down at him, his expression cold.

"I see. And what am I supposed to do about this, particularly?"

Tendrils of power reached up, and Osarion slapped them away.

"In imagery or in words, if you don't mind. I have no intention of allowing you to touch me."

The figure's throat worked.

"Go east."

Osarion raised one eyebrow.

"Why?"

The darkness thinned and soon the Deputy Seer was able to make out a forest and a caravan of tinkers. He Saw Martin fighting an invisible force of gray bands and hammering blows, Saw him pinned to a great web of reflective power strands and Saw a shadowy figure stalking toward him. The figure raised a knife, then fell, a crossbow quarrel buried in his forehead. Martin jerked himself free from the web.

Despite himself, Osarion was impressed. He'd never known the other man was such a good shot. He'd have to remember that.

The scene shifted, and Martin lay curled up behind a dockside tavern his face pale and sheened with sweat. Beyond his hiding place stretched a line of ships, the bright sunlight illuminating their sails with a deep ruddy glow. The nearest carried a figurehead of a brown bear holding a torch. Osarion nodded in understanding. *Kassandra's Pride* was at Breymouth Port this week being outfitted for Prince Marsellus' latest trip to Danelind. So Martin was at Breymouth, and he was ill.

"And?"

The sun touched the edge of the horizon. In the dazzling orange light two paths emanated from Martin's still form. One led to dawn, the other to nightfall. And Osarion knew. He was being asked to save Martin Wrey's life.

He almost laughed out loud. Of all the outrageous things he'd Seen in Vision, this one took the prize. He sent out the first question that came into his mind on a sarcastic thread of images.

"Why should I?"

The gray cyclone rose up again, churning the landscape into a bloody froth.

"I See. So if I let you die, the world comes to an end? Is that it? And if I save your life, what then? Peace, prosperity, and good harvests for all eternity? Think highly of yourself, don't you?"

The cyclone faded away as the Prophetic Realm returned to the clear, crystal plain and the Deputy Seer awoke.

Dawn trickled in through the shutters to cast an array of pale white light across his bed. He considered the dream.

Osarion DeSandra had never doubted a Vision in his life. He'd never denied, ignored, or refused to follow where one led. He'd never even wanted to. Until now. He frowned.

He'd long ago decided that his hatred for Martin Wrey
was entirely justified. Martin was an Apostate and a dangerously unstable force in the Prophetic Realm. His Vision was tainted with madness. But this had not been
Martin's Vision. This had been his own. And his were not
random and chaotic spewings of imagery from the
Prophetic Realm; they were messages from the Living
Flame with clarity, purpose, and direction. They were to
be taken seriously and they were to be obeyed.

Calling for his Acolyte, he rose and began to dress.

The ride to Breymouth was made in silence. Kaliana
DeKathrine had loaned Osarion her nephew, Allen, for the
journey and, overawed by the Deputy Seer, the boy had
constrained his naturally effusive nature. It was just as
well. With his own mood darkening with every mile, Osarion DeSandra was not in the mood to engage in conversation with a Junior Flame Champion. When they reached
the harbor, Osarion didn't even pause. He simply rode
straight onto the pier, stopping at the jumbled pile of nets
and driftwood behind the Drunken Oyster Tavern. There
he could just make out Martin's body, sprawled unconscious under the partial cover of an upturned fishing boat.

Osarion looked down at the other man in disgust, then
gestured at Allen. Dismounting, the Flame Champion
caught the man up and hauled his limp body over his
horse, then mounted behind him. Without a word, Osarion
turned his mount and headed back for the capital, Allen
and his burden following silently behind. Mission accomplished. Whatever he personally thought of his Vision,
Osarion had obeyed it, and the sooner he got back to the
Flame Temple the faster Martin became someone else's
responsibility. Glancing over at the other man, he wondered, not for the first time, why Martin was never capable of being this efficient. No drama, no vague
metaphysical puzzles; just get in and get out. He shook
his head, vowing to himself that the next time Martin

Wrey got himself entangled in this sort of nonsense he could sort it out himself.

Behind them, the signs played out a sarcastic little response, then dissipated with the rising wind.

They were a full day returning home. Osarion directed Allen to give Martin over to the Temple Physician, then went before the Archpriest with the ludicrous task of asking her to take the man in because *the Deputy Seer's Vision required it*. She took Martin back, of course, no questions asked, as she always had, and only Osarion's steadfast obedience to Temple authority kept him from voicing his dissension, even though it was exactly what he'd asked for. The entire situation was making his jaw ache.

After receiving Allen's report on Martin's condition: exhaustion coupled with dehydration; he went looking for signs of this imminent catastrophe yet, once again, found nothing. The Prophetic Realm was as clear and calm as it always was. Hardly surprised, he put it from his thoughts. He had enough to do without chasing down another one of Martin Wrey's wild geese.

Martin himself was unable to shed any light on the Deputy Seer's dream either. He seemed to have used up the last of his sanity calling Osarion to his side, spending most days staring blankly up at the infirmary ceiling, his mind wandering lost in the Prophetic Realm. On other days his Physicians could not even rouse him enough to open his eyes. Finally they'd gone to the Deputy Seer.

"He needs you to bring him back."

Osarion set down his pen very carefully before fixing the senior of the two Physicians with a cold stare.

"You can't possibly be serious?"

She met his eyes, undaunted.

"You were the last to make contact with him in the

*Prophetic Realm. He knows your signature, he reached
out to it once. He will again."*

"Fine." *He picked up his pen.*

She blinked.

"You'll do it?"

"When I've completed my work here, I will attend his
bedside for the fifteen minutes I have before Evening
Mass. If that isn't adequate time to bring him back,
arrange a daily appointment for us with my Acolyte. Now
if you don't mind, I have actual* Temple *business to complete first."*

*Returning to the document he was signing, he pointedly
ignored them until they departed. He would obey his Vision, but he did not have to do it graciously.*

Osarion spent a month coaxing Martin back from the
Prophetic Realm much as one might coax a feral cat into a
cottage. For the first week he simply stood on the edge of
the crystal plain, sending ribbons of calm into the tangled
underbrush that was the other man's mind. When they finally made contact, he let Martin come to him. His presence, hazy and indistinct, hovered just out of reach.
Osarion sent one fine strand of stability toward him and
waited. After a long time, Martin took it.

A flood of images rushed toward the Deputy Seer, only
to smack against his rigid self-control. They fell back,
then rushed forward again, to break against him once
again. Finally they calmed. Osarion stepped forward.

He spent two weeks wading through this seemingly
senseless mishmash of experiences, possibilities, and totally unrelated events, seeking the one image that represented Martin himself. The only constant was a blue-eyed,
golden-haired youth who hovered just out of reach. Each
time Osarion followed him, he disappeared behind an indistinct web of reflective netting, but he persevered and
finally he led Osarion to a shivering brown moth, its
wings frayed and covered in dust, pressed against a

wooden door. Gently Osarion caught the moth up and brought it home.

When he was strong enough, Martin moved into quarters in the south wing tower, as far from the inhabited areas as possible. The Temple servants saw to his needs, and he spoke to no one else save the Archpriest and the Deputy Seer. In good weather he could be seen walking alone through the western end of Collin's Park which butted up against the Flame Temple grounds; in bad weather he sat by his fire, staring blankly into the flames. At night he searched for the boy, but as the months became years, he almost forgot why he was doing it. Then one night the boy burst into his dreams.

There was fire everywhere. Far away he felt the Aristok jerk awake as the Living Flame exploded into the air of the Prophetic Realm. But Martin had no time to wonder at this as, screaming in pain, the boy slammed into his sleeping mind. Without thinking, he jerked him free of the maelstrom. The fire guttered out, and Martin Wrey and Camden DeKathrine stared into each other's eyes.

The boy had grown up. Sixteen, maybe seventeen years old now, his mental abilities shone around him in a brilliant gray light, made that much brighter by the . . . Martin squinted, and the familiar residue of the Potion of Truth snapped into focus. His eyes widened. He turned and, through the link, Saw eight people seated around a bonfire, the flames illuminating their features in a crimson glow. An old woman with gray hair and gray eyes to match sat with her arms around Camden. Across from them, a tall, auburn-haired man supported a girl of similar features, surrounded by a halo of deep sea blue. To the right a beautiful pale-haired man held a boy surrounded by a vibrant green light and to the left an auburn-haired girl with eyes as red as the Flame Itself sat within the arms of a Heathland man whose presence winked in and out of existence. His power covered them all in a reflective net and, with a start, Martin realized that he was staring at the not-thing from within its . . . his protection shield. He grew very still.

Above the bonfire the colors of the Aspects spewed forth in a teetering vortex of unstable energy, Martin's intervention having jerked the gray power of the Wind away from the gestalt. And not a moment too soon. He could Feel the Aspects' Realm hovering perilously close, causing the other Realms to vibrate in time with the spinning vortex.

Martin's fear caused the image of the Archpriest of the Flame to manifest in the Vision, Camden's fear caused it to appear before them both. With a cry, he broke their link and Martin awoke to stare into the darkness, the words "Triarchy Heresy" echoing in his mind.

Around him, he Felt the entire Flame Temple sleeping peacefully, their dreams undisturbed by the events to the north. Camden DeKathrine and his people were trying to raise the Aspects behind the protection of a man who could block the Sight of others. They were dangerously close to succeeding, and the Temple Seers would never sense it until it was too late. Even the Aristok, warned by the movement of the Living Flame tonight, would not be able to pinpoint its source. If they succeeded, it could permanently destabilize the Prophetic Realm, maybe even the Physical Realms themselves, and contact with the Aspects' Realm would most certainly kill the four youths involved. The consequences of this manifestation should be sending a deafening cacophony of warning bells throughout the Prophetic Realm, but no one except one half-mad Seer had even suspected it was happening. Martin wiped the sweat from his face with the back of his hand.

That this Heathland man was powerful enough to hide a gestalt of this magnitude even from the Living Flame's own Avatar was terrifying. Whatever else came of this, he *had* to be eliminated. Half out of bed, Martin paused. The man maybe, but what about the others? Camden

DeKathrine's face hovered before his eyes, and he pulled back under the covers.

"Think, Martin, think, for once in your life," he admonished himself. "You *have* to tell the Archpriest about this, if only because the Aristok will be sending a messenger already, and she has to know why. You know what the consequences will be if you don't."

His mind rebelled sullenly.

"But what about the boy?"

"What about him?"

"They'll take him."

"Would you rather see his mind destroyed by the Aspects' Realm?"

"No, but . . ."

"But nothing. You Saw her face in the Vision, that means she must be made part of this."

"You put her face in the Vision."

"Maybe so. But, either way, you took an oath."

"An oath to the Flame? How many times have you broken that?"

"Not to the Flame. To Her."

His mind fell silent. There was no answer to that. Without the Archpriest's protection he'd be dead by now. He owned her his life, his freedom, his sanity. The boy would be all right. Once the not-thing was eliminated and the gestalt broken up he could protect him, but not before.

Rising, he threw on the first thing he could find and headed out the door.

The Temple bell had long since sounded midnight and, although the Junior Flame Champion at her door had not wanted to admit him, eventually he was shown to the Archpriest's private study. The Champion lit a single candle, then departed, and Martin was left alone to wait.

His thoughts chased themselves around and around in his head, inventing scenario after scenario, all ending badly. By the time the door opened and he heard her firm

footfall on the carpet, he'd almost worked himself into
hysterics. Going to one knee, he forced himself to calm.

"Martin."

As always, her voice sent ripples of imagery dancing
before his eyes.

He took a deep breath.

"Your Grace."

"You have something for me."

"Yes, Your Grace. I've found them."

Ten minutes later the Junior Champion was sent to
rouse the Temple's Senior Priestly Conclave to Chambers.
By the time the Deputy Seer, Coadjutor, Flame Champion
Captain, Chancellory Deputy, and Deputy Adjutant arrived in various stages of undress, the Temple was alive
with rumor. The five entered, the doors closed firmly behind them, and the rest of the Temple was left to hover
nervously about the main hallway, waiting for them to
emerge.

Inside, the Archpriest had already taken her place at the
head of the long Conclave table. Pri Breanne, the Aristok's Personal Priest, and Pri Zarion, the Temple's Liaison
to the Palace, had arrived as quickly as predicted and now
stood together by the window. Martin had taken up a position by the fire. Most gave him a single, cursory glance
before bowing to the Archpriest and taking their seats, except Drusus DeYvonne, the Chancellory Deputy, who
bristled at the sight of him, and Lorien DeKathrine who'd
never really had much against him. The latter offered him
a pipe, accepting a lit taper in return with a nod of thanks,
before taking his own seat.

The Archpriest glanced about the table.

"An hour ago the Aristok experienced a sudden upheaval within the Living Flame," she said without preamble. "It dissipated almost immediately, so His Most Holy
Majesty was unable to identify the source of Its disrup-
tion. He has asked that we do so. At the same time Martin

Wrey has had a Vision of a very dangerous working in a woodlands to the north. It *has* been identified as the Triarchy Heresy."

Her words evoked the expected responses about the table: anger, shock, disbelief. His own expression thoughtful, Osarion glanced across the room at Martin who met his gaze with a cloudy expression of his own.

The Archpriest continued, "Eight people, four acting as Avatars and four in support, have made at least one attempt to raise the Aspects, and have very nearly succeeded. Obviously, we must find these people and stop them as expeditiously as possible. Now, Martin has managed to wrest the name of one of these Avatars from his Vision: Camden DeKathrine."

Rysander, Lorien, and Kaliana all went very still. The Archpriest turned.

"My Lord Coadjutor, are you familiar with this person?"

He frowned. "There's only one Camden in the family at this time, Your Grace," he answered cautiously. "Domitia—the late Duke of Guilcove's—fourthborn. But he's just a child, thirteen, maybe fourteen years old."

"Sixteen," Kaliana amended.

"Old enough to be held responsible for acts of heresy," the Chancellory Deputy pointed out.

"If, in fact, his actions are heretical," Rysander replied coldly.

"Where is he now?" the Archpriest demanded.

Rysander shrugged. "At Kathrine's Hall or in Guilcove most likely, Your Grace. At sixteen, he'd have taken vows of one kind or another. Most of Domitia's side of the family are Sword Knights."

"No, he's not at Guilcove, Ry," Lorien interrupted. "And he's not a Sword Knight either, at least not yet. He's in Kairnbrook. You remember at Domitia's funeral, Kal? He was standing with Celestus—Celestus DeKathrine, Viscount of Kairnbrook, Your Grace." He turned to the Archpriest. "I believe Domitia sent him to foster there after Vakarus died. She needed some time in retreat, so the younger children were sent to different family members."

Kaliana nodded. "The twins, what are their names, Tatiana and Nicholas, are with Lei. Our sister Leilani, Your Grace."

"And Kairnbrook is to the north," Drusus said, a martial light growing in his eyes. "We should send a company of Flame Champions there at once."

"On what grounds?" Rysander inquired with steely politeness. "Celestus DeKathrine is a Peer of the Realm and an acclaimed scholar. Now, I've got nothing against Martin's Vision per se . . ." He glanced across the room but Martin was staring into space, seemingly oblivious to the debate. "However, I'd like to know if we have any outside corroboration? My Lord Deputy Seer?"

His eyes hooded, Osarion acknowledged him with a single tilt of the head. "Possibly. One month ago my Vision indicated that a potential upheaval involving the Aspects might be brewing. As you may recall, Your Grace, we discussed this at the time?"

"Yes."

"*Might* be brewing?" Rysander pressed. "If it was brewing now, wouldn't the Prophetic Realm be writhing like a nest of snakes?"

"Yes."

"And is it?"

"No. However," Osarion continued, his distaste at having to defend Martin making him testy, "I've been made aware of the possibility that a man with the ability to block the Sight of others may be involved."

"That's unheard of," Drusus sniffed.

Rysander ignored him "Do you think it's possible, My Lord Seer?"

Osarion gave a minimal shrug. "I really couldn't say at this time."

"For the moment, we shall proceed with the assumption that it is," the Archpriest said firmly. "With that in mind, is there anything else pertinent that we need to know about Celestus DeKathrine?"

Lorien ran his fingers through his beard with a worried expression.

"Well," he said reluctantly, "he has three other youths living at Tavencroft Keep with him."

"Three?"

"Mm-hm. There's, let's see, his daughter Danielle. Dianne, her mother—that would be Theodor's second girl—she died in . . . when was it now . . . ?"

"It hardly matters," Drusus grated.

Lorien turned a dark gaze on the other man from under his bristling eyebrows. "In eighty-three," he continued pointedly. "She drowned, as I recall, on a voyage to Danelind. So, that's Danielle and um . . . Quinton?" He glanced at Kaliana who nodded silently.

"Our nephew," Rysander added, "by Clairinda, Duke of Cambury." Suddenly he went pale. "And Alisha," he breathed.

Kaliana's eyes widened. "By the Flame."

The Archpriest's jaw tightened. "I take it by Alisha you mean, *Her Royal Highness* Alisha DeMarian, Duke of Lochsbridge, and fourth in line to the Living Flame, not some Alisha DeKathrine, fourth cousin of your grandmother's brother's niece?"

Rysander nodded. "Yes, Your Grace. Celestus is Her Highness' great uncle, brother to the Consort Hadria's father Julianus."

"And Domitia is, or rather was, the Consort Hadria's sister," Lorien added.

"So what you're saying," Drusus asked in growing horror, "is that the Viscount of Kairnbrook has involved one of the Flame's Holy Vessels in the Triarchy Heresy?"

"No," Rysander shot back. "I'm saying that one of the Flame's Holy Vessels is living at Tavencroft Keep, nothing more."

"Regardless," Osarion interrupted, "it puts a whole new and very volatile spin on the situation."

"So to speak," Lorien muttered.

The gathered ignored him.

The Archpriest looked carefully around the table. "That there is a Vessel involved means we must proceed with extreme diplomacy, but also with extreme urgency. I welcome any suggestions."

The room fell silent. Finally Rysander stirred. "A host of Flame Champions descending on Kairnbrook will only alert the countryside. I suggest we send Alexander, Duke of Guilcove, to investigate the charges. Camden is his younger brother, so he can take a fairly large entourage without garnering suspicion. If there's no evidence of heresy, he can simply visit the boy. If there is evidence, he could arrest Celestus and any other adults at Tavencroft and bring the children, especially Her Royal Highness, back to the capital."

"Might I ask, *My Lord Coadjutor,*" Drusus interrupted stiffly, "what the *ages* of these *children* might be?"

Rysander glanced at Lorien.

"Danielle and Quinton are at least seventeen," the older man admitted.

"And are therefore adults under both secular and ecclesiastical law," Drusus stated.

"As is the Prince Alisha," Rysander retorted coldly. "Would you like to arrest Her Royal Highness as well?"

"For all we know she's a hostage."

"Are you suggesting . . ."

"My Lord Deputies, we really don't have time for this," Osarion interjected smoothly. "I imagine that His Most Holy Majesty is awaiting a reply, is he not, Pri Breanne?"

"He most certainly is, My Lord," she answered.

"Then I suggest that our most pressing order of business be what to tell him."

"For now Pri Breanne will tell him that His Flame Priests are aware of the Living Flame's upheaval," the Archpriest answered. "That it is under investigation and that I will personally attend His Most Holy Majesty at His convenience. She will not divulge our suspicions of the

Triarchy Heresy or of Prince Alisha's possible involvement. I will bring that before His Majesty myself when we have more information.

"In the meantime, we will send Alexander DeKathrine to Kairnbrook—and, My Lord Deputy Seer, you will accompany him and his entourage as the Flame Temple's Representative." She turned to Lorien. "How soon can they be in Kairnbrook, My Lord Deputy Adjutant?"

"Two days, if they go by ship, Your Grace."

"You can't go by ship."

The gathered turned as Martin spoke for the first time.

"You have to go by land, or you'll be seen."

Lorien nodded. "That's true. Kairnbrook has a half-dozen towers all along the coast to watch for invasion fleets from Gallia or Bachiem."

"So how do we proceed?"

"On horseback through Clairfield and the Bricklin Forest, Your Grace."

"The Bricklin won't be easy with a mounted party," Kaliana pointed out.

"No. but there are paths. I've Seen them."

"Then you are to accompany them, Martin," the Archpriest said, "to guide them through the forest."

"Yes, Your Grace."

"Then it's decided." She glanced around. "No one is to speak of this, not even with your Acolytes."

Lorien raised an eyebrow. "The Temple's going to go mad with speculation, Your Grace."

"Let it. I don't want the words Triarchy Heresy spoken so much as once beyond these walls. My Lord Deputy Seer, you and Martin are to leave immediately. And Martin, you will speak with the Deputy Seer regarding our earlier conversation before you do."

"Yes, Your Grace."

"My Lord Captain, if you would be so kind as to accompany them to Kathrine's Hall and make our request to the Duke of Guilcove. Tell him only as much as is absolutely necessary."

Kaliana stood. "Of course, Your Grace."

"Very good. The Conclave is dismissed. My Lord Coadjutor, would you stay please."

She rang a small bell as the gathered rose, and an Acolyte put her head through the door immediately.

"Meg, bring the Deputy Marshal and the Temple Herbalist to me at once."

"Yes, Your Grace."

Osarion and Martin made their way down the main hall, ignoring the whispers which followed along behind them like the wake of a ship. As Martin turned toward the infirmary wing, the Deputy Seer glanced over at him.

"You have that constipated Vision look," he said bluntly. "What has you worried?"

Martin shrugged. "I was just thinking that the Archpriest has a lot of DeKathrine advisers involved in this."

The other man snorted. "The Archpriest has a lot of DeKathrine advisers involved in everything."

"Yes, but this time it's a DeKathrine issue."

"You think it will impair their judgment?"

"Who knows. Would it impair yours? If this was a De-Sandra issue?"

"No."

"Then maybe I'm worrying for nothing. But just remember, the leader of this little ride will be a DeKathrine Duke and all the swords at his back will be DeKathrine swords. I'd be on my guard if I were you. I know I will be. Also, we have another problem, one that the Archpriest didn't want to discuss in Conclave." He glanced quickly about to make sure they wouldn't be overheard. "The four who're acting as Avatars got as close as they did because they'd all taken the Potion of Truth."

Osarion froze in his tracks. "That's not possible."

"It is possible. I Saw the residue when I made contact with Camden DeKathrine. I Saw it on all four of them."

The Deputy Seer's face hardened. "How did they acquire the Potion of Truth?" he asked between gritted teeth.

"I don't know, but I'll bet the Deputy Marshal is going to find out."

"By the Flame! This just keeps getting better and better. Do you foresee it becoming a problem for our approach?"

Martin frowned. "I don't think so. If they're using it to gain closer access to the Aspects' Realm, they won't want to waste it on short-range precognition. Also, they won't know how to direct their minds or even how to interpret any Visions they might have."

"Well, that's some good news. Who knows, maybe if we wait long enough, the Potion of Truth and the Aspects' Realm together will so mangle their little brains that our problem will solve itself."

"Unless they succeed."

"Yes, unless they succeed."

Osarion cocked his head to one side. "And what about this man, what did you call him, a not-man?"

"Close enough."

"What of him? Is he a danger to us."

Martin met his eyes. "He is *the* danger to us. Because of him, we're blind. Whatever else happens he *has* to be killed or we're lost."

"Killed?"

"Killed. I'll do it myself if I have to."

They paused at the archway to the infirmary.

"Anyway," Martin added, "if I'm going to spend two days on horseback, I'll need a lot of liniment."

"Fine. I have to speak with my secretary as well. I'll meet you in the stables in one hour."

"Have them find me something docile, will you, one that's not too tall?"

"How about an ass?"

Martin ignored Osarion's pointed tone of voice. "As long as it doesn't fling me into a ditch, I don't care what it is." Turning on his heel, he left the Deputy Seer standing in the hall.

Osarion watched him go with a frown, then headed for

his own suite. If they were going to spend two days on the road, he was going to need a warm cloak. And his sword.

Behind him, the Temple buzzed with wilder and wilder rumors, but no one would have any true idea what was about to take place until the Temple Seers returned with three DeKathrine prisoners and the body of a DeMarian Duke.

12. Alisha DeMarian

THE well-maintained paths of Branshire's largest
Royal Deer Park were unusually dry for the time of
year. The small group of nobles that cantered along behind the Prince Marsellus had been riding since well before dawn, so it was with some relief that they reined up
before the miniature hunting lodge in the center of the
park. Grooms came forward to accept their mounts while,
from within, they could already smell breakfast cooking.
The Royal Duke of Yorbourne might demand an absurdly
early beginning to the day, but at least he set an excellent
table. At the Prince's gesture they dismounted quickly and
crowded inside, his hunting hounds close behind them.
Marsellus glanced over at the man still mounted beside
him.

"Equally eager for a meal," he said with a smile.

Alexander DeKathrine nodded. "You work them as
hard, Highness." Dismounting, he held the Prince's horse
while the other man jumped down. Then, turning, he spotted a mounted figure heading up the path.

"Rider coming, Highness. A messenger from the
Palace?"

Marsellus squinted in the direction he pointed. "I don't
think so. No, you can see the green tabard. DeKathrine.
For you, I'd say, or Nathaniel."

The rider turned out to be Ewan. Dismounting quickly, he bowed to the Prince.

"Excuse me, Your Highness, but Her Lordship Joanne DeKathrine has requested the Duke of Guilcove's immediate return to Kathrine's Hall, if that might be possible, Sir?"

"Nothing too serious, I hope?"

"I don't believe so, Highness, no one in the family is either injured or ill. Her Lordship's message just said: Come home at once if the Prince will give you leave."

"Of course." Marsellus turned to Alec. "Did you want an escort, My Lord?"

The other man shook his head. "No, thank you, Highness. Ewan will do."

"Well, then you'd best be off. Give my love to Jo and bring Anna to supper if you can."

"I will, Highness. Thank you, Sir."

Swinging into the saddle, Alec turned his mount south and headed up the path, Ewan close behind him.

It took just over an hour to make it back to Kathrine's Hall, but instead of Jo, he found two Flame Temple Seers waiting in the chapel and his Cousin Kaliana in his private study. She filled him in on the possible crisis brewing up north. When she finished, he poured himself a stiff drink.

"Heresy," he repeated. "You're certain?"

She grimaced. "No, I'm not certain. In fact this whole thing could be a load of horse shit, but the Archpriest's pet Seer is certain and that's enough to initiate an investigation. Rysander managed to convince Her Grace that it should be conducted quietly at this stage, and she's agreed to let you handle it because Cam's your younger brother. Take enough retainers to make a show of force once you get to Kairnbrook, but not so many that rumor outrides you there."

Alec crossed to the window, watching the clouds gather to the west. "It's a lot to take in," he said. "Cam's always loved the Wind, but the Triarchy Heresy? It was hard enough to teach him his letters; I can't see him studying some obscure religious philosophy." He turned. "You said this Seer saw him in a Vision?"

"That's right. Apparently they have some kind of connection."

"So Cam might have contacted him?"

"Possibly. I really don't know, Alec, but at least we're being given the chance to find out. If Drusus DeYvonne'd had his way, I'd be halfway there with an arrest warrant by now." She frowned. "I have to ask, but for now your answer doesn't have to leave this room. The last time you saw Cam, did he do or say anything that might suggest to you now that he could be involved in heresy, either by force or by design?"

He met her eyes.

"No."

"You're certain?"

"Yes."

Kali stared searchingly at him, then shrugged. "Well then, that's a good sign." She stood. "Can you leave immediately?"

"Define immediately."

"Now."

"No. The Prince Marsellus is expecting Anna and me at the palace tonight."

"The Archpriest will explain your absence."

"What do I tell the family?"

"Only that you've been sent north by the Aristok's command. Tell them nothing about Cam, Alisha, or the reason why."

"And what do I do when I get there?"

"Nothing complicated. Just go and visit your little brother. While the Deputy Seer's questioning Celestus, take him for a ride and ask him flat out if anything's going on. He'll tell you. Cam's always been a very honest boy."

"It's not that simple, Kali."

"Why not?"

"Because I haven't seen Cam but once in four years

and that was at our mother's funeral. He didn't want to talk to me then, and I can't see things having changed."

"What happened?"

"I'm not sure." Turning from the window, Alec dropped into a chair. "After Father died, Cam got very moody. Mother thought it best to send him to Uncle Celestus for the summer, and I thought it best to leave him be, let him get over it in the company of his cousins. Afterward there was war, then Mother's death." He grimaced. "It's my fault. The time goes by so quickly and before you know it, it's almost four years later. Distance becomes a habit. Celestus said he was happy. I left it at that."

"High time to pick it up again, I'd say." She made for the door. "It's probably nothing, anyway, Alec. Martin Wrey's half mad on a good day and, between you and me, the Deputy Seer's not all that eager to follow someone else's Vision, so take them to Kairnbrook, patch things up with Cam, and bring him home. It's time he took oaths, anyway. Make him a Sword Knight, take him with you next time you go to Danelind, and everything else will sort itself out."

"Yes, I imagine you're right."

"Good. Well, I'll see myself out. Contact me as soon as you get back, will you? My oaths are sworn to the Flame Temple, but we're family, and family has to protect each other, especially with DeYvonnes and DeSandras breathing down our necks."

"I will, Kali, and thank you."

She nodded. As she passed the Steward, she jerked her head toward the study. "He needs you."

The weather held for two days as the Duke's small company made their way northeast through Essusiate Mistonshire and Prince Tatarina's Dukedom of Clairfield. The Temple Seers kept strictly to themselves. Subdued by their Lord's brooding silence, the DeKathrine retainers rode quietly, their curiosity over the secrecy of their mission growing as they turned off the main post road and made for the Bricklin Forest. They reached the southeastern edge by midmorning on the second day, and here, with dark storm-clouds gathering to the north, Martin Wrey took the lead.

An hour into the trees, it began to rain. It didn't let up for three days. Undeterred, Martin led them down narrow, briar-choked tracks—barely recognizable as paths, beside slowly swelling streams and through bracken overhung with dripping branches. They paused in whatever forester's cottage or charcoal burner's hut afforded them shelter, but by the time they reached the clearing where Celestus had held the first Circle with the Potion of Truth, they were soaked through and in foul tempers.

The Seers immediately dismounted to examine the remnants of the bonfire, then set about preparing to enter Vision in the hopes that proximity might allow them some glimmer of Celestus' plans before they walked into his stronghold. Forbidden to make a fire this close to Tavencroft, the retainers huddled together in the partial shelter of the ruined tower. Alec handed his reins to Ewan, then made for the footpath just visible through the trees. The Seers would likely be a while and he wanted to get a look at his great uncle's keep. Passing under the trees, he headed up the path.

Meanwhile, in Danielle's Tower, Cam stood by the south window, staring out at the Bricklin Forest. He'd felt restless and claustrophobic all day, unable to go riding because of the driving rain. The keep was cold and damp, the inner courtyard full of water. It ran in rivulets down the tower walls, carving a dozen little streams in the muddy ground and making walking treacherous. Outside the keep was worse. Ross had returned from Gressam to report half the Whroxin River's south bank had collapsed with the other half looking to follow. The road was mud up to the ankles. Everything was gray and wet and dismal.

Cam frowned at the mist-covered trees. Uncle Celestus had planned another Circle for tonight, but with the

weather as bad it was, it would have to be put off. They
were now too powerful to hold a working indoors. That
had darkened Dani's mood, and after a nasty fight with
Quin, she'd stormed off to the gatehouse while he'd shut
himself in the library. Cam and Lisha had spent the morning sparring in the main hall, but the DeMarian girl was
moody and distracted, and after a while, she tossed her
practice sword aside and dropped down by the fire, to
stare mutely into the flames. Cam had wandered up to
their tower intent on taking a nap, but something had
drawn him to the window.

Now, leaning his elbows against the wet sill, he wished
gloomily that they'd never left Heathland. Although the
weather was often as bad, it never seemed so oppressive.
Even the Wind had nothing except rain and flooding to
talk about today.

With a sigh, he sent his mind out to touch the thoughts
of his cousins, but nothing had changed. Quin was reading a long, dull book on siege engines, Dani was playing
skeans with the gatehouse guards, and Lisha was still staring into the main hall fire, her mind unsettled. Cam
watched the flames weave a dancing pattern of signs before their eyes, before gently disengaging.

Lisha had been quiet and withdrawn ever since the
night they'd nearly formed the full gestalt. The Living
Flame's violent reaction had upset her even though Uncle
Celestus had explained that, as the single Aspect with an
absent Avatar, the link to the Flame was bound to be com-
promised. Next time, they would join their minds together
first, with Lisha cocooned in their collective hands—
much as Cam had been before—then, they would reach
for their Aspects as one. Lisha had seemed to accept this,
but Cam, who often took a long time to come to a full understanding of his own thoughts, was certain she was
mulling over reservations she didn't feel comfortable
bringing up. But she would eventually. Lisha wasn't one
to bottle up her feelings.

A shaft of sunlight broke through the trees.

As for the Flame's *True* Vessel, Kether had said the Aristok had reacted to the upheaval but, like the Flame Priests, could not break through the Mirror's protection to pinpoint the source. They were still safe. He hadn't said anything about Martin, so Cam assumed no one else had seen him. He breathed a sigh of relief. Although he was grateful for the Seer's intervention, and glad that his uncle and Pri Gorwynne hadn't actually killed the man, his renewed contact brought back all the old questions and fears: what if the others found out about him, what if he found out too much about them. But that night, when his sleeping mind reached out for him, the Branion Seer was gone again as if he'd never been there. Cam hadn't felt him since.

He sighed, annoyed that he was so disappointed about missing a contact he was afraid to keep in the first place.

The rain began to taper off.

He sent his mind out, absently touching a seagull skimming the shallow waters of the Washe. He smiled as he grew suddenly hungry for fish, then released it and moved up the rapidly flowing Whroxin, dancing across the rain-flattened reeds, to the warrens and over the western edge of the Bricklin.

A familiar presence flitted past his thoughts. He frowned and reached out, but just as he thought he'd caught it again, the wind gusted in through the window, flicking his hair into his eyes. By the time he was able to see again, the presence was gone and the rain had stopped.

Craning his neck, he peered up at the sky. The sun shone through a break in the clouds. They were still heavy with unfallen rain, but for now it looked as if they might have a few minutes' respite. He made for the door.

Passing the main hall, he paused, then put his head in the doorway.

Lisha wasn't one to bottle up her feelings.

"I'm going for a ride. Did you want to come?"

She glanced up, her flame-sparked eyes shadowed.

"Isn't it raining?"

"It's stopped." He took a step into the room. "Don't you want to get out for a bit?"

"I suppose." She stood. "What about the others?"

The sun passed behind a cloud.

"By the time we convince them, it could storm again, and if I don't get out of here soon, I'm going to go mad. You could use the fresh air as well to clear out all the shadows in your head."

"Who says I have shadows in my head?"

"I do; you've been wrapped up in them all day. C'mon. We'll go up to the warrens and check out that tree that got hit by lightning two days ago."

"All right."

She rose, and with one last glance at the dancing flames, followed him from the room.

Once outside, they turned their horses onto the narrow path west around Tavencroft. The surrounding underbrush was thick with thorny bracken. Keeping as far from the crumbling river bank as they were able, they made their way toward the warrens, riding in silence until they crested a small hill which overlooked a rowan tree, splintered beyond recognition. Here they reined up and sat for a long time, staring out at the circular scattering of bark and wood shards.

Breathing in the cool air, Cam stretched in the saddle.

"Nice to get out, isn't it? If this weather keeps up, we might even have our Circle tonight."

Lisha shook her head, her expression clouded. "We won't."

"You don't think so?"

"No."

He glanced over at her with a worried frown.

"Are you all right, Lisha?"

She met his gaze seriously. "I had a Vision, Cam."

"When? Last night?"

"No. Last week. When we linked with our Aspects, I had a Vision about the future."

She fell silent and, after a while, Cam glanced over at her again. "And it wasn't a good Vision," he hazarded.

"No."

"Did you want to talk about it?"

"I don't know. I don't think it will do any good."

"Was it about us?"

"Sort of." She grimaced. "It wasn't that clear. I just know we won't hold our Circle tonight." She turned her flame-sparked gaze on his face. "I don't think we'll ever hold another Circle again."

In the forest clearing, Martin crouched by the bonfire, oblivious to the weather, his hands deep in the wet ashes. He could feel the boy's presence, but the others were still invisible, safe behind the not-thing's protection.

As Alec returned to the clearing, Osarion crouched down beside the other Seer.

"Anything?"

"Just Camden."

"Do you need help?"

Martin breathed out a careful sigh.

"Yes."

Cam's eyes widened. "Do you know why?"

Lisha shook her head. "Something's going to happen. Something terrible."

"What?"

"I don't know."

Osarion held out a flask. "The Potion of Truth. Cold, but still effective. We'll search together," he offered with studied composure.

Surprised, Martin accepted the flask. Taking a long swallow, he then handed it back and, after flicking off the mixture of mud and ash, the Deputy Seer followed suit.

Together they began the ritual breathing that would drop them into the Prophetic Realm.

"Maybe you should tell Uncle Celestus."

"I tried, Cam, but I can't. The Flame doesn't want me to."

"But you can tell me?"

"Sort of."

She stared out at the line of trees in the distance, the flames in her eyes all but obliterating both iris and pupils.

"It's in the Bricklin, she said, her voice suddenly hushed. "I can feel it watching us, waiting for us to make a mistake, like a dragon readying to attack. And it's going to attack soon. It's getting really tired of waiting."

Cam felt the hair on the back of his neck rise.

"What is it?"

"I don't know, but I'll know soon."

He turned his mount around. "We should get back," he tried, but his cousin just shook her head.

"It's too late." She turned to stare at him, her eyes glowing hotly. "It's going to rain again."

As one, the Seers dropped down into the Prophetic Realm, Osarion anchoring their Vision while Martin cast his mind out like a net. Bands of potential appeared before them, but rather than transforming into Osarion's crystal plain or Martin's chaotic jumble of imagery, they took the form of a rain-soaked courtyard, dark storm clouds hovering overhead. With a start, the Deputy Seer recognized the setting of his earlier Vision. Martin turned to look at him, and the other man Saw his eyes slowly fill with blood. Fighting the urge to jerk away, he reached out.

"Martin, what do you see?"

Rain splattering against his face, Cam touched his cousin on the shoulder.

"We really should get back."

Staying perfectly still, Lisha stared into the distance, her crimson eyes blank and staring. "Cam?"

"Yes?"

"Is the river on fire?"

"No."

"Are you sure?"

Cam risked a glance behind them at the swollen Whroxin.

"Yes."

"Then why is it so red?"

Moving very slowly, Cam took the reins from her slack fingers.

"It's not. If you turn and look, you'll see it's the same color it always is."

She shook her head. "I don't dare. If I look, the fire will get me."

"The fire can't get you. You're a DeMarian. Come on, we need to go back." Gently urging his mount forward, he began to retrace their path, her reins held firmly in his hand.

"Martin, tell me, what do you see?"

The ritual question sent ripples of power through the Prophetic Realm. Martin blinked and his eyes cleared for just an instant.

"Camden."

"Anyone else?"

"No, just him. Everyone else is still hidden."

"What's Camden doing?"

"Riding. To the west."

"Is he alone?"

"Yes." He frowned. "No? I don't know. I can't See . . ." He sighed. *"I can't See."*

"Is Camden aware of your presence?"

"No."

A flicker of something touched his mind. "But . . ."

"But?"

The flicker came again, like a single whisper of fire across a nearly spent coal. "Something . . ."

"Some thing or some one?"

"I'm not sure."

"If you reach out, will Camden become aware of your presence?"

"I don't know. I . . . don't think so."

"Then try."

Martin sent his thoughts toward the west. The flicker came again, more strongly this time, then the not-thing's net snapped into being.

Martin jerked back. "I can't." His voice raised in panic as his Sight began to gyrate.

"It's all right, stop trying and disengage. Can you hear me, Martin? Disengage."

A sudden flood of imagery closed over his head. He Saw a copper-haired, fiery-eyed, child running through a field of meadow flowers, Saw her reach out her hand and send a bolt of crimson power into a rye field, and Saw the Living Flame reach out to embrace her as an Avatar only to be thwarted by It's existing link with Its True Vessel. He saw her reach out again, and a shadow the color of flames reflected in blood blotted out his Vision.

"I Saw Alisha DeMarian," he gasped, fear tightening his throat.

The Deputy Seer froze. "What do you mean Saw? What was she doing?"

Martin opened his mouth to speak and an icy cold hand reached out to steal the words as they left his lips. He shuddered. "I can't . . ."

"Is she in danger?"

"I can't . . ."

"Try, Martin. Try to See."

"It won't let me."

"What won't let you?"

Martin shook his head.

"Try!"

*The pressure of Osarion's abilities shoved against his
mind. Martin fought back and suddenly he was thrown
against the not-thing's net.*

In the library, Kether Braithe snapped his head up.
"Did you feel something?"
Quin glanced up from the book he was reading.
"Huh?"
"Did you feel something?"
"No."

*Martin struggled against the sticky bands then sud-
denly something, or someone, jerked him free.*

Quin frowned.
"Like what?
"Like a presence?"
"No. Did you?"
Kether closed his eyes. His net stretched out before
him, taut and undisturbed.
"I suppose not."
"Probably your stomach. Mine always makes its *pres-
ence* known around this time of day."
"Maybe."

A ghostly figure appeared before Martin's eyes.

"Have you ever Seen a ball of fire explode over a
man's head, showering him with rose petals and golden
coins?"

Martin swung his fist at the figure in frustration.
"Not now!"
Osarion blinked. "What?"

"Have you ever Seen a full complement of white ships,
with dragons on their prows, set out on a wind-tossed sea
only to be engulfed by a fiery vortex half a mile high?"

                        *   *   *

"Garius, go away!"
"Who's Garius?"

"Have you ever been to the Flame Temple of Branbridge?"

*Growling low in his throat, Martin made a grab for the
spirit of his former Mentor.*
*"I don't have time for this, old man! Alisha DeMarian
is in danger and if I don't break through this barrier, she
is going to die!"*
"What!"

"There is a way."

The room was on fire, smoke filling the air with a
choking fog. A moment away from death, he caught a
glimpse of a place so primordial it nearly destroyed his infant's mind.

"No."
"You've done it before."
"And I was unconscious for four days."
"I'll help you."
"I can't."
"You can. Take my hand. Reach out."

*In the clearing, Martin's head snapped back so fast he
cracked it against the ground. Blood began to fill his
mouth with warmth.*

"I See the Shadow Catcher!"

Rising, Kether crossed to the window, staring out at the
rain-soaked courtyard. He frowned. Whatever the net
might demonstrate, *something* had touched his mind. He
turned.

"Where are the others?"

"Huh?"

"Where are the others?"

Quin made a sound that might have been a distracted "I don't know."

The Mirror took a deep breath. "Quinton, put the book down. *Where* are the others?"

"I dunno."

"Can you *contact* them, please?"

"Oh, yeah, sure." Quin's eyes flared green. "Dani's in the gatehouse, Cam and Lisha are riding in the warrens. Hey, it stopped raining."

"Are they all right?"

"Dani's pissed. She's just lost three games of skeans in a row."

"And the others?"

"They're . . ." Quin frowned. "I'm not sure."

"What do you mean, you're not sure?"

"Cam's upset about something, and Lisha's . . ."

"What?"

Quin paled. "Something's wrong."

"Wrong? How?"

"There's a huge red cloud hovering over her. It's . . . it's almost on top of her." His voice rose in panic. "If it touches her . . ." He jerked his mind from the link. "She needs help, Kether."

"We have to find your uncle."

Together, they ran for the door.

The very nearness of the Captain of Death made his limbs shake so hard he thought he was about to have a seizure.

Martin shook off the past with an impatient growl.

He'd found the Shadow Catcher the same way he had all those years before. He'd watched It squeeze its way from the Aspects' Realm, then descend upon the world on Its thread of gray shadow. He followed. Together they pushed into the Physical Realm and, between the space of one heartbeat and the next, Martin stood on the bank of the Whroxin River beside two youths on horseback. Reaching into the Prophetic Realm, he formed the strands of potential into words.

"She's to the west, by the river."

"My Lord of Guilcove!"

"They're to the west, by the river."

Kether's shouts had brought Celestus and the other adults running while Quin had contacted Dani. She'd arrived in the great hall seconds after her father. Now, while she maintained a link with Cam, Quin stretched his mind out through the earth in a vast circle around Tavencroft, looking for the presence that had touched Kether's mind. What he found almost made him choke.

"Seers in the Bricklin behind the keep!"

Celestus grabbed him by the shoulders. "How many?"

"Two! They know, I can feel it. And there's others, soldiers and . . . Alec, Alec DeKathrine. They're riding hard for the west." He stared up at his uncle, his green-washed eyes wide with fear. "They're heading for Cam and Lisha!"

Celestus whirled about. "All right, I'll go for them, Danielle, tell Camden I'm coming. Vincent, warn the keep. The rest of you, run; the enemy is upon us."

They scattered.

The rain began to beat down in torrents and the path, already slick with mud, began to crumble away. Cam led Lisha's horse carefully, trying to keep as far from the riverbank as possible. The DeMarian girl rode pale and silent as if she were in a trance. Cam had tried to link with her, but her mind was lost in a heavy fog, impenetrable even in concert with the others. Now, maneuvering over a particularly wide crack across the path, Cam risked a glance at her face.

"Everything's going to be fine, Lisha," he said in as reassuring a voice as he could muster. "Dani says Uncle Celestus is coming. He's going to fix everything, you'll see. So don't worry. All right? Don't worry. Don't worry, Cam," he added in a scared voice. "Uncle Celestus will fix everything."

Again, he tried to link with her, and again the fog thwarted his attempt. Maintaining an open link, he turned back to the path as, beside them, the rapidly flowing Whroxin caught up a willow sapling and tore it from the bank.

It grew cold, the sky darkened, and the rain, driven by the rising wind, beat against his face. Soon his hair was plastered to his skull. He tried to merge with his Aspect to create a small bubble of calm around them, but It eluded him, then, suddenly, warmth passed over his body as he felt Lisha rouse and attempt the same merging. He reached for her mind, then his horse lost its balance as the path disintegrated beneath it. It tumbled into the river, and he was flung onto the slippery bank. He made a desperate grab for a sapling, a twisting branch scored across his forehead, and the last thing he saw before blood covered his vision was Lisha's face as horse and rider went into the water. Her eyes finally cleared as she cried out.

"Cam!"

The word reverberated through the Physical and Spiritual Realms.

"No!"
As one, Cam, Dani, Quin, and Martin flung their Sight into the river after her. In the Physical Realm, the Seer collided with Osarion, both Dani and Quin hit the stable door, and Cam hit the water.

"Lisha!"
"Cam, where are you?"
"I'm here! I . . . I can't see you! Lisha, take my hand!

"Cam! help me!"

The river closed over his head, and his mind shot forward on the Wind as his link with her was suddenly cut off.

At Bran's Palace the eyes of four young DeMarian Princes suddenly flared with power, while in his Council Chamber, the Aristok Atreus the Second's face drained of blood as he felt his fifth-born child die.

"ALISHA!"

Water filled Cam's mouth. He struggled desperately, and then a hand caught him by the hair and pulled him back to the riverbank. Choking and gasping, he looked up to see his Uncle Celestus, with one hand locked around a tree trunk, throw his other hand out and catch hold of Lisha's tunic. As he pulled her lifeless body from the water, tears began to run down his cheeks. Cam started to shake. Inside the keep, Quin and Dani clutched at each other while, in the clearing, Martin Wrey buried his face in his hands.

Time seemed to stand still, forever frozen on the riverbank. Then Celestus slowly released his niece's body and turned toward his nephew.

"Are you all right?" he asked faintly.

Cam nodded.

"You're not hurt?"

Cam shook his head.

Wiping his eyes with a firm gesture, Celestus came forward and took Cam by the shoulders. "All right, then." He took a deep breath. "All right. Camden. I need you to pay close attention to me; this is very important. Camden, look at me."

Desperate to fly away from this terrible spot, Cam reluctantly met his uncle's eyes.

"A terrible tragedy has just happened here. Terrible for

all of us, and we must put it right or all of us are lost. Now, there are soldiers in the woods," Celestus explained carefully. "They will soon be here. If they stumble upon Alisha's body, it will go badly for anyone from the keep that may be captured, so I need you to do something incredibly courageous. I need you to take Alisha to the soldiers. Do you understand?"

"Wha . . . ?"

"It will be all right. The soldiers are your brother Alexander's retainers. They won't hurt you."

"Alec's?"

"Yes."

"Alec's here?"

"Yes. He brought two Flame Temple Seers with him. They must have gotten wind of our workings somehow. I don't know how or why, and that's not important right now. What is important is your safety, yours and Danielle's and Quinton's."

Martin's shadowy features hovered above his head.

Cam paled.

"No."

"Camden?"

Just as he reached out for him, he became the stern and fanatical form of Urielle DeSandra, her hands stained red with blood.

"No!"

"Camden, what is it?"

He met his uncle's gaze, his own expression stunned. "It's my fault," he whispered.

"It wasn't."

"No, it was. I . . ." He swallowed. "I Saw Martin Wrey. We linked. I Saw him and . . . he Saw me."

Celestus grew very still. "When?"

"Last week. During the working. He got me out when

the Flame attacked us. He must have told them. He must have told *her.*"

"Why didn't *you* tell *me?*"

"I don't know!" Cam turned a horrified look on Lisha's body. "It's all my fault!"

Celestus took a deep breath. "All right. Camden, look at me, no, not at Alisha, look at *me.* Now, whoever is at fault is immaterial right now. We'll deal with that when we're all safe. However, I still need you to take Alisha to Alexander. I don't ask this lightly because essentially I'm asking you to give yourself up to the Flame Temple. But it will be all right," he added as Cam's eyes widened in fear. "You will tell them everything, do you understand? Everything except our connection with Heathland and Lochaber Castle. They will have already discovered much of it by now anyway, so you won't be betraying us. You will accuse me of heresy, and you will blame me entirely. You will say that I kept you from communicating with your family and that you were too frightened to defy me. Show relief that you're finally free of my influence. If they demand that you recant, do so at once. Then, when it's safe, come to Lochaber. Even if I'm taken, even if we're all taken, go to Lochaber. Do you understand? Camden, look at me, do you understand?"

"Yes, Uncle."

"Good. Now, I need you to link with Danielle and Quinton. Can you do that for me?"

Cam nodded. His eyes swirled with gray mist.

"They're by the stable door."

"They haven't left yet?"

"No. Quin is crying, and Dani is trying to comfort him."

"Tell them they have to pull themselves together and get out of Tavencroft at once."

Cam was quiet for a moment. "They can't."

"Why not?"

"The Deputy Seer is at the gate."

Celestus stiffened. "No," he whispered. "My Danielle." He stood. "Very well, then. I'll get them out myself."

Cam caught his sleeve. "Wait. There's another way. There's a tunnel under the south range. It leads outside."

Celestus dropped down beside him. "Yes, of course, the old bolt-hole. Tell them, Camden. tell them quickly."

Cam nodded. "They're going."

"Well, that's a relief anyway. Now, Alexander and his people will be here at any moment. Can you do as I ask, Camden? Can you take Alisha DeMarian's body to them and save us all?" He caught Cam in his intense stare. "Do you have the strength?"

Cam straightened. "Yes, Uncle."

"Good." Celestus rose. "Then I'll see you in Heathland, Nephew."

He disappeared down the path.

After a long moment, Cam wiped the rain from his face, then catching up his cousin's body in his arms, he stood and began to carry her back toward Tavencroft and his brother.

"Everything's going to be fine, Lisha," he whispered through the tears that began to track down his cheeks. "Alec is coming. He's going to fix everything, you'll see. So don't worry. All right? Don't worry. Alec will fix everything."

13. Danielle

IWALANI DeKathrine, the Flame's new Liaison to the Palace, stood in the Temple's main entrance watching the frenzy of activity before her with amazement. She'd always known that a forest fire did not move as fast as rumor at the Flame Temple, but this was the first time she'd really seen the old adage translated into action.

In the early hours of the morning Eaglanter, Herald to Maia DeKathrine, Duke of Werrick, had come to the Flame Temple seeking an emergency audience with the Archpriest. The activity which had followed had flowed along two separate but equally important paths.

The official path involved the Junior Flame Champions on guard at the Temple's Administrative Entrance summoning the Night Seneschal who showed the Herald to a private antechamber and then withdrew to rouse the Acolyte to the Deputy Provost. He awakened his master who met with the Herald, determined that her mission was in fact urgent enough to disturb the Archpriest, and sent his Acolyte to rouse her Acolyte who finally awakened Her Grace, Urielle DeSandra. The Archpriest summoned the Herald to her outer chamber and, within minutes, her Acolyte was sent running to invoke the Senior Conclave which involved rousing more Acolytes and their masters at just about the same time the kitchen staff were firing up the bread ovens.

The unofficial path involved semiretired Pri Jacob DeYvonne on his way to the lavatories, observing his cousin Saldra escorting a DeKathrine Herald to a private antechamber at four in the morning. He caught up with her on her way to the Deputy Provost's suite and passed on what little information she had for him to Jarl Ansen, the Senior Floor Polisher, and Randi Lea who worked in the laundry, whom he met when he finally reached the toilets.

Within minutes every servant in the Flame Temple knew that something urgent involving the DeKathrine family was about to erupt. The kitchen staff set about preparing food for the Senior Conclave before the Herald even reached the Archpriest's outer chamber. This delayed the early breakfast and by the time Eaglanter had discharged her mission, every Initiate, Acolyte, and Squire knew they were in for a very long day.

By the time the Coadjutor's new Acolyte, Iwa's cousin Darcy, was sent to the Palace to summon the Flame Temple's Liaison, Iwa was already on her way. Allen, on duty at the Administrative Entrance, had sent her a message before the Herald had even reached the antechamber.

The news that their second cousin Danielle had escaped captivity at Broughard Castle had already spread throughout the Temple when she arrived—thanks to a quick conversation between the Deputy Marshal's Acolyte, Cory DeKathrine, and his Aunt Janet, the Senior Librarian. Every DeKathrine at the Temple was now walking on eggshells, unsure of whether to close ranks as a family or as a Priesthood. Personally, Iwa didn't feel they should have to do either, but then she'd felt the same way four years ago and nobody had asked her opinion then and they probably wouldn't ask her now. Snagging Allen as he made his way across the hall, she headed for the Coadjutor's office.

The Flame Champion Captain and the Deputy Adjutant were already seated in their usual positions by the fire.

Rysander's youthful face was drawn, but when Darcy ushered Iwa and Allen inside, he waved them forward with a strained smile.

"What news from the Palace?" he asked formally.

"Nothing when I left, Father, but the word will have spread by now."

"The Aristok will want a report as soon as he's told."

"Pri Breanne will stall him until I can get back."

"Good enough. What about the city?" He turned to Lorien.

"Much the same, only more so."

"Will there be trouble?"

The older man shrugged. "The North Bank won't do anything foolish as long as the rumors don't interfere with trade. If that happens, with no actual heretics about, some of the merchants may lash out at the Essusiate population."

"I'll send a squad of Champions out," Kaliana offered, "just to keep the peace foremost in everyone's minds."

Rysander nodded. "What about the South Bank, Lor?"

"It's no less interested in heresy as fuel for gossip, but it's less likely to do anything about it. The South Bank tends to mind its own business."

Leaning forward, he tapped his pipe against the hearth. "So how do we protect the family in light of Celestus' latest disaster, Ry?"

"There's no question about Celestus himself," Kaliana growled. "We turn from him completely and, if we hear so much as a whisper about his whereabouts, I send my Champions to haul him in at once."

"That might be easier said than done," Lorien noted, lighting his pipe off a taper and sending a series of smoke rings dancing toward the fire.

"Perhaps, but we have to make the attempt. He can't be allowed to bring the rest of the family under suspicion. Not again."

"Yes, I suppose."

"And Danielle?" Rysander asked.

"She's an adult now, Ry. If she's run to join Celestus, then she's guilty. Period."

"Not necessarily, Kali," Lorien countered. "She might just miss him; he is her father after all. If you hadn't seen your father in four years, you might run to him yourself."

"Not if he'd involved me in heresy and then abandoned me to the mercy of the Flame Temple interrogators," Kaliana retorted. "Face it, Uncle Lor, Danielle was a heretic then, and she's a heretic now. This just proves it."

"Well, with that attitude it's a wonder they all haven't done a bunk years ago, since even their own families are so willing to extend them such a clean slate."

Kaliana glared at him. "Even suspicion of heresy is enough to have someone arrested and sympathy has been viewed as conspiracy in the past. If we don't move quickly on this, it will seem as if we're protecting them from justice. Do you want to face the Archpriest on that charge?"

"Me? I'm an old man. What do I care?"

"Well, I'm not an old man, and I do care."

"So what do you suggest, Captain," Rysander interjected.

"For now all we can do is search for Danielle and hope we find her before anyone else does," she replied. "But if we do find her, we have to bring her in immediately. Any suspicion of a DeKathrine cover-up and the entire family is put in danger, not just those of us at the Temple, but in the other Priestly and Militant Orders, at the Palace, in the Navy, across the country. Nothing could destabilize the realm faster."

"Lor?"

The older man just shrugged. "She's right," he admitted.

"Very well. Kali, ready your Champions to make arrests on the Archpriest's word. Lorien, send out your people. Any rumor of Celestus or Danielle must be reported to both myself and the Archpriest directly."

There was a knock at the door, and Darcy slipped inside.

"Excuse me, Uncle?"

"Yes?"

"The Archpriest is ready to begin the Senior Conclave."

"We're on our way."

He turned to Iwa. "Stay close by. I'll have a message from the Archpriest for the Aristok as soon as we're done."

"Yes, Father."

Now she and Allen stood in their usual place on the main balcony waiting impatiently for the Coadjutor's summons. With a growl, Allen spat over the side.

"Scorchin' heretics," he muttered. "I should be in bed right now, not hovering around waiting to see how many of us are about to get arrested."

Iwa nodded grimly. Leaning an elbow on the railing, she propped her chin up on her hand.

She'd never been close to the Kairnbrook branch of the family—she doubted she'd even met them more than once—but when they'd been implicated in the Triarchy Heresy, suspicion had fallen on every DeKathrine in the Temple, no matter how remotely related. Her own Initiation into the Priesthood had been delayed while the Deputy Marshal, Brenner DeLynne, went over every detail of her service record with a fine tooth comb. In those days she would have willingly executed both Danielle and Celestus herself—along with the Deputy Marshal—and time had not blunted her views. They were still heretics, and he was still a horse's ass. She turned to jab her cousin in the ribs.

"C'mon."

"Where are we going?"

"To wait for Father's summons in the kitchens."

"Why?"

"Because I'm hungry."

"Oh. Good reason."

Together, they returned inside, pausing to watch Martin Wrey and Osarion DeSandra follow an Acolyte across the main hall to the Senior Conclave.

Iwa raised one eyebrow. "Well, that's torn it. It's official now," she said as they made their own way across the hall.

"What is?"

"The end of the world."

He pinched her. "Don't get melodramatic. They've been working together for four years without bloodshed."

"Sure, but now it's different."

"How?"

"Now they're walking in step. I tell you it's the end of the scorchin' world."

"Iwa, just shut up, will you."

"You shut up."

"You make me."

"Don't you think I won't."

"Oh, big talker, *Pri* Iwalani."

Their voices rose as they fell into the old familiar banter, and Osarion DeSandra turned a frown in their direction. As one, they ducked quickly through the south wing alcove.

Beside the Deputy Seer, Martin Wrey didn't even notice them go by. The wisps of imagery around his head had begun to spin like a dozen tiny cyclones, and it was all he could do to see where he was going.

He'd been up most of the night. Once he'd seen the Herald enter the Temple, he'd returned to his rooms and, sitting by the fire, had watched the flames dance across the coals until his eyelids began to droop. The signs had grown and died, spilling over the grate in a constant stream of prophetic imagery, but Martin already knew what they foretold.

Danielle DeKathrine had escaped from Broughard Castle. There could only be one reason why. Celestus DeKathrine had returned to Branion.

*   *   *

A log popped in the grate, sending a shower of sparks across the hearth. Martin jumped. Closing his eyes, he smoothed the beginnings of a headache away with his fingertips. He didn't have time to be jumpy, and he didn't have time to indulge in prophetic headaches. The Triarchy Heresy had risen from the ashes of Celestus DeKathrine's bonfire, and if they didn't douse it soon, it would burn them all up together.

He leaned his head back with a weary sigh.

In retrospect, he supposed they should have expected the residents of Tavencroft to run or fight or lock the doors at their approach four years ago. They had done all three—they were heretics, after all—but the Duke of Guilcove had wanted to believe in his brother's innocence. He'd wanted to enter his uncle's keep peacefully, discover the truth of the matter, and sort it out quietly without resorting to violence. The Flame Temple had wanted that, too. But it had become impossible as soon as Alexander DeKathrine had found his brother Camden huddled on the crumbling Whroxin riverbank with the body of Alisha DeMarian, Royal Duke of Lochsbridge, cradled in his arms.

Everything had sped up after that.

Osarion DeSandra had demanded the keep's immediate surrender. The guards had capitulated as soon as they'd seen Camden. The Deputy Seer had then sent half the Duke's retainers sweeping through the keep rounding up anyone they could find, and the rest out after those who had fled.

Of the seven surviving conspirators in the Triarchy Heresy of 496, three had been arrested: Camden, Danielle, and Quinton DeKathrine, one—a retired Priest of the Wind—had fallen to her death from the gatehouse battlements while resisting arrest, and three had escaped: Celestus DeKathrine, his Companion Vincent of Storvicholm, and the one man they'd desperately needed to capture or kill: Kether Braithe, Mirror of Baltsegar Ness,

Heathland. Of the castle servants and guards, half a dozen were captured; the rest disappeared into the Bricklin Forest.

Martin had stood off to one side, the proximity of the not-thing's protection making his head throb. He could barely even see the keep itself, but when the boy's presence had entered Tavencroft, his Sight had snapped into clarity. Turning, Martin Wrey and Camden DeKathrine met in the Physical Realm for the first time. Martin's eyes had widened.

The boy had grown up. Sixteen years old, he was tall and muscular, with large, strong hands and a sprinkling of golden stubble across his cheeks. His physical presence shimmered with the constantly moving power of the Wind. It wove about him, desperate to give him comfort, but Camden stood, arms limp at his sides, ignoring his Aspect as he ignored everything else around him. His golden hair was plastered to his skull with rain, his expression dull, and his blue eyes, red-rimmed and clouded with gray mist. He nodded slowly when the Duke of Guilcove spoke to him, but otherwise he showed nothing. Martin could almost feel his mind retreating farther and farther into shock. Silently, the Archpriest's Man moved back out of sight. His mind reached out.

"Camden?"

Far away, he thought he could sense a faint response.

"Camden?"

The boy looked up. His eyes cleared for just an instant, then the Wind whipped up between them, knocking Martin's mind away with a sharp slap. Camden's eyes clouded over with a gray mist, and Martin withdrew, his head ringing. The Wind would not suffer anyone else's intervention. If It could not comfort Its Chosen Champion, no one else would be allowed to.

Martin frowned. Alexander DeKathrine was keeping his brother close. So far, the Deputy Seer had not noticed the Wind's activity, but if this kept up, Camden would not be safe from the Flame Temple's interrogators. They

*would See how dangerously close he was to manifesting
as a legitimate Vessel. They would report it to the Archpriest, and she would do what her office required. Mar-
shaling his abilities, Martin reached out again, trying to
work his way around the Wind's protection. He had to
reach Camden's mind to warn him.*

*The return journey to Branbridge took five days, and
for five days, Martin played a cat-and-mouse game with
the Aspect of the Wind. He was nearing exhaustion, but as
the copper turrets of the Flame Temple came into view,
the gray mist in the boy's eyes cleared a little. Calling on
the last of his strength, Martin shot his mind out toward
him.*

"Camden!"

The boy's awareness stirred.

"Camden, we're nearing the Flame Temple!"

*The Wind loomed perilously close, but Martin could
feel that he'd caught the boy's attention.*

"You can't link with the Wind. They'll know."

*The Aspect reared up like a huge cyclone, but before It
could knock Martin away again, Camden's mind jerked up
between them. The Wind held. Slowly, the boy turned his
blank gaze on the Seer's face. Martin reached out more
gently.*

"You have to stay clear for a little while," *he said
silently, forming each word into a single thought.* "Just
until all this is over. Can you do that?"

Very slowly, Camden nodded.

"Good. I'll help you. I'll come to you. You won't have
to do it alone. Just hold out until then."

*Martin disengaged. Camden held his gaze for a mo-
ment and then the gray in his eyes faded completely away
as his mind sank back into shock.*

*It took Martin a week to get permission to see him. It
took two days more for him to get up the courage to go.*

* * *

Suppressing the flood of frightening memories which seven years of freedom had been unable to erase, Martin made his way down the worn steps to the Temple Dungeons. The smell of damp stone caught in the back of his throat, and he could feel his heart begin to pound painfully loud in his chest. The prisoners were being held in individual cells in the north wing. Martin's cell had been in the south. It didn't help.

Pausing at the bottom of the steps, he forced his breath to calm, then pounded on the wooden door.

"Erna."

He heard a chair scrape back and, after a minute, a pale face peered through the grate at him.

"Martin?"

"Open the door."

The jingle of keys made his heart skip a beat, then the door creaked open.

"Didn't ever think I'd see you here again," she observed as she gestured him through before carefully locking the door behind him.

"I'm not staying. Her Grace has given me permission to speak with one of the prisoners."

"Oh? Which one?"

"Camden DeKathrine."

He paused, waiting for Erna's assessment. The retired Flame Champion had commanded the Temple Dungeons for almost a decade and knew every word that was spoken by its prisoners and by its interrogators.

She shook her head. "You won't get much from him," she noted as she fished a jug out from behind her chair. "He's pretty shocky."

"Still?"

"Mm-hm. Poor little bugger. Drink?"

"No, thanks."

"Yeah, Pri Eylla and her Acolyte, what's his name ... Brair something or other, have been trying to get through to him without much success. They can get a word or two

*out of him, but every time they ask about Her Royal High-
ness, he slips away again."*

"What about the others?"

"Their interrogations are coming along." *Fighting with
the cork, she finally worked it free and lifted the jug to her
lips, taking a deep swallow before continuing.* "Brairion,
that's his name. Anyway, they figure they should have
their reports for Her Grace in a day or two."

"What do you think they'll recommend?"

"Hard to say. The servants are Essusiates, and foreign-
ers at that, so they won't get very far in that quarter I'm
thinking. The two other youths, now, they've cooperated
pretty well. If Pri Eylla believes they'll recant and mean
it, they could be out in a week or two. Of course, Her
Grace still has to question them, and she has the Aristok
to answer to on this one." *She took another drink, then
stuffed the cork back in the jug.* "I hear the Prince Alisha's funeral is tomorrow."

"Yes."

"That may well tip the balance against them. Still, she
often follows her own course, and who knows . . ." *Erna
peered myopically at him.* "She let you out."

His jaw tightened.

"'Course that was an Ascension Pardon, wasn't it?"

"Yes."

She glanced over at him. "How're the nightmares?"

"Gone for the most part."

"Glad to hear it." *She led the way down the hall, jin-
gling her keys loudly as she went. Martin swayed for just
an instant, then followed her, his expression tight.*

"Remembered that, did you?" *she asked, glancing at
his face.* "I like to warn 'em someone's coming so they
can get themselves prepared. It's the only dignity I can
offer them, you know?."

"I know."

She stopped halfway down. "He's in here."

"Has he had any other visitors?"

"No one else has been allowed."

"Not even his family?"

She shrugged. "It's heresy, Martin. What did you expect?" Turning a key in the lock, she swung the door open. Martin made to step forward and his feet froze on the stone floor of the hall.

It was dark inside. It was always dark inside.

"Martin?"

Erna's keys jingled in her hand. The cell was cold and smelled of dampness and urine and it was dark inside.

"Martin!"

The retired Champion rapped sharply on the door and Martin jerked awake. For a heartbeat the cell walls closed in on him and then he saw the dawn light trickling through his shutters.

"Your Grace?"

He blinked, hearing the second knock more clearly now. He twisted around in his chair.

"Yes?"

A Junior Acolyte put her head in the door. "Excuse me, Your Grace, but the Archpriest requires your presence at Senior Conclave."

He stared at her for a long moment, then shook himself. "Um, yes, I'm on my way."

"Thank you, Sir."

The Acolyte withdrew.

His breath coming in short, shallow gasps, Martin turned to stare at the fire. He hadn't remembered falling asleep, but the flames had sunk down to a number of pinpoint sparks gleaming sullenly in the ashes, so he must have. Rising stiffly, he splashed some water on his face, then stared into the bowl. His reflection stared back.

"It was just a dream," he told it firmly. "It doesn't mean anything."

His reflection wavered, becoming the blue-eyed visage of Camden DeKathrine.

"I know, but he'll be all right. He survived it before. He knows what to do."

In the water, Camden's eyes went gray.

"It doesn't matter. Alisha DeMarian is dead. The Circle is broken."

A log rolled over in the grate, sending a shower of sparks across the hearth. Spinning about in the updraft, they came together in the form of a dozen DeMarian fire-wolves. Then, one by one, they winked out, leaving a final image staring out at him, its feral gaze burning with crimson fire. He froze.

"Martin."

It was dark inside. It was always dark inside.

"It's heresy, Martin. What do you expect?"

"Martin?"

The cell door loomed up before him.

"Is Camden DeKathrine a heretic?"

"I can't . . ."

Martin, look at me!"

His gaze jerked back to the present, focusing on Osarion DeSandra's impatient features.

"We're about to enter the Senior Conclave," the Deputy Seer snapped. "It's important that you be present. Whatever you're wrestling with, it can wait, do you understand?"

"Yes."

"Then get a grip on yourself."

Martin nodded. With two fingers pressed against his elbow, Osarion pushed him through the door, leaving the last question in Martin's memory unanswered.

"The only news we've been able to glean, Your Grace . . ." Lorien DeKathrine broke off as the two Seers entered the room. Osarion pointed Martin toward a chair by the fire, then took his own seat at the Conclave table. The Archpriest cocked an eyebrow in his direction, and he shook his head minutely. She turned back to the Deputy Adjutant.

"Do continue."

"The only news we've been able to glean, Your Grace," he repeated, "is that, under the cover of darkness, Danielle DeKathrine rode to Breymouth Port, where she took a rowboat out to meet a ship flying a Panishan flag as it passed by Forness Island."

"And the others?"

"The Duke of Werrick has sent word to the Dukes of Cambury and Guilcove that both Quinton and Camden are to be detained until further notice," Kaliana answered. "Apparently neither have received any unusual communications."

"That we know of," the Deputy Provost added pointedly.

"That we know of," the Flame Captain acknowledged. "And neither has shown any sign that they're preparing to flee."

"I can't imagine Danielle did, Kali."

"Likely not."

"And there's still been no word of Celestus' whereabouts?" the Archpriest interrupted abruptly.

"There was a rumor a few months ago that he was under the protection of the Duc Cosme de Cavani, at Casa de Rocco in Panisha, Your Grace," Lorien answered. "But that came to nothing. It's as if he dropped off the face of the earth."

"Obviously not completely," Drusus DeYvonne sniffed. "He must have gotten a message to his daughter somehow. Otherwise she never would have fled, not with the threat of renewed imprisonment for heresy hanging over her head."

Lorien and Kaliana exchanged a glance. It was obvious he'd never actually met Danielle.

"This implicates the Duke of Werrick of incompetence at the very least," Drusus continued, "if not conspiracy. I suggest we summon her here at once to answer to these charges."

The DeKathrines about the table stiffened, but with a

glance from the Coadjutor, they subsided. The Archpriest caught her Chancellory Deputy in a withering stare.

"I have no doubt that the Duke of Werrick will make herself available for a consultation should I feel the need to *request* one," she said icily. "However, until my Senior Conclave provides me with more information, I have no intention of showing the Consort Hadria's first cousin such disrespect."

Drusus subsided and Lorien shot him an evil smile before continuing.

"We *believe* Celestus is the reason Danielle's done a bunk, Your Grace," he said, "but we haven't any proof just yet. For all we know she's just gotten tired of Broughard Castle. We'll know more when we question Quinton and Camden."

"Which will be when?"

"I've sent a rider to fetch Quinton, Your Grace," Kaliana answered. "He should be here in three or four days. The Duke of Guilcove is holding Camden at Kathrine's Hall. I'll go up and fetch him after the Conclave is finished. Then you can question him yourself at your leisure."

"And from the Prophetic Realm?"

"Nothing as yet, Your Grace," Osarion answered. "Kether Braithe is, as always, blocking our Vision of the matter."

"I assume that this is now also true for Danielle's whereabouts?"

"Yes, Your Grace. This is the strongest evidence to suggest that she's reinvolved herself in her father's heresy."

"And the others?"

"Their continued presence in Vision suggests that they're not involved as of yet, Your Grace."

"Keep 'em close and you'll know soon enough," Lorien chuckled. "One moment you'll be looking at them and the next moment, ffftt!" He snapped his fingers.

Drusus glared at him, but Osarion just inclined his head with chilly politeness.

The Archpriest turned. "Martin, do you have anything to add?"

Staring intently into the fire, he shook his head.

"Not now," he whispered.

"Very well. I want this matter discharged as quickly as possible, people," the Archpriest said, returning her luminescent stare to the Conclave. "I want Danielle DeKathrine found and returned here by whatever method possible, and if Celestus DeKathrine has set foot on Branion soil, I want him arrested. I don't think I need to remind any of you that in four months' time His Most Holy Majesty will be officiating at the Living Flame's five-hundred-year anniversary Sabbat Mass. Any bad omen at this time could affect the future of the Flame Temple and the Royal Family for years to come, and the Triarchy Heresy will not be the cause of such an omen regardless of whether Celestus now has the power to do so or not." She turned her intense gaze on Rysander. "My Lord Coadjutor, you may tell the Palace Liaison that I will personally attend the Aristok at his convenience." She stood. "That's all. My Captain, if you would be so kind as to bring Camden now, I will question him at once."

"Yes, Your Grace."

"The Conclave is dismissed."

As one, they filed from the room. Osarion took a step toward Martin, but at a glance from the Archpriest, he, too, withdrew. Once the room was empty, she took a seat across from him, and leaned forward, her gray eyes gleaming.

"Martin, what do you See?"

His closed his eyes, allowing the ritual question to send him into Vision.

"Chaos," he whispered.

"Is the Realm safe from this chaos."

He frowned. "I can't . . . it's clouded, the future is clouded. Maybe, but I don't think so."

"Does it involve the Triarchy Heresy?"

"Yes."

"When will the chaos happen?"

"Soon."

"Can we stop it?"

"Yes."

"How?"

"I . . . don't know."

"Can you See Celestus DeKathrine?"

His face twisted in a grimace of concentration, and then he sighed. "No."

"Can you See Danielle?"

"No."

"Can you See Quinton?"

"Yes."

"Is Quinton DeKathrine a heretic?"

"I . . . can't tell."

"What is he doing?"

"Reading in a tower room at Brackin Castle."

"Can you See Camden?"

"Yes."

"Is Camden DeKathrine a heretic?"

Even though he'd been forewarned, the question snapped him deeper into Vision. For a heartbeat he saw Camden standing in the center of a huge, multicolored vortex. As the world began to shake apart, the youth reached into the Aspects' Realm, and then a dark pall passed between them. Martin looked up into the blank visage of the Shadow Catcher. He froze.

"Martin? Is Camden DeKathrine a heretic?"

He made to speak, and the Captain of the Dead reached out Its skeletal hand to place Its pale, icy cold fingers over his mouth. Behind him the future played out, partially blocked by Its body.

"Martin?"

Air whistled between his teeth. "I . . . can't . . . I See . . . the Shadow Catcher," he choked.

"It's all right, Martin. Disengage. Come up at least one degree."

Using her voice as a drag line, he rose to a more shallow level. The Shadow Catcher faded, and he slumped in his chair, beads of sweat breaking out across his face.

"Is Camden DeKathrine a heretic?"

Closer to the surface now, he was able to give the answer the Shadow Catcher demanded.

"No."

"Can you See him?"

"Yes."

"What is he doing?"

"Sitting." He smiled, weak with relief at finding his voice again. "Throwing rocks at an apple tree at the back of Kathrine's Hall."

"Well, that doesn't sound especially heretical." The Archpriest's voice was dryly sarcastic, allowing Martin to come farther out of Vision.

"No, Your Grace," he sighed. "It doesn't."

Kathrine's Hall, Branbridge.

His back pressed against the wall, Cam stared sightlessly at the line of blossoming apple trees. Sandy's target from two nights before was still a dark stain against the wood. Hefting a piece of core, he threw it in the general direction of the branch. It missed. There was a snicker from behind the wall, and despite everything, he had to smile.

"Shouldn't you be in bed?" he asked loudly.

There was a rustle of dried grass behind him, and Sandy appeared on the top of the wall, dressed in a faded green tunic and oversized pair of breeches which had, in the past, belonged to Jo, Tania, and Kasey before her. For all she didn't want to be a Sword Knight, Sandy had already torn the knees out of them twice.

"It's way past dawn, Cam," she said with the kind of dripping condescension that only a six-year-old could muster. "Besides, everyone's running around like the place is on fire or something. I couldn't hardly sleep through *that*."

She jumped off the wall, plunking herself down beside him.

"What's going on? Nurse wouldn't tell me, but Kasey said he heard that Cousin Kali was coming. Isn't she a Flame Champion or something?"

"Yes."

"What does she want?"

"To ask me some questions."

Her auburn brows beetled into a frown. "Are you in trouble, Cam?"

A dozen answers came and went through his mind.

"Probably."

"What'ja do?"

"Nothing yet."

"Huh?"

"They think I'm going to do something."

"Are you?"

"Probably not."

"So why don't'cha just tell Cousin Kali that?"

"I will."

They sat in silence for a moment, and then he shoved her with his arm.

She ignored him.

He shoved her again.

"Quit it."

He laughed. "So how goes the fight?"

Digging a piece of fruit out from under her, Sandy scrutinized it carefully before answering. "All right, I guess. Papa says I can have the dancing lessons if I learn to use a dagger and I get my pony on my birthday."

"And the dress that goes swish?"

"I'm working on it." She flipped the apple toward her target with practiced ease. It hit about an inch away from center.

"What about Uncle Stephan?"

"Papa says he can wait for my decision." She found another apple. "He's gonna wait an awfully long time," she added darkly.

"I wish Cousin Kali would."

"Yeah, but that's different. I've already told Uncle Stephan no about a hundred times. You haven't told Cousin Kali no even once."

"Do you believe that all four Aspects should manifest a physical representation through a Living Avatar?"
"No."
"Are you actively working to bring this into being?"
"No."
"Do you believe that you are destined to manifest as a living Avatar yourself?"
"No."
"Are you actively working to bring this into being?"
"No."
"Are you a follower of the Triarchy Heresy?"
"No."

"Cam?"
He glanced down.
"Hmm?"
"Are you all right?"
He tried to smile. "Sure I am, why?"
"Your face got all sad."
"Indigestion."
She rolled her eyes. "Is not."
"Sure it is. I'm hung over. I always get indigestion when I'm hung over."
"So why do you get hung over?"
"'Cause I'm stupid?"
"Now that I'd believe. Hey, cut it out!" She flicked her braid out of his hand, then leaned her back up against him. Draping an arm across her shoulders, he tossed a rock toward her target. It hit the direct center. Sandy frowned up at him.

"That's cheating, Cam. You have to use apple bits."

"Says who?"

"Says me. It's my game."

"Oh? And I can't play if I don't play your way?"

"Well . . ." She glanced around, and seeing that there was no more fruit at hand, picked up a rock herself. "I guess you can, but only when I say so."

"All right."

Together, they threw rocks at the apple tree in companionable silence until Ewan came to announce that the Captain of the Flame Champions had arrived. Cam nodded. Rising, he tugged at Sandy's braid.

"Gotta go, Brat."

She craned her neck up to grin at him. "See ya."

"Yeah, see ya." Motioning for Ewan to go on ahead, he crouched. "You know, I may be gone for a while, Sandy."

"Again?"

"Yeah, again, so I want you to do something for me, will you?"

"Sure. What?"

"Just keep saying no for as long as you have to until they listen, all right? Don't ever get tangled up in saying yes when you don't mean it."

"Is that what happened to you?"

"Yeah."

"Are you gonna get untangled?"

"I'm trying to. It's just going to take a while."

"Will you write me?"

He squirmed under her expectant gaze. "Probably not. But I'll think about you every night at dusk, how about that? We'll both stand out and look at the sun going down and imagining having a conversation."

"About what?"

"About whatever you want to talk about. Put your thoughts out on the wind. I'll hear them."

"I can do that." She squinted at him. "You do know that the sun doesn't actually go down, don't you, Cam?"

"Says who?"

"Master Grigori."

"So where does it go, then?"

"It doesn't actually go anywhere."

"So how come we can't see it at night?"

"Because we go up. Or something. It's complicated."

"If you say so." He stood. "I have to go, just remember what I said, and tell your father about these physical sciences of yours. He can't say yes if you never give him a chance, can he?"

"I guess not."

"Good." After planting a kiss on the top of his sister's head, Cam pressed the final rock into her hand and went inside to meet with their cousin Kali.

An hour later he came to the Flame Temple, walking stiffly between Alec and Kaliana and trying not let the closed air of the place intimidate him. They'd entered through a side door—probably to avoid notice—and had made their way through a number of winding halls, painted in a swirling pattern of reds and golds meant to simulate fire. Even the floor was an orange-stained wood. There were no windows and no open doorways to allow light and air through. Cam resisted the urge to link with Wind just to alleviate the growing sense of claustrophobia. He was in the stronghold of the enemy. He couldn't afford to let his guard down even once. Martin Wrey had taught him that.

He allowed one fine tendril of thought to reach out toward the Archpriest's Man. There was a flicker of response and then nothing. In a way, Martin was in the stronghold of the enemy, too. Cam pulled back into his own mind.

Beside him, Kaliana showed no sign that she'd noticed the exchange, but as a Battle Mage, her Sight was limited to the possibility of threat. Cam's relationship with Martin wasn't a threat. Not exactly. To be honest he wasn't entirely sure what it was.

* * *

The day Martin had approached him in the Temple
Dungeons, he'd still been in shock over Lisha's death.
He'd barely remembered his brother Alec breaking
through the trees by the Whroxin riverbank and the look
of horror on the Deputy Seer's face when he'd seen
Lisha's body. The identity of the dark-haired, haunted-
eyed man standing in the courtyard hadn't registered at all
until he'd broken through the Wind's protection on the
way to Branbridge.

Cam had tried to do as he'd asked. He'd turned away
from the Wind's comfort, but the guilt and grief that had
risen up instead was almost too painful to bear. All he
could do was retreat farther and farther into shock. It was-
n't hard. Kether Braithe had taught him how to protect his
thoughts, and Pri Gorwynne had taught him how to overlay false emotions onto his own. The Flame Temple interrogators had tried reason, bribery, and force to reach him.
They'd threatened him with exile and death, told him his
entire family had turned their backs on him, but it was the
sight of Martin Wrey standing pale and shaking in his cell
door that had finally brought him up from his self-im-
posed exile. The distress coming off the other man was so
strong that Cam couldn't help but reach his mind out to
try and help him. They'd linked and some of the grief
faded away. He'd stared at the Seer for a long time before
finally trying to speak.

*"You have a dragon and a two-headed snake fighting
over your head,"* he whispered.
"I know."
"Does it hurt?"
"Yes."
"Martin?"
"Yes, Camden?"
"I can't feel Pri Gorwynne at all."
The Seer took a faltering step into the tiny room.
"She's dead, Camden."
"And . . . Lisha." When Martin opened his mouth to

*speak, Cam threw his hand up. "Don't. I know." He met
his eyes. "I know. It's my fault. I took her out that day."
He drew his knees up to his chest. "My fault."*

*Martin took another step inside. "No. It was your
uncle's fault, Camden. Remember? Your Uncle Celestus?
You didn't feel right about what he was doing; that's why
you linked with me and that's why you hid my presence
from him, because you knew that what he was trying to
make you do was wrong. Remember?"*

Very slowly, Cam nodded his head.

*"All right. Now you have to tell Pri Eylla that, Cam-
den. You have to tell her about all your misgivings and
about how you were afraid to talk to him about them. Will
you do that?"*

Cam nodded again.

*"Good. You tell her that, and I'll come to see you
again. All right?"*

"All right. Martin?"

"Yes, Camden."

"It's dark."

*"I know. I'll see if Erna might leave you a candle.
You're going to cooperate with Pri Eylla now, so she
should be able to." He took a slow, controlled step backward. "I'm going to go now, Camden, but I'll come back.
Just make sure you tell Pri Eylla about how you felt, all
right?"*

"All right."

The worst of it was that it was all true.

Eventually he'd been taken to see the Archpriest herself. Urielle DeSandra had caught him in her luminescent
gaze and Cam remembered being surprised at how gray
her eyes were. Despite his fear of her, that had given him
some comfort so that when she reached inside his mind,
he didn't resist. He answered her questions as honestly as
he could, and when he couldn't, he kept his lies as simple
as possible. Both Osarion and Martin questioned him in
her presence. He behaved exactly the same, and finally

confident in her own abilities and in theirs, the Archpriest believed him.

He recanted. He spent six months in a Flame Temple retreat in Austinshire. He gave the right answers to the Priests. He never dropped his guard. He never linked with the Wind. And he never tried to contact Dani or Quin. They never tried to contact him. Finally Alec came to take him home. He hadn't seen or heard from his brother since the journey to Branbridge, and they didn't speak on the way back to Kathrine's Hall. The evening after he took vows as a Sword Knight, pledging to uphold the Living Flame unto death, Cam crossed the River Mist to the capital's South Bank and got drunk for the first time in his life.

Now, he, Alec, and Kaliana crossed the Temple's main hall quickly, ignoring the stares of those around them. An older man gestured them toward a guarded doorway and Cam was ushered into Urielle DeSandra's presence for the second time.

To Cam's eyes she hadn't aged at all in four years. The power of her abilities and of her position surrounded her like an aura, and he resisted the compulsion to drop to one knee. As her luminescent gray eyes met his, her mind slid into the first layer of his thoughts.

"Camden DeKathrine."

Despite himself, his mouth went dry.

"Your Grace."

"I'm told that you're sworn to the Knights of the Sword."

"Yes, Your Grace."

"But that you rarely attend Muster or Sabbat Mass."

He made himself shrug. "I have a drinking problem," he answered bluntly. Beside him, he could feel Alec wince.

"That's a serious weakness."

"Yes, Your Grace."

She folded her arms inside the sleeves of her robe.

"You know why you've been summoned here."

"Yes, Your Grace."

Her power pressed against his mind.

* * *

"Have you been in contact with Celestus DeKathrine, Danielle DeKathrine, or any agent purporting to represent them?"

The truth came easily enough.

"No, Your Grace."

"Do you know the whereabouts of Celestus DeKathrine, Danielle DeKathrine, or any agent purporting to represent them?"

"No, Your Grace."

"Have you been in contact with Quinton DeKathrine?"

"No, Your Grace."

"Are you aware if Quinton DeKathrine has been in contact or plans to contact Celestus DeKathrine, Danielle DeKathrine, or any agent purporting to represent them?"

"No, Your Grace."

"Are you aware if Quinton DeKathrine knows the whereabouts of Celestus DeKathrine, Danielle DeKathrine, or any agent purporting to represent them?"

"No, Your Grace."

"Are you a follower of the Triarchy Heresy?"

Calling on every lesson Kether and Pri Gorwynne had ever taught him, Cam looked her in the eye.

"No, Your Grace."

The pressure against his mind relaxed. She turned to Alec.

"My Lord Duke, if you would be so kind as to wait with your brother in my antechamber, I will have my Acolyte summon you both when I've made my judgment."

"Certainly, Your Grace."

Together, the two DeKathrine men left the room.

They didn't have to wait long. An hour later they were back in her presence. She came straight to the point.

"I've spoken with my advisers, and in light of past events and present dangers, I believe that it's unwise for

you to remain in Branbridge at this time. Therefore, I,"
she paused a second for emphasis, "request that you return to Guilcove accompanied by an armed escort and
wait until this matter has been concluded."

Alec shot an incredulous glance at Kaliana who refused
to look at him.

"If I might ask, Your Grace, who would make up this
armed escort, Flame Champions?"

"Not at all, My Lord Duke. The escort can, of course,
be made up entirely of Guilcove retainers. Your brother is
not under arrest, nor is he being charged at this time. I
simply wish to keep him out of harm's way. And I hope
that he will cooperate with this wish, as his vows as a
Sword Knight demand."

She turned her gaze on Cam, waiting for his response
He bowed stiffly.

"Very good. I'll send word as soon as Danielle and Celestus have been brought into custody, and you will, of
course, inform the Temple immediately should they try
and contact you."

Cam nodded.

"Very well, then. Thank you both for coming so
promptly."

"Your Grace."

Cam left the next morning in the company of a dozen
armed family retainers. He reached Guilcove two days
later. He stayed a week. On the morning of the seventh
day, he saddled his horse and rode out toward the cliffs in
full view of the castle as he'd done every morning since.
Used to this behavior from both Cam and his brother
Alec, the guards kept a cursory eye on him from the castle
battlements, but remained unconcerned. Cam passed behind a thin line of trees and vanished.

Word of his disappearance reached the Flame Temple
on the heels of a messenger from Cambury. Quinton
DeKathrine had fled from Brackin Castle. Kaliana imme-

diately sent her Champions out scouring the countryside while the Archpriest summoned Martin Wrey and Osarion DeSandra, but it was too late. It was as if they'd vanished off the face of the earth. Kether Braithe's protective net had settled over them like a mantle, and once again the Flame Temple was blind to the workings of the Triarchy heretics.

14. The Shadow Catcher

Kempston Shire, Branion
Spring, Mean Ebril, 500 DR

A RED sandstone ruin, rolling green hills, and a brilliant blue seascape.
Three clear, simple images.

Standing on the southeasternmost tip of Branion, Cam lifted his face to the warm spring sun, feeling the Wind whisper through his thoughts and across his cheeks.

Red ruins, green hills, blue seascape.
Three images.
Two words.
"Come Home."
He opened his eyes with a smile.

He'd been waiting four years for that summons, four years to hear Dani's voice in his mind, as imperious and demanding as always, calling him to Lochaber Castle and what was left of their Circle. Telling him that it was safe, that they didn't blame him for Lisha's death, that he was still trusted, that he was still one of them.

"Come Home."

He looked out to sea. There was a ship on the horizon. His ship. Reaching out, he scattered a handful of Wind against the sails. It would arrive within the hour. He took a deep breath, sending a question out on the exhalation.

"Has anyone followed me here?"

The Wind danced joyfully through his hair, whispering Its answer. No. Kether Braithe's protective net had cast itself over him once again. Closing his eyes, he let the last eight days slip away.

He'd taken a ship much like the one he waited for now to Guilcove as requested—*as ordered*—with no particular plan except to empty his brother's wine cellar. For six days he'd ridden out to the cliffs, bottle in hand, to indulge in one long, unbroken bout of drunken self-pity. The thought he'd been avoiding chased itself around and around inside his head. Dani had run from Broughard Castle. Uncle Celestus had called her home. He hadn't called him. Staring out to sea, the bottle cradled in his lap, he'd let his mind run the full gamut of guilt, pain, and resentment, but on the sixth night he dreamed three images and two words that made him feel a bit like an ass.

"Come home."

He'd left the next morning. Pursuit would go north toward Branbridge and Kairnbrook, but Kairnbrook had reverted to the Crown and Branbridge was too close to the Flame Temple, so Dani had sent a ship to the DeMarian-held shire of Kempston, one day's ride to the southeast. Cam had left his horse at the small fishing village of Weylinge and walked up the coast until he'd reached the spot of his Vision, red sandstone Drayfield Chapel built on a green hill overlooking the Bjerre Sea.

The Wind whispered past his face.

"Soon," he promised It, "very soon." Soon he would give himself over to It as Its fully realized Avatar and then no one would ever keep them apart again.

Far away he felt the faintest sense of pressure against Kether's protection. He ignored it. It came again. He ignored it again.

"Not this time, Martin."

Calling up the Mirror's training, he gently deflected the other man's awareness. Ever since setting out from Guilcove, Cam had felt the Seer's mind pressing against his, seeking contact. At almost any other time Cam would have accepted his touch, but this time Martin Wrey did not reach out for his own reasons; this time he reached out by order of the Archpriest of the Flame.

Closing his mind against him, Cam turned his face back to the horizon. Driven by the rising Wind, the ship drew closer. Soon.

The Flame Temple, Branbridge.

"Camden?"

Across the skies of the Prophetic Realm, a great brown moth flew tirelessly back and forth, calling for the golden-haired boy it had first met years before. The clear, crystal plain of Osarion's Vision stretched out below as calm and undisturbed as it had always been, but the moth knew it was a lie. Spinning about in a frustrated circle, it called out again.

"Camden?"

There was no answer. Seated on the floor in the Deputy Seer's private meditation room, Martin opened his eyes. The room spun about in sickening circles and, ignoring the riot of colors and images thrown up by the Potion of Truth, he tried to focus on speaking past the numbness in his mouth.

"Nothing."

Across from him, Osarion frowned. Coming partially
out of Vision, he opened his own eyes.

"Try again."

"It won't do any good."

"Try, anyway."

With a sigh, Martin closed his eyes and reached out for
Camden for the twentieth time that day.

"Nothing."

In his mind the shining harpoon that was Osarion's
manifestation in the Prophetic Realm shot forward to pin
him to the plain.

"TRY NOW."

The surge of energy that slammed through Martin's
mind sent him gyrating wildly down the link. For an instant the ghostly image of a ship passed across his Vision,
then winked out again. Smacking the harpoon away, the
moth rose shakily into the air.

"He's on a boat."

"What, a rowboat?"

"No, a big boat, a ship."

"Which direction is the ship sailing?"

"I don't know."

"Try to See it."

"No, it's . . . I'm going to be sick."

A bowl was quickly shoved under his chin and, after he
caught his breath, he glared blearily across at the Deputy
Seer. "Enough," he choked, "you'll poison me."

"Fine." With an impatient gesture, Osarion signaled to
the Acolyte holding Martin in her arms. "Help him up,
Devina, then inform the Archpriest about Camden's mode
of transportation. Maybe the Palace can send a ship out
after him." Accepting another bowl of the Potion of Truth
from the Temple Herbalist, he returned his attention to his
fellow Seer. "That went well. I knew there had to be some

detail the Mirror overlooked. Get some rest. Be back here in an hour."

Martin's eyes narrowed. "Drop dead. I'll be back when I'm able to."

"Martin."

"Don't push it, Osarion. This isn't how I work, and you know it."

"The Archpriest has ordered that we work together to find the heretics."

"And we will. You in your way, and I in mine. But your way is only making me want to beat you unconscious. If you need my help, you know how to contact me."

"And if you need my help?"

"I know how to contact you." Ignoring the other man's dark expression, he turned to Devina. "Get me out of here before I pass out."

"Do you want to go back to your room, Your Grace?"

"No, outside. I need some fresh air." Leaning heavily on her shoulder, he stumbled from the room.

Devina left him seated on a stone bench in the Temple's south gardens. His head resting on the bench back, he breathed in the earthy scents of spring with relief. The imagery spinning about his head began to slow.

He and the Deputy Seer had been sweeping the Prophetic Realm for over twenty-four hours, taking dangerously strong doses of the Potion of Truth at Osarion's insistence, ever since they'd been summoned to the Archpriest's Audience Chamber yesterday morning. Her face pinched with anger, she'd come immediately to the point.

"Quinton and Camden DeKathrine have vanished."
The two men stiffened.
"When, Your Grace?" Osarion asked.
"Less than an hour ago. Pri Janice was leading the morning search through the Prophetic Realm, and they simply disappeared. I've sent the Flame Champions out again, but I don't expect we'll have any better luck appre-

hending them than we did Danielle." She strode to the
window then turned. *"Do you?"* she asked sarcastically.

"No, Your Grace."

*"No. Now, I haven't called a Conclave nor have I sent
anyone to the Palace because, quite frankly, I don't know
what to tell them. So please tell me, how the two most
powerful Seers in all of Branion missed the intentions of
three known Triarchy Heretics?"*

Both men remained silent. That both Quinton and Camden DeKathrine had been summoned, questioned, and
subsequently released by the Archpriest herself was not
something either of them wanted to point out right now.
She would be well aware that in order to avoid making
enemies of the two most powerful DeKathrine Dukes, she
had returned two potentially dangerous heretics to what
was ostensibly house arrest outside the supervision of the
Temple. If it was a serious political mistake on her part,
then it was an equally serious mistake on theirs.

"We'll find them, Your Grace," Osarion said simply.

*"Yes, you will. I don't care how you do it, but together
you find some way to pierce through this man Kether
Braithe's protection. And Martin?"*

"Your Grace?"

*"You will make this complex but so far rather useless
link you share with Camden DeKathrine bear fruit of
some kind. I've reached the limit of my patience with it.
Do you quite understand me?"*

He looked up to see nothing but darkness in her eyes.

"I do, Your Grace."

"You are dismissed."

Rising, Martin passed through the garden gate, walking
along the western edge of Collin's Park until he reached
the riverbank. Then, sitting with his back pressed up
against a willow tree, he stared into the water. A fish
swam past, trailing a line of prophetic images behind it.
He cocked his head to one side. The fish would eat another fish and then be caught a mile up the river. Idly, he

wondered if he threw a rock into the water to scare it, would that change its future, or would nothing he did make any difference if its fate were to be eaten.

Prying up a pebble, he tossed it into the river. The fish darted into deeper water out of sight and Martin gave a faint snort. He supposed he'd never know now.

He looked up to see nothing but darkness in her eyes.

He sighed. He'd always thought he'd feel more frightened when this moment came, but all he'd felt at the time was tired. Now all he felt was sick.

"I've reached the limit of my patience . . ."

Staring into the water, he pushed away all thought of what that might mean for his own future. If he were fated to die in a Flame Temple Dungeon, then he was, but for now he was still in deeper water. His eyes scanned the river, searching for the fish he'd suddenly decided to identify with. The water sparkled invitingly at him and, for a moment, he found himself jealous of Camden's freedom even if it was only for a day or two. He closed his eyes, dropping effortlessly back into the Prophetic Realm.

"Camden?"

Again nothing. The crystal plain rose up and, with an impatient gesture, he swept the image away. He wasn't interested in Osarion's Vision. He had Vision enough of his own. At the thought, the Prophetic Realm became the familiar wind-tossed sea of writhing potential, fragments of shipwrecked prophecy floating all around him. Weaving his Sight into a shining net, he cast it out and then gathered it back in. It came up heavy with rats and cockles. He frowned.

"I want the future, not the past," he admonished it.

One of the rats stood up on its hind legs and fixed him with a bloodshot eye.

"Have you ever Seen a ball of fire explode over a man's head, showering him with rose petals and golden coins?"

"Have *you* ever really Seen it, old man, or was it all just some drunken fantasy?"

"Have you ever Seen a full complement of white ships with dragons on their prows set out on a wind-tossed sea only to be engulfed by a fiery vortex half a mile high?"

"The drunken fantasy of a failed poet at that."

"Have you ever been to the Flame Temple of Bran-bridge?"

"Yes, and I wish I'd never gone there." Reaching down, Martin caught the rat up by the scruff of the neck and held it over the sea. "Be useful or back you go. *I've reached the limits of my patience with you.*"

The rat twisted in his grip to become a tiny little amphisbane. Its jeweled eyes stared into his.

"A dozen DeMarian fire-wolves winking out to leave one, its feral gaze burning with crimson fire."

"What?"

It twisted again, and a brilliant white dragon hovered in the air before his face.

"A woman with coal-black hair, the tattoo of a dragon standing out on her left cheek disappears to be replaced by a young man with long golden hair and a glittering sword."

For an instant he felt the heaviness of the pommel press against his hand and then the moment passed.

"Yes, Carla and Camden," he answered impatiently, "but what about the fire-wolves?"

A dark pall passed between them.

Martin burst back into the Deputy Seer's meditation room a few minutes later

"I need your help."

About to drink yet another dose of the Potion of Truth,
Osarion raised an ironic eyebrow in his direction.

"Was that even an hour?"

"A dozen DeMarian fire-wolves winking out to leave
one, its feral gaze burning with crimson fire."

"Pardon?"

"A dozen DeMarian fire-wolves—a dozen DeMarians.
Winking out to leave one—one DeMarian. Its feral gaze
burning with crimson fire—one DeMarian manifesting
the Living Flame."

"Only the Aristok can manifest the Living Flame."

"Alisha DeMarian came within inches."

"Alisha DeMarian is dead."

"There are eleven others."

Osarion's eyes widened.

"Talk."

Seated together in one of the Temple's private dining
rooms, Osarion waited impatiently while the other man
shoved spoonful after spoonful of seafood chowder into
his mouth. Having broken through the cryptic image that
had been haunting him for eight days, Martin'd suddenly
found himself voraciously hungry.

"All right, let's review," he said, picking up a loaf of
bread and tearing a great hunk from the end. "Celestus
DeKathrine has a theory that all four Aspects could and
should manifest in the body of a Living Avatar. It's not a
new theory. In fact, it's a very old theory, one that keeps
cropping up and keeps getting squashed."

"As it should," the Deputy Seer remarked stiffly.

"Immaterial." Martin dipped the bread into the chowder
before continuing. "So he gathers four young people, each
with an affinity to a different Aspect, and raises them in
this theory behind the protection of a man who can blind a
Seer's Vision."

"Yes, we know all this."

"But . . ." Martin bit into the bread, "e goves ong."

"Do you mind?"

He swallowed. "It goes wrong and his Chosen Avatar of the Flame is killed. What does he do?" When Osarion looked at him blankly, he shook his head with impatience. "He gets another one, another DeMarian."

"How?"

"He kidnaps one."

"What? Are you addled? He wouldn't dare."

"He's the leader of a group of convicted heretics, why wouldn't he dare?"

Osarion glared at him. "Go on."

Martin leaned forward. "There are twelve blood Royal DeMarians," he began, ticking them off on his fingers, "the Aristok Atreus the Second, his cousin Gabrielle, Duke of Gaspellier, and his great uncle Tomi, Duke of Anvre with his two boys, Timothy and Jeremy, and His Majesty's seven surviving children, Kathrine, his Heir, Marsellus the Cadet, Margurette, Tatarina, Rosalind, Gabriel, and the baby Demnor. Twelve DeMarian fire-wolves.

"Now he won't touch the Aristok for obvious reasons. Gabrielle, Tomi, and the other two are on the Continent, so you can probably rule them out. It would take too long to reach them and their security's too tight. That leaves the seven DeMarian Princes."

Osarion pursed his lips, convinced despite himself. "He wouldn't go after the oldest three, they're adults and far more than he could handle."

"On the opposite extreme, Demnor's too young and is never out of his mother's sight."

"That leaves Tatarina . . ."

"She's what . . . ?"

"Fifteen. Rosalind, thirteen, and Gabriel, eleven."

"All either just passed into puberty or teetering on the edge."

"And all away from the capital this spring."

The hair on the back of Martin's neck began to rise.

"What? Why?"

"Various reasons. Rosalind's training in Yorbourne.

Tatarina's at her Dukedom of Lanborough. She'll reach
her majority in Mean Lunasa and her formal investiture
will be part of the Anniversary Sabat. Gabriel's visiting
his mother's people in Humbershire."

"All northern shires." Staring at the last of the bread in
his hand, Martin dropped it into the bowl. "When did they
leave?"

Osarion met his eyes. "When the roads dried, three
weeks ago."

"That explains the timing."

"Doesn't it just. But not which child is in danger. Do
you at least know when this is going to happen? Do we
have time to warn them?"

"I don't know, but I think I know how to find out." He
stood. "Let's get back. The Potion of Truth is wearing off,
and I'm going to need a much stronger dose if I'm to do
this successfully."

When they reached the Deputy Seer's room, Martin
dismissed both Devina and the Herbalist. Taking up the
various ingredients, he began to brew a separate batch of
the Potion of Truth, careful to keep his back to Osarion.
The other man frowned.

"What are you doing?"

"Do you remember when I first came to the Temple?"
he asked instead.

Osarion drew his lip up in a sneer. "Clearly."

"Believe me, I wasn't any happier about it than you
were, but I came because a Priest named Pri Garius told
me that it was my destiny." He turned, his shadowed gaze
intense. "But I think he was wrong."

"Martin . . ."

"Hear me out. My family were Essusiates, but Pri Garius dedicated me to the Triarchy. He never should have
done that."

"Maybe not, but Essus doesn't even recognize the
Sight. It's a gift sent by the Living Flame."

"Not mine."

"What?"

"I think mine comes from somewhere else altogether."

"Martin, you're moving dangerously close to heresy."

"Am I? I don't think so. Merrone and the amphisbane have been fighting over me ever since that day and neither one of them have come close to winning out. I think it's because another Being claimed me long before even Essus did."

"What Being?"

"The Shadow Catcher."

His jaw tight, the Deputy Seer took a deep breath. "Martin, you've been imprisoned for apostasy once already, don't make it twice."

"Just try to rise above conventional teachings for once in your life, will you?

"When I was an infant I saw the Shadow Catcher looming over my cradle."

"That doesn't make you one of Its followers. The Shadow Catcher doesn't require worship."

"I'm not saying It does. What I am saying is that, as an infant, long before the Sight should even come close to manifesting, I Saw the Shadow Catcher leave the Aspects' Realm to collect the dead. I've been Seeing It ever since. At my first True Vision I saw it take Atreus DeMarian."

"You did that on purpose."

"Yes, because I could. I wanted a Vision that no one else could have, especially you."

"What?"

"Between us, we were the two most powerful students at the Temple, and you were a little snot. I wanted to one-up you. I specifically asked for it in Vision."

"*I* was a little snot?"

"Whatever. No one approaches the Aspects' Realm. It's far too dangerous, and one of the reasons is because of the Shadow Catcher. But I did, and It allowed me to." He took a deep breath. "When I was sixteen, I rededicated my life to Essus at St. Stephan's Shrine."

"I remember. The Archpriest had to save your arse, and

I had to drag it back. I would have much preferred to let Kaliana DeKathrine run you through."

"I know. My point is that during the battle between Merrone and the amphisbane the Shadow Catcher manifested . . ."

"To take you."

"No, to reclaim me as Its own Seer, but I didn't understand that at the time. I do now."

"I don't want to hear any more of this."

"You have to. You said there must be some detail Kether Braithe missed? There is, the Shadow Catcher. He missed It four years ago when I Saw It take Alisha DeMarian, and he's missing it now. My Vision of the firewolf doesn't come from the Living Flame, it comes from the Shadow Catcher. Celestus DeKathrine is going to kidnap a DeMarian Prince to use in his Circle, and that DeMarian is not going to survive it. Now, do you want to prevent this or not?"

Osarion was silent for a long time. Finally, he looked up, his dark eyes narrowed.

"So, what do we do?"

Taking up the original pot, Martin poured what was left into a bowl, then handed it to the other man. "We go into Vision," he said simply. "With your help I enter the Aspects' Realm and confront the Shadow Catcher. I get the name of the DeMarian under threat and we get out. After that, my future at the Temple is unimportant. Arrest me or not, whatever you choose." Picking up the other pot, he poured the contents carefully through a cheesecloth.

Osarion shook his head. "You're insane. You'll be killed."

"So what? If it works, you know who to ride off to save, and if it doesn't, at least we've narrowed it down to three. I'm willing to risk it. Why aren't you? Afraid you're not powerful enough to survive it?"

Osarion gave a snort. "Yes."

"Don't worry. You won't be going in all the way, I just

need your help to get me there." He caught the other man in his shadowy gaze. "Will you help me?"

The Deputy Seer glared at him. "Fine, but this is the last time. After that, you're on your own, and I think it best if, once this is over, you leave the Temple altogether."

Rubbing at a crescent-shaped scar on his jaw, caused by an interrogator's ring seven years before, Martin shrugged. "The Archpriest is ready to abandon me anyway. Why would I stay."

"All right, then." Osarion jerked his head toward the bowl in Martin's hands. "Drink."

The room was on fire, smoke filling the air with a choking fog. A huge, frightening presence bent over his cradle, and as he screamed in terror, his latent abilities exploded outward, seeking help from someone, from anyone. A moment away from death, he caught a glimpse of a place so primordial it nearly destroyed his infant's mind . . .

Martin threw his power up, freezing the Vision where it stood. Behind him, Osarion gathered his own abilities as the other man reached out to touch the veil between the Prophetic and Aspects' Realms.

Their surroundings began to tremble. The veil parted.

"Now."

Osarion's hands clamped down on Martin's arms. The surge of power that shot between them snapped Martin's head back, driving his teeth into his tongue. His lips stained with blood, he looked up into the blank gaze of the Shadow Catcher. He reached out.

The years flowed over him like a rushing river. Each time he tried to surface, the current closed over his head again. He Saw Pri Garius lying like a broken doll in the back room of the Green Whelk, Saw his grandmother leap from a burning tenement house . . .

                              *   *   *

"Pri Garius is dead. You killed him."

   *"If I stared at you long enough, I could See your death
as plain as if it were just about to happen and . . . it just
might . . ."*

   "No!"
With a jerk, Martin pulled them away. Calling up Osarion's image of the Prophetic Realm, he forced his mind to
calm, as behind him the Deputy Seer took hold of his
crystal plain with an iron grip.
   "Now, slowly."

   *The room was on fire, smoke filling the air with a chok-
ing fog. A huge, frightening presence bent over his
cradle . . .*

   "No. Not that one. Not those deaths." Reaching out,
Martin fought to take complete control of his Vision for
the first time in his life. "His death, Atreus DeMarian's
death."

   *. . . a tall, auburn-haired young man, clad in dark blue
and black, his flame-pooled eyes bright with anticipation.
He carried an iron-tipped spear like a lance and, as his
eyes locked with his prey's, he raised one hand in salute,
then urged his mount forward.*
   *. . . he bore down upon the dragon; it stood as still as a
statue, its eyes glittering with a prophetic intelligence.*
The Prince raised his weapon to strike, and the Shadow
Catcher dropped from the trees.
   The spear took the dragon in the throat. It drove
through and out and, as momentum carried horse and
rider forward, the creature brought its clawed front limbs
streaking down.
   Blood sprayed across the clearing.
   The hunt froze, horror-struck, as their Prince was torn

from the saddle. The dragon clutched him to its breast in a mockery of intimacy, then drove its teeth into his face.

Martin clenched his own teeth against a scream.

The vision engulfed him. He felt an unbearable tearing pain as razor-sharp claws drove into his flesh. There was a wrenching in his head, and then the Living Flame rose up, boiled over, and spewed from his mouth and nose. The Shadow Catcher turned Its empty eye sockets on Martin's face . . .

And Martin stared back.

"Now . . . her death," he gasped, "Alisha DeMarian's death."

The Shadow Catcher stared deep into his eyes and Martin felt his control begin to slip. It loomed over him crowned in flames . . .

. . . and the Aspects' Realm rose up, threatening to drive him insane with the intensity of Its light,

Martin struggled to regain his control. All around him the Prophetic Realm began to shake apart, *then a hand reached down and pulled him to safety.*

The boy.

Martin threw himself down the link.

"I See the Wind dancing on the waves of the Bjerre Sea, and as I watch, the waves become Flame and the Wind takes the form of a child with hair as golden as the summer sun."

"Camden."

I See him standing in the center of a huge, multicolored vortex. As the world begins to shake apart, he reaches into the Aspects' Realm . . .

"Camden!"

* * *

Desperation drove him against the protective net. He felt the thinnest thread of response. Returning to the shape of the great brown moth, he punched through and pulled. Miles away on board the frigate *Capercailie,* Cam was yanked into Vision.

Contact.

"Now," Martin demanded. "Her death, Alisha DeMarian's death!"

A breeze rose up from within his mind, sweeping all other sensations aside. He gave himself up to it, feeling the freedom of the rushing Wind flow through his thoughts and into his body. His arms rose of their own volition, raised by the power of the freest of the Aspects. A pale gray mist rolled in, and he opened his eyes.

Knocked backward by the force of Martin's mind, Cam scrabbled the ship's rigging to keep himself upright as the past swept over him.

A wide meadow appeared, and he heard the ghost of laughter as four youths, covered in daisy chains, chased each other around a wide oak tree. They all had the look of siblings or cousins, hair of varying shades of blond or red flowing out behind them, grass-stained shirts and breeches holding no crest or symbol to interfere with the morning's games. They could have been any four students or Squires stealing an hour's play away from lessons except that the fire-pooled eyes of the youngest girl betrayed their secret.

Desperately, Cam fought against the memory.

The surroundings grew dark. The sky filled with clouds and, from their depths, the wind grew cold. Two of the youths disappeared, while the others mounted up and tried to make their way home as it began to rain. The meadow faded, became a slick and crumbling riverbank. The rain began to pour down in torrents and the remaining boy and girl fought to keep their balance as their horses' hooves slipped on the suddenly unfamiliar path.

"Martin, get away from me!"

. . . the path vanished and they were falling.
Camden jerked as he felt the sharp end of a tree branch score across his forehead. Blood splattered into his eyes, and as Lisha cried out, her voice echoed across the Physical and Spiritual Realms.

"Cam!"

He threw himself toward her and, drawn by his cries, the ship's crew leaped forward to keep him from jumping overboard.

"Lisha!"
"Cam, where are you?"
"I'm here! I . . . I can't see you! Lisha, take my hand!"
"Cam! Help me!"
He felt the catch of gorse bushes through his clothes and the pounding of the rain against his face. He struggled to free himself, to stand, but the earth beneath his scrabbling feet became slick and muddy. He began to slide farther down the ridge, but just as the gorse gave way to gravity, a hand shot out and caught him by the collar.
He shouted out with relief. Alec had come. Despite everything, his brother had come. His mind flung out on the rushing Wind and suddenly he loomed over Martin, his swirling gray eyes furious.

"ENOUGH!"

* * *

Taking hold of a glitteringly golden sword, Camden slashed at the link. Martin was nearly knocked out of Vision but, at the last second, he caught hold of Osarion's power again, forming it into a single question.

"WHO IS THE NEXT DEMARIAN FATED TO DIE?"

The image of Prince Rosalind riding through the hills of Yorbourne filled his mind, then snapped off as Osarion, unable to withstand the proximity of the Aspects' Realm any longer, finally collapsed. Martin came back to himself on the carpet beside him, while on the deck of the *Caper-cailie* Camden's eyes returned to their usual color. The image of Rosalind DeMarian was burned into his sight like the afterimage of the sun. Wondering at it, he waved the sailors aside, and wiped the blood from his mouth where he'd bitten his lip. Angrily he sent five words out on the breeze, not caring if they reached their target or not.

"DON'T EVER DO THAT AGAIN."

Sitting up gingerly, Martin opened his eyes. The room came into focus, the flow of images that had surrounded him most of his life hovering just out of reach. Deep inside, he could feel his now-accepted link with the Shadow Catcher redefining his Sight. With a deep breath, he gave himself over to it, then reached out to pull a random image forward. Studying it for a moment, he released it, and it flowed back like a tiny bit of tide. He smiled and tried again with the same result.

A few moments later he looked down at the Deputy Seer's crumpled body. The man's chest rose and fell slightly, so at least he was alive. His own head was splitting, so he could only imagine what Osarion must be feeling. Or would be feeling when he woke up.

*   *   *

"If I stared at you long enough I could See your death as plain as if it were just about to happen and . . . it just might . . ."

The Shadow Catcher stirred, and Martin shook his head.

"Fortunately I'm not quite that vindictive," he said as he stood up very slowly. Taking up the second pot of the Potion of Truth, he poured it over the fire. The smoke billowed up to form the image of a rheumy-eyed old man.

"Change the ingredients just a little bit, and although it seems the same in scent and taste, you'll keep your wits about you . . ."

Martin scowled at him. "You always knew, didn't you, you old fart," he muttered. "Or did you? Was it the same for you only you never realized it? Was that why you ran off to be a dock-side Seer and drink yourself to death?"

The image twisted in the hearth, then disappeared up the chimney. Martin gave a snort. "So be like the fish. I have business of my own to take care of, anyway."

Beside him, three blurred figures dressed as Heathland Hill Fighters appeared. One touched him lightly on the shoulder, then they turned and disappeared through the door, heading north.

"I know," he growled. "I'm coming."

Everything around him at the Temple seemed different now, cleaner and less chaotic. The people he passed stared at him curiously and he stared back, seeing their lives and their deaths roll out before him like a constantly moving pantomime. He might have warned some of them, but he just passed them by. They were Flame Priests, and their fates no longer concerned him. He had business to the north but first he had to make a stop at Kathrine's Hall.

* * *

He met Iwalani and Allen DeKathrine as he left the Administrative Entrance. About to brush by, he paused, watching the future play out before them with narrowed eyes.

"Let me ask you something," he said suddenly, barring their path, his dark eyes swirling with a strange pale light. "Do you want your family to remain strong and powerful for many years to come?"

The two exchanged a nervous glance and then Iwa shrugged. "Of course we do."

"Then take some advice. Don't let the Captain of the Flame Champions send her people north."

She blinked, and he gave an impatient growl.

"The DeKathrine family is teetering on the brink of political ruin. The Triarchy Heresy could topple it over but only if Kaliana DeKathrine goes north and interferes with what's to come. You can stop it by stopping her. That's all." He stepped around them.

"How're we supposed to do that?" Iwa called after him.

"I have no idea, and I don't care," he said over his shoulder. "It's your family; you figure it out. I've given you a Prophecy, you can make use of it any way you want to—swim into deeper water, or keep going and hope you don't get scooped up by someone fishing downriver."

He headed for the gate, leaving the two of them staring after him.

He reached Kathrine's Hall half an hour later and was shown immediately into the Duke's study.

"I'll be blunt, My Lord," he said as Alec came forward to greet him, his expression wary. "I can save your brother Camden, but only if you trust me and only if you help me."

Alec's jaw tightened. "Why would you do that?" he demanded.

"It's too complicated to explain right now, but I give you my word I'm not lying. I need to get to Heathland as fast as possible, and someone has to go to Yorbourne."

Briefly he explained as much as he was able to.

"I can't make it there on horseback, not in time, I'm not a good enough rider, but I might make it by ship, and you might make it to Yorbourne if you left immediately."

"A big if."

"It's all we've got." He met his eyes. "Whatever may have happened between the two of you in the past, Camden still trusts you and I trust you. Will you help me save him?"

Alec frowned. "The *Sea Bear* is anchored halfway up the Mist," he said after a moment. "Cousin Brittany owes me a favor. I might be able to convince her to take us north."

"Us?"

"I'm coming with you." He held his hand up. "I don't really know you, Your Grace, and based on earlier experiences I can't really say that I trust you, but I'll take the risk on you for Cam's sake, and I'll send my brother Elerion to Yorbourne to warn Prince Rosalind. He's the better rider, anyway. He should be able to make Yorbourne in two and a half days if he stays on the post roads."

"Agreed."

"And Your Grace?" Alec's expression darkened. "Just so we're clear, I will kill you before I let you draw Cam out into the open to be arrested again."

Martin smiled, seeing the truth of the other man's intent played out between them.

"Agreed."

Together the two men left the room.

15. Camden DeKathrine

Ailyth Docks, Abberskine, Heathland
Two days later
Spring, Mean Ebril, 500 DR

CAMDEN stepped onto the docks at Abberskine with a smile. In the last two days he'd put aside his anger at Martin's strange attack and concentrated on watching the smooth shores of Branion become the craggy coastline of Heathland. Now, as the sun shone across the dockyard, he eagerly scanned the crowded wharfs for Dani and Quin. Although he knew Kether could protect their link, he'd resisted the urge to contact either of them before he arrived. He wanted to see their faces first.

"Hey, kelp-for-brains, you gonna stand there and stare at nothing all day?"

The shout snapped his head around to see the two of them lounging against a pile of crates by a nearby warehouse. Seeing she'd gotten his attention, Dani strode across the wharf with a grin.

"Welcome home," she said, throwing one arm about him.

Quin caught him up on the other side.

"Took you long enough, doorknob."

Dani rolled her eyes. "He got in yesterday."

"And besides, I was farther west than you, shrimpo," Cam retorted.

Quin, who'd grown into the family height and bulk in the last four years, aimed a mock punch at his stomach.

"I could take you now, ya soak. I hear you spend all your time in alehouses."

"And speaking of alehouses," Dani interrupted loudly before Cam could react, "I'm parched." Catching both of them around the waist, she pulled them toward a nearby tavern with the dubious title of the Vomiting Dolphin. "We'll drink a toast to the three of us, we'll cry over Lisha, and Pri Gorwynne," she added, "and then we'll go see Da."

Cam twisted in her grip. "Where is he?"

"At Lochaber, of course, waiting for you both with an important surprise. He knew we'd want to get *reacquainted*," she leered at him, "before we got down to business."

"Reacquainted?"

She waggled a small package at him.

"Contraceptive power all the way from Ekleptland. I've been saving it for a special occasion."

"And a proper bed with proper sheets in a room at the Flowing Bowl," Quin added. "Dani's arranged everything."

Cam opened his mouth but, before he could speak, Dani trod on his foot. "There's no time for either brooding or thinking," she said in a stern voice, "so just get in there and enjoy yourself with family instead of strangers for a change, because once we're at Lochaber, you're cut off. Agreed?"

He grinned at her.

"Agreed."

"Then let's celebrate!" With a laugh, she drew both men inside.

They emerged several hours later to make their way, arm in arm, to the nearby stables where Dani and Quin had left the horses, and a few minutes later they were on their way to Lochaber Castle.

They rode steadily westward though a scattering of small villages, the countryside growing increasingly wild

and remote with each passing mile, until they reached the
Flowing Bowl just after dark. The innkeeper had prepared
a huge feast for their coming and they stuffed themselves
on venison pie, braised rabbit, and potted lamprey, soak-
ing up the gravy with the local biscuits as big around as
Cam's fist, all washed down with plenty of mead and
beer. When they finally wove their way up the stairs, Quin
could hardly walk. Cam lifted him the last couple of steps
by the belt buckle and tossed him onto the bed.

"You're a pathetic reveler," he scolded. "We should
make you sleep on the floor."

Quin just grinned sloppily at him as Dani kicked the
door closed behind them.

"Just get him undressed."

That night Cam dreamed that he stood with Dani and
Quin in a coney catcher's hut. Bending down, he touched
one of the sleeping figures, then turned and followed the
others through the door. It made little sense to him and, by
the time the dawn sent little trickles of sunlight to play
across his eyelids, he'd forgotten all about it.

The next morning, sated and well rested, they headed
into the hills around Lochaber Castle. It was a beautiful
sunny day, the sky as clear and blue as Cam remembered
it. Giving himself over to the Wind, he rode along with
half his attention on the rhythm of his horse's hooves until
the others began to sing, and then he joined in with gusto.

They'd just finished the last of a twenty-seven-stanza
doggerel that Dani kept adding ruder and ruder lines to
when Lochaber Castle came into view. Cam reined up,
staring at it hungrily, until Dani jabbed him in the ribs.

"Da's waiting, come on."

Celestus met them at the gate. He had aged in the last
four years, his lean face lined and his dark auburn hair
and beard turned an almost strawberry blond from all the

white in it, but his black eyes sparkled when he saw them. He held out his arms.

Dani urged her horse into a gallop. When she reached him, she leaped from the saddle, catching him in a fierce bear hug before reluctantly allowing Quin to do the same. Cam held back, suddenly uncertain, but Celestus quickly untangled himself enough to turn a welcoming smile in his direction.

"Nephew."

"Uncle."

"It's wonderful to see you again."

Before Cam could answer, Dani grabbed him by the collar and pulled him into their embrace.

They spent the night sleeping on the watchtower battlements, staring up at the stars and reminiscing. Then, tentatively, like new lovers, their minds flowed down the link and merged.

It was different without Lisha. Drifting along on the breeze, Cam could feel the imbalance. The other three Aspects jockeyed about to fill the gap but, with a little effort, the three of them kept their metaphysical footing. Their linked minds hovering above the castle, they sent a gentle good-bye to Lisha, cradled in the arms of the Living Flame, then fell asleep, their minds as entangled as their arms and legs. Cam never woke up until well past dawn.

Over breakfast Celestus filled him and Quin in on the events following the attack on Tavencroft. Most of those who'd escaped the keep had found their way to Lochaber. After six months, realizing that his three charges would not be able to get away individually without suspicion falling on the others, and with the Companion's Guild tight on their heels, Celestus and Vincent had fled to Panisha for three years. They'd returned with the surge of visitors for the five hundredth anniversary celebrations, and with Kether by his side, Celestus had sent a cryptic message to his daughter at Broughard Castle.

"The rest of it you know," he said, sitting back with a cup of tea.

Scratching at the stubble on his chin with one hand, Quin smeared a huge spoonful of jam onto a scone with the other before glancing about the room. "So where is Vincent?" he asked.

Celestus and Dani shared a smile. "Vincent is on a very special errand, but he should be back in time for tonight's working."

"Tonight's?"

"Yes, it's the half moon, there's no reason to wait." He swept his intense gaze across the table. "Are you ready to manifest as True Avatars and finally prove the Flame Temple tragically wrong?" he asked.

"More than ready," Dani answered immediately.

His mouth full, Quin could only nod vigorously.

"Camden?"

Remembering the last four years away from their company, Cam met his uncle's eyes.

"Yes," he said simply.

They spent the day riding over the gorse-and-heather-covered hills. At the edge of a wide track of pine trees, Quin, his eyes as green as meadow grass, called a roebuck from the thicket. Cam stared at it, entranced by the wildness which trickled through his link with the other man. Dani, too, stood enthralled into silence, but as soon as Quin let it go, she immediately rose to the challenge, linking with a huge trout in Loch Carfrae. They spent a moment feeling the water whispering through its gills before she gently released it. They then looked expectantly at Cam. Closing his eyes, he reached out and up to touch the mind of a golden eagle soaring high overhead.

For a long time they stood captivated by its heady sense of freedom, its greed for height and for speed, and its hunger for prey. For an instant, Cam considered pressing it to defecate on Quin's head, but at the other's mental tweak, he released it with a laugh. At noon they lay on the hill overlooking the Loch, eating oatcakes and cold sausages, then had sex on their cloaks thrown over the ground. As they made their way back to the castle, Cam felt the faintest tinge of something ominous on the breeze, but dismissed it. He was home. Nothing bad was going to happen ever again.

That evening the sun set in a symphony of pink-and-orange clouds. The air grew cold. Dressed in heavy hide leggings and woolen tunics, they made their solitary way to the meadow behind the castle. Celestus and the others would come later, but Dani had insisted that the three Chosen go up alone at first. It had been four years since they'd done a true working together and they needed time to get prepared.

The imprint of their bodies had long since been covered over by grasses, but they quickly found their places around a newly stacked bonfire: Quin to the North, Cam to the East, and after she'd lit the bonfire, Dani to the West.

Tentatively, Cam glanced over to the South to the empty space where Lisha should have been, then over at the others. Dani caught him in her dark stare so much like her father's.

"We don't blame you, you know," she said. "Neither does Da. We never did."

"I know, but I blamed me."

"You're going to stop now, though. Right? It'll interfere with the working."

"Yes."

"Good. Then let's begin the breathing. Da will be here soon, and we need to be ready."

As she closed her eyes, Cam could sense an unusual tension in the set of her shoulders. He shot Quin a quick glance, but at the other man's shrug, he closed his own eyes, following her lead in the breathing as he always had. After a few minutes, his mind grew calm.

They sat like that for several minutes, breathing in unison and allowing their minds to flow together, disengage, and then merge again like the tide, feeling the power of the Aspects beginning to rise all around them. When Celestus, Kether, and Vincent came into view, they were ready. Cam opened his eyes to see the Mirror holding a goatskin bag containing the Potion of Truth and his uncle carrying the body of a copper-haired child. Cam stared at him in shock, suddenly recognizing the girl from his Vision on the *Capercailie*: Prince Rosalind DeMarian.

His horrified recoil reverberated down the link. Racing through the hills toward Lochaber Castle, Martin jerked backward from the force of it and would have fallen had his hand not shot forward to grab his horse's mane.

"You go on ahead," he shouted as the wind began to rise all around them, "or we'll be too late!"

Nodding, Alec urged his horse into a faster gallop. Martin followed as best he could, his mind going over the last few days.

It had taken some convincing, but the Duke had finally talked his cousin Brittany into taking them north. Martin had stood on the deck looking out blankly at the passing shoreline for the entire journey. His eyes swirling with the same eerily pale light he'd turned on Iwa and Allen, he stared inward at the veil between the Realms, watching the Shadow Catcher rustle about behind it. It was restless, sensing the future as surely as Martin did but knowing it had yet to come into being. As they passed the border between Branion and Heathland, the sense became an itch. Suddenly Martin Saw the veil shimmer. Seconds later the Captain of the Dead began to emerge like a huge bloated spider birthing itself from an egg sac. Its blank eyes held the image of Rosalind DeMarian.

Martin turned his own blank gaze on the Duke's face.

"They've got her," he said with weary resignation. "Elerion was too late."

"You mean she's dead?"

"No." He frowned. "Unconscious, but in their hands. It's only a matter of time now."

"Can you track her through your link with . . . It?"

"Yes." He turned back to shore.

An hour later he accepted a mug of hot rum, coming up slightly out of Vision to drink it.

"They're moving north through Heathland."

"Can you See their destination?"

"Not yet, but I will."

As the sun crossed the yardarm, he looked over again.

"Tell your cousin to put in at Abberskine."

They debarked immediately, bringing their horses up from the hold and setting out northeast as fast as they could go. This close to Kether Braithe and his net Martin's Sight began to gyrate furiously, but used to that kind of chaos, he kept his concentration glued on the Shadow Catcher's movements as It silently followed Rosalind De-Marian like a great bat above her head.

The sun began to set, filling the sky with a brilliant orange-and-pink glow. When Lochaber Castle finally came into view, it was nothing more than a fine streak of color on the horizon.

"That's where they're headed," he pointed, "hurry!"

Minutes later, Cam's shock reverberated down the link. Martin jerked his head up.

"You go on ahead, or we'll be too late," he shouted over the rising wind. "They're in a meadow behind the castle. You have to stop them before they can call up the Aspects!"

"It feels like they already have," Alec shouted back.

"Trust me, it doesn't!"

His eyes wide, Alec urged his mount into a faster gallop.

In the meadow, Cam stared, open-mouthed, as his uncle carried the Prince to the southern position around the fire. Her chest rose and fell, but there was a blackish lump on her temple, and her eyes were tightly closed. A great weight began to squeeze at his chest.

"What . . . what have you done?" he managed to choke out.

"Vincent's brought us our new Avatar of the Flame," Dani answered bluntly as her father eased himself into a sitting position.

Cam turned his shocked expression on her face. "You knew about this?"

"Of course I knew. Da and I discussed it as soon as I arrived."

"And you agreed?"

"Well, ya. We need a Flame to balance the Circle," she replied impatiently. "Where else are we going to get one from?"

Cam was speechless, the air whistling from his mouth, unable to form words. Finally he turned to Quin.

"And you?"

The other man shrugged. "I didn't know, but . . ."

"But what?"

"But I don't care, all right. She won't be hurt."

"She's already hurt! He knocked her unconscious!" Cam turned to stare at Vincent in horror. "You attacked a DeMarian Prince."

The Companion gave him a sweet smile, but his eyes were dangerously bright. "Yes, I did," he murmured. "How about that."

Cam began to shake. "This can't be happening." He looked around the Circle. "I can't believe you would do this just to prove a theory. She's a thirteen-year-old child."

"The perfect age," Celestus agreed. "Very close to how old you were when you first manifested your true link with the Aspect of the Wind."

"That was different. I did it willingly."

"By the end, she will also be willing. The awakening fire in her blood will be too strong to resist."

"You can't do this."

Shifting the child so that she was tucked into the crook

of one arm, Celestus gestured at the Companion. "Oh, yes, Nephew, I can," he answered bluntly. "Vincent, if you'll pass the Potion around, we'll get started."

His eyes never leaving Cam's face, the Companion gave the skin to Dani. She immediately uncorked it and took a long swallow, then handed it back.

"Quinton?"

He did the same.

After helping Celestus to drink as well, Vincent came around the fire to stand in front of Cam, holding the goatskin out in front of him.

Cam shook his head.

"Camden," Celestus admonished, "after all these years, and all you've been through, you're not honestly going to let something as insignificant as this stand between yourself and your destiny, are you? The Wind awaits. You'll never get another chance like this as long as you live."

"Which might not be very much longer," Vincent added with mock pleasantness.

Cam's face grew red. "I don't know what happened to you in the last four years," he answered, glancing around the Circle. "I don't think I even know you anymore."

"I think, actually," Dani replied, her eyes already misting over with a pale blue light, "that you never really did."

"Lisha would never have gone along with this."

"Lisha is dead."

"But if she were alive," Celestus interrupted, "she would tell you that none of us will ever be safe from the Flame Temple until we're powerful enough to repel it. And she would tell you that Rosalind is in no danger."

"You don't know that."

"I do know that. The Flame won't hurt her, Nephew, nor will It manifest any farther within her. When the Aspects merge, I will link with the Flame through her, taking It into my own body, and the Circle will be complete."

"You're wrong. She'll be killed—and so will you."

"On the contrary. Braniana DeMarian had no more

physical stamina than I when she first took on the mantle of the Living Flame. What she had was the strength of will to reach out and mold her destiny. Now drink the Potion, Camden. You've stood as one of us for a very long time. Don't betray us now on the brink of *our* destiny."

Slowly, Cam got to his feet.

"No, Uncle. This isn't destiny. It's madness, and it's gone too far."

"Too far?" Celestus' eyes began to flash. "What do you know about too far? The DeMarian monopoly on the power we all have the right to share in is too far! The Flame Temple's wholesale arrest and torture of Scholars and Seers for five hundred years is too far! Or have you forgotten your time in their hands? They won't thank you for this last-minute defection, I guarantee you, they'll hang you as assuredly as they would hang any one of us."

"I don't care. This is wrong, and I'm not going to let you do it."

The Wind began to rise about the Circle, whipping the bonfire into a frenzy of sparks and smoke. Cam took a step toward his uncle. Suddenly, he found himself jerked backward. One arm was pulled behind his back while a knife blade pressed against his throat. Vincent's cologne wafted past his face.

"Oh, no, you don't," he purred. "Now calm the Wind, there's a good boy. I'd hate for It to knock my knife into your jugular."

The Wind dropped.

"You see, Camden," Celestus said almost sadly. "It's far too late to have second thoughts now. Danielle, Quinton, begin."

In unison, the two Chosen reached their minds out to their Aspects. Struggling in Vincent's surprisingly strong grip, Cam felt the ground quiver beneath his feet as Quin sank down through the grass and the earth. Across from him, he could see the black of Dani's eyes brighten with a blue glow as rain began to fall all around them, and against his will, the power of the Wind began to rise within him, called forth by the combined might of Sea and Oaks, demanding his participation. They pressed at his self-control and slowly, he felt his eyes mist over as his Aspect tugged at his mind like an unruly kite. Part of him longed to just give in to It, but the sight of Rosalind DeMarian lying still and pale in Celestus' arms, gave him the strength to resist.

The veil between the Realms began to thin. Quin and Dani caught hold of Rosalind's unconscious mind, then flung themselves toward the Aspects' Realm. They hit the veil head on, and the ground rocked beneath their feet, churned into mud by the pounding of the rain, as the bonfire suddenly shot into the sky. The Living Flame took form above the Circle.

Far away in Branbridge the Aristok was flung to the ground by the force of It, and Rosalind went into seizure as It channeled through her young body. His mind wrapped about hers, Celestus caught the full brunt of Its power, but rather than shy away, he opened his mind to It fully, sucking It in like a giant leech. His eyes grew hot, then spilled red fire out into the air. As the Oaks and Sea joined with the Flame, trees and rocks were uprooted into the air. The earth cracked apart as geysers from the many underground springs began to shoot upward. Then they turned their co-joined attention on Cam. The blue of his eyes now obliterated by gray power, Cam fought back.

On the road, Martin was nearly knocked over by the force of the rising storm. Cold rain lashed against his face, and the Wind tore at his clothes and hair. Clinging to his horse's neck, he urged it blindly on with his mind alone. The Duke was far out of sight by now, racing against time, and Martin could only hope he made it before the storm reached its peak.

Above him, the Shadow Catcher began Its slow descent.

                    *   *   *

In the meadow, the three combined Aspects bent all
their will toward the Wind while Cam fought furiously to
keep It from integrating with them, even against Its own
desire. It lashed from side to side, the imbalance causing
the air about them to suck straight up. A nearby tree was
flung into the bonfire in a shower of sparks and Cam
heard Dani shout at him.

"We'll all be killed, you moron. Cooperate!"

Bending all his will against the Circle for the first time
in his life, Cam ignored her. She slammed into his
thoughts like a tidal wave, and, for a moment, he
foundered. Then, calling his Aspect to him, he hammered
back at her, pounding the surf with gale force winds. To
the other side of him, Quin sent great clots of earth flying
through the air, but he deflected them easily; the air was
his domain, not Quin's. The knife pressed harder against
his throat, and without thinking, Cam caught up Wind and
slammed Vincent away from him. The knife blade
scoured across his throat, drawing a bead of blood in its
wake, then it, too, went flying off into the darkness.

Celestus stood, fire pouring from his mouth and nose.
He pointed and a gout of crimson flame shot toward Cam
just as Alec thundered into the meadow.

Everything seemed to speed up. The fire took Cam in
the chest, knocking him backward, Dani and Quin
reached out to jerk him up into the air while, at Celestus'
feet, Rosalind's heart began to falter. The Captain of the
Dead swept Its long arm down to gather the first of Its
crop and, on the road, Martin flung his mind up and out.

Born on the power of the Shadow Catcher Itself, he
hurled himself between It and Its chosen prey and drove
his mind into the chest of Kether Braithe. The Shadow
Catcher spun around.

Everything froze for just an instant, then, his face
deadly pale, Kether collapsed. He was dead before he hit
the ground and, suddenly released, his net exploded
across the Prophetic Realm. The effects spread out like
shock waves, hitting everyone on the Island with even the

slightest sensitivity. At the Flame Temple the Priestly Seers were flung about like rag dolls while the Flame Champions collapsed, writhing in pain. And at Bran's Palace, the Aristok rose up, his face suffused with fury. Sending a bolt of healing energy toward his daughter, he then turned his rage on her captor. Everyone still standing in the meadow was knocked to the ground as a huge crimson fire-wolf, its eye blazing with a feral brilliance, burst into being overhead. Spinning about, it caught sight of Celestus DeKathrine and attacked.

They fought across the Physical and Prophetic Realms, slashing and tearing at each other, equally matched, for although the Aristok wielded the true power of the Flame, Celestus had both the Oaks and the Sea to call on.

The power of the Aspects began to merge under the pressure. The three youths about the Circle rose into the air from the force of it and, his body shaking like a marionette, Cam turned his gray-filled eyes on his brother's face.

"Alec!"

"Cam!" The Duke struggled to his feet as the ground started to heave.

"Save the Prince!"

Alec leaped forward, but Quin, his eyes trailing streamers of green, ivylike energy, reached out to jerk the ground under his feet. He fell, and the meadow grasses flung up to lash about his arms and legs.

"QUIN!"

The Oaks' Chosen turned to see the Wind begin to spin about Cam faster and faster until It rose up as a towering cyclone. Trees and rocks and burning logs were sucking into the maelstrom and Quin could feel his own power being dragged up inside it as well.

"Cam!"

Deep within the heart of the cyclone, Cam stared down at him with blazing eyes and said nothing.

"Cam, stop it!"

Quin's self-control began to erode. The power of the Oaks spewed from his mouth and nose, thundering back into the ground and, with a cry, Celestus flung his mind out to catch it. For the space of one breath Quin hung, trapped between them, then his face twisted in agony as his heart collapsed under the strain. He fell. The Shadow Catcher leaped forward to grab his spirit, and Celestus DeKathrine rose up with the green-and-red bands of his power swirling about him like living things. He dealt the fire-wolf one savage blow, then turned his blazing eyes on his daughter.

"DANIELLE!"

"Da!"

"DANIELLE, COME TO ME NOW. WE CAN DEFEAT THEM ALL, YOU AND I TOGETHER!"

Dani leaped toward him. Their power met through the blood link, and a great plume of water shot into the air as they merged. The Shadow Catcher caught Dani's spirit before her body hit the ground.

"YOUR TURN, BOY!"

Towering over the trees like a huge colossus, Celestus reached out just as Martin stumbled into the meadow. The Seer took in the scattered bodies, the Shadow Catcher crouched in the shadows, and the metaphysical battle, then threw up his arms to protect his Sight as the fire-wolf sprang toward the giant's throat. They connected with an explosion of energy that sent him flying over backward, but before his head could hit the rock-strewn ground, Cam flung a wind out to catch him.

"Help Alec!"

The cyclone thundered toward the two combatants, catching them up, as Martin scrambled over the rough ground toward the Duke. He withered the grasses about the other man with one look, then dragged him to his feet.

"The Prince," Alec gasped.

They raced for the Circle, and as Alec pulled Rosalind to safety, covering her with his own body, Martin turned toward Cam.

The three metaphysical beings were indistinguishable now, giant, fire-wolf, and cyclone churning in a massive vortex of multihued power. It reached out to touch the Aspects' Realm and Martin could see the Shadow Catcher poised to spring. Without hesitation, he threw himself into the link.

In the center of the vortex, a brown moth slammed into Cam. For a second they both foundered, then Cam reached out and pulled Martin from the image.

"Get out of here!" he shouted.

"I can't! He's about to pull you into the Aspects' Realm! You have to stop him!"

"How?"

"Kill him!"

Understanding dawned. "I'll need a weapon, a physical weapon!"

As one, they both turned, shooting their need toward Alec along his blood link with Cam. For a second, the Duke was frozen, outlined in a brilliant gray light, then he jerked his sword from its scabbard and hurled it into the vortex.

Cam and Martin caught it together, their combined ability sending a golden light shooting across the blade. In one motion, they stabbed into the heart of the maelstrom. The power of the Shadow Catcher drove it into the giant's chest. Celestus hung suspended for a single heartbeat, then the Captain of the Dead reached out and plucked his spirit from the blade. Cam released the Wind, and with no physical presence left to contain it, the vortex was sucked up into the Aspects' Realm.

There was silence across the meadow.

                              *   *   *

Cam came to facedown in the mud. Scrubbing at his
eyes, he pulled himself up to gaze blearily across the
meadow. There were dead bodies, uprooted trees, and torn
earth everywhere. Small fires smoldered sullenly in the
sodden grass but, with no wind to spur them on, they
slowly winked out. Beside him, Martin pointed. Across
the Circle, Alec sat, cradling Rosalind DeMarian in his
arms.

Cam struggled to his feet, wincing as one broken rib
scraped across another.

"Alec?"

His brother glanced up, his eyes wide and shocky.

Cam."

"Is she . . . ?" He didn't dare say the words.

"No. She's alive." He glanced woodenly about the
meadow. "She's about the only one. Is it over?"

"Yes."

"What do we do now?"

Cam gave a careful shrug. "Nothing tonight. In the
morning you take the Prince back to Yorbourne. The castle folk can bury the dead."

"They won't attack us?"

"No. When it comes right down to it, this was Branion
business, not their affair."

"Is that why they didn't come running to defend Celestus?"

Martin gave a snort. "Would you have willingly approached this chaos?"

Alec glanced over at Cam. "Only for family."

"Only for family." Cam looked over at the bodies of his
uncle and cousins, feeling a great sadness come over him.
The Wind whispered through his mind, offering comfort,
and he gently set It aside for now. There would be time
enough for that later. Above, the sky rumbled ominously.

"Come on," he said wearily. "Let's get inside. A real
storm is coming."

                              *   *   *

The next morning the three men stood outside Lochaber Castle, unsure of how to say good-bye. Rosalind had woken up in the night and now sat on Alec's horse, wrapped in his cloak. She was still fairly groggy, but Martin assured them she would be all right.

"The Flame protected her," he said. "Her fate won't be for many years to come."

Alec nodded, then turned to Cam.

"You're sure you won't come home with me?" he asked. "Maybe it will be all right. The Aristok knows what you did."

Cam shook his head. "It won't matter, Alec. The Flame Temple would always be watching me, just waiting for me to make a misstep to charge me with heresy all over again, and they'd be right." He raised his face to the Wind. "I am a heretic. I'm the Wind's Chosen."

"Cam . . ."

"Not Avatar, Alec, don't worry, just Chosen. And that's all I ever wanted anyway, just to fly with the Wind. But I can't give it up." He returned his attention to his brother's face. "I won't give it up."

"I understand."

"Do you?"

"I do. I felt it for just a second last night. I'm sorry I pressured you into the Sword Knights. I just wanted to keep you safe."

"I know."

"So what will you do?"

"The Wind's told me the *Capercailie* is still at the dock. Martin and I will take it to the Continent and from there, I don't know, maybe Asharia or even Ekleptland. Either way, you won't see me again unless you follow me yourself."

Alec looked away. "Sandy will miss you," he said after a moment.

"I'll miss her, too. Remind her that she promised to put her thoughts on the Wind. I'll hear her, no matter how far away I am."

"You're really that powerful, then?"

Cam's eyes misted over for just a second. "Yes."

Shaking his head, Alec tried to smile. "Who would have thought it." He looked away, suddenly embarrassed. "*I'll* miss you," he said finally.

"I'll miss you, I'll miss all of you, but if you go out riding in the morning like you always do and send your thoughts out on the Wind like Sandy, I'll hear you, too. Oh, I forgot." He held out Alec's sword.

His brother shook his head. "You keep it. You'll need it if you're heading out to unknown countries, and that other one of yours is too small for you, anyway."

"Thanks."

They stood in silence for a moment, then Cam looked up.

"Sandy doesn't want to be a Sword Knight, Alec," he said. "When you get back, talk to her about what she does want. She'll tell you in no uncertain terms." Both men smiled. "And you and Desmond really listen to her. It's no good to fight against your destiny or keep someone else from theirs, all right?"

"All right."

His brother mounted up behind Rosalind. "If you are that powerful," he said, "contact us on the Wind or whatever when you get settled. Who knows, maybe you can be the family's merchant contact in the far east."

"Who knows," Cam agreed. "Either way I'll send word through Sarah Lambton. She's the proprietor of . . ."

"I know, the Dog and Doublet."

"Right. She has contacts all over. And tell her thank you from me, will you? She was a good friend." He shrugged. "She kept me as sober as she could."

"I'll tell her."

"Thanks. Well, you'd better go. It's a long ride to Yorbourne, and you'll want to stop a lot."

"Yes. Well. See you, Cam."

"See you, Alec."

His brother clicked his tongue, turning his horse on the

south road. Just before he turned out of sight, he twisted around in the saddle, the Wind bringing Cam his final words:

"Good-bye, brother."
"Good-bye. Brother."

He passed out of sight.

Cam stood staring after them for a long time, maintaining the faintest contact, then let it go, feeling it waft away on the breeze.

Martin touched him on the shoulder. "We'd better go, too, Cam. I'm not sure if the Flame Champions are on their way or not, but if they are, they'll be here soon."

Cam nodded. "Will they be all right, Martin?"

"Who, Alec and the rest of your family?"

"Yes."

Watching Carla's misty image wave good-bye from the Shadow Realm, Martin nodded. "They'll be fine. Now."

"Good." His eyes misting over with the faintest hint of gray light, Cam mounted up and, together, the two men headed east toward Abberskine and the Bjerre Sea.

Bran's Palace, Branbridge
High Summer, Mean Lunasa, 500 DR
Four months later.

The evening sun sent a veil of fiery light across the capital city. In the bell turret of Dorian's Tower, a Junior Knight waited for the sound of Bran's Bell tolling in the Sword Tower.

The deep, rich note rolled across the city. The Knight waited for the echoes to fade, then jerked the rope in his hand. The great hammer attached to Dorian's Bell hit the metal side, and the bell tolled.

The sound of Bran's Bell came again and he responded, three times, four, and then, one by one, the subordinate bells of Branbridge added their voices to that of their leaders, calling the faithful of two major religions to their respective services. As the multitude began to leave their homes and businesses for the many temples and churches across the city, the Knight looked down on Atreus DeMarian's capital.

Branbridge shone like a multifaceted jewel in the summer sunlight, a far cry from the fortified village that had once welcomed Braniana DeMarian, first Avatar of the Living Flame and soon to be Aristok of Branion, through its wooden gates so long ago.

Five hundred years had passed since Braniana had planted her flag here on the bank of the River Mist. The twenty-fourth DeMarian to take the Throne and the Mantle of the Living Flame, Atreus the Second, had heralded in a golden age of unprecedented power and prosperity for the Island Realm. The celebrations that had begun last autumn would culminate tomorrow at the Aristok's fiftieth Coronation Anniversary Sabbat Mass and the family that was the Foundationstone of the Crown's Power would play a major role as they had from the beginning.

Releasing the bell rope, Jacob DeKathrine took one last look across the city, noting the many flags and pennants of his family's holding before making his way to the tower's winding staircase and the large Sword Chapel inside Bran's Palace. The Wind ruffled through his dark auburn hair, then swept off down the Mist and across the Bjerre Sea and out to tell Its Chosen all the news.

TANYA HUFF
VALOR'S CHOICE

"Readers who enjoy military SF will love Tanya Huff's
VALOR'S CHOICE. Howlingly funny and very
suspenseful. I enjoyed every word."
—*scifi.com*

Staff Sergeant Torin Kerr was a battle-hardened professional.
So when she and those in her platoon who'd survived the last
deadly encounter with the Others were yanked from a well-
deserved leave for what was supposed to be "easy" duty as
the honor guard for a diplomatic mission to the non-Confedera-
tion world of the Silsviss, she was ready for anything. Sure,
there'd been rumors of the Others being spotted in this sector
of space. But there were always rumors. Everything seemed
to be going perfectly. Maybe too perfectly. . . .

0-88677-896-4 $6.99